FINDING HOPE AT
LIGHTHOUSE COVE

WELCOME TO WHITSBOROUGH BAY BOOK 3

JESSICA REDLAND

Boldwood

First published in Great Britain in 2020 by Boldwood Books Ltd.

A CIP catalogue record for this book is available from the British Library.

Paperback ISBN 978-1-83889-162-6

Ebook ISBN 978-1-83889-164-0

Kindle ISBN 978-1-83889-163-3

Audio CD ISBN 978-1-83889-243-2

MP3 CD ISBN 978-1-83889-753-6

Digital audio download ISBN 978-1-83889-161-9

Boldwood Books Ltd
23 Bowerdean Street
London SW6 3TN
www.boldwoodbooks.com

To my wonderful mum, Joyce, with lots of love xx

1

'Li! Are you ready yet?' Gary shouted up the stairs. 'I thought we were meeting them at seven.'

I glanced towards the digital alarm clock: 18:28. Still twelve minutes till we needed to leave. I took a deep, calming breath then called, 'Just a few more minutes. We won't be late. I promise.'

Squirting another mist of hairspray on my loose auburn curls, I blew a few flecks of make-up off my new teal dress, then pulled on a pair of black strappy, sparkly shoes. Grabbing a black pashmina and clutch bag off the bed, I took a quick glance in the full-length mirror on the wall. Not bad. Perhaps a little over-dressed for a meal at The Bombay Palace with my sister and her fiancé, but surely Gary would be impressed with the effort, especially as the dress was his favourite colour on me. Maybe he'd even pay me a compliment. I shook my head at my reflection. I wouldn't get my hopes up on that one. I'd be lucky if he managed the ultimate cop-out non-compliment of, 'You look nice.'

I paused at the top of the stairs and gazed down at my husband tapping something into his phone, a deep frown creasing his brow. Even in a mood, he was still irresistible with his dark hair, dark eyes and tall, athletic build.

'I'm ready,' I called, preparing myself to do a little twirl so he could appreciate the tightness of the bodice clinging to all the right places – a daring move for someone who normally wore long skirts and maxi-dresses – but he barely managed a cursory glance as he pocketed his phone.

'About time too,' he said. 'I'll get the car started. Can you lock up?' Without waiting for an answer, he went outside.

I reached for the banister and clung onto it as I took a few deep, shaky breaths and willed myself not to cry. It was fine. Timekeeping stressed him out and, even though we weren't actually late, he was understandably tired and irritable. He'd been working long hours with the surgery expansion recently and seemed to be permanently on edge. He'd likely skipped lunch again so was bound to relax when we ate.

'Would you like me to drive back tonight so you can have a drink?' I asked as Gary backed his Lexus off the drive. I reached across to give his thigh a gentle stroke but withdrew my hand when I felt him tense under my touch.

'I'm fine, thanks. We'll stick to the rule.'

'Okay.' Gary's 'rule' was that if it's your family or your friends, you drink and the other drives. I rarely drink so was happy to be the designated driver most of the time, but Gary refused to deviate.

I stared out of the window as he drove along Abbey Drive then guided the car out of the small new-build housing estate where we'd lived for the past six years. Glancing across at his tight jaw as we joined the main road into Whitsborough Bay, he certainly looked like a man who could do with a relaxing drink. Perhaps I'd have one more try at breaking the rule.

'Are you sure? You know I'm never bothered about drinking when we're eating.'

We stopped at the traffic lights, but Gary still didn't look at me. His hands tightly gripped the steering wheel. 'I've already said I'm fine. She's *your* sister so *I'm* the driver. Can we just drop it, Li? Please?'

'Okay. Sorry.' I turned to look out of the window again, blinking back tears. He'd come round when he saw Jess and Lee. He loved their company, even if he didn't seem to love mine at the moment.

* * *

'I have exciting news,' Jess announced when we'd placed our food orders. 'Bay Brides called earlier and the bridesmaid dresses are ready early. They'll be in on Wednesday so I've made an appointment for a fitting a week tomorrow at two. Are you free?'

I grinned at my younger sister – a shorter, slimmer version of myself. 'How exciting!'

'We don't have any plans for next Saturday, do we?' I asked, turning to face Gary.

'I don't know about you, but I'll be going into the surgery.'

I frowned. 'I thought you were going in tomorrow.'

'I'm doing both. Maybe the one after too.'

It was on the tip of my tongue to say, 'But we always spend weekends together,' but what was the point? I had two choices: confront Gary and spoil the whole evening or ignore him and focus on my little sister's news. Forcing a bright smile, I said, 'Two's perfect. Can Izzy and Megan make it?' The wedding was less than three months away on the first Saturday in August. I was chief bridesmaid, supported by Jess's best friend, Izzy, and Izzy's four-year-old daughter, Megan.

Jess nodded. 'I texted Izzy earlier. They've got no plans.'

'Brilliant. Do you know when your dress will be ready?'

'Four weeks later. I managed to order a bigger size just in time and I'm desperately hoping it will still fit on the day.'

I frowned. 'Why would you need a bigger size? You haven't put on weight, have you?'

Jess and Lee exchanged big grins.

'She hasn't,' Lee said. 'Well, not yet anyway...'

I gasped as realisation hit. 'Oh my goodness! Are you saying...?'

'We had our twelve-week scan this afternoon and everything's looking good. In fact it's looking doubly good.'

I gasped again and clapped my hand over my mouth. 'Twins?'

Jess nodded and I let out a little squeal as I leapt up and dashed round the table to hug them both.

'Congratulations you two,' Gary said. 'Wow! Twins? Two kids? That's some news!' He stood up, shook Lee's hand and kissed Jess on the cheek.

'I can't believe it!' I sat down again. 'My baby sister's having her own babies, which means I'm going to be an auntie. I'm so excited for you both. Twins? That's so amazing. And that's cause for celebration.' I signalled a waiter and ordered a round of drinks including a very large glass of wine for myself, then giggled as I added, 'Make that two. One per baby.'

* * *

'I think they'll make brilliant parents,' I said. 'Oopsie!'

Gary took my arm to steady me as I stumbled out of the car a few hours later. 'Those babies will be so loved and so spoiled and so loved.'

'You said "loved" twice.' Gary unlocked the front door and stepped aside to let me in.

'Did I? Are you sure?' I carefully navigated the doorstep, clinging onto the frame for safety. 'Would you like a nightcap?'

'No, and you don't need one either. It's late and I'd like my bed. I think that's where you should be heading too. After a pint of water.'

'You're going to take me to bed?' *Wow! First time in... hmm... don't know how long. Months. Lots of them.* I reached out towards him and he took my hand. Then he placed it on the banister and let go.

'I suggest you hold on so you don't fall. You might want to take your shoes off first.'

'Will you do it?'

'Li! You're not a child. You can manage it yourself. And don't just kick them off and leave them for me to trip over. I'm going to get you a glass. I'll see you upstairs.' He made his way down the hall towards the kitchen.

Scowling, I undid the straps, kicked off my sandals and defiantly left them in the middle of the hallway, before hauling myself up to the bedroom. I flicked the light on, but the brightness hurt my eyes so I flicked it back off, shuffled round to my side of the bed in the darkness and switched on my bedside lamp instead. That was better. More romantic too.

I gently placed my bag and pashmina on my dressing table chair and wobbled slightly as I removed my necklace and earrings. *Oopsie. Had a bit much to drink. Had to celebrate, though.*

'I'm going to be an auntie,' I whispered to my reflection in the dressing table mirror. 'Pretty good, eh? I'd rather be a mum, though. Suppose I'll have to settle for auntie for now. Unless...'

I heard Gary's heavy footsteps on the stairs, then he appeared in the bedroom doorway holding a pint of water and my sandals, which he deliberately placed on the floor by the dressing table with a sigh. 'Drink this.' He handed the glass to me. Then he smiled and his dark eyes twinkled as he added, 'Doctor's orders.'

'Yes, Dr Dawson.' I smiled back. That was my Gorgeous Gary, the man I loved, the one who wasn't all spiky and grumpy. It was such a shame that he rarely made an appearance these days. His evil twin, Grumpy Gary, seemed to have taken up residence instead. He wasn't much fun to be around, but I knew it was short-term. He'd be gone when the surgery expansion was complete and then, with both of our careers where we wanted them, it would finally be time to start that family we'd talked about for years.

I took a sip of my water then put the glass down on the dressing table, taking care to slip a coaster under it first – no point upsetting Mr Neat-Freak unnecessarily.

He wandered over to his side of the bed and put his lamp on.

'Gary, can you help me unzip my dress?'

'Can't you do it?'

'I can't reach properly.'

'Then how did you put it on?'

'Please.'

He sighed but made his way over to me. I imagined him slowly lowering the zipper, his breath hot on my neck. He'd gently kiss just below my ear as he slowly lowered my dress to the floor. He'd kiss my neck as he undid my bra clasp, then he'd...

'Done.'

That was it. One swift tug and the zip was down. He moved away a few paces and unfastened his tie, neatly rolled it up, then wandered into the walk-in wardrobe where I knew he'd carefully put it in its rightful place in the drawer with his other ties, all in their own little cubby holes, arranged in colour order.

'You should really drink that water, Li,' he called. 'You'll be sorry if you don't.'

'Okay.' I obediently took another sip.

He returned to the bedroom and began undoing the buttons on his shirt. Watching him intently, I lowered my dress and willed him to look at me. To notice me. To see I was wearing new underwear. Sexy, lacy, teal underwear. Rip-them-off-me-and-take-me-right-now underwear.

But he didn't raise his eyes. He took off his shirt, tossed it into the laundry basket in the corner and disappeared into the ensuite.

I slowly bent down and retrieved my dress, placed it on a hanger and made a mental note to check for curry stains and cleaning instructions in the morning. Then I waited. And waited.

It felt like hours before Gary finally emerged from the ensuite dressed only in his boxer shorts. 'I thought you'd be asleep,' he said in a voice that sounded like he'd hoped that's how he'd find me. Surely not. Surely I'd imagined that.

'I'm not ready for sleep yet.' I tried for sultry but think I managed slurred. Moving towards him, I wrapped my arms around him and felt his whole body tense. *Ignore it. He'll relax in a moment.* 'You know how you said we needed to wait until the surgery expansion was finished before we could think about starting a family? Well, it's nearly done now and Jess's news is making me extra broody. How about we stop talking and actually start doing?'

'No! Elise!' I flinched at the use of my full name as he backed away. My arms slid off him and slapped back down by my sides. 'I told you I'm tired.'

'You're always tired these days, Gary.'

'And you're always on about having a baby. I told you, I'm not ready. The timing's not right. Can't you just accept that?'

I stared at him for a moment, debating as to whether to fight it, but the angry glint in his eyes told me to leave it. 'Okay. Sorry.'

Gary nodded. 'Night night.' He moved towards his side of the bed.

'Night night.' I bit my lip. *No! This isn't on.* He always had an excuse and I always accepted it, but not this time. I put my hands on my hips, the alcohol making me feel bold. 'Actually, Gary, I can't.'

He moved back towards me. 'You can't what?'

'I can't just accept that. When will it be right? You never seem to want to talk about it. I want a baby. I want to be a mum like our Jess. You know that. She's six years younger than me and she's already pregnant. And I've been married for nearly twelve years. It's not fair!'

Gary folded his arms and shook his head. 'Do you know how childish that sounds?'

'I don't care. We're both thirty now and we said we didn't want to be old parents. At this rate, we're going to be in our forties before we have number three and four. Or maybe even before we have number one if we continue with the excuses. It's time we started trying. I'm ready for a baby now. Aren't you?'

'No!'

I folded my arms too and glared at him. 'Why not? Talk to me, Gary. What's going on? Why are you shutting me out? Why won't you commit to having a baby? What's changed?'

'Everything, Li. That's how life is. Everything changes. I know we originally said we'd start a family in our mid-twenties, but *we* weren't ready then and *I'm* still not ready for a baby now.'

'That's not good enough. We've talked about children for years. There's always been an excuse. University, my promotion, the surgery expansion. What's next? Anyone would think you don't want a baby.'

'I *don't* want a baby,' he yelled.

I stepped back as if I'd been slapped. My heart raced and my head swam. 'What?' I certainly formed the word in my mouth but I'm not sure whether I actually managed to say it. I stared, open-mouthed, at Gary.

A vein throbbed in the side of his head and he looked quite shocked at his own reaction. 'Yet,' he mumbled. 'I meant to say yet.'

'Are you sure?' The words were barely audible.

'I'm sure.'

My heart raced. 'I mean it, Gary. Are you absolutely sure?

Because if you really don't want children, then we have a serious, serious problem.'

'I'm sorry, Li. I didn't mean to... I'm just not ready to be a dad *yet.* Sorry I shouted. I'm just tired. It's been a long few months. I'm... I'm just...'

'It's okay.' I reached for him and held him. He felt rigid in my arms for a moment, then he relaxed and his arms tightened round me. Thank goodness for that. 'I'm sorry I pushed.' I stroked his hair and breathed in the scent of toothpaste, hair gel and CK One: the smell of Gary. The smell I loved. I kissed his neck very gently, then started to trace little kisses round towards his throat.

'Li...' he whispered. 'What are you doing?'

'Sshhh. Just relax and enjoy.' I kissed back towards his ear then nibbled on it slightly – something he'd always loved.

'Li... I...' He tensed again.

I ran my left hand down his back, my nails scratching him slightly. He gasped. 'We don't have to try for a baby tonight,' I whispered. 'I just want you.'

My fingers reached the elastic of his boxers and I slipped my hand inside then edged it slowly round to the front.

'No! Stop!' Gary stepped back so quickly that he collided with the wall. 'I can't do this, Li.'

Was that fear in his eyes? My heart pounded so fast that I felt sick. 'Can't do what? What's going on?'

'I mean tonight. I can't... I've already told you I'm tired. I'm sorry. Do you mind?'

I studied his face. He looked terrified and I was too afraid to explore why. 'It's fine,' I lied. 'I understand. Bit tired myself. Drank too much as you know. Think I'll just brush my teeth and go to bed. And drink that pint of water, of course. Wouldn't want to go against my doctor's advice.' I tried to laugh at my joke, but it sounded more like a hiccup. I picked up the drink and tried to swallow some, but the razors in my throat prevented it from slipping down easily. 'Yummy,' I said. 'Night night.'

'Night night,' Gary said. He climbed into his side of the bed and turned to face the wall.

As I backed into the en-suite, my stomach churned at the familiar sight of the man I loved rejecting me yet again. I brushed my teeth while tears poured down my cheeks like rain and my heart ached at the overwhelming feeling that something between us had just irrevocably changed.

2

'Please say you're joking.' I stopped brushing my damp hair and twisted round on the dressing table stool so I could face Gary the following evening. 'I thought you were showering to get ready for the party.'

He whipped his towel from around his waist and started drying himself. 'No. I was showering because I smell of the surgery. Then I'm meeting Rob for a personal training session. I told you that when you mentioned the party.'

'I thought you were going to cancel it, though.'

'You *assumed* I was going to cancel it. I didn't say I would. I've been saying for ages that I wanted to get back into shape after packing in hockey. This is my chance. Why should *I* cancel?' Gary finished drying himself then wandered into the walk-in wardrobe.

'Because it's Kay's sixtieth,' I called.

I heard the opening and closing of a few drawers then Gary re-appeared with what looked like his sports kit in his hands. 'So what? She's your best friend's auntie, not yours. I barely know her.'

'That's a bit harsh. You know she's always been more of a mother to me than my own has.'

'I know that and I know you think the world of her, but the fact remains that this was last minute and I already had plans.'

'But—'

'Li, I suggest you drop this now unless you want another ugly scene like last night.'

My stomach lurched as my mind took me back to the previous evening. He was right; it had been very ugly. He'd already left for the surgery when I awoke and had been gone all day, jumping straight into the shower on his return. I'd spent the day washing and cleaning and going over everything we'd said or done, trying – but failing – to find some answers. I couldn't shake the feeling that he'd spoken the truth when he said he didn't want a baby and I was too scared to raise the subject again in case I was right. I'd felt sick all day thinking about it. Granted, I'd also had a bit of a hangover, but the uneasy feeling in my stomach was definitely Gary-induced rather than alcohol-induced.

Gary pulled a navy T-shirt over his head. 'This is my first session with Rob. I booked it two weeks ago and I'm not cancelling it for a party that was organised two days ago. End of story.'

I bit my lip and blinked back the tears that seemed to be ever-present these days.

'I'm sorry, Li,' he said in a gentler voice. 'If it was the other way round, I wouldn't expect you to change your plans for me, would I?'

I shook my head. 'I'm just a little...' I searched for the right word, one that hopefully wouldn't start another 'ugly scene', '... surprised that you booked a session on a Saturday night when you knew you'd be at work all day. I thought we'd spend the evening together.'

'I didn't realise there was a rule about it. We spent last night together. With *your* sister. Wasn't that enough?' He pulled his shorts on. 'Sarah will be there. You two always have loads to gossip about. You don't need me.'

Trying my hardest to keep my voice steady and not to sound needy or whiney, I said, 'It's just that I barely get to see you these days. You're always at the surgery or I've got something on at school.'

Gary sat on the edge of the bed and pulled on a pair of sports socks. 'We always knew it would be tough with your departmental headship and the surgery expansion, but we both wanted good careers and to be financially stable, didn't we? We knew this would happen. We knew it meant sacrifices and one of those is time spent together. This just proves how wrong the timing would be to have a baby, though, doesn't it?'

I couldn't agree with him, but I certainly couldn't challenge him on it without another 'ugly scene'. Turning round, I picked up the hairdryer and kept my head down as I switched it on so Gary wouldn't be able to see my tears. What was going on with us? Our days used to be packed with laughter but now it was all tension and, more recently, tears. The sooner the surgery expansion was finished, the better.

In my peripheral vision, I saw him pick up his trainers then leave the bedroom. A few minutes later, the front door slammed, followed a moment later by his car starting. I muttered, 'Bye, Elise, hope you have a great evening. I love you.'

* * *

The function room above Minty's – my favourite bar at the top of town – was packed. There was no sign of my best friend since primary school, Sarah, or her boyfriend, Nick. Thankfully, there was no sign of Clare either: Sarah's close friend from university, and my nemesis.

Sarah's parents, Sandra and Chris, waved at me from the far

side of the room, but were engrossed in a conversation with Kay's best friend and travel companion, Linda. Kay and Linda had just returned from six months travelling around the world. Kay spotted me and also waved, but was chatting to a man I didn't recognise. Normally at ease in a group of strangers – a typical scenario for a teacher – I suddenly felt very lost and alone without Gary by my side.

The beads on my clutch bag dug into my palm, but I couldn't seem to release my grip. Each burst of laughter made me jump, my head thumped, and I still felt sick. Either this was the worst hangover ever or I was coming down with something. Placing the gift bag containing Kay's birthday present by my feet, I hesitated as to what to do next. Go to the bar, hide in a darkened corner or make a speedy exit? Snuggling up under the duvet in an empty house seemed very appealing compared to mingling with strangers and pretending I hadn't just experienced twenty-four hours of hell courtesy of my increasingly distant husband.

'Thank God you're here,' said a voice behind me. 'I don't know about you, but I don't recognise anyone.'

I turned around to face a tall man with big brown eyes, slightly spiky sandy-coloured hair and a cheeky dimpled smile. 'Stevie! I didn't realise you knew Kay.'

'I don't.' He kissed me on the cheek. 'Nick invited me. I usually go out for a few beers with Rob on a Saturday, but he ditched me tonight because he's—'

'—got a personal training session with Gary. That's both of us ditched, then.' Rob had been Stevie's best mate since school but had left the area to go to university in Bristol where he'd stayed, only moving back to Whitsborough Bay a year ago following a relationship break-up.

'You look stunning, by the way.' Stevie smiled, dimples flashing. 'Or is that an inappropriate thing to say to another man's wife?'

I could have hugged him, but instead I kept my hands occupied smoothing down the front of my new dress – a pretty cream maxi dress with flowers and butterflies across the hem and the bodice – that Gary hadn't noticed before storming out of the house earlier. So much for thinking he might pay more attention to me if I splashed out on some new dresses and underwear.

'Not sure, but you've just made my day and I'm very happy to hear it, especially as the husband in question never seems to notice himself these days.' I bit my lip. Perhaps I'd shared too much. Oh well, it was what I felt so why make out that everything was perfect when it wasn't? I couldn't bear lies, even if they were only white ones. They had a way of catching up with people. Stevie was really Sarah's friend rather than mine. I'd only met him a couple of months ago, although I'd warmed to him instantly and, after a few more evenings in his company, had felt like I'd known him for years. I could trust him.

'I'm sorry to hear that.' Stevie's eyes fixed on mine. 'Can I be even more inappropriate and offer to buy you a drink?'

'Best offer I've had all day, although I'm driving so I'm afraid you won't be able to get me drunk and take advantage.'

'Shame. I thought it might be my lucky night.'

I laughed and linked Stevie's arm as we headed for the bar. Sod Gary. He wasn't going to ruin my night as well as my day, although the headache and churning stomach might ruin it instead. The warmth and noise in the function room weren't helping at all.

A few minutes later, Stevie and I managed to grab a recently vacated table near an open window. I closed my eyes for a moment and breathed deeply, grateful for the cool breeze whispering round me.

'I was surprised when Rob said he was still doing PT with Gary,' Stevie said. 'I thought he'd have been here with you.'

Shaking my head, I sighed. 'You and me both, but it would appear that a day at work and an evening of pumping iron – or whatever it is they're doing – is infinitely more desirable than spending time with me.'

Stevie grimaced. 'I don't want to pry, but if you need to talk...'

I took a sip on my tonic water. 'Thank you. There's really not much to talk about. Boy meets girl at fourteen, gets engaged at sixteen, and married at eighteen. He becomes a GP, she becomes a head of department, and they're meant to live happily ever after with three or four children. Except boy seems to find every excuse under the sun, moon and stars not to start a family and girl wonders if the problem is that he doesn't want to be with her anymore, but she's too chicken to ask because she's terrified of the thought of life without him.'

Stevie's eyes widened and he gently touched my shaking hand. 'That sounds like a lot of things to talk about. I'm listening if you want to.'

I blinked away my tears yet again. 'Maybe not tonight. My sister announced last night that she's expecting twins and, while I'm thrilled for her, I'm feeling a little delicate about my own situation and might turn into a soggy mess if I start now. I've also got a really bad headache so I don't think the emotional stuff will help that either. Maybe another time? I'm thinking I might have to bail early tonight.'

'That would be a shame, but the offer's always there.' His eyes seemed so full of sympathy – such a contrast to the anger in Gary's eyes. He held my gaze as he took a sip on his pint. 'I have something to tell you that should cheer you up.'

'It's not about babies, is it?'

'No.'

'Then yes please. I could use some happy non-baby-related news right now.'

'I was chatting to one of my neighbours, Lorraine, last week. Her son's got ADHD. He was doing well in primary school but started senior school this year and got no support. He changed schools this term and has come on leaps and bounds thanks to something called the EGO programme that a certain head of department designed.' He grinned at me.

I felt my cheeks flush at the compliment. 'You must be talking about Brandon.'

'Brandon. That's it! I couldn't for the life of me remember his name. As soon as she realised that I knew you, she couldn't give enough praise. I was nearly late for the dentist.'

'That *has* cheered me up,' I said, smiling. 'Thank you. I mean the praise, by the way; not the being late for the dentist.'

Stevie smiled back. 'Tell me more about this EGO programme.'

'You're sure I won't bore you by talking about school?'

'Of course not. I'm intrigued.'

I took another sip of my drink. 'Okay. You asked for it. You must stop me if I go on for too long because I get pretty passionate about this. EGO stands for Everyone Gets an Opportunity and it's all about making drama accessible to all students, regardless of ability...'

I'd created it when I became Head of English and Drama at Kayley School three years ago. Roles on regular school productions were still fulfilled through auditions, selecting the best students, but the EGO programme ran alongside this. Pupils who were shy, had learning difficulties or weren't naturally gifted at drama were encouraged to participate in shorter performances, mentored by the stronger students. It wasn't about building up to a grand performance in front of parents; it was simply about inclusion and confidence-building.

Running this alongside regular productions meant doubling my after-school commitments, but the rewards for the students and the school had been invaluable. I'd known it would mean another delay to starting a family but, as I'd vacuumed that morning while Gary was at the surgery, I'd started to wonder if that had been the only sacrifice. Had I failed to give Gary enough attention and was his lack of attention towards me the resulting payback for that? Had I brought it on myself?

'That all sounds amazing,' Stevie said when I'd finished explaining. 'You obviously love your job.'

'I *do* love my job, but that's mainly because I love children, which takes us back to the predicament with Gary. I plan to teach for life, but it's not enough for me to just look after other people's children and watch them grow. I want to watch *my* children grow and develop into adults.' I felt the tears welling again. 'Let's not go there.' I glanced around the room. 'I still can't see Sarah or Nick. Can you?'

Stevie turned round and looked. 'No, but they must be here because I can see Clare.'

My heart sank at the mention of her name. 'Where?'

'Opposite the bar. Talking to the guy in the red tie.'

I looked towards where he pointed. 'Oh. That's Chris – Sarah's dad.' And it was probably flirting rather than talking. I decided against saying that aloud, though, because Clare was Stevie's friend and I wasn't sure how much he knew about our mutual contempt for each other.

The paracetamol I'd taken hadn't touched my headache and, with the increasing heat, I now felt even more nauseous. Hopefully Sarah would appear soon because, despite Stevie's great company, handing over my gift and making an early exit for my bed was becoming more and more attractive by the minute.

The sound of a knife tinkling against glass silenced the crowd.

'Good evening everyone,' shouted Kay. 'Thank you all for coming, especially at such short notice. I really appreciate it. Tonight is a very special evening for me. As you know, it's my twenty-first birthday.' She paused for laughter. 'Okay, you've got me, it's actually my sixtieth birthday today and I know you all think that's the reason for the party tonight, but I lied to you as that's not the main reason for inviting you all here. I've had some amazing birthday gifts but I wanted to share the best one of all with you. Nick...?'

Nick, looking very dapper in a dark grey suit with blue shirt and tie, stepped forward and gave Kay a hug. I looked round for Sarah and saw that she'd also appeared and was standing next to her parents. She looked gorgeous in a short, flared, peach dress with silver detailing round the waist, nude heels, and her dark curls tumbling down her back.

'Thanks Kay,' Nick said. 'For those of you who don't know me, my name's Nick. Kay's always believed that I'd be the perfect partner for her niece, Sarah, and I'm delighted to say that she was right. Sarah, will you join me?' Nick held out his hand, smiling. My breath caught. Oh my goodness! Was he about to propose?

'I'm even more delighted to say that, this afternoon, I asked Sarah to marry me. And she said yes!'

The room erupted. I leapt to my feet and turned to Stevie as I applauded the amazing news. 'Did you know?'

He shook his head. 'No. You?'

'No.' I could tell from his huge grin that he was as thrilled as me.

The cheering and applause finally died down.

'The bar staff are making their way round the room with glasses of champagne,' Nick said. 'Once everyone has one, I'd like to propose a toast.'

Stevie took two glasses from a passing waitress and handed one to me.

'How did he propose?' shouted someone, quickly supported by several cries to tell the story.

Sarah beamed as she exchanged a few words with Nick. He nodded, then she turned to address the guests.

'It was very romantic. Nick turned up at Seaside Blooms at lunchtime today with a picnic basket and Auntie Kay. He'd arranged for her to cover the shop while he took me down to

South Bay for lunch. He told me it was to celebrate our first week of living together. There were some beach artists down there who'd drawn the words "will you marry me?" into the sand, using garlands of flowers and hearts. It looked like they were finishing things off so we stood on the prom and watched them for a while, discussing how romantic it was and wondering which of the couples on the beach it was for. They were doing something at the top of the message and it was only when they moved away that I saw that...' Sarah's voice cracked. 'Sorry... I...'

Nick put his arm round her and kissed her head. 'When they cleared the area,' he continued, 'we could see that they'd been writing the name Sarah. Sarah stared at it for a while then turned to find me down on bended knee with a bunch of flowers and a ring.'

Sarah wiped her eyes. 'He's selling himself short. It was a stunning hand-tied bouquet of white roses – our favourites – and there was an open ring box nestling among them containing the most perfect engagement ring ever. And he gave the most beautiful sp...' Her voice cracked again.

Nick laughed and hugged Sarah to his side. 'I think the word was speech, but I'm sure you'll understand that I'm not going to embarrass myself by repeating it in front of an audience. I'm relieved to say that it worked and Sarah said yes.' He looked round the room. 'Has everyone got a glass? Then I propose a toast to Kay on her sixtieth birthday and to Sarah on our engagement. To Kay and Sarah!'

'To Kay and Sarah!'

'And to Nick!' called Kay.

'To Nick!' shouted everyone.

'I can't believe he organised all of that,' I whispered to Stevie. 'What a romantic proposal.'

Stevie smiled. 'It was. How did Gary propose?'

'Nothing quite as romantic as that, but I liked it. Funnily enough, it was on South Bay too but at the other end, near the caves at Lighthouse Cove. Whenever I feel sad or want to think, I go there. It holds good memories for me.'

'Sounds pretty romantic to me.' Stevie stood up and reached for my hand. 'Come on. Let's offer our congratulations.'

'Have you set a date?' I asked Sarah after we'd made it through the crowd of well-wishers and hugged her and Nick.

'Not yet,' she said. 'I don't think it will be a long engagement, though, because I'm far too impatient to wait for long now that I've finally met The One. I know we've always discussed this, but I have to make it official. Elise Karen Dawson, will you do me the honour of being my bridesmaid?'

I beamed. 'Of course I will. Thank you.' I hugged her again. 'I'm assuming Clare will be a bridesmaid too?'

Sarah's smile faded. Perhaps I needed to work on my enthusiasm when saying Clare's name.

'Yes. And Nick's sister, Callie. Can I trust you and Clare to play nicely?'

'It's never me who starts it.'

'Elise!'

'I promise to play nicely and collaborate with her on all things bridesmaid-ish.'

'Sarah! Congratulations!' More well-wishers appeared.

I lightly touched Sarah's arm. 'I'll leave you to it for now, but I want more details. Are you free tomorrow or later in the week? I need to know the contents of that speech.'

She laughed. 'We're going out for a family engagement meal tomorrow so maybe Monday or Tuesday?'

'I'll ring you,' I said. 'I can't believe we're finally going to plan your wedding for real.'

'I know! I was beginning to think it would never happen, but Nick was definitely worth the wait.'

I hugged her again then walked back towards our table with Stevie. As I was about to take my seat, a strong wave of nausea swept over me. Excusing myself, I dashed for the ladies. Another wave hit me as I pushed open the cubicle door. I sank to the floor, stomach heaving, face burning. When the feeling finally subsided, I slowly pulled myself up and sat down on the toilet seat, dabbing my sweaty face with some tissue paper. There was a sickness bug going round school. I hoped I hadn't contracted it – I really didn't have time to be sick.

After splashing some cold water on my face, I headed back to Stevie. My stomach sank when I saw who'd joined him. I spotted the legs first: long, tanned and devoid of any cuts or blemishes. Killer heels. Low cut fitted navy dress. Immaculate blonde bob. Great. I glanced towards the exit. It was tempting to leave, but my bag was on the table next to her drink. I had no choice but to face an altercation with Ireland's bitchiest export.

Stevie spotted me and stood up, reaching out a hand towards my arm. 'Are you okay? You look really pale.'

I tried to avoid Clare's gaze as I reached across the table for my bag. 'That headache's got worse and I feel really sick now so I am going to have to bail after all. Would you make sure Kay gets my present?' I indicated the gift bag by the table.

'Of course. Are you okay to drive?'

I nodded. 'It's not far. And thankfully I have a doctor at home to look after me.'

'Feeling sick?' Clare asked. 'Aw, how sweet. Will the perfect couple be expecting their first perfect child?'

I looked into her mischievous green eyes and scowled. 'I'm *not* pregnant, Clare. Not that it's any of your business.'

'Are you sure? You look like you may have gained a few pounds in that dress.'

'It's a maxi dress. It's meant to be big. And yes, I'm absolutely sure.' Because you had to actually have sex to get pregnant, and that's something I hadn't had for a very, very long time.

3

I slowly steered my beloved lime green Beetle, Bertie, across Whitsborough Bay towards home, hoping that a slow, steady drive would keep the nausea at bay. If I had to stop to throw up by the side of the road, I was bound to be spotted by one of my students who'd instantly share a snap of me mid-vomit on Instagram.

Think positive thoughts instead. I pictured Sarah's radiant beam and, despite the nausea, couldn't help but smile at her news. Hopefully Gary wouldn't be too late home from his session with Rob so I could tell him about the proposal. He'd love it that, like us, they'd got engaged on South Bay beach. Despite the current blip, we'd had a great marriage so hopefully it was a good omen for them.

'Tonight's nineties' party classic comes from March 1994. Take it away Robbie...' announced the DJ on the local radio station, Bay Radio.

Take That's 'Everything Changes' began to play. Immediately, I was back in our bedroom the night before, having that awful baby conversation with Gary. He'd said those exact words: 'everything changes'. What had he meant? Had he been telling the truth when he'd said he didn't want a baby at all, or had he been telling the truth when he'd adjusted that to not wanting a baby *yet? Please let it be the latter.*

By the time I pulled into our estate ten minutes later, I'd made my mind up to sit down with Gary and talk. Really talk. I wouldn't get angry. I wouldn't get frustrated. I wouldn't plead. I'd listen to what he had to say and, if he wanted to wait a couple more years before starting a family, I'd respect and accept his decision. Babies were hard work so the timing had to be absolutely right for both parents.

He'd been right last night when he said I was being childish by moaning that my younger sister was pregnant before me. Had I really voiced that? No wonder he'd been angry with me. Well, we'd have no more anger, and we'd have no more distance. We needed to spend some quality time together, just the two of us. Lately, we always seemed to be out with friends or family. The last few times we'd been out alone, we'd bumped into Stevie and Rob and had ended up spending the evening in their company instead. They were great fun, but Gary and I really needed some alone time to bring the romance and passion back into our relationship.

If I needed to pare back my extra-curricular responsibilities at school to do that, then so be it. The EGO Programme meant a lot to me, but my husband, my marriage and my future family meant a heck of a lot more. A little time and attention and we'd be back on track.

However, if Gary had changed his mind and didn't want a baby at all... Oh my goodness. I couldn't bear to think about that possibility.

As I rounded the corner onto Abbey Drive, relief flowed through me to see the Lexus back on the drive. Having a doctor for a husband certainly had its advantages when illness called.

'Gary? I'm home,' I called, kicking off my ballet pumps and placing them, my bag and my jacket on the bottom stair.

Met with silence, I headed for the large kitchen/diner at the back of the house to get myself a glass of water and to see if Gary was in there. It was deserted. The distinctive smell of pepperoni pizza hung in the air making me gag. It wasn't the nicest smell at the best of times, but for a vegetarian with a churning stomach...

Glancing at the clock above the sink, I frowned. It couldn't have been a very long training session if he'd had time to heat up a pizza and eat it too. I opened a cupboard and took out a glass. *Hang on a minute...*

My heart thumped faster and my stomach knotted as I slowly turned round to look at the dining table again. Two plates. Two wine glasses. And he knew I wasn't going to be back until late. *No, Gary! Please!* I'd have assumed that Rob had come back for pizza if it wasn't for one more item on the table: candles.

Placing the glass down on the worktop, I drifted slowly down the hall and up the stairs, feeling as though I was in a dream... or perhaps a nightmare depending on what I found upstairs. Or, rather, whom I found.

I could hear the shower – the one in the main bathroom. The fact that he was using the large wet-room style shower rather than the single shower in our en-suite added to my feeling of foreboding. I held my breath as I tiptoed tentatively down the corridor towards the bathroom, pulse racing.

He wasn't alone. Every fibre of my being told me so. A deep groan emitting from the bathroom confirmed it. How could he? In our home. In our shower.

I hesitated outside my office door, staring at the closed bathroom door at the end of the corridor. Did I really want to do this? Did I really want to catch him with her?

Another groan curled my toes and sent shivers down my spine. I took another two paces forward then stopped again. Should I wait until they were finished? Sit on our bed and confront them? Wait downstairs with a cup of tea and the TV on to drown out the sound?

But I had to know. Five paces... four... three... two... one... Was I really sure? There'd be no going back once I'd seen them together. I wouldn't be able to un-see that vision. But a little hopeful voice inside me said, 'What if he's alone and you're just imagining things? There may not be another woman in there, you know. He loves you.' I hoped beyond hope that the little voice was right.

Swallowing hard, I reached out with a shaky hand to twist the knob and push the door open. Was the little voice right?

The little voice was right. There wasn't another woman in there. My feet felt like they were encased in cement and my arms felt like lead weights hanging by my sides, threatening to pull me to the ground. 'Run!' screamed the voice in my head. But my body wouldn't obey.

It was Rob who saw me first. 'Shit! Elise!' He let go of my husband.

Gary turned round. His eyes widened and his jaw dropped, but he didn't say a word. What could he say? 'I thought you'd be out till late,' or 'It's not what it looks like,' or 'Hi honey, do you want to pass us both a towel then how about we have a nice cup of tea and a chat about it?'

The water continued to cascade, filling the room with steam. Nobody moved. Nobody spoke. It seemed as though time had stopped.

My gaze flicked from Gary to Rob to Gary again. Rob closed his eyes and hung his head. Gary slowly reached behind him and shut off the water with one hand while tugging his left earlobe with the other. Still nobody spoke. Nobody moved. It was as though the silence and stillness were a protective cloak keeping us from facing what was happening. Don't move and don't speak and we can pretend it's a dream. But it wasn't a dream. It was my worst nightmare and I had to get out.

'Elise, I...' Gary started.

I shook my head, then turned and fled. Stumbling along the corridor and down the stairs, I grabbed my jacket and bag from the bottom step and shoved my feet back into my ballet pumps.

My hands shook so much that I dropped my bag twice before I was able to fish the car keys out of it.

Reversing Bertie off the drive with a screech and turning to face down Abbey Drive, I glanced in my rear-view mirror to see the front door burst open and Gary dive out with a towel round his waist. He ran across the front lawn, shouting my name, but I pressed my foot harder onto the accelerator and turned up the volume on the radio to obliterate his cries. I pulled out of the estate and sped towards town.

My arms shook, jerking the steering wheel, then my legs followed suit. My head pounded, my heart thumped and my stomach churned.

A film of sweat covered my body and my mouth filled with saliva as I drove along the seafront. *Oh shit!* This time, I knew without a shadow of a doubt that I was going to be sick. I swallowed several times on the bile rising in my throat, knowing I had to find somewhere to stop, but this was absolutely not the place. Locals brushed shoulders with early-season tourists enjoying fish and chips, ice-creams and doughnuts. There was no way I could stop and vomit somewhere so public.

Grateful that the traffic lights were on green, I took deep breaths as I sped along the seafront, over the swing bridge and into the car park at Lighthouse Cove, unclicking the seatbelt as I did so. Without switching the engine off, I dived out of Bertie in the nick of time.

An elderly woman perched on the wall of the car park with a yappy Yorkshire Terrier under her arm stared at me then dashed across the road, muttering something about me being 'a disgusting little bitch'. How very charitable of her. What if I'd been really ill and was on the verge of collapse?

My stomach heaved and I vomited again. Wiping my mouth with the back of my shaking hand, I waited a few moments to make sure there wasn't going to be thirds, then slowly clambered back into Bertie, slumping back in the driver's seat, still shaking.

A few minutes later, I reached forward and rummaged in the glove compartment until my hand wrapped round a packet of mints. I sucked on one while I slumped back in my seat again with my jacket draped across my shoulders, staring at the pink sky gradually fading into darkness, listening to the radio on low volume.

The car park I'd pulled into was the closest one to the patch of beach near the caves where Gary had proposed, where I liked to come and think. Ironically, at a time when I needed to do some really serious thinking, my mind was completely blank. The scene in the shower had been so shocking and unexpected that my brain couldn't even begin to make sense of it. Had that really been my husband in the shower with another man? With Rob? I shook my head and closed my eyes, then swiftly opened them when all I could see was the two of them, hands all over each other. I shuddered.

Sometime later, a flash from my open handbag on the passenger seat drew my attention. It was my phone which I'd flicked to silent at the party when Kay stood up to speak. Six missed calls and five text messages, all from Gary. He'd obviously been in panic mode as they'd all been sent within half an hour.

Sighing, I scrolled through the texts:

✉ From Gary
Where are you? Please call me

✉ From Gary
Are you OK? Please call me

✉ From Gary
Li, I'm so sorry. Never meant this to happen

✉ From Gary
Can we talk? Please come home so we can talk.
Rob's gone

✉ From Gary
I'm worried about you. I get that you may not
want to talk yet, but please let me know
you're safe xx

I didn't want to listen to his voice so ignored the voicemail messages. I couldn't bring myself to text him either. Instead, I dropped the phone back in my bag and stared out into the darkness again. Was that it? Was it the end for us? Nearly sixteen years together and my husband was... What was he? Gay? Bi? Confused? It didn't make sense. Gary loved me. He'd always loved me. So what was he doing with someone else? Especially another man! There'd never been anything to suggest he was attracted to men, had there? I clapped my hand over my mouth. *Oh shit! No! Curtis couldn't have got it right all those years ago. Could he?*

4

FOURTEEN YEARS AGO

'I don't believe you.' I shook my head at my new friend, Curtis, as we put our trays on a table and took a seat in the college canteen. 'Surely it's not possible.'

He pulled a shocked expression and dramatically thumped his heart. 'Your words stab me right here, Red.' His blue eyes widened and twinkled with tears. 'Are you calling me a wee liar?' *Wow! Tears on tap? Impressive!* He hadn't been exaggerating when he'd introduced himself as the biggest drama queen I'd ever meet.

'I'm not calling you anything,' I said. 'I just don't think it's possible to tell someone's gay just by looking at them.'

'I'm not unique, you know,' he said. 'Scrub that. I am *incredibly* unique, Red, but my gift isn't. It's called a gaydar. Don't tell me you've led such a sheltered life that you've never heard of a gaydar.'

I shrugged. 'Sorry. I think you're right about the sheltered life. I probably shouldn't admit to such naivety, but you're the first openly gay person I've ever met. Mind you, you're the first Scottish person I've properly met too so I probably need to get out more.'

'Sixteen and oh so innocent to the world around her.' Curtis fluttered his eyelashes. 'I may be the first *openly* gay person you've met, but I'll bet you've met loads of us. You just haven't realised it. In fact, they've probably not realised it themselves. At our age, some know and accept it, some don't realise it yet, and some are very aware but are fighting their calling.'

Within a few hours of meeting Curtis, I'd known that I'd found a truly fabulous and fascinating friend who was going to add a little colour to A Level history classes. After five years of familiar surroundings at my small comprehensive with Sarah by my side, starting at Whitsborough Bay Sixth Form with students from eight feeder schools had been pretty overwhelming. My heart had sunk when I'd looked down the list for my history class and realised I knew nobody. I'd loitered in the doorway before my first lesson that morning, clinging onto my bag and trying to assess whether any of the natives were friendly, when I felt a tug on my sleeve.

'You simply have to make my day by sitting next to me so I can gaze at that fabulous red hair.'

I self-consciously grasped at my auburn curls as I looked into a pair of pleading eyes.

'We gingers must stick together,' he whispered, leading me to an empty pair of desks and indicating for me to sit down.

'But your hair's purple.'

'I know. I'm a traitor to our kind. I could prove I'm ginger, but I'm hoping you won't make me. It would embarrass the hell out of you and it wouldn't do much for me. Girls aren't exactly my thing. The purple's temporary. I felt I needed to make a bold statement for my first week in a new college, new town, and new country.'

'You've just moved here?'

'At the weekend. Traumatic parental divorce and I've been dragged over the border so my mum can seek solace with her parents who retired here.'

'Welcome to Whitsborough Bay,' I said. 'And welcome to the divorced parents club.'

'You too?'

'Last year and not a moment too soon, although my parents still live in the same house – just separate bedrooms – so it's still like living in a war zone.'

He frowned. 'Very strange. Clearly we have loads in common. Might as well do the formal intro thing before the lesson starts. Curtis Duncan McBride,' he said, offering his hand. 'I'm ginger and proud so don't let the purple deceive you. I'm Scottish, but I think the accent gives it away. I'm gay, but you've probably guessed that. I'm a Virgo,' he winked, 'by star sign only... and I'm a vegetarian although I do eat fish and chicken. Oh, and I'm the biggest drama queen you'll ever meet. What about you?'

I smiled. I'd play him at his game. 'Elise Karen Morgan. I'm ginger and also proud, although I prefer to think of it as auburn or red. I'm local, but I think the accent gives it away. I've got a boyfriend called Gary who I've been with since I was fourteen. I'm a Pisces... by star sign only... and a vegetarian too, except I'm a *real* vegetarian because I don't eat fish or chicken. Oh, and I want to be an English and Drama teacher so I'm all for a bit of drama in my life.'

Curtis giggled and clapped his hands. 'Feisty with a sense of humour. I love it. You and I are going to be such good friends, Elise Karen Morgan.'

'I'm still not convinced about this gaydar thing.' I stabbed a cherry tomato with my fork and pointed it at Curtis. 'How about you prove it to me?'

'Okay, you've laid down the gauntlet, Red, and I accept. Let's do it now.'

'In the canteen?'

'It's the perfect place for people-watching. Lots of interactions to observe.'

I worked on my salad as Curtis gazed around the canteen in silence for about five minutes. 'My work is done,' he said, closing his eyes momentarily.

'How many?'

'Four so far.'

'Really? Who?'

Curtis guided me through his choices. He admitted that the 'gay and proud' T-shirt one of them was wearing was a slight clue, but the others were purely on observing chemistry alone and, when I watched, I could see exactly what he meant.

'I'll admit your gaydar seems pretty impressive, but I don't know any of those boys so I'll probably never find out if you're right or not. I'm not going to wander over and ask them outright if that's what you're thinking.'

'You don't need to, Red. Believe me, I *am* right,' Curtis insisted. 'Oh, and I've just spotted another one. And we've saved the best till last by a mile. Hello, young man! Please be single and looking for a bit of drama in your life.'

'Who?'

'Picking up a tray over there. Jeans, Doc Martens, black shirt, dark hair, smouldering good looks.'

I stared across the canteen, and when I spotted whom he meant, I had to bite my lip to keep the smirk off my face.

'So what is it about Doc Martens that makes you think he's gay?' I asked.

'Three things straight off.' Curtis counted them on his fingers. 'The leather bracelets, the way he walks, and the way he can't take his eyes off the wee fella in the denim jacket four ahead of him in the queue.'

I couldn't help giggling. 'What if I told you he's wearing leather bracelets because his girlfriend brought them back for him from her holidays, he might be walking a little differently because he got injured in a bad hockey tackle last night, and the "wee fella in the denim jacket" is his best mate, Dean.'

'You know him?' Curtis looked surprised. 'And he's got a girlfriend?'

'Yes to both questions.'

'Is the girlfriend a recent thing?'

'We've been together for nearly two years.'

His face fell. 'He's *your* boyfriend?'

I nodded and patted his arm gently. 'I think your gaydar may need some fine-tuning now that you've crossed the border. I think it's still in Scottish frequency. Sorry to disappoint, but I saw him first and, believe me, Gary is definitely *not* gay. I think I'd know if he was.'

'Of course you would.' Curtis laughed awkwardly. 'I hope I haven't embarrassed you by lusting after your fella. My gaydar is only right about half the time. I was trying to be too clever. I think I'm just going to get a yogurt. You want anything? No? Back in a mo.'

Curtis nearly over-turned his chair in an effort to escape. Poor lad was obviously very embarrassed, but I was quite flattered. Gary was a catch and Curtis definitely wouldn't be the first or last male to fall for those 'smouldering good looks'.

I watched as Gary made his way over to our table, his dark eyes fixed on mine. He crinkled his nose and smiled his sexy smile.

'Hi Li.' He bent over and kissed me softly on the lips then sat down opposite me. Hmmm. Definitely not gay. Very gorgeous and very mine. 'How was your first history class? Make any friends?'

I smiled. 'One so far. A very interesting purple-haired gay Scot called Curtis.'

Gary frowned. 'Gay? How do you know he's gay?'

'He just came out with it. And you're not going to believe what else he came out with.'

Gary shrugged. 'No idea. What?' He opened his can of cola and took a swig.

'He's been using his gaydar to tell me who he thinks is gay and he singled you out. Can you believe that?'

Gary coughed and spat his drink on the table. 'He did what?'

'He picked you out as being gay.' The colour drained from his cheeks. 'Hey, don't look so worried,' I said, handing him a couple of napkins. 'I told him you weren't gay and that you were with me. Not that being gay is anything to be embarrassed about.'

'Do you think he believed you?'

'Of course he did! He admitted his gaydar isn't always right.'

Gary looked around the canteen. 'Where is he now?'

'Gone to get a yogurt. He'll be back any second. I can introduce you.'

'Sorry, Li.' He stood up. 'I can't stop. I've just remembered a meeting with the hockey coach.'

'Oh. Okay. Will I see you later?'

'I've got that thing with my mum after school.'

'What thing?'

'The thing. With the vicar. I'm sure I told you.'

I shrugged. It didn't sound familiar, but it was very possible he'd told me and I'd not been concentrating. I tended to switch off when he talked about his mother – not one of my favourite people. If there was an award for crappiest mother of the decade, it would be a tightly fought contest between mine and his.

'I'll see you tomorrow, Li.' He kissed me gently on the head then picked up his tray still laden with his uneaten lunch.

'Gary,' I called, as he turned to leave.

'What?'

'I love you.'

He smiled. 'Love you too, Li.'

I grinned as I watched him leave the canteen, butterflies fluttering in my stomach. After two years, he still had the same effect on me, especially when he called me Li. I wouldn't let anyone else shorten my name, not even Sarah. Speaking of which, where was she?

Feeling conspicuously alone, I scanned the canteen. I couldn't see Curtis anywhere, but thankfully spotted Sarah with Mandy, a new friend we'd made in English Language. I waved them over.

'I've got this new friend, Curtis, from my history class,' I said as they both sat down. 'You won't believe what he said about Gary...'

* * *

Three nights later, Gary suggested we skip our usual Friday night cinema trip and go for a walk along South Bay beach. It was a lovely warm September evening – far too nice to spend cooped up in a cinema – so I was more than happy to oblige.

I kicked off my flip-flops and wiggled my toes in the cool sand. 'I'm so glad it's finally Friday.' I hooked my arm through Gary's. 'I feel like I've barely seen you this week. Are you okay?'

He squeezed my arm against his side. 'I'm fine. I've just been a bit busy with starting college and everything.'

We walked slowly in silence, a gentle breeze flapping my long skirt around my legs.

'Do you want to turn back or go over the swing bridge?' I asked when we reached the end of the sand by the harbour.

'Let's continue,' Gary said.

We made our way over the bridge, and down the stone steps onto the beach at Lighthouse Cove. When we reached the caves, I stopped and turned to face him. 'Gary, is there something bothering you?' My stomach churned in anticipation of the answer. What if he'd met someone else already? What if I seemed dull and unattractive compared to the myriad of new faces at college?

He tugged on his left earlobe. Why was he nervous? Was he about to dump me?

'You can tell me,' I encouraged, although I wasn't sure I wanted to hear it.

'That thing your Scottish friend, Curtis, said earlier this week about his... about me being...'

'Gay?'

Gary cleared his throat. 'Yeah, that. Who else knows about it?'

'Only Sarah. Why?'

He tugged on his earlobe again. 'I think there's a rumour going round college. Ever since Tuesday afternoon, when I've walked into a room, it's gone silent and there's been lots of whispering and giggling. I'm hoping I'm just being paranoid. Are you sure only you and Sarah know?'

I put my hand over my mouth. 'No! Another girl, Mandy, was there too. Sorry.'

'It's not your fault, Li. If anything, I blame Curtis, the stupid...' Gary thankfully stopped mid-flow. I hated it when he swore and I sensed a pretty nasty expletive had been on its way. 'He wants to think before he opens his big gob and starts unfounded rumours about people he's never even met.'

'I don't think he was trying to cause any trouble. It was a bit of harmless fun, and he had no idea who you were.'

'If it's only the end of our first week there yet the entire sixth form thinks I'm gay, that's hardly a bit of harmless fun, is it? I hate being the centre of attention anywhere except the hockey pitch. You know that.' He took a deep shuddery breath and looked so vulnerable that I wrapped my arms round him and held him. For someone so gorgeous – and therefore inclined to draw attention as soon as he entered a room – Gary was exceptionally shy. Being the subject of a rumour and having everyone staring and talking about him would be killing him.

'I've just had the craziest idea.' I released Gary and took a step back. 'If a rumour really has gone round that you're gay, I know a way we can quash it.'

His eyes lit up with hope. 'I'd be happy to hear any suggestions – no matter how crazy they are – before the whole town hears about it. And, particularly, before my mum hears about it. You know how homophobic she is and you saw what her racist views did to my brother. What's your crazy idea?'

'You could ask me to marry you.' The second the words left my mouth, I wanted to swallow them straight back down. Had I really just said that? It was right up there with me being the first to say, 'I love you'. Why did I always push for that little bit more?

Gary took a step back, mouth open, eyes wide, looking totally shell-shocked. Not quite the reaction I was hoping for, but at least he hadn't run a mile. Yet.

'It was a joke,' I said quickly. 'Not a very good one either. Maybe we could do a major PDA in the middle of the canteen on Monday? Or maybe we could... why are you looking at me like that?'

Gary wore a half smile on his lips, but his dark eyes sparkled with tears. 'You'd really do that for me?'

'Do what?' My voice caught in my throat.

'Get engaged to stop a stupid rumour.'

I hesitated. Was it honesty time? Yes. I hoped it was the right approach and I wasn't about to scare him away. 'It's a bit sooner than I imagined, but I always hoped it would happen one day. If you do too, why don't we just go for it and quash that rumour? Say something, Gary. Please.'

Gary took a deep breath then got down on one knee in the sand. He took my left hand in his. 'You're the most beautiful, amazing, kind-hearted, generous girl I've ever met and, if you're absolutely sure, I'd love to marry you. Shall we do it?'

I grinned and nodded. 'Yes. Go on, then.'

5

PRESENT DAY

I sat for another hour or two replaying that first week at college in my mind. I picked up my phone again:

✉ To Curtis
Sorry it's been a while and sorry to text so late. Remember what you said about Gary shortly after we met? Turns out you may have been right. I need your advice.

Two minutes later, my phone rang. 'Hi Curtis,' I managed before my voice cracked and the floodgates finally opened.

It was past midnight when I disconnected Curtis's call. He hadn't been able to offer any words of comfort. What words were there in a situation like this? At least he'd stopped short of saying 'I told you so,' which, for someone as tactless as Curtis, must have taken considerable restraint.

Shivering slightly, I pulled my jacket more tightly across my chest. A car pulled into the car park and reversed into the space behind me, the headlights dazzling me as they bounced off my rear-view mirror. I squinted and waited for the driver to switch the lights off but, instead, they applied full-beam. I shivered again, but not from the cold this time. It was late. It was dark. It was deserted. It really wasn't the place for a lone female to be. I started Bertie's engine and pulled out of the car park, praying that the car wouldn't follow. Thankfully it didn't.

Where was I going? There were only three people I knew locally in whom I could confide, who wouldn't treat my news as the gossip of the century, but none of them were options. I could hardly turn up at Sarah's on the night of her engagement, could I? Jess and Lee were visiting friends in Leeds and staying overnight, and Kay had party guests staying at hers. I had no choice. I had to go home.

As I steered Bertie back into Abbey Drive, my heart raced. The house was in darkness. With any luck, Gary would have gone to bed and I could slip into the spare room unnoticed.

I parked Bertie next to the Lexus and gently closed the door behind me. I tiptoed up the drive, slowly turned the key in the lock, and tried to close the door behind me quietly, but failed. The hall light flicked on and Gary ran towards me, arms outstretched.

'Li! Thank God!' He wrapped his arms round me and drew me to his chest where I could feel his heart racing. 'I've been out of my mind with worry.'

For months, I'd longed for him to hold me closely, but not like this. Not a hug laden with worry and guilt. Devoid of the energy to pull away, I remained rigid and unresponsive in his arms.

He squeezed me tightly. 'You're freezing. Where have you been? Are you okay? Do you want a cup of tea? Something stronger?'

'I want tonight never to have happened,' I whispered.

Gary released his hold and took a step back. 'I'm so sorry. It shouldn't have happened.'

My legs felt weak. I sat down on the stairs and looked up into the face I loved. 'You were with a man. I know things have been tense but… a man, Gary. Why? I don't understand.' I had so many other questions, including how long it had been going on, but I was too afraid to know because what if he'd been seeing other men throughout our marriage? I wasn't strong enough to hear that.

He looked down at his feet and shrugged. 'I can't explain.' He looked up again. 'I don't understand either.'

I stared into his dark eyes, took a deep breath, and asked the terrifying question: 'Are you gay?'

He kept his eyes on me. 'I don't know. I don't know anything anymore.'

'Do you love me?'

His eyes softened. 'Of course I do.'

'Then why? Wasn't I enough for you?'

'I don't know. I honestly don't know.'

I took a deep breath, then rose from the stairs. 'I'm going to bed. Do you want to sleep in our room or the spare room?'

'Li…'

'It's not negotiable, Gary. I can't lie beside you tonight after what I saw earlier. Surely you understand that?'

He nodded slowly. 'I'll take the spare room. I'm really sorry.'

'So am I.'

* * *

I couldn't sleep that night. I felt absolutely drained, body, mind and soul, yet I couldn't seem to drift off. Every time I closed my eyes, I could hear the water cascading and see their bodies entwined. I'd stripped the bed – just in case the action had started there – but as I lay between the fresh sheets, I could still smell Gary. At 2.38 a.m. I got out of bed, grabbed Gary's pillows, hurled them into the en-suite and shut the door. The smell had gone, but the image certainly hadn't.

My mind replayed over and over again the day Curtis identi-
fied Gary as being gay and every pivotal moment in our relationship from that point: engagement, wedding, honeymoon,
holidays, anniversaries, birthdays, Christmases. They'd all been
happy. Yes, we'd had the occasional argument, but didn't everyone? They were always about banal things like him hating the
lime green kettle I'd impulse-purchased, or me being frustrated
with him for being a creature of habit and always wanting to
dine out in the same three restaurants in town, including
Sammy's Steakhouse. Hello! Vegetarian here! They were never
arguments about him lusting after other men.

He couldn't be gay. He couldn't be. But could he be bisexual?
Had he always been? What about Rob? What was going on
there? He'd definitely moved back to Whitsborough Bay after
splitting up with his long-term girlfriend. Did that mean Rob
was bisexual?

My head ached from so many unanswered questions. I rose
and swallowed another couple of paracetamol then opened one
of the curtains and stared out into the dark, deserted street. 4.17
a.m. Good grief. I needed sleep. I needed relief from the confusion raging inside me.

* * *

The sensation of someone sitting on the bed beside me awoke
me with a jolt.

'Gary!' I squinted in the sunlight pouring through the
curtain that I'd obviously forgotten to close again during the
night. 'What time is it?'

'Eleven.'

I let out a sigh of relief, realising it was Sunday. Phew. No
work. But a gay husband. Perhaps.

Gary pointed to a mug on my bedside cabinet. 'I've made you
some tea.'

I didn't feel he deserved a thank you. A cup of tea in bed was hardly recompense for what he'd done yesterday.

'We've got lunch at my mum's,' he said. 'Do you want me to cancel?'

I closed my eyes for a moment and shook my head. 'I just want everything back to normal.' Much as I couldn't bear the woman, Sunday lunch with Cynthia twice a month was normality, and I absolutely needed that right now.

Gary frowned. 'Are you sure?'

'I'm sure. What time?'

'We need to leave in forty minutes.'

'Okay.' I peeled back the duvet and smiled sweetly. 'I'll just take a shower, then don my perfect wife clothes. Yippee! Lunch with Cynthia. My favouritest thing ever.'

Gary tugged on his left earlobe. 'You're acting strangely.'

I stood up, stretched and winced at the throbbing in my head. 'Am I? I'm sorry. Is this not how a wife should act the day after finding her husband shagging another man in the shower?' I flinched at the sarcasm in my voice.

'We weren't shagging.'

'Oh dear. Did I catch you during foreplay and ruin the main event?'

'Elise! That's not called for.'

'Neither was your behaviour last night.'

We stared at each other. My head thumped and I felt sick again.

'I'll go to my mum's on my own,' he muttered, turning to leave the room.

'Oh no you won't. I'm coming.'

'I don't think you should. Not while you're like this.'

'It's your fault I'm... oh shit!' I clapped my hand over my mouth and sprinted for the toilet.

* * *

The rest of Sunday passed in a blur of sleep, interrupted by dashes to the toilet. Gary cancelled lunch with his mother to bring me water, hold my hair back while I vomited, and plump my pillows. He was so attentive and caring that I could almost forget that last night had happened. Almost.

Despite his protests, I insisted that Gary went to the surgery on Monday. After a phone call to the Head, Graham, to say I wouldn't be in, I drifted in and out of sleep that morning but, thankfully, had no more toilet dashes. By lunchtime, I felt a lot more human and managed to shower, dress and tentatively nibble on a slice of dry toast. I didn't want to go back to bed, but I had to accept that I had neither the energy nor the inclination to clean the house or mark any schoolwork. An afternoon of lying on the sofa watching films was definitely in order.

Sarah had loaned me a crate full of romcom DVDs, which I'd spotted when I'd helped her move into Nick's the previous weekend. I flicked through the titles, some new, some old, some of which I'd seen many times. I paused as I lifted an old one out and stared thoughtfully at the cover, my memory banks trying to retrieve the story. Was it too close to home? I chewed on my lip as I rummaged further. *Oh my goodness. Another one.* I pulled it out too. Holding the two DVDs, one in each hand, I debated whether I was brave enough to watch them. Sod it. I could do this. Maybe they'd help.

* * *

'Li! What's wrong? Have you been sick again?' Gary crouched by my side; his dark eyes full of concern as he placed his hand on my forehead.

I wiped my eyes and dropped the soggy tissue to the floor where it lay with a pile of fifteen or so others. 'Film,' I whispered.

Gary sat back on his heels and laughed. 'You're crying at a film? I thought something was really wrong.'

'It is.' I grabbed another tissue and blew my nose. 'Us. We're wrong. The films prove it.'

'What the hell have you been watching?' Gary reached for the DVD boxes. '*The Object of My Affection. The Next Best Thing.* Urgh. You've been watching a Madonna film? No wonder you're crying.'

'Read the blurb,' I muttered, slowly twisting on the sofa into a seated position.

Gary sighed and flipped both the films over. He read the blurbs out loud then turned to me and shrugged. 'I'm not getting it. Is this about you wanting a baby?'

I shook my head. 'They're gay. The male leads in both films are gay. They have a relationship with the female lead and it doesn't work out.' A fresh torrent of tears broke free as Gary slumped onto the sofa beside me and drew me into his embrace. This time, I responded, clinging onto him tightly, desperate to cling on to us.

'Oh, Li! What have I done to us?'

When my sobbing subsided, I made no attempt to pull away from Gary. Lying against his chest as he stroked my hair felt so familiar. Comfortable. Normal. Yet nothing was 'normal' about our situation anymore, was it?

'Are you going to leave me?' I whispered.

Gary didn't say a word, but I felt his heartbeat quicken.

'Are you going to leave me for Rob?'

He kissed the top of my head. 'Do you want me to go?'

I sighed. 'Don't put that on me. I asked you a reasonable question.'

The silence was excruciating. Eventually he sighed and said, 'I don't know what I'm going to do right now.'

'Do you still love me?'

He tightened his embrace. 'I'll always love you.'

'Do you love Rob?'

He stiffened. 'I don't know how to answer that.'

'There's only two answers: yes or no.'

'It's not that simple.'

'No. Nothing ever is, is it?' I untangled myself from his embrace, picked up the discarded tissues, deposited them in the bin, then trudged upstairs to the comfort of my duvet.

He still loved me, or so he claimed, but the fact that he hadn't said no when I'd asked him if he loved Rob gave me one very clear message: he loved Rob too, or thought he might. Did I have the strength to fight another man for my husband's affections? And, even if I did, was my husband worth fighting for anymore? If he'd lied to me about his sexuality since school or college – which I strongly suspected he had – I wasn't sure I had enough fight in me or that our marriage was a prize worth winning.

6

✉ From Sarah
How are you feeling? Did you go back to work
today as hoped? I'm guessing you'll be too
tired to come into town for our usual
Wednesday meet-up. Happy to come to you
instead after I close up, if you can cope with
a visitor xx

✉ To Sarah
Yes, back to work today and feeling much
better, but very tired. Would love to see you
tonight. If you don't mind salad, you're
welcome to join me for tea xx

✉ From Sarah
Salad sounds perfect. Got to diet for my
wedding — eek!!! See you at about 6pm Got lots
of wedding ideas I want to run by you xx

'Thanks for coming round here instead.' I led Sarah into the kitchen and flicked the kettle on. 'I don't think I'd have made it into town. I can't believe how exhausted I feel.'

'It's a nasty virus,' she said. 'I've had several customers saying they've been struck down with it and some of them have been wiped out for weeks.'

I lifted two mugs out of the cupboard. 'Sounds like I got off lightly, then, with just a few days.'

'I bet it's great being married to a doctor when you're ill. How is Gary? It's a shame he couldn't make it to the party.'

I stiffened at the mention of his name and swallowed a few times while I busied myself with opening a new box of fruit teabags. Sarah had just given me the perfect opener but I wasn't sure I could do it. I'd contacted Dad, Jess, Sarah and even Stevie to let them know I was poorly but I hadn't breathed a word about my marriage being on the rocks. I knew they'd be supportive, but they'd be shocked and they'd understandably have questions. Questions to which I didn't have answers.

'He's fine,' I said, tossing teabags into our mugs. 'He's at a staff meeting then they're going to The Peking Duck to celebrate the surgery expansion being almost complete.' I handed Sarah her mug and we sat at the kitchen table. 'Enough about Gary. What about you and the wedding? Date? Venue? Dress ideas?' She'd longed for this day for years. It wasn't fair of me to ruin her moment and it would be good to have something positive to talk about.

Sarah grinned. 'The venue's easy. I've got my heart set on Sherrington Hall and we've got an appointment on Sunday.'

'I love Sherrington Hall. Good choice.' Sherrington Hall was an ivy-covered Georgian manor house perched on the cliff top about twelve miles south of Whitsborough Bay. I'd attended a colleague's wedding there a few years before. With acres of land-scaped grounds on three sides and the sea on the other, I'd describe it as fairy-tale perfection. 'I'd imagine it gets booked up well in advance, though.'

'That's the problem,' Sarah said. 'We were hoping for May next year, but I don't think we stand much chance. Nick's suggested we consider other venues, but the thought of holding our reception anywhere other than Sherrington Hall actually makes me feel queasy.'

'I take it you're still planning a church wedding?'

She nodded. 'Definitely...'

Sarah chatted away about her initial plans. She hadn't let the lack of venue or date hold her back from working on the details. She'd known for years what she wanted if the day ever came so it wasn't like she was starting with a blank canvas. I nodded, smiled and laughed in all the right places. I asked questions. I gushed. I drew on all my acting skills to play the role of excited bridesmaid, pushing aside the idea that I could well be attending Sarah's wedding without my husband.

'So, what do you think I should do?' Sarah asked.

I stared at her, cursing myself for tuning out at the moment she'd asked for my opinion on something. 'Sorry, Sarah, I blanked then. Can you repeat that?'

She smiled. 'My fault. I've gone on a bit tonight. I'm just so excited. Have I exhausted you?'

'I am a bit drained, but I promise I'm interested. What did you ask me?'

'I was talking about the top table. Normally the chief brides-maid would sit on the top table, but as all three of you are equal, I can't do that. Should I have no bridesmaids on there or all three of you? And, if it's all three, do I include partners? Would that make it too many people? Clare's unlikely to have a guest, but you and Callie are both married so that's five of you. Is that too much? I could put Gary and Rhys on a friends' table, but I know that Gary isn't very comfortable around strangers so...'

'He probably won't be there so I wouldn't worry about it.' The words tumbled out before I could stop them.

Sarah frowned. 'What do you mean? Why wouldn't he be there?'

I traced a scratch on the table with my forefinger, unable to bring myself to look her in the eyes.

'Elise...?'

'Gary might be gay,' I muttered. 'Our marriage might be over.'

'What?'

I looked up and tears filled my eyes as I repeated the words.

'Gay? Gary? I don't understand.'

'That makes two of us. Actually, three of us because apparently Gary doesn't understand either.' A tear trickled down my cheek and splashed onto the table. 'Sorry, Sarah, I wasn't going to say anything, but it just came out. I don't want to stifle your excitement.'

Sarah reached across the table and took hold of my hand. 'Sod the wedding. This is far more important. What's happened?'

She listened intently as I told her about my discovery on Saturday night, reminded her of the rumour from college and outlined the brief conversations we'd had during the past few days which hadn't moved anything forward.

'Do you believe him when he says he doesn't know how he feels about things?'

I shrugged. 'That's the million-dollar question, isn't it? I want to believe him, but I can't shake the feeling that he's been lying to me all along. What if Curtis was right at college? What if Gary was attracted to men back then? I'm the one who said, "I love you" first. I'm the one who pushed for sex. I'm the one who suggested we get engaged to save Gary from being centre of attention when that rumour started. If he was battling with his sexuality back then, I gave him the easy way out by constantly pushing our relationship to the next level. Except it probably wasn't the easy way out for him because he might have been fighting who he really is for years. We'd be celebrating twelve years of marriage in August and sixteen years as a couple. Has he been lying to me – and to himself – for that long? How does someone find the strength to do that?'

Sarah sighed. 'I don't know. Maybe he hasn't been lying. The Curtis thing could have just been a coincidence. Maybe an attraction to men is a recent thing that's developed as Gary's got older.' I could tell by her glum expression that she didn't believe her own words.

'You develop a taste for olives, red wine or Radio Four as you get older. You don't suddenly develop a taste for same-sex relationships. Curtis said a lot of research indicates you're born with your sexuality – it's not something you become – and I'm inclined to agree with him which means...'

'Which means Gary has always been gay and fighting it,' Sarah finished when I tailed off. 'But how do you do that for nearly two decades? And why? It's not the fifties. We were born into liberal times.'

'I know.'

'So, what happens next?'

'I need Gary to be honest with me. Perhaps for the first time in his life. I don't think I'm going to like what he has to say, but we can't continue like this, pretending nothing's happened.'

'What if he says Rob was a one-off, he loves you, and it will never happen again?'

I traced the scratch with my fingertip again. 'Then he and I should swap jobs because clearly he's a better actor than me.'

7

I didn't get an opportunity to talk to Gary. After Sarah's visit on the Wednesday night, I felt drained so I crawled into bed shortly after nine and didn't hear him arrive home. We'd always been like passing ships during the getting-ready-for-work routine and this was even more the case with him moving into the spare room.

I had rehearsals for the school summer play on the Thursday night and, within minutes of me walking through the door, Gary went out for drinks to celebrate Dean's birthday. I was going out for a colleague's fortieth birthday on the Friday night and had hoped to speak to Gary before leaving the house, but he called to say that the builders had drilled into a water pipe and he was stuck at work waiting for an emergency plumber.

Setting my alarm early on Saturday morning, I hoped to finally catch him before he went to the surgery, but I must have slept through it because I awoke shortly after nine to find he'd already left.

It felt like my life was on hold. I needed answers before I could make any decisions. My thoughts on the future changed with each passing hour. One moment, I'd be convinced that it was a one-off mistake that we could get past because we were soulmates. The next moment, I'd be convinced that he was gay, always had been, had never loved me, and that our sham of a marriage was over.

Tension made my body ache and a shower did nothing to ease it. A bath might have helped, but that meant going into the scene of the crime and I'd been avoiding it ever since.

I tried to mark some year eleven poetry homework but found myself reading the same line over and over again. Action was needed.

✉ To Gary
I can't live like this. We need to talk. I'm with Jess for the dress fitting at 2pm so should be back by 3.30 at the latest. How soon can you be home?

✉ From Gary
I'll try for 5.30, but it's more likely to be 6pm. Sorry, but I've got stacks to do

✉ To Gary
If there's any chance of getting away earlier, please try. This is really important

✉ From Gary
I know, but there's no way it'll be earlier than 5.30. Hope the fitting goes well

'Are you fully recovered now?' Jess hugged me outside Bay Brides that afternoon.

'Still a bit tired, but fine.' I hated keeping secrets from my family, but I still couldn't bring myself to tell anyone else. Sarah had been amazing, but I felt that she had to be judging me for not kicking Gary out after catching him being unfaithful in our own home. To be fair, that was more my own paranoia than anything she'd said or done. Surely throwing him out would be the normal thing to do in these circumstances so why hadn't I done that? I knew the answer, though: I couldn't bear the thought of life without him. He was my husband and I loved him. I knew that if I told Jess, she'd definitely challenge me on it. She was a little more forthright than I was and I wasn't in the right place to cope with a pep talk.

'Are Izzy and Megan still coming?' I asked.

'Yes.' She glanced up Victoria Lane. 'Ah! There they are.' Jess waved then giggled as Megan dropped hold of her mum's hand and sprinted towards Jess, arms outstretched.

'Auntie Jess!' she cried.

Jess bent down, wrapped her arms around the little girl, and cuddled her tightly. 'I'd pick you up and give you a spin, but I can't lift you today.' She stood up and grinned at Izzy before turning back to Megan. 'Did your mummy tell you I've got two babies growing in my tummy?'

Megan nodded and giggled. 'I want a baby brother. Can I have one of your babies?'

Jess laughed and took Megan's hand while she twirled in a circle, her dark curls bouncing and her skirt fanning out like a dancer's. 'I can't give you one, but I promise you can play with them lots. Would you like that?'

Megan stopped twirling, nodded, then turned to me. She cocked her head onto one side as she looked me up and down.

'Hi, Megan,' I said. 'You won't remember me. You were a baby last time I saw you.'

'I'm a big girl now,' she said.

'I can see that.'

She crossed her arms and frowned. 'You look like Auntie Jess, but bigger. Do you have two babies growing in your tummy too?'

'No... er... I...' The words stuck in my throat and I just stared at her, my heart racing. How had it not entered my head until now? If it was over with Gary – and how could it not be after what he'd done – so were my dreams of being a mum. *Shit! No husband. No family.*

Jess took hold of Megan's hand and shot me a confused look before focusing on the little girl again. 'Are you ready to try on your gorgeous dress that will make you look like a princess?' she asked.

'Yes!' Megan bounced up and down then followed Jess into the shop.

Deep breath. Controlled breathing. You can do this.

* * *

Somehow I managed to hold it together. Funnily enough, it was mainly thanks to Megan. She was a bundle of energy and a source of continuous questions so it was difficult to focus on anything but her. Fortunately, there were no more questions about babies.

As we stepped out of the shop into the sunshine and waved goodbye to Megan and Izzy, Jess turned to me and screwed up her face. 'Are you okay? You've been a bit spaced this afternoon.'

'Have I? Sorry. Still tired from that sick bug.'

'Are you sure that's all? You acted very strangely before we went in when Megan asked you about babies.'

I chewed my lip. I wasn't going to get away with evading it completely. 'It's something and nothing. I thought Gary and I would be ready to try for a family soon, but he's not quite ready. We had an argument about it last week.'

'Oh no! Are things okay between you now?'

I smiled and hoped it looked sincere. 'We're working on it.'

Jess looked as though she was going to interrogate me, but we were saved by her mobile ringing. 'Sorry,' she said, fishing it out of her bag. 'Hi you... Crap! Is it?' She glanced at her watch and pulled a face. 'Sorry, I hadn't realised. We're finished now... yeah... yeah... okay... see you shortly. Love you.' She dropped her mobile back into her bag. 'Sorry, I've got to dash. Lee needs the car.' She gave me a quick hug. 'Call me if you want to talk.'

I shook my head. 'As I said, it's something and nothing. Off you go. I'll see you soon.'

I started back towards the multi-storey car park then changed my mind. I had a couple of hours before Gary was home so a bit of fresh air might be in order to clear my head and plan what I wanted to achieve from our talk.

Ten minutes later, I kicked off my flip-flops, turned the waistband of my long white flared skirt over a few times to stop it trailing in the water, and paddled along the shoreline in South Bay. I was planning to continue over the swing bridge to the caves at Lighthouse Cove – my thinking place. I hadn't been able to think about much when I'd parked near there on Saturday night, but now I was definitely ready.

But as I made my way up the sand, I realised that the beach on a sunny Saturday in mid-June was not the place to be. Everywhere I looked there were children: clambering over the rocks, paddling in the rock pools, fishing with brightly coloured nets, splashing water or chasing each other around, squealing. It was an image of the perfect family life. The life that I'd been expecting. The life that my husband had just ruined. Then it hit me. The reason why Gary had been putting off starting a family wasn't because of my promotion, the surgery expansion, or the desire to become financially secure; it was because he wasn't certain he could commit to staying with me. What if he'd been struggling more and more with each passing year to quash his attraction to men and he knew he'd eventually lose his internal battle? What if he'd been planning to leave me all along and he hadn't wanted the added complication of children to stop him? How could I have been so blind?

I couldn't stay there, surrounded by kids, without dissolving into tears. Lighthouse Cove, with its caves and rock pools, was as much a magnet to families as the main beach so no good either. Turning round, I marched across the sand in a diagonal line towards where I'd joined the beach, dodging sandcastles, sunbathers, and games of cricket.

With my head down, I willed myself not to think, not to cry, not to do anything but focus on getting out of there. Fast. I didn't see the Frisbee coming towards me – or the large man diving for it – until it was far too late.

Sprawled out on the sand, I gasped for breath. Talk about being winded! Ouch. I tried to scramble to my feet but collapsed again when a sharp pain seared through my left ankle.

'Oh my God! Elise! I'm so sorry.'

I looked up, squinting. 'Stevie?'

'I didn't see you. I dived for the Frisbee and you came out of nowhere. I'm so sorry. Are you okay?'

'I might have twisted my ankle.' I winced as I tried to move again.

'Gary! Help!' he called.

My stomach lurched. He was with Gary? But Gary had said there was no way he could leave early, the lying little... And if Gary was with Stevie, that surely meant... Stevie moved to the side and Gary loomed into view and... yes, there he was, right behind my husband. Rob. The homewrecker. The husband-stealer. *Shit! Shit! Shit!*

'What are you doing here?' Gary looked shocked to see me. And guilty as hell.

I tried to scramble to my feet again, but he gently pushed me back down. 'Let me check your ankle first.'

Shuffling away from him, I winced with the pain. 'I don't want you touching me.'

He knelt down in the sand. 'Don't be childish. You could

have broken it and I have to touch you to find out. Are you going to let me?'

I scowled at him, as I nodded reluctantly. 'I thought you had to work all day,' I hissed as he gently moved my foot.

'I did.'

'Have you started seeing patients on the beach?'

'I finished early.'

'So I see. And you thought you'd have fun with your boyfriend on the beach instead of coming home to talk about our marriage as promised.'

'Boyfriend?' Stevie said. 'What do you mean?'

I looked up at him. 'You don't know?'

'Know what?'

'Elise!' Gary hissed. 'Don't.'

Ignoring his plea, I shifted my gaze to Rob who was now standing sheepishly beside Stevie, drumming his fingers on the Frisbee. 'So you haven't told your best mate that I found you in the shower with my husband?'

'What?' Stevie twisted round. 'Rob?'

Rob cast his eyes down to the sand.

'Shit! It's true?' Stevie looked back at me. 'I... I don't know what to say. I'm so sorry, Elise.'

'So am I. And, what's even worse, is that I was expecting my husband to come home so we could talk about it but it appears that playing on the beach with his boyfriend was higher on his list of priorities.' I didn't recognise my own voice, dripping with sarcasm.

'Elise!' Gary hissed again. 'This isn't the time or place.'

'Then when the hell is?' I shouted, slapping my hands on the sand.

Gary stared at me defiantly before burying his head about our issues once more and adopting GP-mode. 'Your ankle isn't broken, but we need to get you home, get some ice on it and get it strapped up.' He stood up and reached out his hand to help me up.

I ignored it and reached out my hand to Stevie instead. 'I'm not going anywhere with *you*. Stevie, would you mind?'

Stevie helped me up and put his arm round my waist as I leaned against him. 'My car's in the harbour car park,' he said. 'If I help you across the beach, do you want to sit on a bench while I go for it?'

'That would be brilliant. Thank you.' I reached into my bag and thrust my car keys and barrier token into Gary's hands. 'Bertie's on the second floor of the multi-storey. You can pay the parking and bring him home. It's the least you can do. I've got one condition, though. *He* can make his own way home. I'm not having him in my car.'

Gary shook his head. 'Elise! Don't be so—'

Rob touched his arm. 'It's fine. Leave it. I can get a bus.'

I glared at Gary. 'Don't you dare call me childish again after you've been playing on the beach with your friends instead of being an adult and facing up to the consequences of what you've done. I'll see you at home later.'

Hopping across the sand, even with Stevie's support, was arduous. We hadn't even made it ten metres before he suggested a piggy-back. Clinging onto his back as he picked his way through the crowds in silence, I closed my eyes and tried to hold back the tears. How could he do it? How could he go to the beach and play games with Rob and Stevie as if nothing had happened? But, then again, he seemed to be pretty good at doing what the hell he liked, regardless of others. Just like my mother.

8

I couldn't face going back to Abbey Drive, waiting for Gary to appear, thinking about what he was doing with Rob in the meantime. I'd stupidly assumed he'd have been keeping his distance from Rob while he worked out his feelings. What a mug! Stevie offered to drive me back to his and I gratefully accepted. As we headed towards Little Sandby, a pretty village about ten minutes north of Whitsborough Bay, I told him all that I knew about Rob and Gary. He listened in complete silence.

'I'm shocked,' he said when I'd finished. 'I had no idea. You must be going through hell right now.'

'You could say that.' I chewed my lip. 'Can you fill in a gap for me? Is Rob gay?'

'He's bisexual.'

'Am I right in thinking he had a girlfriend in Bristol?'

'Yes. Sandy. She was his first long-term relationship with a female and they were talking about marriage.'

'Pretty serious, then. What happened?'

'He didn't tell her about his sexuality. Bristol's big, but it's not that big and, about a year ago, they were at a party with all of

Sandy's work colleagues. One of them was gay and had brought along his new boyfriend who happened to be one of Rob's exes. The lad was pretty drunk and still bitter about the way Rob had ended things with him so he decided to have a go at Rob – very loudly – about being the worst boyfriend he'd ever had. Sandy heard everything.'

'Ouch. So she dumped him?'

'Not immediately. She was angry and confused, but she loved Rob. She wasn't exactly... shall we say comfortable... with the idea of him being with other men, but what hurt her most was that he'd hidden something so important from her – something that defined him as a person. Ultimately it was the breakdown in trust that ended it.'

'That's when he moved back up here?'

Stevie nodded. 'He was a wreck as he knew it was his fault. He really did love Sandy and would have been committed to their relationship if they'd got married.'

I gazed out of the window at the attractive stone-built cottages as we entered Little Sandby. 'Poor Sandy. Years together and absolutely no idea that her man fancies other men. I know *exactly* how that feels. It's like somebody's ripped your heart out and jumped up and down on it.'

'I'm so sorry for you. Rob may be my best mate, but I'm pretty mad with him right now. What he did... what they both did... was bang out of order.'

'Tell me about it.'

Stevie turned off the main road and drove up a leafy street with stone cottages either side. He pulled onto a gravel driveway, got out, and opened a low wooden gate in an immaculately trimmed hedge on the driver's side before coming round to my side to help me out. It was a bit easier than it had been on the sand so I hopped after him round the car and through the gate.

'Welcome to Bramble Cottage,' he said.

A large front garden with shrubs and bedding plants opened

up in front of me and a stone pathway curved round towards a stunning old stone cottage with sash windows and climbing roses trained round the door and window frames. I turned to him. 'Stevie, it's gorgeous.'

He grinned. 'Thank you.' He unlocked the door and I followed him into the hallway. A border collie came bounding towards us, claws tapping on the stone floor.

'Hi Bonnie.' Stevie reached out and fussed her. 'Say hello to my friend, Elise.'

Bonnie obediently sat back on her hind legs and stretched her paw out towards me.

'Aw, that's so adorable.' I shook Bonnie's paw. 'Did you teach her that?'

'Yes, but she only does if for people she instantly warms to so that's a good sign. That means you're welcome here any time.'

'Thank you.'

'Come through to the lounge and we'll get you settled with some ice.'

Stevie pushed open a thick oak door and I gasped again as I stepped inside the lounge. What a treat. The floorboards were stripped back and a large burgundy patterned rug added warmth to the room. The wooden floors were complimented by beams across the ceiling. Proper original beams, not fake DIY ones. A wood-burner stood in a stone fireplace and the uneven walls contained various little nooks and crannies to hold books, candles, and photo frames. A pair of dark brown leather two-seaters and a high-backed red tartan-covered chair snuggled round a coffee table. It was incredibly inviting.

'It's a beautiful room,' I said. 'Did you decorate it yourself?'

He nodded. 'An elderly couple had it before me for about fifty years so it needed some updating and TLC. It's taken a while, but I've nearly got it how I want it. I've just got one more room upstairs to do. Can I make you a drink?'

'A cup of tea would be lovely. Herbal if you have it.'

'I might have some green tea.' He pulled a face. 'I bought it a while ago but hated it. I don't think I chucked it, though.'

I smiled. 'It's an acquired taste.'

'One tea and a bag of ice coming up,' he said.

I gazed round the room, taking it all in. I loved it. I could hear Stevie clattering around in the kitchen and curiosity got the better of me. With a lounge that gorgeous, I couldn't wait to see what the kitchen offered. I hopped into the hall and into the kitchen.

Stevie shut the door of a huge American fridge-freezer and turned round with a bag of frozen peas in his hand. 'What are you doing on your feet?'

'Being nosy. Nice kitchen too.' In contrast to the traditional lounge, it was modern and surprisingly huge. The wooden units were a mix of pale sage and cream. A cream Aga with a stone surround dominated one side of the kitchen, with a Belfast sink and the fridge-freezer forming the perfect triangle layout. The other end of the kitchen housed a dining area before jutting out into a glass-ceilinged snug.

'Not the original kitchen as you can tell.' Stevie filled the kettle. 'I got permission to extend about five years ago. The original kitchen was tiny, but when I viewed it, I noticed that the neighbours had an extension so I knew I'd get permission with it being a semi. It seemed like the perfect family home.'

'It is. What made you pick it when you don't have a family?' Stevie's face fell and I wondered if I'd just been really tactless.

'Funny you should say that.' He lifted a couple of mugs off the draining board. 'It was meant to be a family home for Maddy and me.'

'Maddy?'

'My ex-wife.'

'You've been married?'

He nodded. 'I thought Sarah would have said. Let's get your

foot up and iced, make the tea, then I'll tell you my tale of woe. Unless you'd rather talk about Gary...'

'Gosh, no. I've done enough talking about that liar for now.'

Stevie helped me over to the dining table and pulled another chair round so I could put my foot up on it. He returned a few moments later with tea, biscuits, and a towel.

'So, tell me about Maddy,' I said, helping myself to a dark chocolate digestive.

'I was twenty. We'd only been together for six months when she discovered she was pregnant. I was smitten so I asked her to marry me and couldn't believe it when she said yes. Bramble Cottage was up for sale and we'd often talked about how cute it was and how it would make a great family home. I'd inherited some money so I secretly bought the cottage, planning to tell Maddy on our wedding night. We lost the baby at five months, a few weeks before the wedding.'

My stomach sank. 'Oh no! I'm so sorry.'

'It was a pretty tough time.'

'I can imagine. What happened? Did you postpone the wedding?'

He dunked a custard cream in his tea and took a bite. 'We should have. Deep down, I knew she didn't want to go through with it, but I was too young and scared to have the conversation. I still loved her even though I suspected that she didn't feel the same way about me. The wedding went ahead, but it felt more like a funeral than a wedding. As planned, I told her about the cottage, but she refused to move in. She said it was a family home and we didn't have a family anymore. I tried to explore having another baby. Not immediately, of course. But she wouldn't discuss it. She stayed with her parents and I moved in here.'

He dunked his biscuit again and took another bite while I waited for the happy ending that clearly wasn't coming.

'We had no marriage. We barely had a relationship. We

made it to seven months before she told me what I'd known as soon as we lost the baby: that she'd never really wanted me, just a child. God knows why she chose me as the sperm donor or why she'd said yes to marriage. She filed for divorce and emigrated to Australia. I never heard from her again and her parents moved out of the village a year later.'

I shook my head. 'That's so awful. Why do people hurt others like that?'

'Selfishness? Fear? Who knows? It took me years before I felt ready to date anyone else and, ever since, I've been really cautious. As soon as I think it might get serious, I back off. I don't want to get hurt and I don't want to hurt them either. I'm not saying that's how it will always be, but so far I've never met anyone for whom I'd be prepared to take that risk. It's been short-term relationships ever since.'

I shifted the bag of peas off my numb foot and dried it with the towel. 'Do you think you'll ever want to marry again? If you found that special person worth the risk, that is.'

Stevie shook his head. 'I don't know if I believe in marriage anymore after what happened with Maddy. If making promises in front of your friends and family and signing a legal document means so little to some people that they can walk away from it in less than a year, why go through it in the first place?' He smiled. 'I sound very cynical, don't I?'

I winced as I reapplied the peas. 'No. You just sound like someone who's been badly hurt and, after what's just happened to me, I can completely relate to that. Right now, I'm not sure how I feel about marriage either.'

We moved away from the tricky subject of relationships and chatted more about Stevie's plans for his garden, the bedroom he hadn't yet tackled, Sarah's wedding, and my school play. Another cup of tea later, Bonnie padded into the kitchen and put her head on Stevie's lap.

'I need to take her out for a walk. You can stay here if you want or—'

'It's fine. I've got to go home and face him at some point.' I handed Stevie the bag of defrosted peas. 'I hope you weren't planning on having these for your tea. Unless you fancy mushy peas.'

Stevie laughed. 'Tempting. But I think I'll pass. Let me give Bonnie a quick walk round the block so she can do her business then I'll drop you home. I can take her out for a proper walk later.'

After less than ten minutes he returned. I stood up and put my arms out. 'Thanks for this afternoon, Stevie. You've been amazing.'

He hugged me. 'I don't know about that, but you know where I am any time you want to talk.'

'Thank you.' I didn't want to let go. Stevie was shorter than Gary and he carried a bit of weight, making his hold more like a bear-hug. For the first time since shower-gate I felt safe and protected as I relaxed against him and tightened my arms round his waist. Stevie tightened his grip around me. I could have stayed like that for hours, but I had to get home. Reluctantly, I released my hold. 'You give amazing hugs too.'

He laughed. 'In that case, you know where I am any time you want a hug too.'

'Don't say things like that. You'll have me on your doorstep at three in the morning demanding a super-hug!'

9

When Stevie pulled up outside 9 Abbey Drive, relief flowed through me to see Bertie back on the drive, closely followed by anger that there was no sign of the Lexus. The calm I'd felt at Bramble Cottage gave way to rage. How dare he go out and avoid talking yet again? What the hell was wrong with him?

Stevie helped me hop to the door and offered to come in and wait with me, but I insisted he go home so he could take Bonnie out for a proper walk.

After we'd said goodbye and I'd secured another super-hug, I closed the door and hobbled down to the kitchen to see if Gary had left me a note because, to be fair to him, he could have been waiting for me and given up; I'd been at Stevie's for well over two hours. There was no note.

I checked my mobile to see if I was doing him a disservice and he'd texted me to explain his whereabouts, but there was no message either.

✉ To Gary
I'm home. Where the hell are you?

Shuffling over to the dining table, I sat for at least ten minutes, staring at my phone, waiting for a response. None came. I called him instead. It rang five times then disconnected without going to voicemail. So he was choosing not to take my call, was he? Right. That's it. I stabbed at the keypad:

✉ To Gary
Have we really got to the point where you're screening my calls? It's 6.33pm now. I INSIST that you phone or text me by 6.45pm to let me know where you are and when you'll be back to talk. Do NOT ignore this text. I mean it!

I hunched over the phone, watching each agonisingly slow minute pass by, challenging him to dare to ignore the text. He ignored it.

✉ To Gary
Time's up. You asked for it…

Holding on to the table, I pushed myself up, rage propelling me down the corridor and up the stairs, almost oblivious to the pain in my ankle thanks to the greater pain in my heart. I pulled a suitcase off the top of the wardrobe in the spare bedroom, marched into my room and threw it onto the bed. Grabbing a handful of Gary's shirts from the walk-in wardrobe, I shoved them in the suitcase, still on their hangers.

'I should have done this last week,' I muttered. 'I stupidly wanted to give you a chance to explain. To give you a chance to save our marriage. Something you obviously don't care about seeing as you've spent the afternoon with your boyfriend instead of with me.'

As I reached the wardrobe to grab my second load, a thought struck me. What if it hadn't just been the afternoon he'd spent with Rob? What if it had really been the full day and he'd been lying about going to the surgery? What if he'd been with Rob when he'd replied to my text saying that he couldn't get away early? What if every late night and weekend in the surgery had been time with Rob instead? Had the two of them being laughing at me for being so clueless? For being so naive? For being so unassertive?

Well, I'd show him how assertive I could be. I stormed into my office and rummaged in my sewing box for my dressmaking scissors. Returning to the bedroom, I closed my eyes as I stood over his shirts and opened the scissors wide. What should I do? Cut off all the cuffs? Cut them into shreds? Or something more discreet like lots of little puncture holes

I closed the scissors and sat down heavily on the bed, shaking my head. Tempting as it was, itching powder in his pants, cutting up his clothes, or running a key down his beloved Lexus wasn't my style. Changing the locks was, though. I put the scissors away then searched on my mobile for an emergency locksmith and made the call.

* * *

Ninety minutes later, there was a new lock on the front door and I'd packed most of Gary's clothes into two suitcases, a holdall and a suit-carrier. I'd also filled a crate with his favourite CDs and films along with his office in-tray and a couple of files. He kept most of his paperwork at the surgery so hopefully he wouldn't need access to the house for anything else.

The locksmith had taken pity on me struggling up and down the stairs with my poorly ankle and had kindly carried everything into the garage, no questions asked, although the sympathetic look in his eyes told me that he knew exactly what was going on. He probably encountered the same sorry tale on a regular basis.

☒ To Gary

```
Thank you for spending the day with your
boyfriend, ignoring my texts and refusing to
come home to talk. This has made things really
easy for me. The lock has been changed and
your stuff is in the garage to collect at your
leisure
```

My phone rang moments later.

'Hi Gary.'

'What the hell are you playing at?' he shouted.

'Gaining back control of my life.'

'By kicking me out of my own home?'

'What did you expect? That I'd continue living in limbo while you decide whether or not you're in love with another man? That I'd cook and clean while you spend your weekends playing Frisbee on the beach with him? That I'd give you all time in the world to decide whether you want in or out of our marriage?'

He sighed. 'I can come home and we can talk now.'

'It's too late for that. You've had your chance all week and you've had several chances today, but you've screwed up every time. Collect your stuff and find somewhere else to live.'

'But—'

But I didn't want to hear it anymore.

He appeared at about half nine. I watched through the bedroom blinds as he slammed the car door shut, stormed up the garden path and tried the door, probably hoping I'd been lying about changing the locks. He rang the bell several times, rang my mobile, rang the landline, rang the bell again, but I ignored him. Eventually, he gave up and lugged his stuff out of the garage and into the boot of the Lexus, got into the car, and started the engine. I released a shaky breath as I watched his car disappear round the corner.

I'd just brushed my teeth and crawled under the duvet when the doorbell rang again. Gary? I limped to the window and cautiously parted the blinds. The Lexus was back on the drive.

'I know you're in there,' Gary shouted through the letterbox. 'We need to talk. I'm sorry I didn't come home earlier. It was wrong of me. Please come down and let me in.'

I hovered near the top of the stairs.

'I'm not leaving so you might as well let me in.'

'How do I know it's not a trick to get access to the house again?' I shouted.

'You'll just have to trust me.'

'Trust you? Really? Because it transpires that you're such a trustworthy person, aren't you?'

'Please, Li. I'll answer your questions.'

I hesitated before slowly limping down the stairs. If he was being honest and this wasn't a trick, I *did* want answers, even if those answers were going to hurt. I was already assuming the worst – that he'd been gay when he married me – so what harm could it do having that affirmed?

'You promise you'll leave when you've said your piece?' I said, opening the door on the chain.

'I promise.'

'Go through to the kitchen,' I said, fully opening the door. This wasn't a curl-up-on-the-sofa discussion. It was a hard-wooden-chairs-so-you-won't-outstay-your-welcome discussion. I exhaled slowly and rubbed my tired eyes as I followed him down the hallway, pulling my dressing gown tightly round me.

'So, how are you?' he asked as he sat down in his usual dining chair.

I sat down too. 'How do you think?'

He nodded. 'Sorry. Stupid question. Is the ankle okay?'

'It hasn't fallen off.'

'Good.'

I sighed. 'You didn't come here to check out my injury. You wanted to talk. So, talk.'

'You asked me some questions this week and I realise my answers were very non-committal. Rob made me realise—'

I flinched. 'You've been discussing me with Rob?'

'Well, he just thought—'

'I don't give a shit what Rob thinks.'

'Elise!' Gary banged his fist down on the table. 'I'm not here to have an argument. Rob told me I'd been unfair to you when I know the answers to the questions, so he insisted I come here and tell you the truth, which is why I came back.'

I stared at him for a moment. 'Go on then. Let's have the truth. Are you gay?'

'Yes.' It was barely a whisper.

'Gay as opposed to bisexual?'

He nodded slowly.

Shit! Worst-case scenario. My heart thumping, I could scarcely form the next question. 'How long?'

He tugged on his earlobe. 'I suspected it when I was about fifteen.'

My empty stomach churned and my breathing came fast and hard. So did the tears. I quickly wiped them away, but it was too late.

'I'm so sorry, Li.' He reached across to wipe my tears, but I backed away. I didn't want him touching me. It was too intimate. I swallowed hard a few times, those razor blades slicing in my throat. 'So everything about us was just a lie. You never loved me...'

'I did love you. I still do, but—'

'You're just not *in love* with me? That old chestnut.'

'Li—'

'It's Elise! You've lost the right to shorten my name. If you knew you were gay, why the hell did you marry me?'

'Because I loved you. You were my best friend. I thought that would be enough to make it work. And it did work for a long time. We had a great marriage. You know we did. But you were so desperate for a child and... I don't know... it just felt wrong somehow to bring a child into the world. It felt like a lie.'

I scraped my chair back over the quarry tiles as I leapt up. 'A lie? A baby would be a lie, but our marriage wasn't? That's absolute bullshit.'

Gary screwed up his face. 'I'm sorry. I didn't explain that very well. Will you sit down?'

I slowly lowered myself on to the chair, but I didn't pull it back under the table. I needed the distance. 'Explain it then.'

'It's hard to. I suppose it was the thought that you didn't just want one baby. You'd always wanted three or four. I'd been happy with just you, but the reality of playing happy families felt like a step too far.'

'A step too far?' I cried. 'We talked about kids from day one. This isn't something I suddenly sprung on you. I adore children. I'm a teacher, for goodness' sake. Everything I've ever done has been about building up to my own family and I thought that's what you wanted too.'

Gary stared at the table. 'I thought I did too. Until...'

'Until you met Rob,' I suggested when he tailed off.

He nodded. 'I'm sorry.'

'Is it love?'

He nodded again.

My stomach lurched. 'Was he the first?'

'Does it matter?'

'Of course it does. I know we hardly ever had sex, but I think I have a right to know whether my husband was shagging another bloke at the same time he was hardly ever shagging me.'

Gary's shoulders sagged and he looked at the table as he muttered, 'There were two others before Rob.'

I put my hands to my face and shook my head, my stomach twisting and turning. 'Gary! When?'

He looked up at me. 'Last summer. It was nothing serious.'

'Nothing serious? You were having sex with another man... with two other men... and you call that nothing serious?'

'It wasn't sex. It never went that far. It still hasn't.'

I shook my head. 'You can spare me the details.'

We sat in silence for a while as I tried to digest his revelations.

'I've got one more question,' I said, 'because you haven't given me a proper answer. If you knew you were gay, why did you marry me? Don't give me that best friends bullshit again.'

'I thought it was the right thing to do.'

'For whom?'

Gary tugged on his left earlobe. 'I can't... It's complicated. I'm sorry. It's... I...'

I stood up. 'I think you know, but seeing as you're refusing to tell me now, it's time for you to go.'

He lowered his eyes, nodded, then stood up. 'Okay. Sorry.'

I headed down the hallway towards the door and waited for him to follow me.

'If my mum calls, you won't tell her about any of this, will you?' he said.

It was on the tip of my tongue just to say 'no' when it struck me that I didn't need to be diplomatic about his mother anymore. 'The fewer words I have to utter to your mother, the better. *You* can have the pleasure of telling her. I don't imagine she'll be too devastated that I'm out of your life, and I certainly won't shed a tear that I never have to cross paths with her again.'

'Tell me how you really feel about her,' he said, sounding surprised at my reaction.

I turned round to face him, hands on hips. 'Oh Gary, you so don't want to challenge me to do that. That little comment didn't even represent a fraction of how I feel about your mother, which you'd have known if you'd ever listened to me instead of constantly jumping to her defence any time I opened my mouth.'

'I'm sorry. I didn't realise.'

I shook my head. 'You did but you chose to do nothing about it and I, like always, didn't push the issue. It's how it's always been with the two of us, isn't it? I stay quiet and keep the peace and you ignore your mother's appalling behaviour.'

He looked down at the floor, which showed me that he agreed.

'I won't say anything,' I said again, 'but I suggest you don't leave it too late to tell your mother yourself. We live in a small town and word has a habit of getting round.' I opened the front door.

He remained in the hall. 'You think she'll find out about Rob?' he whispered, panic etched across his face.

'Of course she'll find out. The woman's a walking gossip column.' I closed the door again as realisation hit me. 'That's it, isn't it? That's really why you married me. So she didn't disown you like Lloyd.'

Gary's silence and downcast eyes said it all.

I opened the door again. 'I'll text you or email you next week about the practical stuff and I'll text you if your mother rings, but don't get in touch with me. You've got what you want, but I need some time to get my head round the huge lie that our life has been and decide what I want.'

'But—'

I raised my hand in a stop gesture. 'No! Listen to what I'm saying for once in your life. I mean it. Leave me alone and this can remain amicable. Keep pestering me and things will turn nasty. That's not a threat, by the way, it's a statement of fact. I need time and I need space. Goodbye.'

The moment I closed the door, my jelly legs gave way and I sank to the floor, sobbing. It was a lie from the start. Right from the very start. Exactly what I'd feared the most. He'd never loved me, except as a friend. He'd just used me. And I'd let him.

It was cold by the front door. Making my way upstairs, I curled up under the duvet, shivering. What a mess. And all because of what happened with his brother. Nine years Gary's senior, Lloyd had moved to London with his job shortly after I started seeing Gary. I remembered his mum being overly dramatic about it and sounding off about big cities being smelly, unsafe and far too multicultural. Gary once told me that she was terrified Lloyd would meet someone who wasn't a white, middle-class, Tory Christian. She was therefore thrilled when he announced a year later that he was bringing his girlfriend, Zoe – a practising Christian – home to meet the family. What he'd failed to mention was that Zoe hailed from Jamaica. I could vividly remember sitting in Gary's parents' lounge with Gary and his dad, Malcolm, while Cynthia fussed round us, straightening doilies and handing out hors d'oeuvres. She was at a critical point with cooking lunch when the taxi pulled up outside so she couldn't go to the door. When she returned to the lounge, Lloyd and Zoe were taking off their coats. 'Darling!' she cried, holding her arms out towards Lloyd. Then she stopped, the smile slipping from her face as her hand clutched her throat. 'Good Lord! She's coloured.' Half an hour later, Lloyd and Zoe were in a taxi heading back to the train station.

I'd tried over the years to forget what I'd witnessed that day. I'd had no idea that anyone could possess such abhorrent views based purely on the colour of someone's skin. My parents had called each other names, but it had been tame compared to the venom that exploded from Cynthia. Gary had tried to defend her later, saying it was just the surprise, but I knew her behaviour had shocked him to the core too. A few days later, Malcolm had a mild heart attack. A few weeks after that, he had a fatal one. Although she'd treated him like a minion, Cynthia had been devastated by Malcolm's passing. She blamed Lloyd and Zoe for it. She wrote to Lloyd to tell him his father was dead, that it was his fault, that he was dead to the family, and he wasn't welcome at the funeral.

After the coffin was lowered into the ground, Cynthia, Gary and I had all stepped forward and dropped a rose onto it. Cynthia turned to Gary, took his hand, and said, 'Promise me you'll never let me down like Lloyd. You're all I have left now, Gary. Promise me you'll be a good son and never break my heart like he did.' Gary had remained silent. 'Please, Gary. It's only the two of us now. If you're going to turn out like Lloyd, you might as well push me in to join your father.' Gary had pulled her into his embrace. 'I promise, Mum. I'll be the perfect son. I won't let you down.'

And he hadn't. Instead, he'd let me down and he'd let himself down. He'd pretended to be someone he wasn't to keep the peace and for what? He'd messed up his life, he'd messed up my life and Cynthia was going to find out sooner or later. And, when she did, I wouldn't want to be around to witness it. For a brief moment, I felt sorry for Gary and actually understood why he'd done what he'd done. Then I reminded myself that he'd had a choice and that he should have been strong like his brother, sticking by what he wanted out of life. He should never have made that promise. And he should never have dragged me into it.

10

I woke up a little after nine the next morning. It felt strange knowing that Gary wasn't in the house and hadn't been there all night. I wondered where he'd stayed. It wouldn't be his mum's because that would lead to too many questions. His best mate Dean's? Rob's? I shuddered at the thought of the latter.

My eyes focused on the large wooden frame on the wall opposite the bed, filled with photos of us as a couple through the years. How could I not have known?

Rolling out of bed, I moved closer to the frame and squinted at each image, looking for some sort of clue to show me that Gary wasn't happy, that he didn't want to be with me, that he wanted to be with a man instead. Nothing. I shook my head. What had I expected? To see Gary holding up a rainbow placard stating, 'I am gay'?

I turned and reached for the large framed photo on my dressing table. It had been taken on holiday in the Maldives and showed us clinking champagne flutes as we celebrated our tenth wedding anniversary. We looked happy and in love, didn't we? I squinted my eyes as I focused on Gary's face, then my eyes widened and my stomach churned. 'His smile doesn't reach his eyes!' I whispered.

I dashed out of the bedroom and onto the landing where there were more large framed photos and snatched each one off the wall. Smiling, but not happy. Down the stairs. More of the same. Dining room. Lounge. Every image told the same story on the face of it; a couple in love, a couple devoted to each other, but scrutinise closer and it was clear that only one felt that way. It was subtle. Very subtle. But now that I knew our marriage had been a lie, I could see it.

Stumbling into the lounge, I dropped the bundle of frames on the sofa and, with shaking hands, grabbed at the sparkly silver frame on the mantelpiece. I stared at my favourite wedding photo of Gary standing behind me with his arms round my waist and his head nuzzled into my neck. Even on our wedding day. Smiling, but not happy.

'How could you live that lie?' I yelled at Gary's image. 'You said you realised when you were fifteen. That's fifteen years. *Fifteen years of lies!*' In a frenzy, I pushed open the clips on the back of the frame and tossed the velvet backing onto the carpet. I snatched at the photo and let the frame drop to the floor with a smash of glass on the hearth. A tear dripped onto the photograph then, sucking my breath in, I ripped it in half, then again and again. I threw the pieces up in the air and watched as they floated to the floor like confetti. How ironic.

I spun round, taking in the contents of the lounge: the leather suite we'd splashed out on when I secured my departmental headship; the lamps we'd bought from Greenwich Market on a 'romantic' mini-break to London; the carved wooden box Gary had bought me for our fifth 'wood' wedding anniversary and the wooden chess set I'd given him; the pair of prints we'd bought on holiday in Tuscany. Every single item in the room held a memory and every single memory involved Gary.

Sagging against the doorframe, I gasped for air. I'd been wrong to kick Gary out and stay in a place full of memories. *I should have left instead.*

I had to get out of the house and away from the lies. I ran up the stairs to the bedroom, wincing with every other step, pulled off my nightie and grabbed the first skirt and top I saw in my wardrobe. They didn't match, but I didn't care. I didn't care that my hair was a mess or that I hadn't brushed my teeth. All I cared about was escaping. I just hoped I could still drive with my injured ankle.

* * *

Sitting cross-legged on the cool sand at Lighthouse Cove, my arms loose by my sides, a breeze chilled my wet cheeks, but I didn't have the energy to wipe the tears away. Wispy clouds floated lazily across a cornflower blue sky indicating the start of another gorgeous day on the Yorkshire Coast. The weather felt wrong. It felt like there should be a storm and crashing waves to match the turmoil in my life, not the sort of weather that could elicit a smile from even the grumpiest person.

I closed my eyes and tried to clear my head of any thoughts, focusing only on the soothing lapping of the waves. *No thoughts. Focus on the waves. Relax.* The warm sun on my face felt like a hug; just what I needed. I breathed in and out slowly. *In through my nose, out from my mouth. In... and out... In...*

'Elise?'

Startled, I opened my eyes. 'Kay? What are you doing here?' I quickly wiped at my cheeks.

'Taking photos of the rock pools.' She knelt down beside me. 'What's wrong?'

'Nothing.'

'I saw the tears. You know you can tell me anything, sweetheart.'

The tears tumbled at her kind words. 'It's all gone wrong. My husband's gay and our marriage was a sham...'

* * *

'I'm so very sorry,' Kay asked when I'd brought her up to date between sobs. 'Where do you go from here?'

I shrugged. 'Arrange to see a solicitor, start divorce proceedings and somehow try to re-build my life. That's not going to be easy given that Gary's been the most important part of it since I was fourteen.'

'I'd ask whether there's any chance of a reconciliation, but under the circumstances...'

'After I caught them together, I knew it was over. After his revelation last night that he's always known he was gay, what would be the point? If we did stay together, it would be a marriage of convenience and that's not going to make anyone very happy. It's not what I want and, let's face it, he wants Rob, not me.'

'Will you keep the house?'

I sighed. 'The house has too many memories. There are photos of us everywhere and we picked everything together. Every piece of furniture and every item in the house right down to the utensils pot in the kitchen symbolise our life together. A lot of couples set up their own homes then meet so they've got their own stuff, but we were childhood sweethearts so we started from scratch together. Nothing's *mine*. It's all *ours*. Even if I removed everything and started afresh, there's still the house itself. We were the first people to live in it. We had our offer accepted early enough to pick out the kitchen and bathrooms and make alterations to the layout so it was exactly what we wanted. I remember meals and barbeques and parties... and, worst of all, I remember him in the shower with Rob.'

Kay took my hands in hers. 'Then you know what you must do. Come and live at Seashell Cottage with me.'

I shook my head. 'I couldn't impose on you like that.'

'Nonsense. You wouldn't be imposing. After more than six months travelling the world and sharing a room with Linda, I'm finding it a little too quiet on my own again so you'd be doing me a favour.'

'You really mean that?'

'You know I've always thought of you as a surrogate daughter. I want to help.'

What a lifeline! Yes please! I looked into her eyes to make sure she was genuine and not just being nice and saw the loneliness. I could use a mum figure in my life right now. 'Would tonight be too soon?'

She grinned. 'You can move in right now if you want.'

I dug a shell out of the sand with my bare toes as I contemplated her offer. 'It's very tempting, but it will take me a while to pack. Plus, I haven't broken the news to Jess, Dad or Mother yet. I really need to do that today before anyone else does.'

'Tonight it is, then,' Kay said. 'Good luck with your mother. Do you want me to come with you for some moral support?'

'Also tempting, but I prefer to face the enemy alone.'

* * *

I didn't bother trying her flat. I knew I'd find her in The Flag Inn, her run-down local; Flag Inn by name and flagging by appearance. The stale smells of beer, sweat, and years of nicotine abuse before the smoking ban made me gag as I pushed open the heavy wooden door.

When my eyes adjusted to the gloom, I spotted a woman on her own at a table by the jukebox, nursing a tumbler of amber liquid. She wore a sky-blue cotton nightie with daisies embroidered across the top, a pale grey threadbare cardigan and a pair of navy canvas shoes. Matted auburn curls hung round her haggard face. If I didn't know better, I'd have placed her in her late sixties, not fifty-one.

'Hello Mother.' I pulled out a stool and sat down opposite her.

'Jess,' she slurred. 'What are you doing here?'

I took a deep breath. 'It's Elise.'

She squinted. 'Oh. Forgot my glasses. I'd offer you a drink, but...'

'It's fine. I'll get my own.' I stood up again.

'Whiskey,' she said. 'Double. No ice.'

There was no point protesting. Over the years, I'd tried it all – reasoning with her, shouting at her, enveloping her in love, shock tactics, GP appointments, counselling – but at the end of the day, she didn't want my help or anyone else's. I'd ended up turning to counselling myself. I'd believed that I needed to 'fix' her, but my counsellor, Jem, had helped me see that she didn't want to be fixed. He was right. Only she could make that decision.

A few minutes later, I placed the double whiskey on the table in front of her. 'I'm not staying long.'

She smiled after staring at the glass for a while, as though she'd managed to focus for long enough to register that it really was the double measure she'd demanded. 'You don't have to stay at all if you don't want.'

I took a gulp on my apple juice. 'I've come to tell you some-thing and then I'll leave you in peace because I can see you're very busy.' The sarcasm was lost on her, but it made me feel a little better. When she showed no interest in what I had to say, I hesitated about telling her. 'I see you've got a new nightie,' I said.

She stroked the embroidered daisies. 'Prettier than a dress and at a fraction of the price. You got a problem with that?'

'Would you do anything about it if I had?'

'No. I'd probably start coming out in my slippers too.'

She would too, just to spite me. 'No Irene?' I asked. Irene was Mother's drinking partner and, from what I'd seen of her, equally as self-centred.

'Her daughter dropped a sprog and has dragged her to some hideous family photoshoot, poor bugger.' She knocked back the rest of her drink and picked up the one I'd bought, then stopped before she took a sip. 'Ah. Penny drops. Is that what you've come to tell me? Are you finally sprogged up?'

I cringed at the phrase. 'No. I'm not pregnant.'

'Is that doctor of yours shooting blanks?'

'Mother!'

'He is, isn't he? He's shooting blanks. Or, worse still, he can't even get it up.' She took a sip of whiskey.

'I've come to tell you that Gary and I have split up.'

She laughed, or should I say cackled. 'He's finally had enough of your pathetic "yes, Gary, no, Gary, three bags full, Gary" spineless attitude, has he? No man likes a woman with no opinions or interests of her own, you know. Men need someone they can spar with, not someone who follows them round like a lost puppy dog.'

My stomach churned. 'Is that really what you think of me?'

'Yes, and you've just proved it in the ten minutes you've been here. You've bought me a double without question and you've just rolled over and accepted that your own mother goes out dressed in a nightie without trying to debate it. For God's sake, Elise, why don't you grow some?'

I stood up, picked up the rest of her whisky and tipped it into my almost-full glass. 'How's that for growing some? I'll see you at Jess's wedding. If you can drag yourself out of the pub for such a "hideous family photoshoot", that is.'

Shaking from head to foot, I drove to Lighthouse Cove and sat on the sea wall above the beach, gasping for fresh air and soaking up the heat of the sun in an effort to cleanse myself of Mother's hurtful words. The worst part of it was knowing that, although tactlessly put, she was absolutely right. At some point during our marriage, I'd completely lost sight of me and had become all about pleasing Gary. I'd carved out a great career and knew I was good at my job, but it was like I was a different person at home: no interests of my own, no challenges, no passion for anything that wasn't about Gary. Why had I done that? Had it been an attempt to become the exact opposite of my selfish mother and somehow I'd gone too far the other way? Or, even more alarming, had it been that I'd known that things were wrong between Gary and me some time ago and, as the falling apart of my relationship would have meant no baby, I'd tried to become 'the perfect wife'. If I kept the peace with his awful mother, ran a tidy and ordered house, and avoided arguments, surely there'd be no reason to ever leave me and therefore the family I craved would be just round the corner.

Yet he'd still left me.

Bending my head over, I held it in my hands. What a mess!

I sat on the wall for about half an hour before texting Gary to tell him that he could move back in that evening because I was moving out. Then I drove back to Abbey Drive where I Skyped Dad then phoned Jess to give them the news. Dad offered to get the next flight over from Spain, but I insisted he stay put. I'd see him at Jess's wedding and we'd spend some quality time together then. Jess, after calling Gary every name under the sun, said she would offer to help me pack, but was looking after Megan for Izzy and there'd be no chance of packing anything if she brought Megan over.

I texted Stevie with an update and called Sarah. Despite me insisting I could manage, Sarah pulled up outside half an hour later. 'You helped me move twice in less than a year,' she said as I hugged her gratefully. 'It's the least I can do.'

Ten minutes later, Stevie turned up too. 'Don't want you taking too much weight on that bad ankle,' he said, giving me another of his amazing bear-hugs.

Three pairs of hands made light work of it and packed up all my summer clothes, the essentials from my office, my toiletries and anything else I might need in the foreseeable future. I'd return another weekend to pack up the rest of my belongings when I'd worked out where to live on a more permanent basis.

Closing Bertie's boot, I took one last look at 9 Abbey Drive and sighed. It was over. My marriage was over. I'd never really known the man I'd loved since I was fourteen. As a result, I no longer knew who I was. Well, it was time to find out and, thankfully, I had some great friends around me who'd help me do just that.

Sarah put her arm round my waist. 'It'll be okay. You'll get through this.'

I swallowed hard on the lump in my throat. 'Do you think so?'

'Not overnight, but it *will* happen. I guarantee it.'

As I backed Bertie off the drive, I hoped she was right because, despite everything that had happened, the thought of life without Gary terrified me.

11

The next two weeks flew by as I settled into my new home, Seashell Cottage. A cosy white-washed eighteenth-century cottage in The Old Town, I'd often enjoyed school holiday sleep-overs there with Sarah when we were kids. We used to tell each other stories by torchlight as we snuggled under the blankets and listened to the waves from the distant shore. I'd never imag-ined back then that I'd be sleeping in that same room, on that same bed, at the age of thirty because my marriage had fallen apart.

The EGO programme and play rehearsals kept me occupied for a couple of evenings a week and, on the others and during weekends, I joined Kay for walks along the coast. Sometimes we talked about Gary. Sometimes we talked about Charlie, the love of her life who'd died when his car left the road on his way to propose to her on her twenty-first birthday. She'd closed herself off to relationships ever since. Sometimes we shared compan-ionable silence while she took photos and I stared at the sea, trying to work out what I wanted from life without Gary.

I avoided everyone else, though. I didn't want sympathetic looks or clichés about time being a great healer or there being plenty more fish in the sea. I didn't want a new fish; I wanted my old one. I wanted my life back the way it was meant to be: happily married to Gary, looking forward to starting a family, and basking in the excitement of being bridesmaid for my sister and my best friend.

Sarah asked to meet up on several occasions but I fobbed her off with a myriad of excuses. It was a self-preservation thing because I didn't have the strength in me to be excited about two weddings and, as Jess's was soonest, I needed to inject the limited wedding excitement I could muster into hers. I had the luxury of time before Sarah's so I could make it up to her later. It was also a friendship-preservation thing. What sort of friend would I be if I rained on her parade with my current negativity towards the sanctity of marriage? The occasional text or email was definitely the way to go until I felt more positive about things.

Stevie texted me several times and invited me out for a drink. I felt bad for putting him off, but what if he told me news about Gary and Rob that I didn't want to hear? It was hard enough psyching myself up to opening texts from him, just in case, without meeting him in person as well – even though I really needed one of his super-hugs.

A couple of days after I moved in, Sarah managed to set up an appointment for me with the solicitor from Bay Trade, a business club she attended, including negotiation of a large discount in exchange for me giving some confidence coaching to his painfully shy ten-year-old son.

Sitting in front of a stranger one evening and saying, 'I want to divorce my husband,' felt very surreal, but Richard was reassuring and guided me through every step of the process. Providing Gary didn't dispute things, it should be fairly straightforward. Surely he wouldn't dispute it. How could he?

At school, I received some amazing news. Graham had secretly nominated me for 'Exceptional Teacher of the Year' for my work on the EGO programme and I was invited at very short notice to attend a black-tie dinner. To my surprise, I won the award for Yorkshire. Clutching the glass plaque as cameras flashed, I didn't know whether to laugh or cry. The EGO programme had been the catalyst that turned Gary's attentions elsewhere, yet it had also brought a close to a sham marriage. Ultimately that had to be a good thing, hadn't it? A marriage built on lies wasn't a marriage at all.

I must have gone through every sort of emotion during that first fortnight at Seashell Cottage. Some nights I drifted off to sleep feeling really positive about the future. Other nights, I sobbed myself to sleep instead. I missed Gary. I missed his friendship. I missed his presence. I missed our routines. I missed giggling with him over some of the hilarious mistakes some of my students made in their homework, and I missed hearing about the latest embarrassing medical complaint he'd encountered or the ridiculous ailments dreamt up by his hypochondriac patients. Most of all, I missed the possibilities that our future together had held. The longing for a baby grew stronger every day, perhaps because of the Gary-shaped gap in my life.

On the Sunday of the final weekend in June, three weeks after Gary's betrayal, I found myself drawn to my laptop to research my options. Insemination. Adoption. Fostering. What a minefield! I read several pages on insemination, shaking my head. Aside from the expense and the complications brought on by legislative changes, could I really start a life using a donation from a stranger? It felt wrong considering anyone other than Gary as the father of my children.

I gazed down at the engagement, wedding, and eternity rings that I still wore. When Gary had placed each of them on my finger, I'd truly been happy and in love. I'd believed we were two who would become three, four, five... To me, those three bands symbolised our love and our intention to create new life. The love had gone – or at least it had on his part (if it had ever been there) – but I hadn't been able to bring myself to remove the rings. Was it because I still saw Gary as the father of my children? I'd come to terms with him not being my husband... sort of... but until I came to terms with him not being the father to my children, I couldn't think about other options. And I couldn't remove the rings.

I closed my laptop and went for another long walk, on my own this time, to try to clear my head. I have no idea whether I did it consciously or unconsciously, but I found myself outside the community centre where my former counsellor, Jem, ran a Sunday morning yoga class.

'Elise! How wonderful to see you.' Jem kissed me on one cheek then the other when he emerged from the building.

I sat down on the bench again. 'I'm sorry for turning up like this. I should have phoned and made a proper appointment.'

He sat beside me and ran his fingers down his strawberry-blond goatee while he studied my face. 'I've been thinking about you a lot this week. I had a feeling I'd see you soon.' Jem had always made it clear that he wasn't officially psychic, but he did possess some form of sixth sense. 'It's not about your mother this time, is it?'

I sat on my hands and swayed back and forth a couple of times. 'No. Gary and I have split up.'

'He's seeing someone else?'

'Yes. A man.'

'Oh.' Jem stood up and reached for my hand to help me to my feet. 'I have an hour. Do you want to come to the office to talk about it?'

'Yes please. I'm not coping very well. I need your help.'

On the Thursday night that week, a text arrived:

✉ From Gary
Please can we meet at the house later tonight?
I need to talk to you. It's urgent

I pushed aside my half-eaten bowl of risotto and sighed as I stared at the message. What did he want?

'I take it that's from Gary,' Kay said.

'How did you guess? He wants me to go to the house tonight. Says it's urgent.'

'Are you going to go?'

I shrugged. 'I suppose I should. I've managed to avoid anything face to face since I moved out, and I've always known we'd have to talk eventually.'

'Could be a good chance to tell him you want a divorce,' she suggested.

I'd asked Richard to hold off sending Gary a letter, feeling that I should give the news in person. 'You're right. It all seems so final, though. Oh gosh, what if he wants to tell me that *he's* going to start divorce proceedings?' My stomach churned at the thought of another nail in the coffin if he divorced me rather than the other way round.

'I don't think he'd do that. He knows it's your place to initiate things.'

'Maybe he wants to discuss the house,' I said. 'Maybe he wants to put it on the market. It's a family home. It's far too big for just him. Unless he wants Rob to...' I couldn't bear the thought of Gary having his happily ever after with someone else in the house *we* chose, surrounded by *our* belongings. It was abundantly clear now that we hadn't been heading for our own happily ever after, but that didn't stop it hurting that he might be heading for his while I still struggled to get over our marriage being a lie.

Kay put her fork down and smiled reassuringly. 'I'm sure it's not that, sweetheart. I don't think Gary would move Rob in. Not yet. It's too soon. He'll know that. Although you do know it may happen one day, don't you?'

Picking up my fork again, I stabbed at a mushroom. 'I know. It's just not a reality with which I thought I'd be faced.'

'I'm sure it will be about selling the house,' Kay said. 'What else could it be?'

* * *

I parked Bertie on the drive next to the Lexus and slowly walked towards the front door. It felt weird being back home, knowing it wasn't my home anymore.

Gary must have been watching for me as the door flung open. 'Li!' He held out his arms to give me a hug, but I stepped backwards.

'I'd prefer if you called me Elise from now on.'

'Oh. Okay. I'm glad you came, Li... Elise. Come in. Ignore the mess.'

My heart raced as I stopped into the hall, an uncomfortable feeling in my gut, worried that I might see signs of Rob all over my former home. But there was nothing to suggest he'd moved in. Instead, I frowned at the unprecedented sight of several pairs of shoes and trainers discarded on the floor instead of neatly stacked on the shoe-rack. Gary must be really struggling if he'd veered from his neat-freak status. The thought gave me a little comfort and satisfaction, and then I felt guilty for being so mean.

'Lounge or kitchen?' he asked.

'Kitchen.'

'It's a bit messy too. Sorry.'

Talk about an understatement. There couldn't have been any glasses, plates, or mugs left in the cupboards; they were all piled high on the worktops. Pans soaking in some dubious-coloured water filled the sink. Empty yogurt pots, spilled cereal, breadcrumbs and banana peels were strewn everywhere, and an obnoxious smell emanated from the direction of the overflowing bin.

'It's bad, isn't it?' he said. 'Sorry.'

I nodded. 'Gary, I...' I genuinely didn't know what to say. I looked at his face and, although I longed to feel hate and anger still, my heart went out to him instead. He clearly hadn't shaved for a couple of weeks. He often sported stubble, but this was a beard. The dark rings under his eyes, the hollow cheeks, and the haunted eyes reminded me of how I'd looked just before I moved into Kay's.

'I'm no good without you,' he whispered.

He reached out towards me, but I stepped back, unnerved by the intimacy.

'Look at me, Li.'

'It's Elise. You really should load the dishwasher after each meal, you know. It takes seconds, but if you pile stuff up like this, it becomes a mammoth task. And there's a funny smell coming fro—'

'Li! Stop!'

My heart raced as I turned round slowly and raised my gaze to meet his. 'It's Elise!' I cried.

'Sorry. I'll try to...' He shook his head. 'I miss you. I'm lost without you.' His dark eyes, so full of pain, filled with tears and the next moment he was sobbing. I'd only seen Gary cry twice before: when his dad died and when he received a card from his brother, congratulating him on becoming a qualified GP and enclosing a photograph of the four-year-old nephew and two-year-old niece he hadn't known existed.

My hands twitched. I didn't want to touch him, but every instinct in me screamed out to comfort him. I couldn't just stand helplessly by the fridge and let him cry. 'Come here. It'll be all right.'

As I held Gary tightly, I willed myself not to start crying too.

He'd said he was lost without me. What did that mean? Surely there was no going back. No matter how much it hurt both of us, we were better off apart. We had to be. Living a lie wasn't healthy for either of us.

'I'm so sorry,' he whispered into my hair, still clinging onto me.

'It's okay. We'll get through this.' I didn't want him to hold me anymore. It didn't feel right. I steered him towards one of the chairs. Thankfully, he didn't resist. 'You said you needed to talk and it was urgent,' I prompted.

Gary sat back against his chair and wiped his eyes, then he turned to look at me. 'You look really well.'

I shrugged. 'Thank you. And...?'

'I like your hair like that.'

I self-consciously reached up to my hair, which I'd let Kay straighten for me for the first time ever when I'd got in from school. I hoped he didn't think I'd done it for his benefit. 'Thank you again, but I wasn't fishing for another compliment. Why am I here?' I sat down, waiting for his answer.

He stared at me as he twiddled with his earlobe and I held my breath while the kitchen clock ticked, the fridge-freezer hummed, and my heart hammered. What was he building up to? It was going to be about Rob moving in, wasn't it? I tried to mentally prepare myself not to flinch, cry, or scream.

'I'm struggling. Will you move back in?' He reached for my hand, but I pulled it away.

'I'll give you anything you want,' he said. 'We can even have a baby if that's what you really want. We can act like a normal family.'

Oh my goodness! He'd just offered me the one thing I desperately wanted. At my session with Jem on Sunday, I'd admitted I still wanted Gary's baby and he'd challenged me on why I needed a man – particularly Gary – to fulfil my dreams of motherhood. He'd really pushed until I'd broken down in tears and cried, 'Because one parent isn't enough. You need two for when one of them can't cope with life anymore and finds the answer at the bottom of a bottle of gin.' 'You're not like your mother,' Jem had assured me. 'You'll never be like her.'

I stared at Gary as my body stiffened and my nails dug into my palms. Jem had insisted that a baby with Gary wasn't the way forward and I hadn't wanted to hear it, but, now that the offer was on the table, I realised he'd been right. He was always right. Gary was gay and, although he might be struggling right now, he'd get through it and what would happen to me if I agreed to have a baby with him? I'd be pregnant and he'd be with Rob, or someone else and I'd be even more messed up than I was right now because of it.

'Are you still seeing Rob?' I asked.

With his eyes down, he nodded. 'He thinks I'm still in love with you. We've had a huge argument about it.'

'And are you?'

'No... yes... I don't know.'

I swallowed hard on the lump in my throat. 'You don't love me, Gary. I'm not going to debate whether you ever did, but you definitely don't love me now. Not in *that* way. You do love Rob, though, and I think you've panicked about what this means after years of lying to yourself and everyone you know. Getting back with me and having a baby would be like putting a sticking plaster on a broken leg: ineffective in solving or covering up the real problem.' I reached for my bag and stood up. 'I realise this is hard for you too. You've been fighting who you are for sixteen or seventeen years. I can't imagine what that must feel like, but you've found the person with whom you want to be, the person with whom you can be you. Why not just accept that and stop fighting against who you really are? I know you're worried about keeping up appearances and I'd be lying if I said there won't be some gossip, but it will mainly be because people will be surprised rather than because they're being malicious. 'If you've lived a lie and fought against who you are for more than half your life, you must be made of pretty strong stuff, so you can ride out whatever storm hits you when this all comes out.'

'You really think so?' Tears sprung in Gary's eyes again.

'I know so.' I reached out and lightly touched his arm. 'Let's pretend this conversation never happened.'

He nodded.

'Don't *ever* put a proposition like that to me again,' I said sternly. 'I may desperately want a baby, but if it happens, it'll be with someone who loves me and who'll be around as a father *and* as a husband. It won't be to keep up appearances.'

'I'm sorry. I've really screwed things up, haven't I? Not just today.'

I nodded. 'Quite spectacularly as it happens. You'll always hold a special place in my heart, so it hurts me to see you in this state. Look at the house. Look at yourself. Look at the crazy places your mind is taking you. You're better than this. You said I look well, but don't let a different hairstyle deceive you into thinking I've found it easy to walk away. I'm devastated that our marriage is over, but the last few weeks has given me the time and space to realise that the last couple of years together have been tough. Really tough. So, in some ways, I'm relieved it's over. I'm equally devastated that we haven't had the family that we planned to have, but I'm relieved about that too because it's less complicated.'

'I should never have let it go on so long, should I?'

'Let's not go there, shall we? What's done is done.'

'Sorry.' He held out his hand. 'Friends?'

I stared at his hand but kept mine firmly by my side as I shook my head. 'I'm sorry, but I can't give you that. Not yet. Friends support each other through tough times and I can't support you through this. It's hard enough getting through it myself. To put it bluntly, you've lied to me, you've betrayed me, and you've taken away my hopes and plans for the future. Friends don't do that.'

'You hate me, then?'

'Of course I don't hate you, although I did when I found you together. I really hated you both at that moment, but I've got past that initial shock, and that's not how I feel about you now. I'll always love you, but I don't like you very much at the moment. You have to know somebody to like them and I don't know you anymore. I'd like to think that one day we can re-build some sort of friendship, but for now I need time and space. I asked you once before to stop texting me and you ignored it. I mean it this time. I really need you to stop getting in touch. I need you to let me fully get over us and build a new life for myself. Once I've done that, we can consider whether friendship might be back on the cards. Okay?'

'Okay.' He put his hands in his pockets and looked down at the floor. It hurt to see him so down, but it also felt so good to be finally standing up to him. My mother was wrong. I wasn't that much a pushover. Well, not anymore, I wasn't. It would have been easy to say yes to his offer of moving back in and having a baby, but I was stronger than that now. Much stronger.

I pushed my shoulders back and stood even taller. 'I'm going now, but there's two more things I have to say. Firstly, I don't want to kick you when you're down, but you probably won't be surprised to know that I've seen a solicitor. I want a divorce and I need you to do whatever's necessary to make it a speedy one. I think you owe me that, don't you? Will you promise to co-operate?'

Gary nodded. 'I never thought I'd be divorcing you.'

'You're not,' I snapped. '*I'm* divorcing *you.*' I sighed then added in a gentler tone, 'Sorry, but you asked for that. Will you co-operate with the speedy divorce?'

He ran a hand over his beard then nodded. 'I promise. I'll find a solicitor and ensure everything's handled quickly.'

'Thank you.'

'I'm so sorry. For everything.'

'I know.' I lifted my bag onto my shoulder. 'I need to go now. Sort it out with Rob. I think your present state of mind is more about what's going on with you two than us two, isn't it?'

He didn't answer.

'Can I make a suggestion?' I said. 'Don't tell Rob what we talked about. There's no need to hurt him too. Make sure he knows that you don't love me anymore and it's him you want before you lose him as well.'

Gary nodded then followed me down the hall to the front door. 'You said there were two things you wanted to say...?'

'Oh yes. I don't want to live here again, but I can't stay with Kay forever so I need my share of the house. It's up to you whether you sell up or buy me out. I'll give you until next weekend to decide. Okay?'

'Okay.'

'Goodbye, Gary.' I opened the door then hesitated on the doorstep. I gazed down at my left hand. It was time. We weren't husband and wife, we weren't lovers, we weren't even friends. And we certainly weren't going to be parents together. The rings no longer represented the future to me. I had a new future to write.

'These are yours,' I said, placing the three rings in his hand.

Gary looked down at them, his hands shaking slightly. 'No! Please don't do that.'

'You'll find the boxes in the top drawer of the dressing table.'

'They're yours. I know we've split up, but I want you to keep them.' He tried to hand them back to me, but I backed down the path and onto the drive.

'I can't keep them and I don't care whether *you* want me to because the important thing is that *I* don't want to.' Because that part of my life was now over and, somehow, I needed to find the strength to start over again. New home. New life. New routine.

New beginnings. 'Text me when you've made your mind up about the house.'

I heard his strangled sob as I opened Bertie's door. It took every ounce of strength I had not to rush back and scream 'yes' to his offer because what if I was walking away from my one and only opportunity to have a baby? The thought terrified me. But so did the thought of having a baby and being forever connected to the man I'd loved and trusted since I was fourteen who'd lied to me all my life. And that fear was even greater.

12

✉ From Curtis
Get your dancing pants on, Red. I've got
cover for the salon tomorrow so I'm on my way
right now. Meet me at the station at 8, ready
to go. If you don't look slutty, you'll be
marched home to change, so choose carefully!
Xx

'Curtis!' I flung my arms round him.

He picked me up and spun me in a circle in the middle of the platform.

I patted his biceps when he put me down. 'Someone's been working out.'

'That's nothing. Check this out.' He swiftly removed his shirt, revealing a ripped stomach. A group of giggling girls wolf-whistled as they passed. Curtis licked his finger then rubbed one of his nipples with it in an extremely camp Austin-Powers-style pose.

I laughed. 'I've missed you, but I'm going to regretfully ask you to put your clothes back on before you get us arrested for indecent exposure.' The Station Manager was marching towards us with a face like thunder.

'Spoilsport.' He pulled his shirt back on. 'Enough about me, though, let's look at you, Red.' He stepped back while I did a twirl. 'Not bad at all. Not slutty, but I approve.'

I smoothed down the short flared skirt on the emerald green halter-neck dress. 'I think you know me well enough to know that I have nothing in my wardrobe that fits that description.'

'Even if you did, I don't think "slutty" is a word that could ever be applied to you. You are, and always have been, classy. Shall we?' He offered me his arm.

'Don't you have a bag?' I asked, registering the absence of any luggage.

'No. Even a wee bag would get in the way. I'll borrow your toiletries and buy a new T-shirt tomorrow.'

'And some pants,' I suggested.

'Why? I'm going commando now. I'll do the same tomorrow.'

I laughed again. 'Too much information.'

'You asked. So, where first? I haven't been out drinking in Whitsborough Bay since college and I'm desperately hoping the place has changed since then. Is there anywhere that does cocktails?'

'Blue Moon. Follow me.'

* * *

'To the most stunning woman in Whitsborough Bay.' Curtis clinked his 'Flirtini' glass against mine.

'To the hottest man in Scotland,' I toasted back. 'And to a great night out.'

'I guarantee that, but I can't guarantee you'll remember it all because I intend to get you absolutely paralytic tonight. If you don't puke your guts up, I'll consider it my personal failure.'

'Can we just stick with the paralytic and avoid the puking

part? I promise I'm a cheap date because paralytic will probably only take three of these.'

Curtis took my hand and brought it to his lips. 'You, my beauty, could never be referred to as cheap.'

'Gosh, Curtis, I've missed you so much. Why have we left it so many years?'

Curtis did a dramatic shrug of his shoulders and flung his arms out, nearly spilling his drink. 'Life, Red. Life got in the way. Plus, setting up what I'm sure will become Glasgow's finest hair salon requires working your arse off at weekends and makes catching up with fabulous friends like you a wee bit tricky. But I'm here now. Do you want to talk about your gay husband?'

'Not really.' And especially not after his surprising offer last night.

'Good, because neither do I. Instead, I have a wicked plan. Down these then take me to a quiet pub.'

'A *quiet* pub?'

'Yes. I have very specific requirements. No music and quite a lot of people, preferably middle-aged to old.'

I frowned. 'You're describing The Grey Goose which hasn't changed since you left. I can't imagine that's your kind of place.'

'Oh, it isn't. I hate that pub. But we're going to play a wee game and it's the perfect venue for it. Now down that in one and let's go.'

* * *

'You see that couple over there,' Curtis said while we waited for our drinks at the bar of The Grey Goose.

'What, the couple who aren't speaking, but clearly feel an obligation to come out to the pub given that it's Friday night?'

'That's the ones. Do you know them?'

'No.'

'Do you know anyone in the pub?'

I looked round. There were twenty or so drinkers scattered around the place in couples and singles. The minimum age was late fifties and the dress code was beige. 'No. Nobody.'

'Brilliant. We can have some fun, then, without sullying your reputation as an upstanding department head. We're going to give those two something to talk about. Play along.' Before I could ask to what I'd be playing along, he'd taken a seat next to the silent couple and I felt I had to follow.

'So, it burns when you pee?' he announced.

I spat my drink back into the glass. It was either that or the table. 'Curtis!'

'Sorry,' he said. 'It's just that I've had a burning sensation too and I wondered whether it's because a brother and sister shouldn't sleep together...'

The evening quickly descended into depravity from that point.

* * *

We burst through the doors of Minty's, clinging to each other and giggling hysterically.

'I seriously can't believe you came out with all of that,' I said. 'You're a sick, sick puppy, Curtis McBride.'

'Elise? Curtis?'

I looked up. 'Sarah! My best friend!' I flung my arms round her. 'It's been weeks. Why's it been so long?'

Sarah let go of me and wrinkled her nose. 'Because you've been avoiding me?' she suggested.

I nodded. 'Good point. S'nothing personal. It's just... cos of Gary... and weddings... you know...?'

'I know. But we didn't have to talk about either of those subjects unless you'd wanted to, did we?'

Even in my drunken state, I could hear the edge to her voice and knew that I'd hurt her. So much for friendship-preservation.

Staying away had probably caused more damage than moaning about Gary instead of wedding-planning would have done. Damn! 'Sorry. We'll go out soon. I promise.'

She smiled. 'I'll hold you to it. Speaking of long time, no see, how are you, Curtis?' She spoke in the forced pleasant tone that I knew she reserved for awkward customers. She didn't dislike Curtis; she just worried that he tended to land me in trouble whenever we were together. It was a legitimate concern because he usually did.

Curtis grabbed her and twirled her round like he'd done with me at the station earlier then gave her a big smacker on the cheek. 'All the better for seeing you. I believe congratulations are in order.'

'Thank you.' She held out her hand so Curtis could admire the ring.

'Stunning. Just like you. I'm liking the soft curls by the way. Perfect for your bone structure. Gorgeous.'

The flattery had clearly worked because her tone changed to genuinely polite. 'Would you like to join us? We're over there.' She pointed towards the back of the bar then pulled a face. 'Clare's here, though. So if you don't want to...'

Curtis put a protective arm round my shoulder. 'I'll protect her from The Rampant Leprechaun.' We both howled with laughter. Talk about an echo from the past. I'd completely forgotten that Curtis has christened her that. What a great memory he had.

'O-kay.' Sarah looked like she was already regretting the invite.

'We'll get some drinks then join you.' Curtis shooed her away. 'Give us ten minutes or so.'

With a worried look, Sarah returned to her group. I could see Nick's head and there was another man with them, but I couldn't see him properly. I bobbed about to get a better view. Stevie? He nodded his head towards me and smiled. I gave him a little wave as a pang of guilt shot through me for turning down his offers of a shoulder to cry on since he'd helped me move.

'Tequila time!' Curtis placed two shot glasses in front of me, alongside a saucer of lemon pieces and a salt cellar.

'Oh no.'

'Oh yes. One, two, three…'

* * *

I'm not entirely sure how my unsteady legs managed to carry me across the bar to Sarah's group, but Curtis's supporting arm certainly helped. Sarah jumped up when she saw us and did the introductions while Nick pulled up extra chairs. I was relieved to sit down before I collapsed in an undignified heap on the floor.

'Clare. Great to see you as always,' I said, pointing to her.

'Elise!' Sarah hissed. 'Be nice.'

'I *am* being nice. I said it was great to see her.'

'It's the way you said it.'

'Shhhh.' I put my finger to my lips and missed. 'Anyway, it's rude to whisper.'

'How are you, Elise?' Clare said.

'It turns out my husband's gay and it's taken him fifteen years to admit it so my whole marriage has been a lie. I only found out because I found him shagging *his* best friend in our shower.' I pointed at Stevie. 'So we've split up and I'm living in Sarah's auntie's spare room. So, as you can probably imagine, I'm feeling pretty shit right now. But thanks for asking. Or should I just have given the standard answer of fine?'

I waited for some sarcastic comment about it serving me right for marrying so young or a statistic about how many marriages ended in divorce, but all Clare said was, 'I'm really sorry. Nobody deserves to have that sort of bollocks happen to them. Your man Gary's an eejit.' It sounded like she genuinely meant it. Clare being nice? That was certainly a first.

'We're going to throw some shapes in Stardust,' Curtis announced. 'Anyone fancy joining us?'

'Me!' Clare said. 'Don't look at me like that, Sarah. It'll be grand. You've been promising me a trip to Whitsborough Bay's finest nightclub since you moved home.'

'I know. And I *will* take you... if I must... but not on a Friday,' Sarah said. 'I've got an early wedding tomorrow. I've got to be at the shop by seven.'

Clare pouted.

'I don't mind going,' Stevie offered. 'I can see Clare back to yours.'

'Are you sure you both want to go?' she asked. They nodded so Sarah reached into her bag and handed Clare her key.

* * *

Two hours later, Curtis had well and truly achieved his goal of getting me paralytic. I knew that if I had even one sip more of alcohol, he'd achieve his other goal of making me throw up. Staggering off the dance floor, I ordered a pint of water then made my way unsteadily towards a quiet corner where I slumped onto an unexpectedly hard sofa. My head felt fuzzy, my feet throbbed, and it surely had to be past my bedtime. I rummaged in my bag for my mobile to check the time and spotted a text from Gary. What now? More propositions to play happy families? With shaking hands, I opened the message and concentrated hard on focusing my eyes:

✉ From Gary
Thanks for your understanding yesterday. Not
sure what I was thinking. I don't need a week
to decide about the house. Too many memories
for me too so let's both start over. I'll get
some estate agents to value it next weekend

```
and, if you're happy with the price, I'll get
it on the market the week after. Really sorry
it's come to this
```

I sipped on my water as I stared at his text. How should I feel? Happy? Angry? Numb?

'I'm guessing you've had plenty if you've moved onto water.'

I looked up to see Stevie holding a short glass.

'Can I join you?' he asked.

'Be my guest. But the sofa's rock hard. Be warned.'

He sat beside me and shuffled his bum. 'You're right. It's like a breeze block.'

'Told you.'

He took a sip of his drink then put it down on the table. 'It's great to see you enjoying yourself. You deserve a good night out after what you've been through.'

I stared at Gary's text again and frowned as I put the phone down on the sofa beside me. 'Sorry I haven't seen you since I moved, but thanks for the offers of drinks. I wouldn't have been great company. Needed to get my head straight.'

'That's okay. I understand. Bad news?'

'What is?'

'You keep staring at your phone and frowning, so I'm wondering if it's bad news.'

'Sorry. Text from Gary. We're putting the house on the market.'

'Big step. How do you feel about it?'

I shrugged. 'Bit strange. I thought Gary would buy me out.'

'Maybe there are too many memories for him to stay there.'

'That's what he said.'

'It's a big house for one person too. I can't imagine Gary rattling round there on his own. Can you?' He smiled.

'Probably not.' I stared at his dimples. 'Can I touch them?'

'Touch what?'

'Your dimples. They're so cute.'

His smile widened and his dimples indented even further. Very cute. Actually, quite sexy. Why hadn't I noticed that before?

'If it turns you on,' he said.

'Oh, it does.' I reached out my right hand and gently stroked the side of his face. His skin felt smooth whereas Gary's was nearly always stubbly. My lips parted as I ran my fingers from his dimples into his hair. It felt very soft whereas Gary's was usually hardened with product.

'Elise...'

'Shhh! I don't want to talk.' I reached out my other hand and touched his thigh. He didn't tighten it like Gary had last time I touched him. My heart thumped along with the baseline of the music. My breathing quickened as I stared into his eyes. I'd never stared into anyone's eyes except Gary's. Stevie had beautiful eyes like melted pools of chocolate with flecks of gold in them. Why hadn't I noticed them before either?

'I don't think this is such a good idea,' he said.

'What isn't?' I brazenly leaned forward and gave him a gentle peck on the lips. They felt soft, moist, and incredibly kissable. I'd only ever kissed Gary before. My body shook with anticipation.

'This. You've been drinking...'

I kissed him gently again. 'I know what I'm doing.'

'I'm sure you do. But...'

'But what?' I pulled back. 'Don't you want me?'

'You're gorgeous. You must know that. But...'

'*But what?* Don't tell me you're gay too.'

'No. It's just that... it's not right. You've only just split up with Gary. I don't want you to do anything you might regret. I don't want to lose you as a friend.'

'Friend?' I snapped. 'Friend? Is that what I am to you?'

'Yes. A good friend.'

'Good friend. Yes, that's me. Everyone's best friend. Can I ask you a question, Stevie? What's wrong with me? Why does every man I meet want to be my friend? Why does nobody want to rip my clothes off and enact *Fifty Shades* with me? Do I score zero on a desirability scale?'

'You'd score top marks. You're very desirable.'

'Then how come I just handed myself to you on a plate and you said no?' I grabbed my bag, stood up and shoved past him. 'Don't answer that. Tell Curtis to meet me outside.'

Then I fled.

✉ From Curtis
This time last week, I was travelling home
after an amazing weekend with a gorgeous
woman. What would they say at work if they
knew? Just had a very tame weekend in compari-
son. No idea The Bay had so much going on!
Please tell me you've been in touch with
Dimples this week and sorted out your misun-
derstanding xx

✉ To Curtis
I miss you, but my liver doesn't! I swear it
took me till Wednesday to recover. I haven't
been in touch with Stevie. I was hoping he'd
make the first move

✉ From Curtis
He's probably thinking the same about you.
Remember you were the one who propositioned

him & you were the one who ran out on him. Be
brave. Don't lose a friend over this xx

✉ To Curtis
Easier said than done. I feel like a prize
idiot, but I also feel hurt and humiliated.
What's wrong with me?

✉ From Curtis
Nothing's wrong with you. Except your timing.
Chin up xx

I put my mobile down on the worktop and returned to the task of washing up the breakfast pots. Curtis was right. It had been a great weekend and, other than the incident with Stevie, it had been exactly what I needed. Waking up late on Saturday morning, my head had felt like it may spontaneously combust. Thankfully a walk round The Headland, a bottle of Lucozade, and a bag of hot sugared doughnuts from the seafront returned me to the land of the living. Curtis promised to be gentler with me the following evening so, after a quick trip into town to buy him some fresh clothes, we had a Chinese followed by a walk along the beach.

He wouldn't accept my story that I'd left Stardust because I felt sick. Eventually I confessed, cringing as I re-lived my failed attempt at seducing poor Stevie. I still had no idea why I'd done it. I could only plead drink-induced temporary loss of sanity. It wasn't like I fancied the guy. He was just a friend. Although he did have cute dimples, very sexy eyes and gave the best hugs ever.

My mobile beeped again. I wiped my hands on a tea towel and checked my texts:

✉ From Sarah

Can you meet me at The Chocolate Pot at 2pm
today? Got some exciting news!

My stomach churned. It had to be wedding news. Perhaps
they'd found a venue and set the date. Feeling very guilty after
her comments in Minty's at the weekend, I'd dropped by Seaside
Blooms after school on Wednesday like I used to and had asked
how the plans were going. Sarah had refused to talk about it at
first, but after I managed to convince her that I wasn't about to
collapse in hysterical sobs at the mention of anything wedding-
related, she'd admitted that there was very little news. Sherrington Hall was fully booked for the next eighteen months, as
expected, so she needed to get over that disappointment before
she started looking for alternative venues. She didn't want to go
dress-shopping or plan anything else until she had a venue and
date.

I read her text again. It had to be wedding news. Something
had obviously changed and, as I'd recently experienced, a heck
of a lot could change in the space of a few days. I replied to say I
was free and, after a light lunch, took a slow meander towards
town.

I'd just reached the top of The Old Town when my phone
beeped. Gary. Which meant one thing: the final valuation on the
house was complete and he'd made a decision as to who would
sell 9 Abbey Drive. This was it; the next key step in our
separation:

✉ From Gary
Lawtons have just gone. The agent from there
seemed most switched on so I've instructed him
to put the house on the market. He took the
measurements and photos while he was here.
Don't panic — I got my act together and
cleared up after you came round! I'll get the

details to approve by the end of Tuesday so the house could be on the market by Thursday at the latest. Are you sure you want this?

✉ To Gary
I'm sure. Thank you. Keep me posted on viewings. This is it then

✉ From Gary
Looks like it. Feels strange

✉ To Gary
I know

I put the phone back in my bag and sat down on a bench overlooking The Old Town and the harbour. Above me, fluffy white clouds floated across the blue sky and seabirds squawked as they caught the thermals and soared into the air. Below me to the left was the River Abbleby, where sailing boats jostled for space with small powerboats and canoeists. In front of me, the tide was in on South Bay beach and the remaining stretch of sand was packed. The Ferris wheel turned in Pleasureland and one of the jet boats bounced across the waves beyond the harbour. I couldn't hear them, I couldn't properly see them, but I knew that everyone would be having fun in the sun while I struggled with another key milestone in the collapse of my marriage while on my way to meet my best friend to no doubt talk about the start of hers. Could the timing be any worse?

* * *

'Thank you for all for coming,' said Sarah.

As soon as I spotted Clare, and Nick's sister, Callie, at a table with Sarah, my suspicions about it being wedding news were confirmed. My heart sank and I admonished myself immedi-ately. *Don't be so selfish. You know how much she's longed for this day. Be happy for her. You've managed to be supportive for Jess. You can do the same for Sarah.*

I plastered a smile on my face. 'You're welcome. I take it you have wedding news.'

'I do,' Sarah said, giggling at the wedding pun. 'We've set a date.'

Callie squealed and clapped her hands together. 'Please tell me it's next year. I can't bear to wait until the one after.'

Sarah grinned. 'As you all know, Nick and I have been venue-hunting over the past few weeks and we'd set our hearts on Sherrington Hall, but they were fully booked. However, they phoned on Friday with a cancellation, which nobody seems to want. It's quite a bit sooner. We're not having a spring wedding anymore. We're having a winter one. We're getting married on the twenty-first of December. This year. Can you believe that?'

Callie squealed again and hugged Sarah. Clare offered her congratulations and all I managed to say was, 'That's a bit close to Christmas, isn't it? People might not come.' I looked at three shocked pairs of eyes. *Did I really just say that out loud?* 'That came out wrong. I meant that's probably why nobody wanted it. I'm sure all your guests will come. I'm delighted for you.'

'Thank you.' Sarah smiled, but it didn't reach her eyes, just like Gary's smile on all those photos at home. I'd hurt her. Again.

'I'm so excited,' Callie said. 'Have you booked the church too?'

'Yes. All done...'

Sarah gushed about the church she'd booked, what time the service would be, what time the reception would be, their thoughts about going to Canada for their honeymoon. I felt as though I was having an out-of-body experience throughout the discussion, as if my usual 'nice Elise' persona was floating above me and this nasty, bitter individual was left in her place, pretending to be delighted for her best friend. I hoped desperately that the feeling wouldn't continue for five months of planning because if it did, I knew I would screw up my friendship with Sarah forever. This was a woman who'd dreamed of her wedding day since she was a little girl – a woman who, after finding her single uncle dead when she was only thirteen, had made it her mission to find her soulmate so she didn't end up all alone like him. How could I begrudge her a perfect day, especially when I'd enjoyed twelve years of happy marriage myself? Or so I'd believed. No, they were happy. Or ten of them were. Even Gary admitted that. I had to stop thinking about the whole thing as a disaster.

'I have a little surprise if you're all free for another hour or so,' Sarah said when we'd finished our drinks.

We settled the bill, headed out of the café, and turned left along Castle Street. Sarah stopped a few paces later outside The Wedding Emporium, a wedding dress shop that had opened earlier that year next-door to The Chocolate Pot. She knocked on the door.

Callie squealed. 'Have we got a private appointment?'

'We shop owners like to do each other a favour or two,' Sarah said as a petite dark-haired woman in her mid-thirties opened the door and welcomed us inside. 'Thanks for doing this, Ginny.'

'No problem at all. Thanks for that great deal on my sister's wedding flowers.'

Callie squealed again and grabbed Sarah by the hand, dragging her across to a mannequin wearing a big sparkling wedding gown – the sort of dress I envisaged Sarah wearing. I felt my throat tighten and my eyes moisten. *Don't cry. Not now. Pull yourself together. Smile. Play happy bridesmaids.* I reminded myself that I'd longed for this day too. How many hours had Sarah and I spent over the years talking about her dream wedding? This was the start of it. *Join in. If you can't do it genuinely, act your heart out!*

A cool hand touched my arm, making me jump. 'I know that this will be hard for you,' Clare whispered. 'But can you not just pretend? For her sake?' There was a tenderness to her whispered tones that suggested she really did understand.

'Gary's just put the house on the market,' I whispered back. 'I'm feeling a bit sensitive.'

'Ah, that's just bollocks. I'm sorry.'

'Thank you.'

'Champagne is served, ladies,' Ginny announced.

'How lovely,' I said, reaching for a glass. *Smile.* 'So, Sarah, what's the plan? Wedding gowns or bridesmaid dresses first? Or all together?' I glanced across at Clare. She nodded her head approvingly. I could get through this. It was only an afternoon. I did it for Jess. I could do it for Sarah. Just as long as nobody announced they were pregnant because that might just tip me over the edge and no amount of acting could cover how I felt about that.

14

✉ To Curtis
Been bridesmaid dress shopping with Sarah. Not
an easy afternoon, especially as Gary texted
en route to say the house is now on the
market. Another brick in the wall. Now feeling
guilty for being so unsupportive towards Sarah

✉ From Curtis
And she probably feels guilty for doing
wedding stuff, but you don't expect her to put
it on hold, do you? Chin up, Red, one day at a
time. What colour are the dresses? Are they
fabulous? xx

✉ To Curtis
Champagne and teal. They're gorgeous. We've
all got the same skirt, but a different style
top. I'm having halter-neck, Callie's having
floaty sleeves and Clare is having strapless.
I'll send you a picture later xx

⊠ From Sarah
Tried you at Auntie Kay's, but you're not
home. Your mobile's switched off so sorry for
the informality of a text. I'm worried about
you. I know you said you were OK about wedding
stuff on Wednesday, but that was when you
expected me to get married next year. I'm
concerned that this afternoon may have been
insensitive and too soon for you. I didn't
mean it to be, but I had to kickstart things
because of the date. I promise not to witter
on about the wedding all the time. I know it's
hard for you at the moment. Please let me know
you're OK and I haven't screwed up xxx

Whoops! Curtis was absolutely right. Poor Sarah. I'd better call
her. Then I stopped. I couldn't do it. If I spoke to her, I'd cry, and
I needed to stop crying. Wallowing wasn't doing me any good.
I'd have to text her and I was going to have to lie. She'd be devastated if she knew I'd deliberately ignored her calls earlier.

⊠ To Sarah
Went for a walk round The Headland. Must have
been no signal as my phone's on. It's not the
easiest having my two favourite people getting
married while I get divorced, but I want to be
involved. I may not look it, but I promise I'm
over the moon for you. Please keep telling me
your plans and slap me if I start to wallow!
The dresses are stunning. Can't wait to see
which dress you finally select. I hope I
didn't spoil your afternoon. Gary texted to
say the house had gone on the market on my way
into town so I was a bit distracted. I'll come

to the shop after school on Wednesday as usual
if that's OK xxx

✉ From Sarah
No! So sorry to hear that. Why didn't you say?
Glad I haven't messed up. Remember that, just
because I have a wedding to plan, it doesn't
mean I'm not here for you with a big hug and
shoulder to cry on any time you need me and
you don't have to wait till Wednesday if you
need me sooner than that xxxxxxxxxxxxxxxxxx

How guilty did I feel? I suspected she'd gone home and cried because of my behaviour. It wasn't only Gary and me who were affected by our break-up. It was affecting my friendships too and that wasn't fair.

A sharp knock on the front door echoed and made me jump. I reluctantly rolled off the bed and headed downstairs as the knock sounded again.

'Keep your hair on,' I said under my breath as I opened the door.

'So it's true. You *are* here.' Gary's mother pushed past me.

'Come in, Cynthia,' I muttered. I looked up and down the street then closed the door. *Deep breaths.*

I found her standing in the lounge looking immaculate, as always, in a straight navy skirt, crisp white blouse, short-sleeved red cardigan and nude stilettos. Her dark hair was scraped back into a sleek chignon and she wore a slash of red across her lips. Her very angry-looking lips. Which parted and uttered one word: 'Well...?'

I really wasn't in the mood for this. 'Well, what?'

'Don't play games with me, young lady. You know why I'm here.' She crossed her arms and glared at me.

I wasn't going to make this easy for her but I also wasn't

about to drop Gary in it. I didn't know how much she knew. 'I have no idea why you're here, Cynthia. Why don't you enlighten me? I'd offer you a drink, but I'm hoping you won't be staying long enough to need one.' *Go Elise!* After years of keeping quiet and accepting her criticisms in order to keep the peace, I no longer needed to and, if it was a fight she wanted, I was going to defend myself for once. I'd stood up to Gary. I could stand up to her. This worm was turning.

Her eyes widened with surprise. 'I don't want a drink. I have better things to do than be here. I demand to know what you're playing at by moving out and leaving my son.'

'That's what Gary told you, did he?'

'Gary won't tell me anything, but I have contacts and I discovered you've been living here for about a month.'

'That's right.' I folded my arms and raised my eyebrows, challenging her to continue.

'Your place is at home with my son.'

I laughed. 'Doing his cooking, cleaning and ironing, I suppose?'

'That's what a wife is for.'

'I can't believe you just said that. What century do you think this is?'

'Perhaps if you'd concentrated a bit more on those things – and more important things like raising a family with my son – perhaps you wouldn't be living in a stranger's spare room.'

My fists clenched and I had to keep my arms tightly folded to stop me from slapping her. 'Firstly, I'm not living with a stranger and, secondly, Gary and I having children or not is none of your business.'

She narrowed her cold eyes at me. 'Did you leave or did he throw you out?'

When I didn't answer, but simply stared at her, I could almost hear the cogs working.

'You haven't, have you?' she said.

'Haven't what?'

'Have you committed the ultimate sin of seeing someone behind his back?' She gasped. 'That's it isn't it? You dirty little—'

'I suggest you stop right there and leave my house.'

I hadn't heard the door open, but I'd never been so grateful to see anyone in my life. 'Are you all right, sweetheart?' Kay asked.

I nodded. 'Cynthia decided to pay me a little visit, but she's leaving now.'

'I'm not going anywhere until I get some answers.' Cynthia's beady little eyes narrowed to slits to match her mouth. 'Tell me straight. Have you cheated on my son?'

'Oh, for God's sake. Get out. She's not the one who's been cheating. Your precious son's the unfaithful one.'

'Kay! Don't...' I pleaded with my eyes: don't tell her about Gary.

Kay nodded. 'It's him you should be confronting,' she said. 'Now leave.' She marched into the hall and I heard the front door being yanked open.

Cynthia didn't follow. She glared at me instead. 'If Gary's had an affair, it's all your fault.'

'How do you work that one out?'

'You work ridiculously long hours at that school, you're always out with that friend of yours – the shop girl – and you haven't given him any babies. Is it any wonder he looked elsewhere?' She gave me one final withering look then stormed towards the lounge door.

I wasn't going to let her get away with insulting me like that. Not anymore. 'Not so fast.' I grabbed her arm and she spun round; shock etched across her face. 'I'll admit to one thing. Gary and I *are* getting a divorce. If you want to know why, you can ask your son. I'm devastated that our marriage is over because, despite your influence, Gary is a good man. However, I'm also delighted my marriage has ended because it means my relationship with you is over. You truly are a hateful woman, Cynthia. You're a snob, you're racist, you're homophobic, and... well, from what I've seen, you have no redeeming qualities whatsoever. I'm glad we didn't have children who'd be tainted by a cold-hearted grandmother with prejudiced views. You drove your husband to an early grave and you drove your eldest son away. If you're not careful, you're going to end up a very lonely and bitter old woman. And when you do, you can look up the word "karma" in the dictionary and you'll see "Cynthia Dawson" written next to it.'

The colour of Cynthia's face matched her cardigan. 'How dare you—?'

'I dare very easily. You can leave now. You're not welcome here.'

Cynthia's mouth opened and closed a few times then she turned and stormed out of the cottage, heels clicking on the tiled floor in the hall.

As soon as the door slammed, I slumped onto the sofa, shaking. Through the shock and anger, one little ray of positivity shone; I'd finally stood up to her and it felt good. If only Gary had had the strength to do the same when we were teens, we wouldn't be in this mess.

'Are you okay, sweetheart?' asked Kay, returning to the lounge. 'That woman's vicious, but you certainly gave her what for.'

I smiled. 'I did, didn't I?'

Kay nodded. 'You look happier than I've seen you in ages.'

'I feel it. Cynthia Dawson is not my problem anymore and I can't tell you how good that feels. Do you know what? I've never stood up to that woman in sixteen years. First I was too young and respectful, then I was too scared of her, then I was too scared of upsetting Gary. Every time I let her say something nasty about me or someone else, I think a little part of me crumbled. I lost who I was. I think the real me might have just returned.'

'Does that mean you're going to start telling everyone what you think of them? Should I be scared?'

I laughed. 'Don't panic. I'd never be that blunt with anyone except Cynthia. Or my mother. Or Clare perhaps. I just meant that the strong, confident woman that I used to be is clearly still in there somewhere. She's always been present at work, but she never appeared at home. Until now.' Perhaps the future wasn't so bleak. Coming up were a house sale and a divorce, but were those really bad things? No. They were lines in the sand ready to face a new future. A new life. A new me.

15

✉ From Curtis
I hope you've given our conversation some
thought. You know I'm right!

✉ To Curtis
I've thought of little else! Don't know if I
dare, though! Xx

✉ To Sarah
Is it still OK to drop by after school? Maybe
we could nip to Minty's for a quick drink xx

✉ From Sarah
You've twisted my arm! See you later xx

'What's this?' Sarah asked as I thrust a sparkly silver gift bag into her hands on Wednesday evening after she'd locked the door and turned the sign round to 'closed'. 'It's not my birthday for a while yet.'

'It's a little peace offering,' I said. 'I've been a rubbish friend recently.'

'Hey, don't say that.' She shook her head. 'You've always been there for me and I'd be a rubbish friend if I didn't understand why you've been a little...' She paused as if trying to find the right word, '... distracted lately.'

I smiled. 'Distracted? I like it. It's a good description. Open it, then.'

She gently placed the bag on the counter and pulled out some crumpled lilac tissue paper followed by an A5-sized notepad bound in ivory silk with a teal ribbon round it. 'My Wedding Planner,' she read. She flicked it open. Soft cream, beige, and pastel blue pages revealed headings such as, 'My Bridesmaids', 'My Cake', 'My Dress'. 'Elise! It's gorgeous. I love it.' Still holding the planner, she threw her arms round me and I hugged her back tightly, relieved that things weren't awkward between us after my 'distracted' behaviour.

'Thank you,' she whispered into my hair. 'And thanks for coming round. I've missed you.'

'I've missed you too.' I gave her another squeeze then released her. 'Now get cashed up while I vacuum, then we can get to the pub. There's something I want to run by you.'

* * *

Over a bottle of Pinot, we discussed Sarah's wedding in the same sort of detail we used to when we were younger only, this time, it was for real instead of a fantasy. She'd been a little reluctant to talk about it at first, but I managed to convince her that I was genuinely interested and that I might have been a little too 'distracted' to take it all in on Sunday at The Chocolate Pot. It soon became apparent that I'd been a little more than 'distracted'; I hadn't listened to a word because hardly anything she told me rang a bell. No wonder Clare had felt the need to have a quiet word.

When we'd exhausted wedding talk, she asked me how I felt about the house going on the market. 'It's officially up for sale tomorrow,' I said. 'I feel quite relaxed about it at the moment, but I suspect I'll feel differently when we get an offer.'

'It's a big step.'

'I know. Speaking of big steps, I took a huge one with the delightful Cynthia on Sunday evening.'

Sarah listened, eyes wide, as I told her about my confrontation. 'You go girl!' she said. 'I'm impressed. It must have taken some restraint not to tell her about Gary.'

'It did. Despite what he's put me through, I'll always care about him. I still want him to be happy, even if that means without me. I warned him that he should bite the bullet and tell her before she found out through her evil little coven of spies, but it was his choice. I suspect the whole truth will come out soon. It won't be pretty when it does.'

'Have you seen him recently?'

I shook my head. 'Not since he begged me to go round two weeks ago and asked me to move back in and have his baby.'

Sarah clapped her hand across her mouth. 'Oh my God! No way!'

I relayed my unexpected encounter with Gary and figured I might as well fill her in on my epic fail with Stevie in Stardust too. 'I take it by your shocked expression that Stevie hasn't told you about it.'

'I've seen him a few times since then and he hasn't breathed a word. Is there anything else you want to confess?' Sarah asked. 'Because I might have to order something stronger to cope with the shock.'

I laughed. 'I think you can close the confession box now, Priest Peterson. I'm done. I hope.' I leaned back on the chair and rolled my shoulders a few times. 'I can see why Catholics go for this confession malarkey. It's very therapeutic.'

We both sipped on our wine, smiling.

'What?' I said, as Sarah narrowed her eyes at me suspiciously.

'There's something else, isn't there? You said earlier that you wanted to run something by me and it feels like you've been evading it all evening.'

I chewed my lip as I thought about the phone conversation I'd had with Curtis the night before. I leaned forward again. 'Okay. You've got me. I *do* have one more confession, but before you run for the hills, this is something I'd *like* to do rather than something I've actually done. Or at least I *think* I would. But I don't know if I dare. I need your take on it.'

Sarah sat forward too and picked up her glass. 'Sounds intriguing. Confess away.'

'This getting over Gary malarkey is hard work. Some days I'm fine and other days I'm a mess. Saying no to his baby, initiating divorce proceedings, putting the house on the market and standing up to his evil mother have all been huge steps in my journey towards a Gary-free future. The problem is, I still love him. Or at least, I think I do. Curtis has come up with a cunning plan that might help me move on a bit more quickly and put my feelings for Gary behind me.' I took a deep breath. 'I want to get laid.'

Sarah's wine sloshed all over her hands as she tried to put it down on the table. 'Oh my God! Did I hear that right? You want to get laid? Have you been spending too much time with Clare?'

'I know.' I passed her a tissue from my bag to mop up the spillage. 'It sounds more like something Mrs Potty Mouth would come out with. I told Curtis it was at the top of his crazy ideas list, but I'm not sure it is that crazy after all. I've been thinking about it a lot. There's no way I'm ready for another relationship, but as you know, Gary's the only man I've ever been with. I hadn't even kissed another man until Stevie and that wasn't what you'd call a proper kiss. I'm not saying I'm going to morph into Clare and jump into bed with anything with a pulse, but maybe a one-off one-night-stand is in order.' Looking at Sarah's shocked expression, I put my hands over my face. 'I think I've had too much wine. It *is* a crazy idea isn't it?'

She shook her head. 'No. I get what you're saying and, funnily enough, I was having a very similar conversation with one of my reps today.'

I lowered my hands. 'Really?'

'Yeah. I get a lot of my gifts from this rep called Daniel. He's about our age and he's lovely. He didn't seem his usual cheerful self today so I asked if he was okay. He told me he'd recently separated from his wife after discovering she'd been unfaithful. They'd been childhood sweethearts, just like you and Gary, and a friend had suggested that he go out and sew his oats. He said he liked the idea in principle, but he's only ever been with his wife and wouldn't know where to start. He jokingly asked if I had any nice single friends who'd be gentle with him and not laugh at him for being so inexperienced.'

'You're not just making that up?'

She shook her head. 'I don't think I have that good an imagination. I'm not suggesting you two should jump into bed together. I'm not about to pimp you out! But if you fancied an introduction to someone who's going through something similar to you...?'

Interesting. An introduction to someone who Sarah knew and liked would surely be better and safer than meeting a stranger in a club or online. 'I don't know,' I said eventually. 'I think I would feel a bit like I was being pimped out. You wouldn't tell him I wanted sex, would you?'

'God no! What do you take me for? It really wouldn't be like that. Just two people who've both been crapped on by their partners getting together to talk things over and maybe offering each other some emotional support. And if it leads to a quick tumble, so be it.'

Sarah took another sip of her wine while I mulled over the idea. 'There's no need to make a decision now,' she said. 'Have a think about it and let me know what you decide. Remember that you started this conversation saying you want to get laid and wondering about a one-night stand. This is just me offering something that isn't quite that extreme, but which could help you achieve your goal.'

I nodded. 'It's not a no. It's not a yes either, but I'll definitely give it some thought.'

'You do that.'

* * *

I gave it a lot of thought as I walked back to Seashell Cottage. Sod it. What did I have to lose?

✉ To Sarah

Thanks for a great evening. It was so good to catch up rather than sit at home and think about the next big step of the house going on the market tomorrow. Speaking of big steps, I've given it some thought. If you really rate this Daniel, I'd like to meet him to share stories. Not sure I have the nerve to go through with anything else, despite what I announced in Minty's! xx

✉ From Sarah

Yay! I'll set something up. Who knows what might develop? He seems like a great guy. I promise I won't tell him you only want him for his body! xx

I grinned as I put my phone down. I suspected that I wouldn't have the courage to take it further with Daniel, even if I really liked him, but it would be good to share stories with someone going through the same thing. Oh well, wherever it took me, the next part of Operation Getting Over Gary was underway. Curtis would be proud of me. Actually, I was proud of me and, bizarrely, I had Cynthia to thank for it. Having the guts to stand up to her on Sunday had done wonders for me. It had made me take control of my life again. The first step had been to get my friendship with Sarah back on track which the evening at Minty's had definitely done. The next step had been to fall out of love with Gary and I was one step further towards that too. I'd love to see Cynthia's face if I told her that her visit had had the opposite effect on me than she'd desired; instead of running back to her son, I was probably running into the arms of another man.

16

My heart raced so fast, I thought I might pass out at any moment. Every time the restaurant door opened, my stomach churned and I shivered in anticipation wondering if it could be him. I'd never been on a blind date before. In fact, I'd never been on a first date. Gary and I had been part of a group from school who met at the cinema most Saturdays. One day, when we were the only two who turned up, he'd put his arm round me and kissed me. I hadn't realised until that moment how big a crush I'd developed on him and how much I'd been longing for him to make a move. There was therefore no first date build-up, and we didn't have to play the 'getting to know you' game because we were already friends.

Staring at the door, I sighed. This was hideous. How did people do this regularly? Sarah had said that Daniel looked a little like Gary. I'd always been drawn to dark hair and dark eyes so that was a good thing. It could equally be a bad thing if the resemblance was too strong.

I looked at my phone: 7.42 p.m. He was only twelve minutes late. It wasn't that late, was it? He may have had trouble parking. I glanced around the restaurant, hoping I wouldn't catch any sympathetic glances from other diners who suspected I'd been stood up. It had started raining so that could have slowed traffic down.

Daniel had chosen Salt & Pepper Lodge and I was impressed. It wasn't on Gary's shortlist of favourite restaurants so this was my first visit. The vegetarian and vegan selection was extensive and I'd already chosen my meal... if Daniel ever showed up.

Fiddling with the salt, I tried, but failed, not to look at my phone again: 7.51 p.m. I'd give him until eight. If he hadn't shown by then, he wasn't going to, and I wasn't going to humiliate myself by staying any longer. Then I panicked. Surely twenty minutes late was a definite no-show. Did I really need to give him thirty? Why was I even debating? I already knew I was going to wait until eight. He was Sarah's friend and she'd never have set us up if he was unreliable. Something must have happened.

'Thank you,' I said to the waiter ten minutes later as I handed over a ten-pound note for my drink. 'Please keep the change. I'm sorry I hogged a table.'

'It's no problem. Tuesdays aren't usually busy,' he said. 'I'm sorry your friend didn't show.'

I smiled and hoped the tears pricking my eyes wouldn't make it down my cheeks. 'Thank you.'

Standing up, I picked up my bag and cursed myself for not bringing a coat or a brolly. I was going to get very wet walking back to Seashell Cottage. Perfect end to a perfect evening.

'Elise! Thank God you're still here.' I looked towards the door to see a tall, athletically built man dashing towards me. His dark hair was plastered to his head and there was muck on his face and down his soggy pale blue shirt.

'Daniel?'

He nodded. 'I'm so, so sorry. My car had a blow-out and I had to change the tyre and, as you can see, it's peeing it down. I'd have phoned the restaurant because I don't have your number, but I forgot to charge my phone. I kept praying you'd still be here. Have I screwed up? I'll understand if you want to leave, especially given the state of me, but I'm really hoping you'll stay.' He finally paused for breath.

I glanced at the waiter hovering nearby who smiled and nodded then discreetly moved away. There was something instantly attractive and vulnerable about Daniel and I knew I'd regret it if I walked away.

'I'll stay,' I said. 'But on one condition.'

'Anything.'

'You get yourself to the bathroom and give your face a little scrub.'

He put his hand up to his cheek and wrinkled his nose. 'It's a deal. Thank you. I'd give you a hug, but I don't want to drench that gorgeous dress. Sarah wasn't wrong when she said you were stunning.'

I blushed. 'Sarah said that?' I looked down at my long, floaty coral dress with a delicate print of seashells and seahorses on it.

'Yes. And she also said that if I mess you about, she'll never order from me again and she'll rip my bollocks off and mount them in her next floral arrangement. So please don't tell her I was late because I'm a little bit scared of her right now.'

The thought of that made me laugh. 'Get yourself cleaned up. I promise I'll still be here when you get back.'

When Daniel emerged from the gents, his hair was dry – presumably from the hand-dryer – and sticking up slightly. He had a look of a younger Colin Farrell about him. Very nice. His face was scrubbed and he'd somehow acquired a clean white shirt.

'Do you always have a spare shirt in your back pocket?'

Daniel laughed. 'One of the waiters took pity on me and loaned me his spare.' He sat down. 'I'm so sorry again. I've been looking forward to meeting you all week. I'm glad you could come out on a school night. Or did term finish last week?'

'We broke up on Friday, but I was in school yesterday and today for training. I'm finished now, though.'

'They didn't have teachers who looked like you when I was at school,' he said. 'I might have done better if they had.' He clapped his hand over his mouth. 'I can't believe I just said that. That was unbelievably cheesy, wasn't it? Again, I apologise. Sarah probably told you that I've only ever dated my wife... ex-wife... so I'm completely out of practice when it comes to dating. Not that this is a date. Unless you want it to be.' He shook his head. 'I think I might just stop talking.' He took a swig of his wine.

I laughed. 'Firstly, please relax. Secondly, I'm out of practice too as Gary was also my childhood sweetheart. Thirdly... about that chat-up line... don't ever, ever say anything like that again or I may have to ask Sarah to carry out her threat.'

Daniel laughed too.

'How about we start over?' I said. 'I'm Elise. I'm thirty and I'm the Head of English and Drama at a local comprehensive. Next month I'd have been celebrating my twelfth wedding anniversary with Gary who I've been with since I was fourteen. Unfortunately, I found him and his new partner in our shower six-and-a-half weeks ago so I'm now living with Sarah's auntie and going through a divorce. And you are...?'

'I'm Daniel, I'm thirty-two and I'm a sales rep. I work for several different companies including Gorgeous Gifts who supply to your friend Sarah's shop. I met my soon-to-be-ex-wife, Amber, when I was sixteen and we married at twenty-one. Unfortunately I discovered she'd been having an affair with my friend and neighbour, Jake, and I found out because she miscarried our baby. Only it wasn't *our* baby, it was Jake's. So now I'm living in my nan's holiday cottage in the middle of nowhere with my brother Michael who hates me and, like you, I'm going through a divorce.'

'I'm so sorry to hear about the baby,' I said. 'I think you may have just trumped me on the sheer crap-ness of it all.'

'I don't know. I didn't have the dubious pleasure of catching them in the act.'

'True,' I said. 'And at least Amber was having an affair with someone of the opposite sex.'

'No!' Daniel's eyes widened. 'He was with a guy?'

I nodded. For a moment, I panicked that I'd told Gary's secret, but Daniel wasn't from Whitsborough Bay originally so he wasn't going to know Gary. Plus, if Gary had any sense, he'd have confessed all to Cynthia by now.

'Wow!' Daniel raised his glass. 'How about a toast to despicable exes and new beginnings?'

I clinked my glass with his. 'I'll drink to that.'

* * *

After a poor start, the hours whizzed by. We noticed the waiters looking anxious to close for the evening just before eleven so decided we'd better settle the bill and let them head home.

Sarah, Kay, Curtis and Stevie (before the incident) had been great listeners and Jem had worked his counselling magic during a couple more sessions but speaking to somebody who was going through the same thing was ever so cathartic. We'd both been betrayed by the one person we trusted more than anyone else and we'd both had our world thrown into turmoil. We laughed, we cried, we flirted, we laughed some more.

The rain had stopped by the time we left the restaurant.

'Did I do okay?' Daniel asked. 'Are my man-bits safe?'

I laughed. 'You've more than made up for the shaky start. I wish the evening didn't have to end, but there's nowhere to go on a Tuesday night.'

'It doesn't have to end.' Daniel took my hand. My heart raced at his touch.

'What do you propose?'

'You could always come back to mine,' he said. 'We don't have to do anything. We can just continue to chat.'

I bit my lip. 'And what if I want to do something?'

* * *

Daniel had only had one glass of wine during the meal. He told me his nan's holiday cottage was in the grounds of a farm about twenty minutes' drive up the coast towards Shellby Bay and it was easier and cheaper to drive than travel by taxi.

That twenty-minute journey felt like hours as he drove along the coast road in silence, the tension between us fizzing. I had to sit on my hands to stop me from touching him and causing an accident. Watching his profile out of the corner of my eye, my mind raced with all the things I wanted to do to him. I really shouldn't have read *Fifty Shades of Grey*. I'm a voracious reader, but the series hadn't sounded like my kind of thing so I'd avoided it at the time. About eight months ago, desperate to try something... anything... to garner Gary's interests, I'd relented and borrowed the first three from a colleague at school. I hadn't been converted to erotica as a preferred reading genre, but I'd certainly learned a thing or two. Needless to say, it hadn't worked on Gary. At least I now knew why.

Daniel steered his car into a courtyard. A security light came on, illuminating a large farmhouse straight ahead, a cottage to the left, and a barn to the right. Daniel stopped his car in front of the cottage, switched off the ignition and took a deep breath. He touched my arm and a wave of desire ran through me. 'Are you sure?' he asked.

I nodded. 'Very sure.' I surprised myself at how much I wanted this.

We opened our doors at the same time and stepped into the

cool air, which had been freshened by the earlier downpour. My whole body felt on fire so the breeze was soothing.

'Michael's back.' Daniel indicated the jeep parked next to his car. 'We'll need to be quiet.'

He unlocked the cottage door and flicked the switch on a lamp just inside. I followed him into a large open plan kitchen/diner/lounge, but I had little chance to take in the surroundings because, the moment the door closed behind us, Daniel took me in his arms and kissed me, softly at first, then more urgently. I responded with the same urgency, clinging tightly onto him. We stumbled into the lounge area. He unzipped my dress and eased my arms out of it, letting it fall to the wooden floor. His eyes flashed with desire. Thank goodness I was wearing matching underwear. I unbuttoned his shirt and tried to pull it off him, but it had long sleeves and buttons and his hands got caught in the cuffs. We giggled as he tried to release himself. He finally tugged his arms free and pulled my face towards his, running his fingers through my hair, but I squealed as his watch got caught in my curls.

'Oh my God! I'm so sorry.' He unclasped his watch and carefully worked on my hair until he'd untangled it. 'Are you okay? Did it hurt?'

'It's fine.' I rubbed my sore head.

He gently kissed my scalp. 'Are you sure you're okay?'

I reached up and took his face in my hands and moved it close to mine. 'Where were we?'

He kissed me again, gently at first then with more passion. He lowered himself onto the sofa and pulled me towards him, but my foot got caught on a table lamp, which went crashing to the floor along with what sounded like a glass smashing.

'What the bloody hell's going on?'

I peeked over the sofa towards the staircase where I could make out the shape of a man in a pair of trunks.

'Michael! Sorry. I'll clear it up. We were just—'

'So I see,' Michael interrupted. 'Show some respect and use your room.' He turned round and stomped up the stairs again. I cringed as a door slammed.

'Sorry,' Daniel said. 'That was my brother. I didn't think it was the right moment for introductions. This isn't going very well, is it?'

I stroked his cheek. 'I'm beginning to feel like something's trying to stop us.'

'Do you want me to drive you home?' He looked disappointed.

I shook my head. 'No. Unless you want to.'

'No. I'd really like you to stay. Do you want to head upstairs while I get this lot cleared up?'

I nodded.

Daniel grinned. 'There's only three rooms. The bathroom's on the side, Michael's room's at the front and mine's at the back so you can't go wrong.' He helped me to my feet and picked up my dress. 'I don't think I've ever said sorry so many times in one evening, but I really am very sorry for the crap start and end to the evening.'

I gave him a gentle kiss on the lips. 'It's been different, but it's been fantastic so you have nothing to be sorry about. Plus, the evening isn't over yet. I'll see you upstairs.'

17

I awoke desperate for the toilet and immediately kicked myself for having fallen asleep before Daniel came upstairs last night. He could only have been about ten minutes clearing up yet I hadn't managed to stay awake that long. What must he have thought?

To my left, he lay spark-out, hair mussed up, lips pouting. I had an overwhelming desire to kiss him, but I also had an overwhelming desire to pee and that was stronger. It was still dark, but the blinds I'd drawn last night had been black-out ones so it could have been the early hours or mid-morning for all I knew. I carefully peeled back the duvet and slipped out of bed. Through the gloom, I spotted a towel draped over a radiator and wrapped it round me in case I encountered Michael on the landing.

A small clock on the windowsill in the bathroom read 6.32 a.m. After using the toilet and freshening my breath with some toothpaste, I crept back along the landing, noting that a strip of light had appeared under Michael's doorway. Darting into Daniel's room to avoid Michael, I'd just closed the door behind me when Daniel flicked on a bedside lamp, startling me.

'I woke up and you were gone.' I looked towards the bed

where he was propped up on his arm. 'I thought you'd done a runner.' Gone was the confidence from last night. Instead, he looked sad and perhaps a little afraid. My heart went out to him.

'I wouldn't do that to you,' I said. 'Call of nature.'

'That's a relief. I'd have been sad if you'd gone.' He folded back the duvet on my side of the bed and his eyes beseeched me to join him. I dropped the towel at the very last moment and quickly dived under the covers.

'Thank you,' he said.

Those two words sounded so full of emotion and gratitude that I just wanted to take his pain away. 'It'll be all right,' I tried to re-assure him.

'Will it? Is that how you feel?'

'No. But I have to try and make myself believe it will be, or I wouldn't be able to get out of bed each day.'

'What hurts you the most?' he whispered.

'The lies. I trusted him and he lied to me pretty much from the moment we got together. I'm such an honest person and I thought Gary was too. Apparently not.'

'It's the same for me,' he said. 'Amber was so excited about the baby, you know. I thought we had our whole future ahead of us. Together. When she started bleeding, I'd never felt so scared in my life, but when it was over she wouldn't let me comfort her. She kept asking for Jake and I couldn't understand why. I went next door to tell him about the baby and he looked so shocked and hurt that it dawned on me. It was like a million unexplained things suddenly made sense. Five years. They'd been lying to me for five years.'

We lay for a moment staring into each other's glistening eyes. My heart began to race and my breathing shallowed. I heard his do the same. Next moment, we were in each other's arms and, this time, there were no clothing-removal disasters, no lamps or glasses to kick over, and no angry brother.

* * *

'Are you okay?' Daniel asked, holding me tightly. 'You're shaking.'

'That's because I'm in shock,' I admitted.

'Oh God! Was I that bad?'

'No. The complete opposite. I had no idea that... well, with Gary I... it was never... he never... Sorry, I think you may have turned me into a gibbering wreck.'

Daniel loosened his hold so he could look into my eyes. 'Really? You're saying you've never climaxed?'

Colour rushed to my cheeks as I shook my head. 'I thought I had and I didn't get what the fuss was all about, but now I know I was way off. That was amazing. Thank you.'

He laughed and stroked my damp hair. 'You don't have to thank me. But if you give me a moment, we may be able to make up on some more lost experiences.'

'Again? But Gary...'

'Gary never made love to you more than once a night?' Daniel suggested when I fell silent. 'You're stunning, Elise. How did he manage to keep his hands off you?'

'I think we both know the answer to that question, don't we?'

'Sorry. Completely inappropriate.'

'It's fine. I was lucky if Gary made love to me once every six months, never mind more than once in a night. I have a feeling I've missed out on a lot, but I also have a feeling I may have found a good teacher. And you know I have a lot of respect for the teaching profession.'

Daniel laughed and dived under the covers. 'Let the lesson commence.'

Ooh yes, definitely a fantastic teacher!

* * *

I felt a little uncomfortable rooting around in the kitchen cupboards to find a mug and teabags, but Daniel had said to make myself at home while he showered and got ready for work so I'd padded down to the kitchen in my knickers and one of his work shirts. I'd heard the front door go and an engine start so assumed Michael had gone out and I was safe.

Finally finding the right cupboard, I leaned against the units, having a good look around the room while I waited for the kettle to boil. I instantly loved the cottage. Colourful seaside prints adorned exposed stone walls and a deep bay windowsill was covered in shells, pebbles, wooden boats and a lighthouse. A shabby chic dresser painted bright turquoise and loaded with paperbacks and board games took pride of place on the wall opposite the window. Next to it another smaller cream dresser displayed bright mismatched crockery. Brightly coloured scatter cushions adorned the navy wrap-around sofa and I blushed as I thought about what had nearly happened on it the night before. Then I blushed even more as I thought about what had happened in the bedroom just now. Twice. Wow! Who knew?

The kettle boiled and I was squeezing my teabag when the door opened and Michael walked in carrying a camera bag. He carefully placed it on the sofa and fiddled with something inside it. He obviously hadn't noticed me. What should I do? Cough. Say 'hello'? Stay quiet? Run upstairs? Damn!

'Er, hi,' I said. 'You must be Michael.'

He looked up, startled, then frowned as he saw what I was – or should that be wasn't – wearing.

'You're still here then?' he said.

I chose to ignore the attitude. 'I'm Elise. Can I make you a drink? Kettle's just boiled.'

'I was on my way out.' He picked up his bag again and headed back towards the door.

'I'm sorry about disturbing you last night,' I said.

He stopped and stared at me. He was taller and slimmer

than Daniel, but I'd definitely have picked them out as brothers in a line-up. They certainly came from a good gene pool. 'Elaine, is it?'

'Elise.'

'Elise, you have nothing to be sorry about. He's the one who should be apologising. Bringing you back here was completely inappropriate and disrespectful. As usual.' Then he stormed out of the cottage, slamming the door. I heard an engine start up and the screech of tyres.

Sipping on my tea, I wondered what he meant by 'as usual' and my stomach clenched.

Daniel appeared five minutes later, looking handsome in a sky-blue shirt and coordinating tie. 'I bet you can convince your lady customers to spend a fortune when you're dressed like that,' I said.

He laughed. 'Speaking of clothes, I'm liking what you're wearing. Or not wearing.'

'Thank you.' I did a twirl.

'I'm going to have to stop looking at you because I'm getting very turned on right now and I will be so late for my first client if I do all the things I'd like to do to you.'

A shiver of delight ran down my body and I knew immediately that I'd do anything for an action replay of our morning together. 'Fancy taking a rain-check on that?'

'Tomorrow night?'

I nodded. 'Give me two minutes to gather the rest of my clothes then are you sure you're okay to drop me in town?'

'My first appointment's in York so it's not too much of a detour. And I can't leave a beautiful lady stranded.'

* * *

As we drove back towards Whitsborough Bay, I thought about Michael's comment. I knew that if I didn't ask Daniel what he meant, it would niggle at me and then doubts would creep in about whether he was being honest with me. After what I'd just been through with Gary, I had to know.

He laughed when I told him. 'He really said that? My brother's such an arse.'

'You know we were talking this morning about how the lies were the worst part of what we've been through? You have been honest with me, haven't you?'

'About what?'

'About your sex life since splitting up with Amber. If there've been others, I don't mind. Just be honest. I wouldn't blame you if you'd slept around.'

Daniel pulled into a side-road, stopped the car and turned to face me. 'Do you really think I'd lie to you after what you've been through?'

I shook my head. 'No. It's just that—'

'It's just that my idiot brother's done what he likes to do best: screw things up for me.' Daniel banged the palm of his hand on the steering wheel. 'He's such a shit.'

I wished I hadn't said anything. 'Sorry,' I muttered.

He turned back to face me. 'Don't be. It's him. I told you we don't get on and I think you've seen plenty of evidence of that last night and this morning. I didn't tell you why, though, did I?'

I shook my head. 'You don't have to if it's too personal.'

'It's fine. I want you to know. Michael's two years older than me. When we were kids, we got on as well as most siblings do. You know how it is? Play great one minute, fight the next. Everything changed when I brought Amber home. Michael was eighteen, single and desperate to find a girlfriend. I could tell he liked her instantly. I only found out how much when we were at a family party and I overheard him trying to convince her to dump me and see him instead. He tried to make out he was joking, but he wasn't. He made a pass at her a few years later.

This time his excuse was that he was drunk, it was dark and he thought she was someone else.'

'But you didn't believe him?'

'No. I saw the way he looked at her. We had a huge fight about it one day and he told me I wasn't good enough for her, never would be, and he'd never stop trying to convince her of it. We've barely spoken since. I know he's my brother, but I can't stand him.'

'I'm not surprised. Why do you share a house, then?'

He rolled his eyes. 'Good question. Nan decided she was too old to deal with the hassle of renting it out as a holiday home so was looking for a permanent let. Michael's a photographer like my dad. They'd returned from a shoot in South Africa and Michael needed a place to rent so Nan agreed to let him have the cottage on the proviso that I could use it too. I'd stay over occasionally if I had appointments in this area or further north, rather than trek back home to Lincoln. Then, when Amber and I split up, it made financial sense for me to move in permanently. Work-wise it's better because I now live in the middle of my patch instead of at the bottom. As for Michael, my dear brother is happy to take half the rent off me, but he still likes to swan about as if he owns the place. The comment he made was nothing to do with me bringing other women back. You're the first. He thought it was "inappropriate and disrespectful" when I couldn't sleep and put the TV on too loud. And when I burned a pizza. And when I forgot to take my washing out of the machine so he had to. It's his favourite phrase. I think it makes him feel important. I'm sorry if he made you uncomfortable and dragged you into our little war.'

'Why didn't you move in with your dad instead of Michael? I thought you said he was local.'

'I don't get on very well with my dad either and I don't like being in that house. My mum had leukaemia and he didn't want her to go into a hospice, so she died there. Too many memories.'

'I'm sorry about your mum.'

'It was years ago.'

I leaned over and gently kissed him. 'Thank you. I didn't mean to question you.'

'Feel free to question me any time,' he said. 'I'd rather you did that than you worried I was about to hurt you like Gary did because that's the last thing I'd ever want to do.'

When we pulled up outside Seashell Cottage he checked I was still okay for a date the next night before kissing me again.

Curtis had been right. I really had needed a 'damn good shag' as he'd put it and Daniel had absolutely delivered the goods. I danced up Kay's path, feeling all light-headed and girly.

18

✉ From Daniel
Can't stop thinking about you. Counting down
the hours till I see you tonight. Bad news,
though. Michael isn't going out after all. If
I cook for you, he'll only make things
awkward. Can I take you out for a meal again
instead? xx

✉ To Daniel
Sounds great, but a bag of chips on the
seafront would be fine by me xx

✉ From Daniel
A meal it is then! I'll book a table at that
vegan place by the harbour so perhaps we can
have a walk along the beach afterwards. Can't
wait to see you later xx

'Wow! You look stunning,' Daniel said as soon as I opened the
door to Seashell Cottage. He gave me a gentle kiss and, as I

wrapped my arms round his neck, my heart fluttered and so did other parts of my body. I liked the sensation very much.

'I don't look too casual?' I'd opted for some sparkly flip-flops and a long, floaty cream summer dress with small burgundy flowers embroidered round the hem and bodice.

'You look perfect.'

'As do you.' He looked sexy in dark jeans and a light grey short-sleeved shirt. He smelled good too.

Daniel took my hand as we strolled into town. I was surprised at how natural it felt to be holding another man's hand after years of only Gary. Mind you, I'd been surprised at how natural it felt to have sex with Daniel after only ever being with Gary. I wondered whether it would have felt that way with any man or whether Daniel was extra special.

A waitress led us to a small booth in Bean Cuisine, a restaurant overlooking the harbour at South Bay. A trio of candles in the middle of the table and a string of fairy lights across the wall provided mood lighting. The whole place had a very chilled, relaxed ambiance thanks to the lights, cushions and ambient music. 'Good choice,' I said.

While we pondered the menu, my phone beeped in my bag. 'Would it be rude if I checked that while you're still deciding?' I asked.

'Go for it. I may be some time. It all sounds delicious.'

⊠ From Gary
Had a last-minute viewing on the house
earlier. They seemed keen. Sitting here
looking at everything we've collected over the
years and feeling melancholy. I know it's the
right thing, but I hate the thought of a
stranger living in our beautiful home. Hope
you're coping better than me

'Something wrong?' Daniel lowered his menu.

I released the grip on my phone and tossed it back into my bag. 'Just Gary about the house. Emotional stuff that I'm not going to dignify with a response.' I understood that we needed to maintain some level of communication while we were selling the house, but why couldn't he have stopped the text after the word 'keen'? Why add in all that other stuff? I looked up at Daniel and smiled. 'Sorry. It's fine. Have you decided?'

'Yes. Decision definitely made.'

* * *

After we'd finished our main courses, I left Daniel looking at the dessert menu and nipped to the ladies, which were on a mezzanine level up a narrow metal staircase. When I came out, I waited on the landing, looking down on the restaurant, while another customer ascended the stairs. Daniel was still studying the dessert menu in our booth and a young couple were taking their seats in the next one along. I glanced at the final booth and I swear my heart skipped a beat. Gary was in it. With Rob. Gary was eating in a restaurant he'd refused to take me to. With Rob.

Gripping onto the railing, I watched them talking animatedly. The beard had gone and Gary looked relaxed and happier than I'd seen him in years. Our waitress appeared with desserts for them. When she'd gone, Rob picked up a spoon and dipped it into his then leaned across the table and offered it to Gary who eagerly took the spoonful. Rob offered him another spoonful then Gary did the same with his dessert. He laughed and pointed at Rob's face, indicating a bit of mess on his chin. Rob put his hand up but missed it so Gary leaned across and wiped it away with his thumb. The look that passed between them was one of absolute adoration.

If they were on their desserts already, they had to have been in the restaurant when we arrived. Which meant that Gary hadn't been sitting at home getting melancholy over our house selling when he'd texted me; he'd been dining with his boyfriend ten feet away from me. So we'd split up and still the lies continued. Why? What did he possibly have to gain from sending that text?

My legs shook with each stair I descended and I clung tightly to the handrail, desperately hoping that my legs wouldn't betray me and give way altogether.

I stupidly stole one more glance in their direction and, at that very moment, Gary looked across. The smile faded from his face and I saw his lips move with my name. Rob turned too. Gary stood up and started towards me, but I put my hand up in a stop signal and shook my head. He nodded and slowly backed towards his seat, keeping his eyes on me.

Daniel stood up. 'Are you okay? You don't look well.'

I reached for my bag. 'May we skip dessert? Actually, can we go?'

'Of course. Do you need some water?'

'Just some air. I'll meet you outside.'

* * *

'Do you want to talk about it?' Daniel sat on the bench beside me, overlooking the harbour.

I bit my lip. 'Yes. But can we go for that walk?'

'We certainly can. Where do you want to go? Along the beach? To the lighthouse?'

'The tide's out so Lighthouse Cove, please,' I said. 'I'll explain what happened when we get there.'

I held Daniel's hand as we silently and slowly walked over the swing bridge. The anger eased with each step and I felt much calmer by the time we made our way down the steps onto the beach at Lighthouse Cove.

'Gary was in the restaurant,' I said as we stepped onto the

sand. The beach was deserted – exactly how I liked it.

'Oh.'

'In his text, he said that he was at home and feeling emotional about selling up yet he had to have sent it from the restaurant.'

'More lies.'

I nodded. 'You know how I feel about lies. The one he told in the text was so pointless.' I kicked at a half-collapsed sandcastle. 'The text was bad enough, but what really threw me was seeing them together behaving in a way that he never behaved with me. They were sharing desserts. He always refused to share food with me. He said you should be satisfied with your own choice and not expect to take someone else's and that sharing a spoon passed on germs. Mind you, he also said showers were for soaping not shagging. And he never deviated from his three favourite restaurants when we dined out yet there he was eating in a restaurant he refused to take me to.'

We'd reached the caves. I stopped walking and turned to stare at the dark waves lapping onto the distant shore. The tide was fully out and the sun had set, leaving an orange tinge in the darkening sky. The beauty around me helped to soothe my mood. Keeping my eyes on the sky, I said, 'What really hurts is that he's doing all these things with Rob that he would never do with me and he looks so relaxed and happy about it. It's more proof that our marriage was obviously a living hell for him. I had no idea I was making him so miserable so I feel like such a failure.'

Daniel stood behind me, wrapped his arms round my waist and put his cheek against mine. 'Just remember that it wasn't you who made Gary miserable. If he felt that way, it was because he was lying to himself about his sexuality. You could do nothing to change that.'

I sighed. 'I know. But it still hurts.'

'I wish I could take your pain away, but only time will do

that,' he whispered. 'But if you're willing to give me time, I'll do everything I can to try to make things better for you.' He gently kissed my cheek. The touch of his lips was so tender that it sent butterflies fluttering throughout my whole body again.

'Are you cold?' He ran his hands up and down my bare arms. 'You're shivering.'

'I'm not cold. It's the effect you have on me. I mean that in a good way. Do you really want to try and take my pain away?'

'Of course.'

I twisted round to face him. 'Can we re-enact yesterday morning? Right here.' With Gary, it had always been the missionary position in a bed and, if he could try different things, so could I. And what I was suggesting was far more adventurous than a vegan restaurant or sharing desserts.

Daniel's eyes lit up. 'You want to partake in a little sex on the beach? I think I can be persuaded. Are you sure? What if someone sees us?'

'Isn't that part of the excitement?'

* * *

'You're an amazing woman, Elise.' Daniel kissed me on the forehead as we lay on the cool sand looking up at the dark sky. 'And you're full of surprises.'

'Good ones, I hope.'

'Very good ones.'

'I might actually have surprised myself tonight,' I admitted. 'I've never done anything like this before. Not only was my sex life pretty much non-existent, it wasn't very adventurous either.'

'We'll have to rectify that, then. Assuming you want to.'

I kissed his bare chest. 'Definitely. But tell me if I do things wrong, won't you?'

Daniel laughed and held me tightly. 'God, I love you.'

I gasped. 'What did you say?'

'Erm... Something I didn't mean to say out loud so soon. I haven't scared you, have I?'

'No, you haven't scared me.'

We lay there in silence, hands entwined, looking up at the stars. At that moment, I felt happy, which was a surprise given how low I'd felt an hour earlier. Love or not, Daniel was good for me. As was hearing it from the man first. I would always regret being the first to tell Gary I loved him.

I turned onto my side and traced my finger across Daniel's lips. 'This is really short notice, but I don't suppose you'd be my plus one at my sister's wedding a week on Saturday? I've been dreading going alone.'

He kissed my fingers. 'I'd be honoured to.'

'Really? You'd do that?'

'Of course.'

'Thank you. I was worried about being bombarded with questions about Gary. Hopefully having you by my side will mean some of the guests are a bit more tactful.'

'Did you say you're a bridesmaid?'

'Yes.'

'Then I'm sure you *will* be the centre of attention, but it will because you outshine the bride rather than because you're the subject of the latest gossip.'

I laughed. 'I don't think I'll outshine our Jess, but I appreciate the sentiment.'

Daniel shivered. 'I'm a bit cold now. Can we relocate? I know a little place up the coast. One of the occupants is a bit grumpy, but the other one has some moves he'd like to show you.'

I giggled. 'Now there's an offer I can't refuse.' I grabbed my bag and flip-flops then scrambled to my feet. 'Race you to the car.'

'Oi! Cheat!' Daniel grabbed his belongings and raced after me as I squealed like a little girl. Suddenly, next Saturday didn't seem like the terrifying ordeal I'd started to build it up as.

19

✉ From Gary
Lawton's have just booked a viewing for 3pm.
Still no offer from that other couple. They
obviously weren't that keen after all. I wish
you'd respond to my texts. I've already apologised a million times. It was wrong of me to
send that text, but I can't change what's
done. You must really hate me to keep ignoring
me like this

✉ To Gary
I don't hate you. I just hate what you've
done to us. It's Jess's wedding today so it's
about them, not you. Please don't text me
again today unless it's to say we have an
offer

✉ From Gary
Sorry. The date hadn't registered. Please
congratulate Jess & Lee. I hope they have a

great day. Hope you don't get too many questions about us

⌧ To Gary
They can ask as many questions as they want,
but I'll just introduce them to my gorgeous
new boyfriend and they'll be able to see I've
moved on. Please stop texting

I bit my lip as I put my phone back in my bag. That had been a
bit mean, but then again, it wasn't as mean as making out that he
was devastated about the house selling when he was really out
having fun with his boyfriend.

Megan giggling in the lounge made me smile and instantly
snapped me out of my dark mood. She had such an infectious
laugh and it was so much better to hear that than the excitable
high-pitched squealing she'd been doing ten minutes earlier as
she raced around Jess's bedroom. Suspecting it was only a
matter of time before she fell, smashed something, or ripped
someone's clothes, Izzy had lured her daughter into the lounge
with promises of *Peppa Pig* and a tub of grapes.

Knocking lightly, I pushed Jess's bedroom door open. 'It's
only me and I promise not to run laps around your room.'

She was on her own, standing in front of the full-length
mirror, looking quite emotional. 'I still can't believe it's my
wedding day today.'

'Well, it is, and you look absolutely stunning.' I flounced her
veil. 'That dress is so flattering.'

She smiled and twirled. 'I must have had some sort of sixth
sense when I picked an empire line dress. Perfect style for hiding
my stomach.'

'You can't tell that you're pregnant with twins at all.'

'Only because I ordered a bigger size, thank goodness.' She
pulled the dress tightly across her stomach, revealing a small

baby bump, and looked down. 'Now, you two, listen to Mummy carefully. I know you've started your flutterings, but Mummy doesn't like them. Makes me feel like I'm on a rollercoaster. So please be nice to me on my wedding day and hold off on the weird stuff. Can you do that?' She cocked her head. 'I'll take the silence as agreement. Thank you.'

I laughed. 'You've really started flutterings?'

'Tuesday was the first. I like being able to feel the babies, but I don't like the actual sensation. It freaks me out a bit.' She reached out and took my hand, her face suddenly serious. 'Are you really okay about today? Without Gary, I mean.'

I sat down on the edge of the bed and indicated that she should join me. I took her hand. 'Today is your day, Jess. Enjoy it. Please don't spend a single moment of it worrying about me.'

She squeezed my hand. 'If you're sure...?'

'I'm sure.'

Jess smiled. 'And your new man, Daniel, is serious?'

'I don't think I could cope with "serious" after what I've just been through. I'm enjoying it, though. He's good for me. I think you'll like him.'

'If *you* like him then *I'll* like him.'

'Thank you. I'm in a good place right now, so you really don't need to worry about me.'

'I'll always worry about you,' she said. 'That's what sisters are for.'

I laughed as we hugged each other. I really meant it when I said I was in a good place. Daniel was helping, a couple of nights out with Sarah had helped too, and that old cliché of time had worked wonders. The only major blip at the moment was the delights of a day with my mother.

Right on cue, the bedroom door opened. 'Ah, there's the two of you. The divorcee and the pregnant one. I couldn't be prouder.'

I gritted my teeth and fought the urge to correct her

appalling grammar. 'Hello, Mother. You made it! And here was me thinking the wedding car would be making a stop at the pub to collect you en route.'

She scowled at me. 'I've no idea what you're talking about.'

'Come on, Jess,' I said. 'It's nearly time to say, "I do". Are you ready?'

'I'm ready.' Her eyes shone brightly as she stood up and flounced out her skirts.

'You don't look *too* fat in that dress,' Mother said.

'I'm not fat. I'm pregnant.'

Mother shrugged. 'Same thing. Your body's ruined for life now.'

I reached for Jess's hand. 'I think she looks stunning and, as her mother, you should be telling her that.'

Mother cleared her throat and, for once in her life, I thought an apology might be on its way or perhaps even a compliment. But that would have been far too much to expect. 'That colour you're wearing,' she said, pointing at my dress. 'What *is* that?'

'It's sage,' I said.

'Sage? That's not a colour. That's a herb.'

I wanted so much to give her a mouthful of abuse. It would ruin Jess's day, though, and Mother really wasn't worth it. I would have my Cynthia-style confrontation with her one day. But today wasn't that day.

It was late afternoon by the time we'd finished the wedding breakfast then the speeches. I smiled across at Daniel from the top table as I took a nibble out of my sliver of wedding cake. 'Okay?' I mouthed.

'Perfect,' he mouthed back. He was seated at a table with Sarah, Nick, and some of Jess's friends. Judging by the shrieks of laughter, everyone had gelled well and Daniel seemed to be playing a lead role in keeping them amused. I loved that he was making such an effort to fit in. Gary would have looked lost and uncomfortable in the same scenario. He hated big social get-togethers like this.

Dad appeared by my side and asked Lee's dad if he wouldn't mind swapping places while we had our coffees.

'How are you holding up?' he asked, pulling his chair in.

'I'm fine thanks, Dad. I'm not the poor bugger who's had to sit next to Mother for the whole meal.'

He smiled weakly as he shook his head. 'Where is she?'

'Do you really need to ask?'

His eyes flicked in the direction of the bar. I nodded and he sighed.

'How are you holding up without Gary?' he asked.

'Surprisingly well. I know it's only been eight weeks, but things hadn't been right for quite some time so it was a long time coming. I've had my ups and downs, but I'm definitely getting there. The house is on the market, the divorce is going through and I've met someone else. It's change. It's unexpected change. But it's good change.'

Dad poured cream into his coffee and stirred. 'I'm sure I'll be able to chat to him properly later, but first impressions are good. Is it serious?'

I shrugged. 'Jess asked me the same thing. He's told me he loves me.'

Dad stopped stirring and turned to me, mouth slightly open. 'How long have you been together?'

'Less than two weeks. You can close your mouth. I didn't say it back.'

'Do you feel it?'

'I don't think so, but I like him a lot and I don't want it to end. Right now, it's exactly what I need it to be and that's something without a label.'

Dad laughed. 'Something without a label? I like that.' He

took a sip of his coffee. 'You know you can say the word anytime and I'll fly straight home, don't you?' His voice cracked as he spoke.

I reached for his hand. 'I know.'

He took another sip of his coffee. 'Much as I don't want to, I think I'd better go and track down your mother and make sure she's not working her way across the optics.

'She's been gone about twenty minutes. She may be on her second trip by now.'

✉ From Curtis
How's the event of the year? Everyone asking about the ex?

✉ To Curtis
Surprisingly not… although I'm sure there's plenty of whispered gossip

✉ From Curtis
I challenge you to really give them something to gossip about by another risky liaison in the great outdoors. The gauntlet has been laid down, Red. Do you accept?

✉ To Curtis
Hmm. Interesting. I accept. When we were having our photos taken in the garden earlier, I spotted a hidden rose garden with a bench waiting to be christened! xx

Guests had started to move into the bar so the room could be cleared ready for the evening do. Daniel stood up and made his way towards the top table, his eyes fixed on mine. I downed the last sips of champagne, picked up my dolly bag and wrapped it round my wrist, then stood up to meet him, my body fizzing as he ran his hands up my arms and gently kissed me.

'Having fun?' I asked.

'I am, actually, but I'd be having even more fun if it was just the two of us. I don't suppose we can escape to our room for some private time, can we?'

I grinned. 'Hold that thought. I think my bridesmaid duties are over, but I need to check on my mother before I can properly relax. Why don't we go to the bar? I might need to abandon you if Mother isn't there or if she's there and a bit worse for wear.

Daniel nodded and gave my hand a gentle squeeze, suggesting he understood. I'd warned him that she liked a few drinks, but I'd shied away from giving him the full details. I'm not really sure what had stopped me. Perhaps a gay husband was enough to confess for the early stages of a relationship without throwing in the bleak truth about an alcoholic mother and a damaged childhood.

The bar was packed with wedding guests but there was no sign of Mother or Dad. My shoulders slumped. 'Sorry, Daniel. I'd better go and find them.'

'That's fine. Come and find me in here when you're done,' Daniel said. 'How long do you think you'll be? Ten minutes?'

'Hopefully no more than fifteen and I promise I'll make it up to you. I've got a big surprise for you.'

'I can't wait. I love surprises.'

'Believe me, you'll definitely love this one.'

But I never got to give him his surprise because I was about to get a big surprise myself. And not a good one.

20

'Are you looking for someone, dear?' I turned round to look into the pale watery eyes of Dad's older sister, Auntie Grace. 'You look a bit lost.'

'I'm looking for Mother and Dad. I don't suppose you've seen either of them, have you?'

She tilted her head to one side and sighed. 'I'm sorry, dear, but your mother was inebriated and making a scene. Trevor took her outside.'

She had to do it, didn't she? She couldn't just behave for one afternoon and evening. 'Thanks, Auntie Grace. Which direction?'

'That way.' She pointed towards the front of the hotel. It made sense. Guests had spilled out onto the patio running alongside the back of the bar, but there was only a car park out the front. She could create a scene out there without an audience.

I made my way down the stone steps and along the edge of the car park then stopped when I heard their raised voices coming from a grassy area to the side of the building.

'She's your daughter, Marian. Can't you just lay off the drink and show you care for one day? For one *special* day?'

'But I *don't* care, so why should I pretend I do? If it hadn't been for the free bar, I wouldn't have bothered coming.'

I gasped. How cruel could she be? I gingerly peered round the corner. Mother had kicked her shoes off and was lounging on a wooden bench, clutching a hip flask in one hand and a roll-up cigarette in the other. Dad stood beside her, hands over his mouth in obvious shock at what she'd just said.

'How could you say something like that?' he cried. 'She's your flesh and blood.'

Mother took a swig from her hip flask and shrugged. 'So?'

Dad shook his head slowly. 'What happened to you, Marian? How did you become so bitter and twisted? I look at you like this and I don't see any of the person I loved in you. Not even a tiny glimmer.'

She laughed bitterly. 'What happened to me? Do you really need to ask? Kids, Trevor. Bloody kids. Two squawking, demanding, blood-sucking leeches who ruined my life. That's what happened to me.'

I felt sick. Leaning against the wall, I gasped for breath. I didn't want to hear any more, yet my feet felt like they were encased in a block of cement, rooting me to the spot.

'How can you say that about our daughters?'

'Easily. I should never have had them.'

'You wanted kids. I didn't force you into it.'

I peeked round the corner again as she took a long drag on her roll-up. 'It was the done thing, to have kids, but I didn't know what I was letting myself in for. If I'd had any idea what it was going to be like, I'd have marched you straight down the clinic for the snip. I hated being a mum. Hated it. From the moment Elise was born, I knew we'd made a mistake.'

'Then why have a second one?' Dad paced up and down in front of the bench, shaking his head. 'Why have Jess?'

'There was never meant to be a Jess. I was on the pill, for God's sake. There was no way I wanted to spawn another brat. The only way I could cope with Elise was with vodka. Or gin. Both worked for me. Seems I was a bit too pissed to remember to take my pill regularly. Next thing I know, I'm up the duff and that one was worse than the first. Like I had the time and energy to cope with a sickly baby. Now she's having her own brats and she expects me to be happy about being a grandma. Twins? Yuck.'

I watched in horror as Dad sank to his knees. 'You never told me,' he said.

'Told you what?'

'That you hated being a mum.'

'You wouldn't have listened if I had. You were smitten with them. You didn't need me anymore. You had your perfect little family.'

'I *did* need you. *You* were my family too.'

'Yeah, well, I didn't need any of you.' She waggled her hip flask in front of his face. '*This* is my family. *This* is all I need.' She pulled herself to her feet. 'Now bugger off and leave me in peace.' She staggered across the gardens and through an arch in a hedge, disappearing from view.

My heart raced as I debated what to do next. Should I rush forward and comfort him? If I did, he'd know that I'd overheard the ugly truth that my mother hated her own children. Would that hurt him more than the pain of coming to terms with the revelation on his own? I closed my eyes and breathed deeply. Yes, it would. I needed to leave him to his grief. I slowly edged my way along the side of the building and up the steps, gripping onto the handrail for support.

I needed to be alone while I gathered my thoughts. Spying a high-backed leather armchair tucked away in a dark corner of the reception area, I gratefully sank into it as my mind whirred with memories of growing up with a bitter alcoholic for a mother. With tears streaming down my cheeks, I unbuckled my sandals and curled my bare feet under me.

Daniel would be waiting for me in the bar but I couldn't face him. I wasn't strong enough to explain it to him, but I needed to tell someone. Sarah. I couldn't look for her in case Daniel spotted me so I rang her but it went straight to voicemail. I tried Nick's phone, but his did the same. Who else could I speak to? Gary. He'd been by my side through every battle with my mother and would understand exactly how I was feeling. Even better, he'd know exactly what to say to take the pain away. He always had.

'Elise? Are you okay?' Gary asked.

'No,' I sobbed. 'I need you Gary. It's my mother. She's... she said... it was...' I couldn't say it aloud.

'Where are you?'

'At the wedding.'

'The Forester's Arms?'

'Yes.'

'I'll be there in ten minutes.'

Sinking back in the chair, I clenched and un-clenched my fists as images swam round in my mind of Mother screaming at me, screaming at Jess, screaming at Dad, hurling insults, hurling vases, throwing my treasured wooden jewellery box down the stairs, throwing Dad's belongings out into the street, burning mine and Jess's books and toys. I remembered some of the names she'd call us over the years and how distraught Dad had been as he'd tried to cover our ears and whisper reassurances that she didn't mean it and that he loved us as big as the universe and beyond.

From my hidden corner, I watched Dad shuffle back into the hotel like a broken man. He picked up his room key from reception then clung onto the bannister and hauled himself up each wooden stair as if he had no strength left in his body. I wanted to run after him and comfort him, but it would break his heart into a thousand pieces to know that I'd overheard their altercation. I couldn't do it to him.

I thought about Daniel waiting in the bar, no doubt wondering where the hell I was. He wouldn't be alone, though. He knew Sarah and had bonded with the rest of the table during the meal. As a rep, he was also used to chatting to complete strangers. And he hadn't come looking for me because I'd have seen him so I didn't need to worry about him being all alone.

Waiting on the steps a few minutes later, it felt like my knight in shining armour had arrived when I saw Gary's Lexus turning into the drive. I ran towards the car, desperate for his comfort. As soon as he'd pulled into a space, he leapt out and wrapped his arms round me. My body racked with sobs as he held me close, stroked my back, and whispered soothing words into my hair. When the tears were spent and I felt ready to talk, we sat in the car and I opened up about what I'd seen and heard.

'I'm so sorry for ruining your evening, but I couldn't find Sarah and you were the only one who'd understand.'

Gary squeezed my hand. 'Forget about my evening. You did the right thing to call me. I know we're not together anymore and I know I've hurt you really badly, but I'll always be here for you any time you need me. You know that, don't you?'

I nodded, silent tears raining down my cheeks. He'd told me a lot of lies, but at that moment, I knew he was telling the truth and I felt comforted and safe.

21

'Where've you been?' Jess planted her hands on her hips and tried to frown, but the grin on her face and the sparkle in her eyes stopped her from pulling it off. 'You missed the first dance.'

'Did I? I'm sorry, Jess. Something came up.'

'Are you all right? You look like you've been crying.'

After saying goodbye to Gary, I'd nipped up to the bedroom and quickly re-applied my smudged make-up, but no amount of mascara or eyeliner could mask my red eyes. I smiled. 'It's an emotional day seeing my baby sister get married. I'll admit to having a little weep.'

Jess hugged me. 'Aw, you're such a softie.'

Glancing round the bar, there was no sign of Daniel. It was past eight, which meant I'd abandoned him at a wedding full of strangers for about an hour and a half. That was pretty unforgivable. I wouldn't have blamed him if he'd thrown a strop and caught a taxi home, but his bag was still in our room so he had to be here somewhere.

'He's fine,' Jess said. 'He was outside chatting to Izzy last time I saw him.'

Phew! He hadn't been alone. 'Is Megan still around?'

'Her grandma picked her up about ten minutes ago. She was shattered, poor thing.'

'How are you feeling?'

'Also shattered, but I'm having an amazing time.' She stroked her stomach. 'Try as they might, I'm not letting these two put me to bed early.'

'Don't overdo it.'

'Yes, mum!'

Inwardly, I flinched at the mention of the word 'mum'. How could our mother feel so much venom towards this beautiful woman in front of me with twins growing inside of her? It beggared belief.

A group of Jess's friends arrived for the evening do so I said goodbye and headed off in search of Daniel. I was relieved to see Dad in the bar with Auntie Grace and a handful of other relatives. Although he was laughing and joking with them, I could tell that he wasn't really in the room. Mother had well and truly broken him.

Daniel wasn't in the bar. He wasn't on the terrace or the dance floor. I made my way back up to the bedroom, but he wasn't there either. I looked towards the bed. What I wouldn't give to crawl under the duvet and pretend this evening had never happened. But I couldn't abandon Daniel for the whole night and I certainly couldn't bail early on my sister's wedding.

It was another hour before our paths crossed. His face fell when he saw me and I prepared myself for a lecture – rightly so – for abandoning him for so long. I didn't expect him to say: 'So are you and Gary back together, then?'

'What? Of course not!'

'I saw you together in the car park.'

I took his arm and steered him out onto the deserted terrace, away from earwigging relatives.

'What did you see?'

'Him speeding into the car park in his posh car and you all

over him. Were you having such a crap time with me that you had to call your ex to rescue you?'

'It wasn't like that.' To be fair to Daniel, I could see exactly why it would look like that, but I couldn't even begin to explain what I'd witnessed and the complicated history with my mother.

'We said no lies,' he challenged. 'If it's not over with Gary, you need to tell me. I can't be number two again.'

I reached for his hand. 'There's nothing going on with Gary. He's gay. He's with someone else.'

'But you'd have him back if he wasn't gay, wouldn't you?'

'He *is* gay so that's not even an option.'

Daniel let go of my hand and took a step back from me. Damn! I should have just said 'no'.

'But you'd have him back if he wasn't. Go on. Admit it.'

'I'll admit no such thing. You're being ridiculous.'

'Ridiculous? I'm not the one who invited my new partner to their sister's wedding, abandoned them for two or three hours, and spend part of that time in the arms of my ex.'

'It wasn't like that.'

'How was it then?'

'It's complicated.'

'That's crap and you know it.' He crossed his arms and narrowed his eyes at me. 'You need to choose. It's Gary or me.'

'Don't be stu–'

'Stupid *and* ridiculous? I wonder why you bother with me.'

'We're getting divorced, Daniel. It's over. Completely and utterly over.'

He fixed his dark eyes on me. 'Are you sure about that?' Without waiting for an answer, he stormed off.

I slumped into the nearest chair and sighed loudly. I couldn't blame Daniel for his reaction because it was justified in the circumstances. It would probably be a good idea to chase after him, but I didn't have the energy.

Shortly after eleven, the party was still in full swing but I couldn't take any more dancing or socialising with a fake grin plastered across my face. I hadn't seen Daniel again so I headed back to the room, assuming he'd gone home. I was therefore surprised to see his bag still there.

I got ready for bed and crawled under the duvet, willing sleep to come quickly to dull the pain of Mother's revelations, Dad's devastation and the bust-up with Daniel. But, of course, sleep didn't come.

I stiffened when I heard a key in the lock a couple of hours later. I pretended to be asleep as Daniel clattered around the room, dropping things, banging into the furniture and swearing.

After he'd visited the bathroom – also very noisily – he slipped into the bed beside me and lay on his back in silence for a while as I continued to feign sleep on my side, facing away from him. Then he rolled onto his side and clumsily draped a heavy arm over me and nuzzled close into my back. I could feel his erection prodding against me through my nightie and, despite the weariness in my body, I felt a zip of electricity. Why did he have such an overpowering effect on me?

He wriggled closer and ground himself against my backside as his hand moved across my arm and gently massaged my breast. 'Are you awake?' he whispered.

I remained silent, but my damned body gave me away. As he continued to massage my nipple, I arched in response and a soft moan escaped.

'I'm sorry,' he whispered. 'I know you're not going to get back with Gary. I was jealous. I was scared of losing you.'

His hand drifted across my stomach and down my thigh until he found the bottom of my nightie, then his hand travelled back up my thigh under the material. I wanted to be angry with him. I wanted to shout at him for throwing a strop because he didn't understand the hell I'd been through that evening and how I'd needed Gary or I'd have fallen apart. But even stronger than that, I wanted him. I widened my legs and gasped as his fingers entered me, then I turned my head so I could kiss him.

'I love you, Elise,' he muttered as his fingers caressed me.

'I know.' I still couldn't bring myself to say it in return. 'I'm sorry too. I've heard that make-up sex is meant to be the best.'

'You'd better believe it.'

And, as always, it was incredible with Daniel. He pushed every button and then some. But, as I lay awake in the darkness, listening to his gentle breathing beside me, I couldn't shake the feeling that something between us didn't feel quite right. We'd had our first fight, which concerned me so soon into our relationship but the reason for the fight concerned me more. Why hadn't I been honest with him about my childhood and my toxic relationship with my mother? Yes, it would have been an uncomfortable conversation but, if I loved Daniel or even if I thought I could grow to love him, I should have let him in.

22
___

The next week and a half passed, during which I saw Daniel every other night. I felt as though something had changed between us, although he clearly hadn't noticed. He was as attentive as ever, telling me he loved me, complimenting me, and being the most incredible lover. We tried new positions, new places, and even introduced a bit of role-playing. It was new and exciting, but I missed the conversation, deep connection and understanding I'd had with Gary. I knew that how I was feeling was my fault for not opening up to Daniel. I kept my past hidden, and I didn't share any hopes for the future, which I'd surely have done if he was Mr Right. Our relationship was definitely all about the here and now and, let's face it, lots of sex. Was that enough?

I spent the rest of my time with Dad, who was house-sitting for Jess and Lee while they were on their honeymoon. We went out for day trips or sat in the garden chatting. I loved spending time in his company, but he seemed to have aged a decade since the wedding and it tore me apart that I couldn't tell him that I knew why.

Jess and Lee were due back on the Tuesday night and had

invited me round for tea on the Wednesday so they could tell me all about their trip and have a last evening with Dad before he flew back to Spain on the Thursday morning. Given that Wednesday was my evening to visit Sarah, I asked her if we could meet for lunch instead.

'I had a small world moment at Bay Trade on Monday night,' she said over lunch in The Chocolate Pot. 'We had two new members and one of them turned out to be Daniel's brother, Michael.'

'Michael? The grumpiest photographer in the world? I bet that was fun for you.'

Sarah shook her head. 'He seemed quite friendly, actually, but he said something really strange before he left. He said Daniel isn't what he seems and you should be careful.'

I wiped my mouth and pushed my empty plate away. 'Michael really said that?'

She screwed up her nose and nodded. 'Sorry. What do you think he meant?'

'Trouble,' I said. 'He hates Daniel, and every time I've been to the cottage, he's made it pretty clear he's not enamoured with me either. Not that I care because the feeling's mutual.'

Sarah stirred her hot chocolate. 'You're normally so positive about people. What's he done to upset you so much?'

I shrugged. 'Nothing major. He had a go at us the first night we were at the cottage, but to be fair, I had just kicked a lamp over and smashed a glass. But he was really cold the next day and couldn't get out of the place fast enough when I saw him. Since then it's been dirty looks and little jibes all the way, although he's not been around much lately which is a relief. Plus, I know why he fell out with Daniel so I'm holding that against him too.'

Sarah leaned forwards on the table, eyes glistening with mischief. 'Ooh, do tell.'

'Okay, I concede, he is a bit of an idiot,' she said when I'd finished the story. 'He seemed nice enough when I met him on Monday. A bit shy and nervy, perhaps, but pleasant. I suppose it's only when you get to know someone that you find out what they're really all about.' She sighed. 'I understand why you don't like Michael, but can you do as he says and be careful? Neither of us really knows Daniel. Who says he's the one being honest and Michael's in the wrong?'

I prickled and nearly snapped back that it was none of her business, but a voice in my head told me she was right. I'd been with Gary for sixteen years and he'd lied throughout that time. What was to say someone whom I'd only met three weeks ago was going to be a pillar of honesty? He *had* to be honest, though. Surely nobody would be cruel enough to make up the stuff he'd told me about Amber and the baby?

I smiled at Sarah. 'Thanks. I'll be careful. I promise.'

* * *

As I walked back towards Seashell Cottage to start on some teaching prep for next term, I replayed what Sarah had told me about Michael. By the time I reached the front door, I was fuming. How dare he? How dare he say something like that to someone he'd only just met? He must have known it would come back to me. I might have doubts about Daniel being The One but he had done nothing but show me kindness and respect... and a damn good time in bed! Michael had tried to split Daniel and Amber up and clearly he was trying again with me. What a horrible person.

It took a very strong cup of camomile tea to calm me down. It was just as well I wasn't going to the cottage that night because, if Michael had been there, I might have given him a Cynthia-style piece of my mind.

✉ From Gary

Estate agent just phoned. Two second viewings
at the weekend and he says they both sound
very keen

✉ To Gary
Thanks. Hopefully we'll get an offer and can
complete quickly so we can both move on. Keep
me posted

On the Friday morning that week, I took a break from planning and was running a duster round the lounge when the doorbell rang.

'Can you get that?' Kay shouted from upstairs. 'I'll be down in a minute.'

I opened the front door and could not have been more astonished if my mother had been stood on the doorstep with news that she'd joined the AA. 'What the hell are you doing here?'

For a moment, Michael just stared at me open-mouthed. 'Erm... have I got the right place? I'm looking for Kay Summers.'

I nodded. 'It's her cottage. How do *you* know Kay?'

'I don't. My dad's going to give her some photography tutoring and I'm going with them to do some shooting myself. Is she your mum?'

'No. She's my friend's auntie. Actually, I think you know my friend, Sarah, from Bay Trade. I believe you two had a nice little *tête à tête* on Monday night.' I tried to give him a dirty look.

'Yes. I told her to tell you to be careful and I'm happy to say it to your face too. My brother isn't everything he initially seems.'

'Meaning what exactly?' I crossed my arms and leaned defiantly against the doorframe.

'You'll have to ask him.

'I'm asking you.'

He shook his head. 'I shouldn't have said anything. I'm only trying to protect you.'

'Rubbish,' I snapped. 'You're trying to drive a wedge between Daniel and me just like you did with Amber and him.'

Michael shook his head again and rubbed his hand over his unshaved face. He looked like he was about to blurt something out then clearly thought the better of it. 'That's what he told you, is it?'

I nodded.

He sighed and, for a fleeting moment, I thought I detected vulnerability in the gruff package on the doorstep. 'I guess we have nothing more to say to each other, then, do we?' he said.

'I guess not.'

'Hi. Sorry about that. I couldn't find my watch.' Kay appeared in the doorway. 'You must be Philip.' She stretched out her hand to shake Michael's.

He grinned. 'Close, except I'm the younger and more ruggedly handsome version. I'm Michael. Philip's my dad. He's waiting in the car. I hope you don't mind me tagging along.'

'The more the merrier. Thanks for doing this at such short notice.'

'No problem at all. I think my dad's quite excited at the thought of passing on his expertise again. He couldn't wait to get started.'

I watched Michael in amazement. He seemed so friendly and at ease speaking to Kay – a complete contrast to the grumpy person I'd come to know and avoid. Had I misjudged him?

'Now, Michael,' Kay said, 'I've got my camera and a packed lunch. Do I need anything else?'

'I'd grab a waterproof just in case, but camera and food are the essentials. I'd better warn you, if you have any chocolate in there, you may find it goes walkies.'

Kay laughed and punched him lightly. 'You nick my chocolate; you'll be wearing my coffee.'

Michael laughed and I reeled. I didn't think he knew how to

laugh. Who was this charming person? A smile and twinkling eyes completely transformed him.

'I'll probably be back late so you enjoy having the cottage to yourself,' Kay said. 'See you later.'

They set off in the direction of a grey 4x4 at the end of the street, then Michael paused and turned round. The smile had gone. He held my gaze for a moment, shrugged, then turned his back again.

I watched him load Kay's bags into the boot, open the front door so she could take a seat, then climb into the back. As the car pulled away, he turned round once more and looked at me through the back window. He looked sad.

The sound of my mobile ringing in the lounge brought me out of my trance. I closed the front door and dashed to answer it before it clicked into the answer service. 'Jess, hi, how are you?'

'Fat,' she said. 'I swear I've doubled in size since the wedding.'

'You're not fat. You're five-and-a-half months' pregnant with twins. You weren't expecting to stay a size eight, were you?'

'No, but I wasn't expecting to be a size eighteen either.'

'Ooh, someone's exaggerating.'

'What are you doing this afternoon?' she asked.

'Nothing much. Kay's just gone out for a photography lesson and I might go for a walk.'

'Scrap the walk. You can spend the afternoon buggy shopping with me.'

'Why aren't you at work? You've only just got back from your honeymoon.'

'I know, but I had some lieu time due from before the wedding. My boss said I could take it this afternoon. We're moving offices and I think he's terrified that a pregnant woman hauling boxes of files around is a lawsuit waiting to happen. It's the perfect opportunity to go buggy shopping and I want your opinion.'

'I know nothing about choosing a buggy.'

'You know more about children than I do,' she said.

'That would be children aged eleven to sixteen. They're not generally known for being pushed around in buggies.'

'Pretty please,' she whined.

* * *

'Having twins means the choices are limited,' Jess said as we stood in front of the area containing all the double buggies. 'Which do you like best?'

I shrugged. 'I haven't a clue. I don't know why you'd think I can help.'

'Because you're the practical one.'

I shrugged again. 'Which one do you like best?'

'Probably that one.'

Glancing at the £1000 price tag, I whistled. 'I think we can rule that one out. Second favourite?'

'That one.' She pointed to a wide buggy.

I shook my head. 'It's enormous. I doubt you'd fit that in your hall, even collapsed down.'

'See! I knew you'd be able to help.'

'What colour?' I asked after we'd found a winner. 'Neutral?'

She grinned at me. 'It will have to be seeing as we're expecting a boy *and* a girl.'

I gasped and grabbed her arm. 'You've found out? I thought you weren't going to.'

'We weren't and I wouldn't have done if there was only one baby, but it seemed so much more practical to know when there's two.'

'That's brilliant news. How do you feel?'

'Couldn't be happier. I thought I might like two girls, but as soon as I found out it was one of each, I realised I had my perfect ready-made family. I'm so lucky.'

I hugged my sister and said all the right things about being a delighted auntie with my first nephew and niece to spoil, but her words cut right through me. She wouldn't have meant anything by it, but 'perfect ready-made family'? I should have had one of those by now instead of a gay husband and an impending divorce.

It didn't end with the buggy. My head thumped as I placed the third armful of bags in the boot of Jess's car. My face ached from the forced smile, and my throat burned from the restrictive lump in it. It had been harder than bridesmaid dress shopping. Much harder. With every purchase, the reality hit home more and more that my dreams of motherhood were just that – dreams. Daniel was fun, but it was lust, not love. He wasn't my future, which begged the question as to whether I should end it and find someone with whom I could see myself settling down and having a family? Every day I stayed with him was a day that I wasn't working towards my dreams of being a mum.

Jess slammed the boot of her car shut. 'Are you sure you don't want a lift home? It's no bother.'

I shook my head. 'Look at that blue sky. I fancy a walk along the beach.'

'As long as you're sure.' Jess hugged me. 'Thanks for today. I'm really glad you were there to help me.'

'Me too. It was fun.' I smiled and hoped it looked sincere.

I waved her off then strolled the ten-minute journey down the hill towards South Bay, dodging tourists draped in soggy sandy towels, their arms loaded with buckets, spades, and picnic hampers. It was a muggy day and I paused to buy a drink before continuing along the seafront and over the swing bridge to Lighthouse Cove.

The beach at Lighthouse Cove wasn't very busy due to families heading back to their hotels and caravans for dinner so I managed to find a quiet spot among the sand dunes just beyond the caves. I sat down and wiggled my bare feet until they were buried under a small pile of sand, and gazed at the twinkling azure ocean.

Closing my eyes, I willed my busy mind to empty, but all I could see was Michael's face staring out of the back of the 4x4 and hear his warning. *Stop thinking about it. He's trouble.* But what if he wasn't? What if Michael was right and it was Daniel who was trouble? I opened my eyes and glanced across to where I'd had my first ever experience of sex outdoors. My body tingled at the thought of it. If Daniel was trouble, he was pretty good trouble.

My phone beeped and I smiled. Were his ears burning?

✉ From Daniel

My last customer cancelled so I'm back early. Had the day from hell. Missing you so called round at yours, but there's nobody in. I know we weren't meant to be seeing each other tonight, but I could use the company. Are you free later for a drink, a cuddle, or both? xxx

✉ To Daniel

Was just thinking about you. Sorry you've had a rough one. Me too. I'm on the beach now if you want to come and find me. I'm near the caves, but I think it's a bit too light to re-live what happened last time we came here ;-) xx

✉ From Daniel

LOL. Got a couple of errands to run then I'll come and find you. Thanks. You're my saviour xx

I put my phone back in my bag. Had it been the right thing

to do? Should I have said I was busy and taken advantage of some me-time instead? We'd seen so much of each other lately that I never seemed to have a moment to sit down and take stock of what I wanted from life after Gary. He'd sounded so down, though. I couldn't be so selfish when he clearly needed me.

The sound of a crying baby pushed Daniel from my thoughts and Jess into them. I closed my eyes again and held my head in my hands. My mind swirled with the news about the genders of the twins, our shopping trip, my own longings for a child and how Daniel didn't seem to be the one for that next step.

A shadow blocked the sun and I looked up.

'Elise? Are you okay?'

I scrambled to my feet. 'Stevie? Hi. Erm... long time no see.' Oh gosh, I never had got round to texting him after the Stardust incident.

'I wasn't sure whether to come over or not. I kept meaning to get in touch after Stardust to say sorry.'

I shook my head. 'You've got nothing to be sorry for but I do. I kept meaning to text you but the longer I left it, the harder it became.'

'Same here,' he said. 'What a pair we are. So, we're good?'

'We're good.' I noticed his attire. 'I take it you're out for a run?'

'I'm meant to be, but it's still too warm for me. I normally run with Sarah on an evening when it's cooler, but it's my Uncle George's birthday so we're going to The Apple and Peach tonight.'

'Wow! You lucky thing.' The Apple and Peach was a Michelin-starred restaurant up the coast near Daniel's cottage.

'It's his seventieth so he's pushing the boat out. Have you got any plans tonight?'

'I'm not sure. Did Sarah tell you I've been seeing one of her reps, Daniel?'

Stevie lowered his eyes. 'She mentioned something.'

'He's going to join me shortly so we'll probably do something together.'

'You don't sound too pleased about that. And you looked pretty deep in thought just now. Penny for them?'

'Believe me, Stevie, they're not worth that much.'

'Ha'penny then?'

I smiled. 'You really want to know? You'd best take a seat then.'

We sat on the sand and I drew swirly lines in it with my fingers as I told him about my shopping trip with Jess, my longing for a baby, turning down Gary's proposition and my concerns that I'd never become a mum.

'You don't see Daniel as dad material, then? Sarah said it was going well between you two.'

'It is. He's been great for me and we have fun together, but...' I searched around for the right words.

'But he's not Gary?' Stevie suggested.

I shook my head. 'No. It's not that. I don't actually miss Gary the husband. Maybe that's because we'd already grown apart when I found him with Rob. What I miss is Gary the best friend and, even though I really like Daniel, I don't feel like he's my soulmate like Gary was. But then I remind myself that we haven't known each other very long and it wasn't instant with Gary.' I brushed my sandy hands on my dress. 'I don't really know what I want right now. I don't want to end it with Daniel as he's doing me the world of good, but I'm wondering if I should cool it a little and see less of him. I was looking forward to an evening to myself tonight, but it looks like we're spending it together.'

'Why didn't you tell him you had plans?'

Because I was doing it again. I was pushing aside what I wanted for the sake of someone else. Same old default mode. 'I felt guilty,' I said. 'He's had a bad day and needs the company. I don't want to let him down when he needs me, especially after he came to Jess's wedding when I needed him. I just worry that I never seem to have any time to discover me.'

Stevie picked up a shell and twiddled with it. 'What do you mean?'

'I've been part of a couple since I was fourteen. We did everything together. I don't have any hobbies or interests of my own outside of work so I don't know who *I* am or what *I* like instead of what *we* like. I used to manage the house, plan our weekends and organise holidays. I don't have any of that to do now, but I have nothing with which to replace it. I'm probably noticing it more because it's the summer holidays so I have more time on my hands and I actually feel quite lost.'

'Hey, don't cry.' Stevie put his arm round me and I cuddled gratefully against his side. We sat in silence for several minutes, watching the sea. I felt the tension easing away from me, replaced by a feeling of calm as I snuggled into his super-hug.

'What did you do before you met Gary or maybe while he was studying to be a doctor?' Stevie asked after a while, still holding me. 'Did you have any hobbies back then?'

I thought for a moment. 'Actually, I did. I used to write.'

Stevie let go and turned to look at me. 'Really? What sort of stuff?'

'Fantasy books about a unicorn whisperer called Ashlea. It didn't start out that way, though.' It had actually started by me making up stories to distract Jess from Mother's increasing reliance on drink and the horrific arguments with Dad. I found that I needed the escapism even more than Jess and started to write my stories down accompanied by a few basic illustrations during the times when the screaming matches were so loud that I couldn't concentrate on words. Before long, the fantasy world of Ellorinia had developed; a beautiful land far removed in time and place from the warzone at home.

'It sounds like you loved writing,' Stevie said when I finished explaining. 'What made you stop? Meeting Gary?'

I shook my head. 'No. He was really supportive. He encouraged me to write regularly and even gave me a few ideas. He bought me a wooden unicorn called Serenity for my sixteenth birthday.' I smiled. I hadn't thought about my writing in so long. Then I sighed. 'It was Mother who stopped me.'

When I was sixteen, Mother went on a drunken rampage one summer's night after overhearing Dad on the phone telling his best mate, Bryan, that he planned to move to Spain when Jess turned eighteen and could leave home. Dad, Jess and I returned from an evening bike ride to find Dad's clothes strewn all over the front lawn, clinging to shrubs and trees, and Mother emptying more out of the front windows while necking a bottle of vodka. I vividly remember dropping our bikes and dashing towards the front door. Dad had no sooner unlocked and opened it when there was a loud crash as my precious hand-carved wooden jewellery box – a gift from Dad on my twelfth birthday – landed on the parquet floor in the hall and smashed to smithereens. Vases and various other ornaments of Jess's or mine swiftly followed. Dad slammed the door before anything hit us. And then we smelled the burning. We dashed down the path at the side of the house to find a large fire in the middle of the back garden; a fire burning books and toys. Dad grabbed the hose, but it was too late. Nothing could be saved.

While Dad tried to reason with Mother in her bedroom to stop her wreaking any further damage, I had the heart-breaking task of leading my little sister by the hand and taking her into our shared bedroom to see what – if anything – had escaped from Mother's attack. Fortunately for Jess, most of her belongings had survived. Mine hadn't. The three things I cared about the most were Marmite my teddy bear, my jewellery box, and the exercise books containing my stories. Marmite had been hidden under the duvet so had thankfully survived. I already knew my jewellery box's fate, but there was no sign of my stories. Distraught, I stormed across the landing and demanded to know where they were. Mother pointed towards the back of the house – where the bonfire had been – and cackled.

My voice cracked as I finished the story, a memory I'd buried for years now so vivid in my mind. Stevie put his arm round me again and held me close.

'Gary tried to encourage me to write them again, but I couldn't do it. I couldn't risk recreating that world and having her destroy it again.'

Stevie kissed the top of my head. 'I'm so sorry about your mum. That's such—'

'What the hell are you doing to my girlfriend?' I fell back into the sand as Stevie was yanked away from me.

'Daniel? What are you doing?' I scrambled to my feet.

'What am *I* doing?' he yelled. 'What are *you two* doing? I thought this was our special place or do you bring all your conquests here?'

'Don't speak to her like that,' Stevie shouted. 'We're just friends.'

'I wasn't talking to you.' Daniel shoved Stevie.

'Daniel! Leave him alone!' I pulled on his arm. 'This is my friend, Stevie. I was upset and he was comforting me.'

'I bet he was.'

'What's that supposed to mean?'

'It means he's a man and men don't do friendships with women. They always want something and, if I hadn't shown up, I bet he'd have made his next move. And you'd have let him, wouldn't you? Not quite the innocent you pretend to be, are you?' He took a step towards me and I backed away, shaking. Who was this person? He certainly wasn't the fun, caring Daniel who'd helped me through one of the darkest times of my life.

'Stop it!' Stevie stepped between Daniel and me. 'She's done nothing wrong.'

'Move out of my way or I'll—'

'You'll what? Hit me?'

And that's exactly what he did. I cringed at the crack of Stevie's nose before he fell to his knees, blood spurting onto the sand and down his white T-shirt.

'Shit! Stevie!' I knelt down, grabbed some tissues out of my bag and held them to his bloody nose. I turned to Daniel. 'What the hell were you thinking? He's a *friend* and, even if he was more, you don't go around punching people.'

Daniel's face was pale. His mouth kept opening and closing, but no words came out. Then he turned and ran up the beach.

I put my arm round Stevie. 'C'mon. Let's get you to your feet. Is your car nearby?'

'Yes. Why?'

'Because I need to drive you to A&E.'

He fished in his pocket and handed me his keys. 'Good plan,' he said. 'But promise me one thing.'

'Name it.'

'You'll dump that bastard before the next person he hits is you.'

23

Stevie's nose was definitely broken. I'd suspected that as soon as I heard the crack, but a three-hour wait in A&E confirmed it.

'I'm so, so sorry,' I said as I drove his car back to Bramble Cottage.

'Eighty-seven,' he said.

'What is?'

'The amount of times you've said sorry since the beach.'

I smiled weakly. 'If I've said it that many times, then you'll know I mean it.'

'It really isn't your fault,' he said. 'Although it's just as well I don't have any hot dates lined up this weekend because the nurse said I'll be bruised and swollen by the morning, possibly sporting two black eyes.'

I opened my mouth to speak, but Stevie beat me to it. 'Don't you dare say you're sorry again.'

'Okay, sorry, I won't. No! I just said it. Sorry!'

We both giggled then Stevie groaned. 'It hurts to laugh.'

It was just after nine when we pulled up outside Bramble Cottage.

'Cup of that disgusting green tea?' he suggested.

I laughed. 'You need to work on your sales technique. I'll politely decline although I could really do with using your loo if you don't mind.'

'Be my guest.'

Bonnie came bounding towards us as soon as Stevie opened the door and she obediently lifted her paw for me again.

'The bathroom's up the stairs and on your right,' Stevie said. 'Feel free to have a look round while you're up there but excuse the mess.'

The bathroom was lovely: neutral tiles, large shower cubicle, and a roll top bath. Opposite the bathroom was a small bedroom which acted as Stevie's office. At the end of the corridor, taking up the full width of the house was a spare bedroom and, judging by the peeling floral wallpaper and swirly carpet, this was obviously the room that he hadn't yet tackled. It would make a gorgeous child's bedroom.

At the other end of the cottage was the master bedroom. The external wall had been stripped back to stone and the remaining walls were painted a warm cream. A sturdy oak sleigh bed took pride of place in front of the exposed stone wall, flanked by a matching oak chest of drawers and a wardrobe. Glass doors at the back of the room opened onto a small balcony with views over Stevie's garden and the fields beyond. *Wow! Just wow!*

Feeling suddenly self-conscious about staring at another man's bed, even though I'd been given permission, I made my way back downstairs and found Stevie in the kitchen tidying away some pots.

'When can I move in?' I asked.

'You like it?'

'It's gorgeous. I'm not a hundred per cent taken with the carpet in the spare bedroom, but the rest is stunning.'

Stevie laughed. 'Oh, but that's the template for the rest of the house. How could you not like it?' He pointed to the kettle. 'You're sure you don't want a drink?'

'I'm sure. I'd best be going. Will you promise me you're going to get some rest?'

Stevie pointed towards Bonnie nuzzling against my leg, 'I know a certain border collie who's not going to let that happen.'

I stroked her head. 'Do you want me to do it for you?'

'Will you stop worrying about me? I'll be absolutely fine. I'll walk her round to my Uncle George's. I need to check he's had something to eat.'

'His birthday meal. Oh my goodness, I'd forgotten. I'm so—'

'Don't you dare say you're sorry. Uncle George won't mind. If I know him, he'll have seen it as the perfect excuse to go to the chippy instead which, if I'm honest, would be his preferred option over a Michelin-starred restaurant any day. We'll celebrate another time. Maybe you could join us?'

I smiled at Stevie. 'That would be lovely, thanks. Although I'm not sure your Uncle George will want an evening in my company after he sees the state of you.'

'Elise...!'

I put my hands up in surrender. 'Okay, I'll stop taking the blame. I'd best let you get round to your uncle's. I'll call you in the morning to work out how I get your car back to you.'

Stevie drew me into a hug and I gently squeezed him back, taking care not to knock against his nose. 'Thanks for staying with me at the hospital. I really appreciate it.'

'I was never going to abandon you there. It was the least I could do in the circumstances.' I released my hold. 'Is there anything else I can do for you?'

'One thing.'

'Name it.'

His eyes took on a puppy-dog appearance as he said, 'Dump Daniel.'

'Stevie! I told you in the hospital that I don't know what I'm going to do yet. There has to be an explanation for what he did.'

'Does it matter? Surely nothing excuses behaviour like that.

Please, Elise. Dump him and go out with...' He stopped and looked away.

For a moment, I thought he was about to add 'me'. I bit my lip. 'Go out with whom?'

He smiled as he looked back at me. 'Someone who will treat you like you deserve to be treated.'

'Like a princess?' I joked.

'If that's what you'd like. I was thinking more like a beautiful, intelligent, funny woman who deserves respect and understanding.'

'Oh. Is there such a person? Right now, I'd settle for someone who doesn't lie.'

He held my gaze. 'Not all men lie, you know.' Bonnie nudged his leg, making him look down. 'Looks like nature calls.'

'Please send my apologies to your Uncle George and I'll call you tomorrow.'

* * *

As I passed a turn-off to Shellby Bay ten minutes later, I knew what I had to do. I checked nobody was behind me then slammed on the brakes, reversed down the road, turned left and sped towards Daniel's. I wanted an apology. And I wanted answers.

Daniel's car was parked in front of the cottage alongside Michael's jeep. I banged on the door. No answer. I banged again. Still no answer but the downstairs was lit. Exasperated, I lifted the letterbox and shouted through it, 'I know you're in there, Daniel. We need to talk.' I let the letterbox slam shut then banged on the door again.

'All right, I'm coming. Keep your hair on,' yelled a man's voice. The door flung open. 'What the hell...? Oh, it's you.'

'Sorry. I was after Daniel.' I tried to avert my gaze from

Michael's wet, naked torso and the towel fastened loosely around his hips.

'He's not here.'

'His car is.'

'Well, he's not.'

'Then where is he? You live in the middle of nowhere. He can't be far away.'

'I don't know where he is. Come in and search if you don't believe me.' Michael stepped aside.

'I will if you don't mind.'

'Be my guest. As you know, I'm not exactly his biggest fan so, believe me, I'm not hiding him from whatever it is he's done to upset you so much.'

I paused at the bottom of the stairs. 'Who says I'm upset?'

'Erm... perhaps the beating the crap out of the door and the screeching through the letterbox like something possessed might be a clue?'

'Sorry about that.' I bit my lip. 'Am I okay to go upstairs?'

'Help yourself. Don't forget to check under his bed, under my bed, the shower and the airing cupboard.'

I'm ashamed to say that I did. I checked everywhere, but Michael was right; Daniel wasn't there. My legs shook as I made my way back down the stairs, cheeks burning. 'I feel a bit silly now. Apologies for the irrational behaviour.'

'Don't worry about it. You look like you could use this.' Michael handed me a cup of tea. I breathed it in. Camomile. I could have done with a stiff drink but this was the next best thing.

'Why don't you sit down and drink that while I put some clothes on?'

'Oh, you don't have to.' I felt heat rush to my already flushed cheeks and squirmed. 'That came out wrong. I just meant don't put yourself out. Continue with your shower or whatever you were doing. I'll just drink this then leave you in peace.'

Michael smiled then sprinted upstairs. When he came down less than ten minutes later, he'd shaved and put on a pair of jeans and a plain royal-blue T-shirt, which accentuated the blue of his eyes. I found myself staring at him thinking that he was actually better-looking than Daniel when he wasn't scowling.

'So what's he done?' He curled up on the other end of the corner sofa.

I looked at my tea instead and blew on it to keep me from staring at him. 'He punched my friend Stevie and broke his nose.'

Michael whistled. 'I'm assuming it wasn't an accident.'

'Do you think I'd have been "beating the crap out of the door and screeching through the letterbox like something possessed" if it had been?'

'Fair point. Is your friend okay?'

'He will be.'

'Why did he do it?'

I shrugged. 'He saw Stevie hugging me and went into what I'm assuming was some sort of jealous rage. Stevie and I are just friends. I was upset and he was comforting me, but even if it had been more than that, it doesn't excuse what he did.'

'In my mind, there's never an excuse for violence. He didn't hit you, did he?'

'No. I don't think he would have done.'

Michael ran a hand through his damp hair then shook his head. 'I can't believe he got jealous and hit your friend. How hypocritical can he get?'

I put my tea down. 'What do you mean?'

'Sorry, Elise, it's between you and Daniel. I don't want to get involved.'

'Seriously, Michael, you have to stop this.'

'Stop what?'

'The cryptic comments. On Monday you told Sarah to tell me to be careful, then you repeated the warning to my face earlier, and now you're saying Daniel's hypocritical for being jealous, but you won't expand.'

'Can you forget I spoke?'

'If you've got something to say, I'd rather you just came out and said it. I'm a big girl. I can take it.'

Michael gazed into my eyes for a while and I found myself holding my breath. 'No,' he said eventually. 'I can't. There's a big enough wedge between us as it is. I'm not going to cause any further problems.'

I toyed with pushing it but changed my mind. I felt emotionally drained and wasn't sure I really wanted to know. 'Does he have a history of violence?' I asked.

Michael laughed. 'You sound like the police! He used to beat me up when we were kids and I wasn't allowed to touch him because I was older and bigger, but beyond that, I've never known him to hit anyone so I'm a bit surprised. Something must have really riled him. Not that I condone what he's done, even if he was wound up.'

I sighed. 'I guess there's a first time for everything. Let's change the subject. How was photography today?'

Michael's eyes lit up. 'The best. We went to Kittrigg Forest then on to Shellby Bay. It was one of those days where everything seems to come together: the weather, the colours, the wildlife...'

Curling up on the sofa with my tea, I listened to him enthuse about his day. I asked him about the greatest photography experiences he'd had and he told me about amazing trips to South Africa, the Galapagos Islands, South America, and Russia. At one point, he jumped up and ran upstairs, returning with a MacBook.

'These are incredible, Michael,' I said as we scrolled through his online albums. 'You're very talented.'

'Thank you. Dad's a good teacher. Kay's in very capable

hands. From what I can see, she's got a real eye for photography so Dad's in his element. Do you ever—?'

A loud clatter outside stopped him. He stood up and cocked his head. There was another clatter followed by a string of expletives.

'Daniel's back.' His shoulders drooped and the light left his eyes. 'I'll leave you to it. Unless you want me to stay.' He closed his laptop.

'It's fine. Thank you. I'm only here for an explanation and an apology then I'm out of both of your lives for good.' Stevie was right. I needed to dump Daniel.

The door burst open. Michael put his hand on my shoulder and whispered, 'Good luck,' before dashing up the stairs.

'Bollocks,' mumbled Daniel, trying to pick his keys up off the floor, but stumbling onto his knees instead. He pushed the door shut with his foot, crawled a few paces then hauled himself up, clinging onto the kitchen worktop. He swayed a little then surveyed the room. 'Elise? Ish that you? Oh God, babe, I'm soooo sorry.' *Babe? Really?* He staggered a few steps and flopped onto the sofa. 'Sit still,' he said.

'I'm not moving. I take it you've been to the pub.'

'Farmer Bill gave me a lift. He's a nice bloke. Really nice bloke. But I'm not. I hit your friend.'

'I noticed. Care to explain why?'

He looked at me with big sad puppy-dog eyes and shook his head.

'Then I'll be off.' I stood up and walked towards the door.

'Don't go.' He grabbed my hand. 'Please don't go.'

'Then tell me why you hit Stevie.'

He flopped back and closed his eyes. 'Amber. Saw her with Jake.'

I felt a rush of empathy towards him. 'When?'

'This morning. Went to Lincoln. Still got clients there. Saw them together and she's...'

'She's what?'

'She's pregnant.'

'No! Oh Daniel, I'm so sorry.' My voice softened.

He opened his eyes again and tried to pull me down onto his knee. I resisted and sat down on the edge of the sofa instead. 'I was so jealous,' he said. 'They looked so happy. Then when I saw you and him... I didn't know he was your friend. I thought it was happening all over again. Should have known you wouldn't do that. Should have trusted you. Please say I haven't lost you.'

His words were a boost to my fragile ego, but could I trust him? 'I can't promise you that, Daniel. I understand how tough today must have been, but do you understand how wrong your actions were?' I felt like I was speaking to one of my students instead of a grown man.

He nodded. 'It won't happen again.'

'Damn right it won't.'

'I love you. Don't dump me. Please. I couldn't bear it.'

I looked into his sad eyes, wondering what on earth to do next. I couldn't bear violence, but Michael said it wasn't like Daniel and he certainly wouldn't be covering for him. I knew I didn't love him back and I knew I needed some me-time, but it was flattering having someone who loved me and wanted me after what I'd been through. What was the stronger pull? Dump him now and discover myself or have my fragile ego flattered for a bit longer? Was there any point when it would end eventually? I needed to sleep on it. Not with Daniel, though. Not tonight. I decided to avoid the subject altogether. 'I think somebody could do with some coffee,' I said.

'Yes please.'

I stood up and wandered into the kitchen area. When I returned, he was snoring. I crept upstairs and knocked on Michael's door. He opened it in just a pair of trunks. An unexpected tingle of excitement ran down my spine.

'All sorted?' he asked.

'I wouldn't say that, but he's apologised. He's asleep on the sofa. I'm going to take his duvet down and put it over him, but I'm not staying. Will you tell him I'll call him tomorrow, but it probably won't be till early evening?'

Michael nodded. 'I'll tell him. Night.' He moved to close his door then stopped. 'I know the circumstances weren't ideal, but I just wanted to say that I enjoyed spending time with you this evening. I'm sorry I've been off with you. It was nothing personal. It was about Daniel.'

I smiled. 'I know. Oddly enough, I enjoyed this evening too. Thanks for showing me your photos, especially the local ones. You've somehow put beauty into places I'd previously thought were quite drab.'

'Thank you.' We stared at each other for a moment.

'Right, well, I'd better get this duvet down to your brother. Good night, Michael.'

'Good night, Elise.'

As I walked out to Stevie's car a few minutes later, I glanced up at Michael's bedroom window. He was silhouetted in the window, and I could feel him watching me. My stomach did a flip. *Oh-oh! What's this? Please, no!* If I was going to dump Daniel, it was to discover me, and not to jump straight into another relationship. Especially with his brother! I had some serious thinking and decision-making to do over the weekend.

When I closed my eyes that night, though, it wasn't Michael I pictured. It was Stevie.

✉ From Sarah

I've chosen the dress… I think! Mum says it's perfect, but there was a close second and I want to be absolutely sure by getting the opinion of my fabulous bridesmaids! I know it's a bank hols weekend so I understand if you have plans. Clare's up for the weekend so she's free, Callie can do 2pm and Mum can cover the shop. Would that work for you?
xxxxxxxx

✉ To Sarah

Can't wait to see it! Got no plans so see you there xx

✉ From Gary

One of the couples who viewed on Sunday have offered £10k below the asking price. Lawtons are trying to negotiate it up

✉ To Gary
Promise me you'll accept if they won't budge.
I want to move on

✉ From Gary
I promise

✉ From Sarah
Just heard from Callie. She says can you and
Clare join her for drinks afterwards to
discuss my hen do?

✉ To Sarah
OK. See you on Saturday xx

✉ From Gary
An extra £5k. I've said yes. The house is now
officially sold STC. Hopefully it will be a
smooth one

✉ To Gary
Let's hope so. Thank you

'I'm so relieved you all liked my first choice best,' Sarah said as we left The Wedding Emporium. The first dress she'd tried on had been lovely, but the second one was definitely the one. It rendered us all speechless, even Clare.

'You looked so stunning in it,' I said. 'I'm so excited for you.' I was too. I was in a very different place to where I'd been when we'd shopped for bridesmaid dresses.

'Have you got time for a quick drink with us or do you have to go back to work now?' Callie asked.

Sarah looked at her watch. 'I'm probably good for another half an hour max.'

'Minty's it is, then,' Callie said.

Clare and Callie went to the bar while Sarah and I secured some seats. I could have done without it. I'd been struggling to shake a headache the past few days and would have preferred to go home. The champagne in The Wedding Emporium hadn't helped so goodness knows why I'd asked Callie to get me a glass of wine. Dutch courage to face an afternoon with Clare?

'I saw Stevie on Tuesday,' Sarah said.

'Oh.'

'Why didn't you tell me?'

'Because I thought you'd worry. Because I thought you'd tell me to dump Daniel. Because I couldn't think of how to tell you without it sounding really bad.'

'Is there a way?'

'Probably not. It's complicated. There's still no excuse for what he did, but I understand why he reacted in that way. He's really sorry. He insisted on meeting with Stevie so he could apologise in person.'

'I know. Stevie said.'

'Are you going to lecture me?'

Sarah shrugged and looked at me with pity in her eyes. 'Do I need to? Do you want me to tell you that you're playing with fire going out with someone who goes around punching people? Because I can do that quite easily. But I suspect you've lectured yourself enough already, haven't you?'

I fiddled with a beer mat. 'I know what I'm doing. He won't do it again and he'd never lay a finger on me.'

'How do you know that?'

'I just know. There was a reason why he reacted the way he did. I know it doesn't justify it. He was mortified, you know. But please don't worry. He really won't touch me.'

'I hope not. Or *he'll* end up with more than a broken nose.'

I smiled, but a battle raged inside me. Stevie thought I should dump him, Sarah thought I should dump him, and I'd already been questioning whether it was time to say goodbye before the incident, knowing that I liked him but didn't love him. Since the incident, I wasn't sure I even liked him that much. Why was I still clinging on by the fingernails?

Sarah placed her hand over mine. 'It's only because we care, you know.'

'I know and I appreciate it. But I'm really okay.'

She removed her hand and sat back in her chair. 'Okay. Subject dropped. I haven't seen Auntie Kay since I sorted out that photography tutoring for her. How's it going?'

'Brilliantly.' My shoulders relaxed and I put the part-shredded beer mat down. 'She went out with Philip and Michael last Friday and I've seen her photos. They're amazing. I think she may have a hidden talent.'

'Who has?' asked Clare, returning with our drinks.

'Auntie Kay.' Sarah explained, then I told them about Michael's photos and how talented he was.

All too soon, Sarah announced she had to get back to the shop. She hugged Callie goodbye and agreed to meet Clare at home later. As she hugged me, she whispered into my ear, 'Are you sure you've picked the right brother?' I stiffened. What was that supposed to mean?

'Thanks for helping me choose the dress,' she said to us all. 'Please don't scheme anything too embarrassing for my hen do. Callie, you may need to act as referee between these two, so good luck with that.'

'It'll be grand,' Clare said. 'Go and do some work, you big slacker.'

Was I sure I'd picked the right brother? My stomach churned as I twisted in my seat and watched Sarah walk back down the precinct towards Castle Street. Why had she said that? Probably because I'd just spent twenty minutes gulping down my wine and raving about how talented Michael was. What an idiot. It wasn't like I fancied him. But then I pictured him looking out of the back of his dad's 4x4 after they picked up Kay, answering the door with the towel round his waist, and while he talked animatedly about his photography projects. Oh my goodness, was that it? Was that why I was hanging onto Daniel, because it gave me an excuse to see Michael? Why else would I still be with someone I didn't even like anymore? No!

'Elise! Have you heard anything we've just said?'

I turned back round to face Clare. 'I... No. Sorry. What were you saying?'

'Are we keeping you from something?'

'No. I'm concentrating now. Fire away.'

Callie shuffled awkwardly in her seat as I scowled at Clare. 'We were discussing what Sarah did and didn't want for her hen do,' Callie said.

'Oh, right. And what did you conclude?'

Clare sighed loudly. 'Sarah said she doesn't mind what we do or where we go as long as it's something everyone will enjoy. She doesn't want any silly challenges but she doesn't mind wearing a veil and L-plates.'

'She liked the sound of some of the things I did on my hen do,' Callie added. 'We went to Wales for an adventure weekend. We did laser clay shooting, whitewater-rafting, gorge-walking, tank driving... all sorts of stuff. It was amazing. I don't think she was too keen on the gorge-walking but she liked the sound of the other stuff.'

'I'd love to drive a tank,' I said. 'That sounds like fun.'

'It's brilliant,' Callie said, grinning. 'There's a place in Northumberland called The Adult Playground. It's a disused airbase and it's got different vehicles like tanks, army trucks, racing cars, steam rollers, diggers. You name it, they've got it. They've also got things like laser clays, grass sledging, and this really wet, muddy assault course.'

'Wet mud? That sounds like something that Clare would hate.'

Clare raised her eyebrows at me. 'Would I now? And how will you be coming to that conclusion?'

'Look at you.' I indicated the short, tight, navy dress, high heels, perfectly manicured nails and immaculate make-up. 'I don't think I've ever seen you in jeans or without make-up. Somehow I can't see *you* driving a tank or scrambling over a cargo net.'

Clare leaned forward on the table and swirled the remnants of her wine around her glass. 'And you'll have come to that conclusion purely from how I look?'

'Yes. There's no way you'd be seen dead in a boiler suit covered in mud.'

'You're saying that because I dress a certain way, get manicures, spend time on my hair and make-up, that it somehow defines me? That you know exactly the type of person I am?'

I nodded. 'Yes! The type of person who doesn't like to shake her hair loose and get covered in mud.'

Clare knocked back the last of her wine then stared at me. 'Well, no wonder,' she said.

'No wonder what?'

'Given that you're so quick to make assumptions about people and put them in boxes, it's no wonder your poor husband didn't dare tell you he was gay. No wonder he lied and found real love behind your back. Being married to someone as judgemental as you must have been hell on earth.'

I heard Callie gasp. In slow motion, she turned from Clare towards me, her mouth open and her eyes wide. 'Oh, Clare,' she whispered. 'That was—'

But I didn't stick around to hear the end of the sentence. 'Excuse me,' I muttered, then fled. I could barely breathe as I ran through the bar and down the stairs to the ladies. My chest felt tight, my stomach felt tight, my eyes were blurred. I threw myself to my knees in the first cubicle and vomited. Tears rolled down my cheek as I vomited again and again.

'Elise? Are you in here? It's Callie.'

I tried to shut the door but wasn't quick enough.

'Ooh, not pregnant, are you?' she said.

'Of course not. I'm struggling to shift this gastric flu that I've had for weeks.'

Callie nodded. 'Sorry, I was only kidding. I talk too much. Open mouth, don't engage brain. That's me. Especially when I'm nervous. And I'm really nervous right now around you two. I told Sarah I could handle it, but I'm way out of my depth.'

I didn't know what to say. Did she want me to say everything was okay because it really, really wasn't and I wasn't going to lie? I pressed down on the toilet seat and heaved myself to my feet. 'What do you want, Callie?'

'To check on you. What Clare said was way out of order and she knows it.'

I grabbed some more loo roll and blew my nose, wiped my eyes then flushed it away. 'So she rushed down here to apologise, then. Oh no, she didn't. She sent you to do her dirty work instead.'

'She *was* coming, but I stopped her. I told her you probably wouldn't want to see her right now.'

'You're not wrong there.' I squeezed past her to the sinks where I washed my hands and splashed some cold water onto my face.

'Are you coming back upstairs?'

I dabbed my face dry with a paper towel and turned to look at Callie. She looked terrified. Who could blame her? That had been an ugly scene upstairs – the worst ever exchange I'd had with Clare and poor Callie had been caught right in the middle.

'Give me a minute and I'll be up, but I won't be staying. I hope you understand that.'

'And I hope you'll understand this. It's the same thing I've just said to Clare. I barely know either of you, but I do know you've got years of bad history between you. I don't know what it's about and I don't really care. What I *do* care about is Sarah. The reason the three of us are in Minty's this afternoon is because you two also care about Sarah. Or at least I hope you do.'

'Of course I—'

'I haven't finished.' Callie pushed back her shoulders, stood a little taller, and fixed her eyes on mine. 'Sarah loves you both but, as I understand it, you've done nothing but cause heartache for her with your constant bickering and sniping at each other over the years. I hope the performance upstairs was not an example of how you usually behave when you're together because, if it was, you must have put Sarah through absolute hell. If you were my friends and you behaved like that, I'd have ditched you both because what I've seen is toxic. It would wear down even the most patient person.'

I opened my mouth, but she silenced me with a raise of her hand.

'I'll tell you when I'm finished. Don't say it's all Clare's fault. Yes, what she said upstairs was inexcusable, but I've seen you dish it too and she was right; you were being rude and judgemental about her just now. There are less than four months until the wedding. I don't give a damn whether you tear each other to shreds after that, but for the next four months, you're going to act like the grown-up, mature women I know you both are and not the childish idiots you become when you get together. Sarah's dreamed of this day all of her life and you're not going to ruin it for her. When we go upstairs, I'm going home. I know you want to leave too, but I urge you and Clare to get a coffee, sober up, and talk instead. Really talk. Work out why the hell you hate each other and find a way to turn that around. Can you do that?'

I looked down at the woman who was a good head and shoulders shorter than me and two years my junior, and I felt ashamed. Weren't you meant to become more mature and wiser as you aged? 'Give me two minutes,' I said.

'I'll wait upstairs with Clare until you appear, then I'm off.' She opened the door. 'Did you know that Sarah toyed with not having any bridesmaids for her wedding? Nick told me that she had a panic about it. She couldn't pick between you, but knew you'd tear strips off each other if you were bridesmaids together. She was in tears about it. That's why they were late to their own engagement party.'

'No,' I muttered. 'She didn't say.' Poor Sarah. Had we really caused that?

'Of course she didn't. She doesn't want to lose either of you so she ties herself in knots trying to keep the peace. And did you know that she originally turned down the December date at Sherrington Hall because she was devastated about what had happened with you and your husband? She was worried that you might think she didn't care if she started planning her dream day. Nick had to beg her to accept the cancellation because he knew they'd have to wait a couple of years if she didn't. I know that what you're going through right now is one of the shittiest things that could happen to someone, but don't punish everyone else because of it.' She visibly relaxed. 'I've said my piece. I'll see you upstairs.'

I rested my hands on the sink unit and drew a few deep breaths. That was me well and truly told. She was right, though. She'd told some home truths and it was finally time for Clare and me to do the same and address whatever it was that had caused a wedge between us for over a decade. Best get this over with...

25

Clare stood up as I tentatively approached the table. Her eyes were red as though she'd been crying. Surely not. Sarah said Clare never cried. Callie stood up too and pointed to a pot of tea and a glass of water on the table. 'On me. Clare says you don't drink coffee. I hope you two can sort things out.'

'Sorry, Callie,' I said.

'Don't be sorry. Just sort it out. Now.' She sighed, shook her head, then left.

Clare indicated for me to sit. My legs felt very weak so I was grateful to take a seat before they buckled. I gulped on the water, hands shaking. Were the shakes from being sick, my lecture from Callie, or the confrontation I was about to have? Probably all three.

'I'm so sorry,' Clare said. 'I mean that genuinely from the heart.' Her green eyes pleaded with mine. 'I've no idea what made me say something like that. You hit a raw nerve and I lashed out.'

'It hurt.'

'I know. It was meant to. It's a gift of mine. Or an affliction.' She pointed two fingers to her head as if holding up an imaginary gun. 'Quick brain, quick to dish out insults, but also quick to regret them. Like just now.'

I'd need to accept her apology or we'd never move on. I took a sip of my tea. 'You said I hit a nerve. I don't follow.'

Clare picked up a beer mat and tore thin strips off it. 'I don't have many friends,' she said. 'I have lots of acquaintances, but not many people who I would call genuine friends. I find it hard to trust people and very hard to let them in. Sarah's the only person I've let get close to me, but even then, there's a lot I'm guarded about.'

'About what? About your past?'

'Yes. And I'm not going to confess all about it to you either just now.'

'I wasn't asking you to.'

Clare looked up for a moment and caught my eye. 'Good. Because I don't want to talk about it.' She cast her eyes down and continued shredding the beer mat. 'Let's just say that some bad stuff happened when I was younger. I didn't want to spend the rest of my life being the sort of person to whom bad things happened so I imagined the type of person I wanted to be: someone strong and confident who took no shit. I liked that person so I became her, particularly at work. It's worked for me. I've just been promoted as a result. But that person's not the whole me. Clothes, cosmetics, manicures… it's just an image for that person, but it's one that makes me feel comfortable and safe. It's the one I want the outside world to see. It doesn't define me, though. When I'm in on my own, I wander around make-up free wearing a Minnie Mouse onesie. That's more the kind of person I am. But don't you dare tell anyone that. Especially the onesie thing.'

I smiled. Clare in a Minnie Mouse onesie was not an image I found very easy to conjure up. 'I'm sorry. As you said, I don't really know you. I didn't think.'

Clare pushed aside the scraps of beer mat and looked up. 'Ditto. Must be an epidemic.'

I took another sip of my water. 'I have a tricky question. Why are we like this with each other? Maybe addressing that will help us move on.'

Clare shrugged. 'It's how it's always been.'

'I know that. I vividly remember the first time I met you and the filthy looks you kept giving me.' It had been Sarah's second term at Manchester University and I'd finally agreed to visit for a weekend. Sarah had been so excited about introducing us that she seemed oblivious to the snarls from Clare the second we met. I'd never felt so uncomfortable or unwelcome in my life. It had deteriorated from there with Clare sneering at me for marrying so young and me defending my actions, swearing that we may be young, but we knew it would last. Hmm. Didn't manage to prove her wrong on that one.

'That was because you'd upset Sarah,' Clare said.

'What? How?'

'By not visiting her sooner. It had been a big thing for her moving from here to a huge city. She was homesick for her family and for you and she was worried about the two of you drifting apart by living at other sides of the country, not to mention her being single and you being married. A visit from you in her first term would have reassured her that everything was okay. You kept promising you'd visit and you never followed through. She was devastated, you know. She thought there was no space for her in your life anymore now that you were a mature, married woman.'

Oh, the irony! She was right about me deliberately avoiding Sarah and her new life, but not about the reason. 'I didn't know she felt that way,' I said. 'Do you want to know why I didn't visit in her first term?'

'Enlighten me.'

'I was scared to. I'd just married my childhood sweetheart, I was renting a flat in the only town I've ever lived in, was studying here, and planned to teach here when I graduated. My life wasn't exactly filled with adventure. By contrast, my best friend who was originally going to do teacher training in Whitsborough Bay with me had decided it wasn't the career for her, had changed to Business Studies at Manchester, and was about to start an exciting new life without me. I was scared of visiting her in case she saw me as the boring, unadventurous person I was, sticking out like a sore thumb against all these exciting new friends with whom she was living.'

Clare stared at me for a moment, her green eyes soft with understanding. 'That's pretty ironic,' she said eventually. 'What a pair of eejits you two were.'

'Tell me about it!'

Clare sipped on her coffee. 'I'm sorry I judged you. I never paused to think there could be another explanation for you not coming.'

'Thank you. And thanks for telling me about Sarah. I only thought about myself, not how it affected her.'

'What made you visit in our second term, then?'

'We spent time together over the Christmas break and I realised she was still the same Sarah, but if I didn't make an effort to fit into her new life, our relationship might not stay the same. I was dreading meeting you, though.'

'Why?'

'Because you were the new me. You were the person with whom she did everything. Up until that point, it had been the two of us against the world.'

Clare shook her head. 'You're saying you were jealous of my friendship with Sarah?'

'If you want to put a label on it...'

Clare laughed. 'Yet more irony because I was jealous of you too.'

I smiled. 'Really? Why?'

'I've already said I don't make friends easily, but there was something about Sarah. I warmed to her the minute I met her. She's the only person I've ever fully trusted. She's also the sort of friend I wish I'd had when I was younger to support me through...' She tailed off and stared out of the window.

I cleared my throat and she looked back at me, a distant look in her eyes, then continued. 'She was the friend I'd have wanted and, childish as I can see it is now, I was jealous that she'd had you and you'd had her at a time when I hadn't had anyone. I wanted to make the most of my time with her and not share her with you.'

'Wow!' I said. 'So we were both jealous of each other and we've let it drag on for twelve years. Pretty stupid, eh?'

Clare rolled her eyes. 'Eejits. I don't think that's all, though. I think we're very different personalities so we clash. Sarah's somewhere in the middle.'

'True.' I held out my hand. 'Do you think we can call a truce for Sarah's sake?'

'I'm willing to give it a go if you are.'

We shook on it. As I sat back in my chair sipping my tea, I realised that I'd finally seen something vulnerable about Clare and instantly I didn't feel threatened, inferior, ugly or undesirable next to her. How could I? She was just as insecure and messed up as me. Something had clearly happened to her when she was younger that had scarred her for life. I suspected we'd draw a line in the sand and tolerate each other going forwards – too much water under the bridge to become friends – but I wondered if she'd ever fully open up about her past to Sarah because it sounded like she had demons to face. Only time would tell.

26

'I really appreciate you helping me to re-stock.' Sarah set a box of gifts down on the shop floor next to me. 'It's not the most exciting way to spend a Friday evening, especially when we were meant to be going out for a meal.'

I smiled. 'I honestly don't mind.'

'You're a star. I've got so many new lines to get out that there's no way I can do it during shop hours. Let me put off the lights nearest the window so nobody can see us.' She wandered over to the door and flicked a couple of switches. 'That's better. Probably shouldn't take too long with two of us. We could go for a curry afterwards if you like.'

'Maybe not curry,' I said, pulling a face. It was nearly two weeks since I'd been sick in Minty's following my altercation with Clare and I hadn't felt right since. In fact, I'd felt ill on and off since Sarah's engagement party. Sarah had said that some of her customers had found the bug sticking around for weeks. They weren't wrong about that.

'Are you still feeling sick?'

'It comes and goes. I think it's that gastric flu thing that I had last term. That's the problem with being a teacher – you work so hard and so intensively all term then you take your foot off the pedal in the holidays and wham! If I don't feel better when I start back at school next week, I'll make a doctor's appointment, although I need to find a new GP. I don't want to go to Gary's surgery.'

'Can't say I blame you. Could be awkward.' She ripped the tape off the box and pulled a few small boxes out. 'If I give you one of each type of gift, can you unwrap it and put it on the counter? Then we can decide what to move to make way for the new stuff.'

I did as she asked. My phone beeped and I fished it out of my bag. 'It's Daniel. Apparently he misses me and wishes he could see me tonight. He hopes we enjoy our meal and think of him with beans on toast and a DVD for one.'

'Didn't you tell him we'd ditched the meal?'

'Must have forgotten to mention it.'

'How's it going after the incident with Stevie?'

Good question. 'It's not the same. To be honest, we've not seen much of each other. He's been extra attentive when we've been together, but I'm not feeling it.' I knew exactly what the obvious next question would be.

'Then why not just end it? What's the point in stringing it out when your heart's not in it?'

Another good question. I switched my phone to silent and put it in my bag, then busied myself rearranging the boxes on the counter into a straight line to avoid looking at Sarah. 'I don't want to end it. I know I should and I will, but not just yet. I'm not ready. I will be soon. I'm just... Actually, can we change the subject? You wanted me to unwrap each of these, yes?'

'Yes please.'

We both worked in silence for a while. I knew she'd be desperate to challenge me more about Daniel, but my tone had clearly said 'drop it' and she'd have picked up on it.

Stevie and I had spoken on the phone a few times and he'd

challenged me too... but he'd also known when to drop it. I'd even had a lecture from Curtis: 'No shag's *that* good. Dump the tosser!'

'Clare told me she's got a promotion and is moving to Leeds.' I called down the shop. 'Is it this weekend that she moves?'

'Yes. She officially starts on Monday. She's staying with my brother while she looks for somewhere to rent.' She wandered over to the counter with a few more gifts and started unwrapping them.

'How *is* Ben?' I asked. 'I didn't get a chance to speak to him at your engagement party with going home early.'

'I haven't seen him since then, but I've spoken to him a few times. Nick's asked him to be an usher and he's well chuffed with that, although Lebony can't come to the wedding, of course.'

'They're still going strong?' Lebony and Ben had starting seeing each other years ago but, because Sarah hadn't mentioned her in ages, I'd assumed they'd called it a day. Lebony worked for a charity overseas so limited time together had surely put a strain on things.

Sarah shrugged. 'If you can call a distance relationship of thousands of miles where they never see each other strong, then I guess they are.'

I unwrapped another gift. 'You *really* don't like her, do you?'

'No. Actually, that's a lie. There's nothing to dislike about her. She's a lovely person, but she never seems to have time for Ben and it winds me up. I get that she goes abroad a lot with her various humanitarian endeavours and I think it's amazing that someone can be so giving, but she comes back home often too, and she doesn't always bother meeting up with Ben. How can you call that a relationship?'

She looked at what I'd unpacked and frowned. 'I'm missing some. Can you do me a favour and go into The Outback and see if there's another box in the store cupboard? I'll check that I've definitely got one of each out of this box.'

I headed into The Outback – a storage area out the back of the shop – and found a taped-up box dumped on the floor.

'Found it!' I picked it up and walked back into the shop. 'Or at least I think this is it.'

But Sarah wasn't paying attention. She was staring out of the window.

'What are you looking at?'

She turned to me, eyes wide. 'Oh, Elise, don't…'

I looked out of the window to where a young blonde woman and a dark-haired man were passionately kissing and groping each other in the middle of Castle Street. 'Wow! They should get a room!' It was only when they moved slightly that I was able to see him clearly. I gasped. 'That's Daniel. That's Daniel kissing another woman.'

'I know. I'm so sorry.'

I felt the energy drain from my body as I witnessed, once again, an act of complete and utter betrayal. I caught hold of Sarah's arm to steady myself.

'Are you going to confront him?'

I let go of her arm, stood tall, and shook my head. 'What's the point? What could he possibly say that would make this situation any better?' I turned away from the window, teeth grinding. 'Let's get on with the re-stocking. Shall I open this box?'

'We can do this later,' Sarah said gently. 'It's not important.'

'It is. I promised I'd help and that's what I'm going to do.' I knelt down, ripped the tape off the top, then looked out the window again. They'd set off down the street, arms round each other. 'So it turns out that, as well as thumping people, Daniel can add being a two-timing cheating little shit to his CV, just like my ex-husband. But I picked myself up after Gary and I'll pick myself up after this.'

'You're not upset?'

Was I? I was upset that I'd been lied to. Again. But was I upset at seeing Daniel with someone else? Not really. Just a bit resigned. 'I don't think I am. I don't think I'm in a place where I trust men at the moment. I think part of me expected this to happen.'

'Not all men are like that, you know.'

'I know. Nick isn't. Stevie isn't. Our Jess's Lee isn't. Unfortunately, I seem to be a magnet for them.' I started removing the contents of the box.

'Elise…'

I sat back on my heels and looked up at her. 'Do I have a tattoo on my forehead that says, "Please betray me"? What's wrong with me?'

Sarah sat down beside me and gave me a gentle nudge. 'You know it's them and not you. There's nothing wrong with you. You've just been really unlucky.'

'I won't rush out and buy a lottery ticket then,' I said. 'Look, Sarah, I'm actually okay with this. It's not like I was head over heels in love with him, is it?'

Poor Sarah looked like she was about to cry.

'Honestly. I'm fine. I don't really want to talk about it now, although I may do later. I need to think it through and work out how I feel first. Right now, I have no idea if I'm angry, upset, or relieved it's over.'

'It's definitely over?'

'Oh yes! Definitely. I know you and Stevie must think I'm crazy to have stayed after the incident and maybe I was, but he seemed so genuinely sorry and I never, ever felt threatened by him or I'd have been out of there like a shot. This time, I don't care what excuses he has, it's over. Can you just promise me one thing?'

'Anything?'

'After Rob and now Daniel, promise me you'll never introduce me to any more of your friends.' I winked at her so she could be assured that I wasn't angry with her.

'I promise.'

* * *

The re-organising took us a lot longer than expected so I dipped out to buy a couple of bags of chips when Sarah's stomach rumbled loudly. It was a relief to escape from her sympathetic glances and unspoken questions.

It was past eleven when I got back to Seashell Cottage, but Kay wasn't home. The empty cottage seemed to amplify my troubled thoughts. I sat in the lounge in darkness trying to make sense of what I'd seen that evening and, more importantly, how I felt about it.

Deep down, I'd known it was over when he punched Stevie. I'd been having doubts anyway, and that was really the final straw, yet I hadn't ended it. I'd steadily pulled away, though. We'd kissed, but I'd managed to avoid going any further. I'd wanted to be clear in my mind whether I really enjoyed Daniel's company or just our sex life. I'd been fairly sure it was the latter. My resigned reaction to Daniel's PDA outside Seaside Blooms confirmed my suspicions that I wasn't into him anymore. As I'd said to Stevie before Daniel thumped him, he wasn't my soulmate and, having had that with Gary (despite how it ended), I wanted that again. I wasn't prepared to compromise and settle for 'like' instead of 'love'.

I took my phone out of my bag and switched it off silent. It instantly beeped. Six missed calls and three texts from Jess all insisting I ring her whatever time I picked up the message. My pulse raced and I paced the lounge floor as I waited for the phone to connect.

'Are you okay? Are the twins okay?' I cried as soon as she answered.

'We're all fine. Sorry for scaring you. I should have said it wasn't baby-related.'

Phew! I slumped onto the sofa. 'Thank goodness. So why the urgency?'

Jess sighed. 'I'm sorry, but there's no easy way to say this other than to come straight out with it.'

I sat forward, my stomach churning. 'Come out with what?'

'I only found out tonight and, believe me, I've given her a right mouthful.'

'Who?'

'Izzy. I'm really sorry, but she had sex with Daniel at my wedding.'

Wow!

I think Jess was more upset than me, but the news hadn't really surprised me after what I'd witnessed earlier. I was angry with him – with them both – and I felt sickened that he'd returned to our room for sex with me too. I bet he'd loved that conquest. Two bridesmaids in one night? Sick.

Having reassured Jess that I was fine, I stood up with the intention of going to bed to put a close to a hideous day, but my phone beeped again:

✉ From Daniel
Hope you had fun with Sarah. Nice meal? I
pushed the boat out and had spaghetti on toast
LOL! Watched the latest Bond film again but
would have rather been snuggled up with you.
Missed you loads xx

You lying little... Right, that's it! I grabbed my bag and keys and stormed out of the cottage. I don't think I've ever driven so fast in my whole life or ground my teeth so much. My jaw hurt by the time I screeched to a halt outside Daniel's cottage. I leapt out of Bertie, ran to the front door, and banged on it just like I'd done after the incident with Stevie.

Michael opened the door. 'Elise? What are you doing here?'

'Is he in?'

Michael shrugged. 'I've just walked through the door myself. Are you okay?'

'No. I'm fuming with Daniel right now. Can I come in?'

He stepped back to let me pass then closed the door. 'He hasn't thumped another of your friends, has he?'

'No. Worse. Well, maybe not worse. Different. Still bad.'

'Do you want to go up to his room?'

Did I? A flashback of Gary and Rob in the shower entered my mind. I really didn't want to add Daniel and Whoever She Was to that album of images I'd rather forget. 'No. Can you shout him down? Don't tell him I'm here, though.'

I could tell from the concerned expression on Michael's face that he wanted to ask more questions. With a sigh, he headed to the bottom of the staircase and shouted, 'Daniel. Get your arse down here. Now!'

Silence.

'Daniel!' He ran up a few stairs and banged on the wall separating the staircase from Daniel's bedroom. 'Daniel! Down here. *Now!*'

He ran back down the stairs and whispered, 'Do you want me to leave?'

'No. This won't take long.'

'What the hell's got into you?' Daniel stomped down the stairs wearing only a towel round his waist. 'What do you think you're—' His eyes widened as he spotted me. 'Elise?' The quick shift of his eyes back up the stairs told me exactly what I'd suspected; he'd brought her home.

'You don't look pleased to see me,' I said.

'Sorry. Of course I am.' He moved towards me but didn't touch me. 'I'm a bit surprised, that's all. I was just dozing off.'

'Oh, I very much doubt that,' I said. 'Unless that's a euphemism with which I'm unfamiliar.'

'You've done it again, haven't you?' Michael snapped, shaking his head at Daniel. 'What the hell's wrong with you?'

I flinched at his tone. And the use of the word 'again'.

'I don't know what you mean.' Daniel looked at me, all wide-eyed and innocent, but then Whoever She Was ruined it for him.

'Danny? What are you doing down there? Come back to bed.' She appeared round the corner of the staircase, dressed only in one of Daniel's thin white work shirts, which left nothing to the imagination. Hmm. Not a natural blonde.

Daniel looked at her then me.

'I think we're done,' I said. 'Don't you?'

'Elise, I—'

I raised my hand to silence him. 'Spare me the apologies. Just answer me one question. Why did you do it?'

He shrugged. 'Because you weren't giving me any.'

'And whose fault was that? It's not a good enough excuse, Daniel. Got any more?'

He shrugged again. 'Because I could.'

I heard Michael's sharp intake of breath beside me.

'Because you could?' I said. 'Really?'

'I didn't promise you anything, babe. I thought you knew it was a bit of fun, but you took the fun part away so what do you expect?'

'What about at Jess's wedding? I hadn't taken the "fun part away" then?'

'You know about that?' He looked shocked and perhaps a little guilty. Then he crossed my arms and gave me a smug grin. 'Well, we never agreed we were exclusive and you *had* abandoned me if you remember.'

Not exclusive? What did he think being in a relationship meant? It was on the tip of my tongue to say that and to remind him that he'd said he loved me on several occasions and had begged me to stay after he'd punched Stevie, but it might hurt Whoever She Was hovering on the landing looking very embarrassed and uncomfortable. What was the point?

'Yes, well, fun's definitely over now. Goodbye Daniel.'

I turned and paced towards the door. I'd almost closed it when I heard Michael say, 'You stupid fucking idiot. Don't you ever learn? Elise, wait!'

He caught me as I reached Bertie. 'I'm so sorry,' he said.

'Don't be. You tried to warn me, but I snapped at you for interfering.'

'I should have tried harder. Direct approach instead of subtle hints. Just like you asked.'

'Please don't beat yourself up about it. I probably wouldn't have listened to you. I'd like to listen now, though. Tell me, did Daniel's marriage end because Amber was having an affair? Or because Daniel was?' I felt I needed to know the truth so I could get absolute closure... and know exactly how much of a mug I'd been. Again!

'Given tonight's little episode, what do you think?'

'I think you need to tell me what you know. Hop in. Is there somewhere nearby where we can park and talk?'

'There's a car park about a mile further up the coast road. I don't know everything. As you know, I try to have as little to do with my brother as possible, but I'll tell you what I can.'

We drove to the car park, which I recognised as a popular starting point for a walk over the moors, and Michael told me what he knew about Daniel's marriage. Apparently Amber hadn't been Daniel's girlfriend; she'd been Michael's. Daniel had made it clear from the outset that he wanted her, but Michael was confident that his little brother would get over it and find his own partner. After they'd been together for four years, Michael had an amazing rare opportunity to join his dad for a six-month photography project in the Galapagos Islands. He didn't want to leave Amber, but she insisted he went. To ensure she was clear of his love for her, he proposed to her first, but while he was away, Daniel took it upon himself to make sure she wasn't lonely. Literally. When he returned, Michael could tell that something had gone on between them. It didn't take much probing. Wracked with guilt, Amber told him she'd been unfaithful and didn't deserve to marry him. She returned the ring. Devastated, he accepted another overseas project and was in South America within a week.

'It took me a few months to acknowledge that, even though she'd slept with my brother, I still loved her and wanted to marry her,' Michael said. 'I knew what Daniel was like and I knew he'd have worn her down and filled her head with doubts about my fidelity while I was away. I decided to come home and beg her forgiveness. But when I phoned Dad to tell him my plans, he told me that I was too late. Amber had discovered she was pregnant and had married Daniel.'

'No! That's awful. What did you do?'

'I stayed in South America for another three months. Amber miscarried the baby. A few weeks after I came back, I bumped into her and she looked terrible. I insisted on taking her for a drink and she told me that she believed Daniel was seeing someone else. Somehow she and I made it back to being friends. We'd regularly meet for coffee, but every story about my brother's infidelity was like a knife through the heart.' His words were thick with emotion and I could tell he still really cared for her, despite everything she and his brother had put him through.

'He told me she'd been seeing a neighbour,' I said. 'Jake, I think.'

Michael shook his head. 'Amber *was* seeing Jake, but as his client. He's a counsellor. She started suffering from anxiety attacks and a form of agoraphobia brought on by fear of being out and seeing Daniel with another woman. A friend referred her to Jake and he was amazing with her. It took a couple of years, but he got her to the point where she was strong enough to throw Daniel out and demand a divorce.'

I sighed. So many lies. 'Daniel said Amber's pregnant with

Jake's baby now and that seeing them together triggered the incident with my friend Stevie. All lies?'

He nodded. 'He really said that? Amber's not with Jake and she's certainly not pregnant by him or anyone else. She was expecting again three years ago, but my wonderful brother forced her into having a termination. She wasn't in a good place with her nerves and he convinced her that she'd be a terrible mother. I think it was the regret from that which spurred her onto finally agreeing to an appointment with Jake.'

Michael sighed, sat back in the passenger seat, and ran his hand across his stubble. 'I know he's my brother, but I hope you can see why I hate him. I hate him for taking Amber away from me, but the part that really grinds is that, once he'd won her, he didn't want her. He turned a lovely, caring woman into a nervous wreck. What sort of person plays with someone else's life like that?'

I didn't know what to say. What *could* I say to him? Daniel hadn't just played with Amber's life, he'd played with Michael's too and now he was doing it all over again with me, Izzy, Whoever She Was, and anyone else he might be stringing along.

Michael twisted round in his seat. 'Sorry, Elise, I think I may just have gone off on one and wallowed in my own sorrows, completely forgetting that he's hurt you too. How are you feeling?'

'Like all men are liars and I'm a really bad judge of character.'

'Sounds like Daniel isn't the only one who's done a number on you. Feel like off-loading?'

We sat in Bertie with only the moonlight to take the edge off the darkness and talked about Gary and Rob, and Daniel and Amber.

'I hoped you'd see sense and ditch him after he thumped your friend,' he said. 'I could see you were better than all the others.'

I squirmed. '*All* the others?'

'Sorry. They usually only lasted a night or two, but there've been at least four since you met him, although that one back there may have been a new one. They start to blend together after a while.'

'Four? Wow! I am *such* a mug.'

'No, you're not. Daniel's the mug.'

Silence engulfed us as I stared into the blackness and digested Michael's revelations. At least I didn't love Daniel. What an idiot I'd been, though. Four or five since we met? Was Izzy included in that? Good grief!

'I'm sorry I was off with you when we first met,' Michael said, breaking the silence.

I smiled. 'I understand why. I have a confession to make, though.'

'Oh yes?'

'I was a little bit scared of you.'

Michael laughed loudly. 'Sorry, I probably shouldn't laugh at that. I've been called a lot of things in my life, but I think scary is a first for me. And how do you feel about me now?'

I felt a shift in the atmosphere, as though my next words could forever change things between us. My pulse quickened and my lips dried. I looked into his moonlit eyes. 'Still a little scared,' I whispered. 'But perhaps for a different reason.'

We stared at each other. His breathing was rapid like mine. His face edged closer. Mine did too. Any moment, our lips would meet.

Then some idiots screeched into the car park with their windows down and music blaring. 'Woo hoo!' shouted the passenger. 'Dogging time.' With a beep of the horn, they screeched out of the car park again.

And the moment was well and truly lost.

'Erm… I should probably get you back home,' I said.

'Yes, and, er, you should probably get to bed. Your bed. For some sleep.'

We clicked seatbelts on and I drove Michael back to the cottage in silence.

'Good night then,' I said. 'And thank you for being honest. It's about time someone was.'

Michael undid his seatbelt then paused. I wondered if he was going to make a move, but if he was, he obviously thought the better of it. 'Night, Elise.' He opened the car door and got out.

Damn! Were we going to kiss? Had my thoughts from earlier been right; that I'd stayed with Daniel after the incident so I could still see Michael? Did I have feelings for him? I hoped not. Because, if I had... Oh goodness, what would I do? I didn't want to drift from one relationship straight into another. I needed time to get to know myself. Me. On my own. Not one half of a couple.

I reversed Bertie out of his space then drove towards the main road. I could do this. Even if I'd somehow developed a crush on Michael, I could fight it. I needed to be alone. Not forever. But definitely for now.

27

'Do we really have to spend the next hour or so mingling with a wee bunch of business stiffs?'

I grabbed Curtis's arm and dragged him up the steps of The Ramparts Hotel, Whitsborough Bay's only five-star hotel. It was Bay Trade's fifth anniversary. Nick and his friends Skye and Stuart, the founder members, had decided to celebrate in style with a huge members, ex-members, friends and family party and awards ceremony and I'd felt very proud to receive an invite.

'It's an important night for Sarah and Nick so I promised I'd support them. Besides, I'd already said yes before you decided to grace us with your presence again.'

'You're sure there'll be food?'

'I'm sure. And it's a five-star hotel so the food will be exquisite. Can we go in?'

'Aye. But only because of the food, mind.'

'Tell me how you manage to eat like a horse yet you have the body of a Greek God?'

'It's in the genes, Red. And a strict mayonnaise-avoidance technique. That stuff is evil.'

I shook my head and pulled him towards The Castle Room.

They'd certainly pulled out all the stops. Tables adorned in crisp white cloths ran down one side of the room, ready for the buffet. Round tables with balloons, flowers, and candles were filled with guests of all ages, dressed in their finery. I was relieved I'd worn a calf-length green satin dress and heels. I'd have looked out of place in anything else.

Sarah waved and made a beeline for us. Her dark curls were piled up on her head with loose spirals round her ears. She wore a long, flared, midnight blue dress with crystal-covered spaghetti straps and floaty net short sleeves. A spattering of crystals across the waist matched both the dress straps and the ankle straps on her midnight blue heels.

'I'm so glad you could come,' she said, hugging me then Curtis. 'You look stunning, Elise.'

'And so do you. I love that colour on you.'

'Thank you. The first drink's on the house. The buffet will be served in about an hour. Are you okay if I find you in a bit?'

'Yes, go and mingle,' I said, smiling. 'Enjoy.'

Curtis turned towards the bar. 'On the house? Mine's a bottle of tequila, then.'

'I'm not doing tequila shots again tonight. I'm on soft drinks. I'm still not over that gastric flu.'

'Spoilsport. You used to be fun.' He winked at me.

'I'd like to think I'm still fun, but those shots tipped me over the edge last time and, if you cast your mind back, it was as a direct result of them that I tried to seduce Stevie. Epic fail.'

'Have you made your peace?' Curtis steered me in the direction of the bar.

'Yes, although I'd understand if he hated me forever because, the next time I saw him, Daniel broke his nose. Since then, we've only texted.'

We reached the bar and Curtis ordered a bottle of lager and a soda water.

'When was this display of testosterone?' He passed me my drink.

'Four weeks ago.'

'And you really haven't seen Dimples since?'

'No. I just said that. We've made arrangements to meet up a couple of times, but one of us has had to cancel each time. Why?'

'Because he's heading our way right now.'

I turned round so abruptly that I spilled some of my drink down Stevie's shirt.

'Oh no! I'm so sorry.' I grabbed a bar towel and tried to mop his shirt. 'It's only water. I promise.' I blushed as my hand slipped off the towel and onto his chest and I had a sudden desire to wrap my arms round him and get lost in one of his super-hugs. My cheeks burned even more.

'It's fine,' he said, seemingly oblivious to my colour-change. 'As long as you weren't aiming for my face. My nose couldn't take it.'

'Of course I wasn't. I—'

Stevie grinned. 'You're nearly as easy to wind up as Sarah. It's great to see you.' He gave me a kiss on the cheek then shook Curtis's hand. 'Good to see you again, mate. Didn't think this would be your kind of thing.'

'I'd rather hack my eyes out with a wee spoon, but I've been promised food and an early pass out of here. I plan to eat, drink, and completely ignore anyone except you lot because I'm anti-social like that. If we were in Glasgow, I'd be schmoozing like hell to try and get them to the salon. Here, I have nae need to kiss ass.'

Stevie laughed. 'At least you're honest.' He turned to me. 'Apparently one of the Bay Traders is in a band and they're pretty good. You'll stick around for that, won't you?'

'Sounds good.' I winced at Curtis's pained expression and

put my arm round him. 'I promise you can bail if they're dire. Sarah already knows we'll probably leave early so I won't feel too absolutely, completely, hideously guilty for running out on her big night.'

'You're very manipulative when you want to be, Red,' Curtis said. 'I'll try and last beyond the buffet. Just for you.'

The three of us moved to an empty table. Sarah came over and dumped her bag to secure her seat, then went to play host again. I felt a stab of pride watching her. I genuinely hadn't seen her so at ease or so animated for a long time. She was glowing and she had so much to glow about with a successful business and fantastic fiancé. Lucky thing. Mind you, I loved my job and I didn't want a relationship right now so I wasn't in a bad place either.

I chatted to Curtis and Stevie, relieved that the four weeks since the incident on the beach hadn't made things awkward between Stevie and me. While Curtis told Stevie about his salon, I took a moment to gaze around the room. The door opened revealing Sarah's brother, Ben, and Clare. My stomach clenched. It had been three weeks since our altercation in Minty's. Even though a tentative peace had been declared and a few messages about hen do ideas had been exchanged with her and Callie since then, this was the first time we'd come face to face. She looked stunning, as always, in a short, tight burgundy dress and killer heels. Nick and Sarah welcomed them, pointed towards the bar, then pointed towards our table. Ben smiled and waved, Clare nodded her head in my direction, then they headed for the bar.

'Are you okay?' Stevie asked a few moments later.

'Yes. Why?'

'Could I have my hand back then?'

'What?' I looked down. I hadn't realised I'd taken hold of his hand or that I'd squeezed it until his knuckles turned white.

'Sorry,' I whispered, letting go. 'I hope I haven't just added a broken hand to your collection of injuries caused by me.'

'The nose wasn't your fault and you know it.' He fixed those warm hazel eyes on mine. 'I heard about Daniel. I'm not sorry it's over, but I am for how it ended. What a tosser!'

'Thanks. I should have taken your advice and dumped him after he hit you, but he seemed so genuinely distraught about it. It seems he's a pretty good actor. I should give him a part in one of our school productions.'

'Who's a good actor?'

'Ben!' I stood up and hugged him. 'It's been far too long. How've you been?'

'Pretty good. Well, apart from a house full of women's products and lacy undies thanks to this one moving in.'

'Oi. It's just grand having me there. You're getting a new kitchen on my company thanks to me slumming it with you instead of living the life of Riley in a hotel, so just you be grateful.' Clare playfully punched him on the arm. 'Hi Elise. Hi Curtis.'

'Hi,' we said together.

Stevie stood up and hugged her. I found myself wishing it was me and shook my head. I had to stop obsessing about his super-hugs.

Ben and Clare sat down. Thankfully the question of who was a good actor wasn't raised again. I didn't want talk of Daniel to sour what promised to be a great evening.

'Do you mind if I join you?' said a familiar voice about fifteen minutes later.

My pulse quickened when I turned round and saw him all smart and sexy in a suit instead of his usual jeans and T-shirt combo. 'Michael. Hi. Of course.' I quickly did the introductions round the table. 'Sit down. You're in luck. There's one seat left.' I saw Michael glance across to the far side of the table where the empty seat was. Was that a look of disappointment?

Curtis stood up. 'You can have mine for a moment, mate. I'm nipping out for a wee smoke.'

'Curtis! I thought you'd given up.'

'I had, but I've fallen off the wagon. I've had enough stick off my staff about it so zip it, Red. I'm on holiday.' He headed for the door, pulling a packet of cigarettes out of his suit pocket.

Michael sat down beside me and asked me a question so I turned to answer him, but then Stevie asked me a question so I had to turn to face him. Then Michael asked another, then Stevie again. Feeling increasingly awkward, I pushed my chair away from the table so I could get eye contact with them both.

Curtis returned and hovered nearby, watching. I caught his eye and shrugged apologetically. 'It's okay,' he said. 'I'll sit next to Legs. I want to see if she's up for clubbing again later.' He sat in the spare seat beside Clare.

By the time the opening of the buffet was announced, I felt quite exhausted from the barrage of questions coming from both men and excused myself to go to the ladies. On my way back, Curtis grabbed me and steered me towards the queue for the buffet table. 'Well, well, well,' he said. 'Who's got the boys fighting over her?'

'What?'

'Don't play Little Miss Innocent with me. Dimples and Camera-Boy are falling over each other to get your attention. So who's going to win?'

Colour flooded my cheeks and butterflies took flight in my stomach. Could he be right about them? Michael and I had almost kissed and there was definitely some chemistry there. But Stevie? He'd turned me down in Stardust, but he had said that I was attractive and it was only a bad idea because I was drunk and on the rebound. I had no idea whether that had been a gentle let-down or whether he had been interested. And if he had been, was he still interested now? Surely he'd have said something if he was.

Back at the table with plates of food, everyone had switched seats. Curtis sat down beside me. While we ate, he kept whispering in my ear to let me know that one or the other was either staring at me, giving each other evil looks, or laughing a little too loudly then glancing across to see if I was watching. Allegedly.

'Stop it, Curtis,' I hissed. 'You're being ridiculous.' I chased a piece of potato salad around my plate then gave up and pushed the plate aside. I didn't want two men fighting over me. I didn't even want one man after me. I wanted to be my own person. Single. Strong. Happy being me.

'Game time,' he whispered.

My stomach lurched. 'No! Don't start stirring.'

He coughed loudly to grab everyone's attention. 'Seeing as we're all back from the buffet and food's nearly finished, who's up for a wee game?'

Everyone looked intrigued and I cringed.

'I'll give each person the name of another person on this table. You have to say two things that you think are fabulous about that person then one thing you'd change about them. I know some of us have just met this evening so you'll have to be creative. I'll start to give a demo. This is directed at Legs over there.' He blew a kiss towards Clare.

Clare smiled, placed her elbows on the table, and clasped her hands under her chin. 'Bring it on!'

'The first fabulous thing is obvious. You have legs that even I, as a gay man, would love to have wrapped round me.' Clare beamed and everyone laughed. 'The second fabulous thing is your hair. If I could do to all my clients whatever your hairdresser does to you, I would be able to retire next year.'

Clare tossed her hair which fell back perfectly into position. 'And the thing you'd change?' she challenged.

'You've got a wee bit of chilli sauce on your cheek.'

Clare grabbed her napkin and everyone laughed again.

'Do you want to play?' Curtis asked.

His offer was met with an enthusiastic response, but my stomach churned again. I smelt trouble.

'In that case,' he said, 'we'll start with Nick. We need two fabulous things and one thing you'd change about Sarah.'

Nick smiled and took Sarah's hand. 'The first fabulous thing is your personality. You're funny, intelligent, passionate, vibrant... I could go on and on. The second fabulous thing is that you agreed to be my wife and I get to spend the rest of my life with you. I'm the luckiest man on earth.'

A chorus of 'awwww' went round the table.

'As for what I'd change, I was going to say absolutely nothing, but there is one thing. I wish you could see yourself through my eyes because you'd never again worry about your weight or your business being successful if you could see yourself as I see you: absolutely perfect.'

A tear fell down Sarah's cheek at that point and she hugged Nick. I wiped at my eyes. Wow! I wanted to be alone for now, but if and when I felt ready to try another relationship, I wanted what they had. It reminded me of how things had been between Gary and me in our early days.

'Ooh, pressure's on,' Curtis said. 'Who can top that? I think we'll go to Sarah who can tell us all what she thinks of...' He paused for dramatic effect, '... her brother.'

Sarah played the game then Curtis pretended to scan round the table as if deciding who was next. But I knew it would be one of two people and they'd be talking about me. 'Next up is... Michael. Telling us about... Elise.'

Michael's eyes widened and he chewed on his thumbnail. 'I haven't known Elise for very long, but two fabulous things about her are...' He looked down, no doubt thinking, 'Ground, swallow me up, now.' Poor Michael.

'Go on...' Curtis said.

'Erm... It would be her gorgeous red hair and her brilliant laugh. And I'd change the first few times we met so that I wasn't so hostile towards her because she didn't deserve that.' He grabbed his pint and gulped it as the group clapped.

Curtis put Clare on the spot next about Nick. Then, with a sinking feeling in my stomach, I knew where we were going next. 'Stevie. Your turn to tell us about Elise too.' No! Curtis was such a childish idiot sometimes.

Stevie fixed his eyes on me and smiled. Gosh, I loved those dimples.

'Everything about Elise is fabulous,' he said. 'If I had to really narrow it down to two things, the first would be the fact that she tries to see the good in everyone and every situation, even with people who don't really deserve that consideration. The second thing would be her amazing passion for her job and the huge difference she's made to others like my neighbour's kid, Brandon. As for something that I'd change, I wish I could take away the last few months of pain and hurt because someone as lovely as Elise doesn't deserve to have gone through what she's gone through.'

Curtis nudged me under the table. I ignored him, but I did notice the look on Michael's face. He looked like a man whose lottery numbers had come up on the one day he'd forgotten to buy a ticket.

Waitresses appeared to clear our plates, which thankfully brought a natural conclusion to the game.

'Did you see Michael's face?' whispered Curtis. 'I bet I can tell you exactly what was going through his mind: "Shit, why didn't I say that?" Round One to Stevie I think.'

'I'm going to the ladies,' I whispered back. 'And, when I come back, this stops. This is *not* a game. Playing with people's emotions is *not* a game. I should know. Gary played with mine for years.'

My legs shook as I lowered myself down onto the cool lid of the toilet and rested my hot forehead against the cold tiles, taking deep breaths. A wave of nausea swept over me. I leapt off the seat and raised the lid just in time. Damn! Why couldn't I shake this illness? I dabbed my face with toilet paper and flushed. It would appear that Curtis was going to get his wish for an early pass, only it would be to go to bed instead of a pub crawl and clubbing. I felt a bit guilty that he'd travelled all this way, then I reminded myself of his childish behaviour and the guilt dissipated.

'Elise? Are you in here?'

I opened the cubicle and smiled weakly at Sarah.

'Oh my God! Are you okay? You look terrible.'

'Thanks a lot! I spent ages getting ready.'

'I didn't mean it like that. It's just—'

'I'm joking.' Exiting the cubicle, I washed my hands and glanced up at the mirror. Sarah was right. My eyes were red with huge shadows under them, my face pale and blotchy, and my hair was sticking up. I certainly didn't do illness with dignity. 'I've been sick again.'

'No! Did you make a doctor's appointment?'

I shook my head. 'I got as far as picking up the forms to register with a new surgery, but I've been so busy with back to school that I never got round to it. I will, though, because it's not improving.'

'Good. Illness aside, are you okay after... well, after that little game?'

I shrugged. 'I'm pretty mad at Curtis right now. He's convinced that Michael and Stevie both fancy me, and I know he contrived that game to put them on the spot and embarrass the hell out of them. It embarrassed *me*, though. As if they'd both fancy me.' I turned the hand drier on.

When the drying cycle finished, Sarah said, 'I think he may be right.'

'Really? Why? Have they said something to you?'

'Not as such. Or at least not something outright, but now that I think back, they've both asked after you quite a bit recently. When I was at Bay Trade on Monday, I got the distinct impression from Michael that something might have happened between you and—'

'We nearly kissed the night I found out about Daniel.' I leaned back against the sink unit and briefly told her about the night in the car park. 'What about Stevie? You said he'd been asking after me too?'

'Just general interest and concern for you, which I didn't really think anything of until I saw the way he was looking at you tonight which was mirrored by the way Michael was looking at you.'

Damn! How had that happened? I put my hands over my mouth and shook my head. 'What a mess.'

'You don't like either of them?'

I removed my hands and looked at Sarah. 'That's the messy part. I think I may like them both, but I don't want to have jumped from Gary to Daniel to one of them. I want some time alone. I *need* some time alone.' I shook my head. 'I think we'd better be getting back. 'Curtis is going to hate me for it, but I just want to go home. Would you mind me leaving early?'

'Of course not, especially when you're ill. You get home and get an early night. You look done in.'

I felt it. 'Thanks.'

'And maybe you'll feel clearer about things after a good night's sleep. You know where I am if you want to talk.'

'Could be a plan. How about The Chocolate Pot at some point tomorrow afternoon, providing I haven't been sick again? I might need a sounding board to make sense of things.'

'What about Curtis? Won't he still be here?'

I shook my head. 'He's got something on so he's booked on the nine-forty to York.'

Sarah smiled. 'I've got no plans so I'm happy to help. I may even bring my Post-it notes. People laugh, but they're really helpful.'

I smiled as I reached to open the door. Sarah had made a couple of major life decisions using Post-it notes and I have to say that they were two of the best decisions she'd ever made. Perhaps there was a method in her madness. 'You know what, that might actually be a good idea.'

28

Curtis was surprisingly compliant when I told him I wanted to call it a night. I didn't even have to plead illness; he accepted the suggestion immediately, saying that he had a headache and could do with an early night himself. He also apologised if he'd taken things too far. Curtis never apologised. He'd done some pretty bad things over the years like abandoning me when he'd pulled, spiking my drinks to the point where I lost use of my legs and he had to call Gary to my aid, and making me spend the night in a neighbour's shed after he lost his keys in a club in Glasgow. He'd always laughed and called it 'an adventure' rather than actually saying sorry, so this was unchartered territory. I decided to accept his apology with good grace and not have a go at him, especially as I suspected Sarah might have already done that before she found me in the toilets, judging by the dark looks they'd exchanged when we said goodnight. Good for her!

As I finished removing my make-up back at Seashell Cottage, Curtis knocked on the bathroom door. 'I know I came with luggage this time, but I've forgotten my toothbrush. Can I borrow yours? I promise I have no dodgy mouth infections.'

'I can do one better than that. I've got a spare. I'll leave it out for you.'

I opened the under-sink cabinet. Kay had cleared a shelf so I could store my spare make-up and toiletries. 'Come out, come out, wherever you are,' I muttered as I rummaged around at the back of the cabinet, trying to put my hand on the toothbrush. 'Ah, got you!' As I closed my hand around the toothbrush, I knocked a bottle of shower gel and a box of tampons out of the cupboard. Tutting, I picked up the gel and put it back, then picked up the tampons... and my stomach lurched.

Heart racing, I sat down heavily on the toilet seat. *Relax and think.* I'd started my period the day I moved in with Kay. I was near the end of my next cycle when I'd tried on the bridesmaid dress for Sarah's wedding because I could remember Clare joking about my big black knickers showing through the material. What date was that? I shook my head. Mid-July? And now it was the middle of September. I flashed back to Callie in the toilets at Minty's asking me if I was pregnant. No. The sickness was that gastric flu sticking around and the skipped period was simply the stress of splitting up with Gary and selling the house. I had form with that. The situation with Mother had wreaked havoc with my periods but, within months of leaving home, I'd settled into a regular cycle. I'd skipped periods since then at times of heightened stress such as applying for my departmental headship and a couple of particularly problematic school plays.

I jumped up and tossed the tampons back in the cupboard, shaking my head. 'Not pregnant. Just stressed,' I muttered. 'Very stressed.'

* * *

It was raining the following morning so I drove Curtis to the train station rather than walking.

'You're very quiet this morning,' he said as we waited at some lights.

'Am I? Sorry.'

'You're not still mad at me for last night?'

I gave him a reassuring smile. 'Consider it forgotten. I just have a lot on my mind at the moment.'

He nodded. 'Aye. I get that. You know where I am if you want to offload.'

'Thanks, Curtis. You're a good friend.'

After I dropped him off, I drove to a nearby supermarket to get something for dinner. Wandering aimlessly with a basket hooked over my arm, I found myself in the health and beauty section, staring at the pregnancy tests on the shelf in front of me. What the heck. I was certain I wasn't pregnant but, for a tenner, I could confirm for sure. I grabbed a single test and hid it under a bag of grapes.

I paid for my shopping, then nipped to the toilets. No time like the present.

Staring at the testing kit in my hand moments later, I took a few deep, calming breaths. Not stress, then. And not gastric flu either.

I drove to the car park at Lighthouse Cove and switched off my engine as I stared across the road towards the sea. Rain battered my windscreen with increasing ferocity and the waves ahead of me seemed to leap in protest at the addition of more water. It seemed apt that the waves were in turmoil – a fitting metaphor for my life.

A beeping from my phone disturbed my trance.

✉ From Curtis
Sorry again about last night's game. Maybe it is time I grew up a bit. Been single too long. Makes me tamper in other people's relation-ships, oblivious to their feelings. For what

it's worth, they both seem like great wee
fellas. But remember you don't have to pick
either if they're not right or you're not
ready for a relationship! Hope to see you
soon, Red. Any time you fancy a trip to
Glasgow and the best haircut you've ever had,
give me a shout (((((hugs)))))

'Not ready for a relationship?' I muttered. 'Oh Curtis, you have no idea!' I placed my phone back into my handbag, beside the box containing the positive pregnancy test, and stared out at the wild sea again.

✉ From Unknown
Hi Elise, it's Michael. Hope you don't mind,
but I made Daniel give me your number. Just
wanted to drop you a quick text to say I hope
you're OK. You didn't look well when you left
last night. Hope you managed to get a good
night's sleep and feel better for it this
morning. I know I probably should ring to do
this, but you might be having a lie-in and I
don't like to disturb you… would you like to
go out for a drink with me one night next
week? Hope to hear from you soon. Michael x

✉ From Stevie
Morning. How are you feeling? Was really
worried about you last night. Sarah says
you've still got that gastric flu. Can you
face a visitor this afternoon or this evening?
Would love to see you if possible xxx

I leaned back in the car seat and flicked between the two text messages. Michael was definitely asking for a date, but was Stevie? Hard to tell. Stevie and I knew each other better so perhaps it was just the more informal approach of his text. I could easily put Stevie off a visit today by citing illness, but how would I tell Michael I couldn't see him at any point next week? And, speaking of not seeing people, I couldn't meet up with Sarah this afternoon. I needed some alone time to get my head around things:

✉ To Sarah
Hope you had a brilliant evening. Sorry again for bailing early. And another apology… can we take a rain-check on Operation Post-it Notes today? I'm feeling a bit rough so think a duvet day's in order. I'll see you after school as usual on Wednesday. Spend the day with that gorgeous man of yours instead. That's an order! xx

My shoulders sank. I hated lying. Hated it. But what else could I say? I wasn't ready to tell anyone that I didn't really still have gastric flu because, surprise, surprise, what I actually had was a little more long-term than that.

I flicked back to Michael's and Stevie's texts and reality hit me. Michael had just asked me on a date, oblivious to the fact that I was pregnant with his brother's baby. The brother he hated. The brother who'd impregnated Michael's fiancée then married her while he was overseas. The brother who'd made her abort her second pregnancy. That all-round nice guy. I certainly didn't do things by halves.

I stared out at the sea again, twiddling my phone round in my hand, and eventually came to a decision. Gary had effectively strung me along for years. I wasn't going to do the same to Stevie or Michael. Before my discovery, I'd already been 90 per cent sure I didn't want another relationship, but now I was 100 per cent sure. I'd arrange to meet them and let them down gently. If it was a date, that was. Stevie's message could be read either way and, coming to think of it, Michael could just be showing friendly concern after his brother's infidelity.

✉ To Stevie
Thanks for your concern. Still feeling a bit icky today so just want to rest. How about we meet up on Tuesday night?

✉ To Michael
Thanks for your concern. Feeling a bit sick today, but hopefully better soon. How about we meet up on Wednesday night?

Switching my phone to silent, I stared at my stomach and shook my head. I'd finally got what I'd desired for years, but this wasn't the way I'd planned or expected. I recalled telling Gary that, if I had a baby, it would be with a husband who cared about me rather than the sperm-donor situation he'd suggested. That hadn't happened. Maybe I should have taken him up on his offer after all as I might not have had a husband that way, but at least my baby would have had a devoted father. My current situation brought me neither. There was no way Daniel would want to be involved; just look at his track record with babies. And I certainly wasn't going to get involved with him again but I couldn't get involved with anyone else either because that would hardly be fair on them. Well, I'd just got the me-time I wanted and I'd better make the most of it because, in seven or so months' time, it would be in very short supply!

I drove back to Seashell Cottage where I rummaged in my drawers for an A4 notepad and pen. Sitting on my bed, I wrote 'THE NEW ELISE' at the top of a fresh page. Right. What did I want to achieve between now and the birth? What had I always wanted to do that was purely for me? Hmm.

I stared at the blank page as the minutes ticked past. I put the pad down and stared out of the window. I picked it up again. Put it down. Picked it up. I sighed and began doodling in the margin while I willed some sort of plan to present itself. Half an hour later, the page was full... of doodles. Great. I was about to scrumple it up when my eyes were drawn to an image in the centre of the page. An image from the past.

'The sword of Ellorinia. Oh my goodness. That's it! I want to write again.'

29

For someone who hates lying, the following week seemed to be one lie after another as I embarked on my two evenings of 'dates' with Stevie then Michael, and fed Sarah yet another excuse for not visiting after school on the Wednesday.

I enjoyed both 'dates' and, under other circumstances, would have found myself torn as to whom I was most drawn towards. Stevie was great fun and my sides had actually hurt from laughing so much. Michael also had a good sense of humour, but he had an intensity to him so the evening wasn't quite as light-hearted. That was no bad thing, though. I liked that he could be serious about things when his brother clearly viewed life as a big joke.

Keeping focus and steering the conversation to avoid any sort of acknowledgement that we were on a date had been pretty exhausting. I'd then probably confused them both with a speedy end to the evening, citing fatigue and work the next day.

By Friday night, I was exhausted, confused, and very much looking forward to a relaxing evening while Kay was out taking photos with Philip. A WhatsApp message popped up on my phone from Callie:

✉ Hi Elise & Clare
Hen do update: Contacted that adult playground
and I've managed to negotiate a great deal
that I'd like to run by you both.
Clare — I'm assuming you'll be over in 2
weeks' time for Sarah's birthday meal. Can we
meet up then? Unless you're over sooner????
How are you both getting on with your
tasks? xx

Damn! I'd been so wrapped up in my own little world that I'd completely forgotten that I had bridesmaid responsibilities. After our aborted meeting, Callie had set up the WhatsApp group so we could agree on the format for Sarah's hen do. I scrolled back up the messages to shed some light on what I'd been allocated, because I couldn't for the life of me remember. Oh yes, I was apparently going to look into reasonably priced accommodation and meals for two nights. It wasn't exactly a difficult task. Best get my act together.

Another message arrived from Clare:

✉ Moving into my new flat tomorrow so this
weekend's out and got a work thing the one
after. Will deffo be across for Sarah's
birthday meal. I wasn't planning to drive over
till Saturday afternoon but can come across
earlier. Done my research.

Clearly I was the weakest link on Team Bridesmaids. I cringed as I typed my response:

✉ I'm free that day. Research is going well x

More lies, but I couldn't face the risk of a lecture from Clare if I confessed I'd forgotten. We needed to maintain that truce. Callie replied:

✉ Brilliant! How about 10.30am in The Chocolate Pot two weeks' tomorrow? Bring all your info and we'll get it finalised. And I'll bring red cards in case you two kick off again! xx

I responded with a laughing emoji then put my phone down and rolled my weary shoulders. It was only eight, but my PJs were beckoning. I padded upstairs and changed, then loosened my hair clip, shaking my curls out. That felt good.

As I wiped cotton pads over my eyes to remove my make-up, I reflected on my midwife appointment after school. It had felt so alien actually saying the words, 'I'm pregnant' to someone for the first time, especially a complete stranger. I'd always imagined the first time I said those words aloud would be to Gary, having discovered I was expecting his baby. How things had changed.

I headed down to the lounge with a notepad and pen, flicked the TV on, then lit a couple of scented candles before curling up on the sofa. I wrote the dates on the top of the page but my mind kept drifting. I imagined the conversation with Daniel to tell him I was expecting his baby and how he might react. Definitely not very well. I imagined telling Sarah and having her lecture me for stealing the thunder from her wedding. I imagined not being able to fit into the bridesmaid dress we'd ordered and made a mental note to discreetly ask Ginny if she could change mine to a bigger size. That was a point. How pregnant would I be at the wedding?

I rolled off the sofa, wandered into the kitchen, took Kay's calendar off its hook and counted down the weeks. Twenty-one weeks or thereabouts. Five months. Did you show at five months? Jess was nearly that with the twins at her wedding and barely showed, but I had no idea if that was typical.

Logging onto my laptop, I asked Google. After checking out several sites, it seemed that, for a first baby, I probably wouldn't show too much although, of course, every pregnancy was different. Then I remembered a colleague looking heavily pregnant at that stage. Hmm. My baby would weigh about three quarters of a pound, be about twenty-six centimetres long and be properly kicking. I lifted my PJs top and stroked my stomach. Wow! That was hard to imagine. I wondered what baby was doing now. Clicking on another link, I discovered that, at about eight weeks pregnant, baby would be the size of a kidney bean.

'It's just you and me, baby bean,' I whispered. 'I promise I'll be a good mummy. I'll be completely different to my mother. I'll be such a good mummy that you won't miss having a daddy because I doubt very much that Daniel's going to want anything to do with you. In fact, I bet he'll want me to get rid of you like poor Amber's baby and there's no way I'm doing that. It's not your fault. I don't think we'll tell him for a long time yet. I don't think we'll tell anyone. We'll keep it as our little secret.'

A knock on the door startled me. I was in my PJs! I closed my laptop and grabbed a long grey cardigan Kay had left draped over the armchair. I pulled it tightly round me as I answered the door. 'Stevie? Hi.'

'Hi. Sorry for dropping by unannounced, but I was in the area.' He shook his head. 'That's a lie. I came especially to see you and to give you these.' He handed me a stunning bouquet of orange, yellow, and cream flowers.

'Thank you.' My heart thumped as I took them. 'They're beautiful. But what are they for?'

'Lots of reasons. Because you've been poorly, because you've had such a tough time lately and because you deserve to be spoiled. And I'd like to be the person to spoil you... if you'd let me.'

It wasn't fair. It was a good line and, under other circumstances, would have worked very well.

'Do you want to come in?' I was going to have to make it clear to him that a relationship wasn't on the cards. It wasn't fair of me to have avoided the subject on Tuesday night.

He nodded. 'Only if it's not too inconvenient.'

'You could never be an inconvenience.' His eyes caught mine and he looked hopeful for a moment. I imagined him giving me one of his super-hugs, but this time the feeling was accompanied by butterflies in my stomach. I hadn't had those before around Stevie. What was happening to me? It must be the hormones. Yes, that was it, a mix of hormones and vulnerability. It would go. Soon. I stepped back and indicated that he should step past me.

'Cup of tea?'

'Yes please.'

'Go through to the lounge and make yourself comfortable.'

Butterflies continued to dance as I gently placed the flowers in a vase while the kettle boiled. I jumped at another knock on the door. 'I won't be a minute,' I shouted to Stevie. 'I'll just see who that is.'

Pulling the cardigan round me again, I opened the front door. 'Michael?'

'I'm sorry to interrupt your evening,' he said, 'but I haven't been able to stop thinking about you. I bought you these.' He handed me a bouquet in pinks and purples.

'They're gorgeous, Michael, but—'

'Sorry, Elise, but can I just say something because I'm going to chicken out like I did on Wednesday if I don't get on with it?'

I gulped. 'Okay.' I glanced back down the hall towards the lounge. Could Stevie hear? Oh my goodness, what could I do? I couldn't shuffle up the hall and shut the lounge door without making Michael suspicious, I couldn't tell Michael to shut up, and I couldn't step outside in only my PJs and a cardigan.

Michael took a deep breath. 'I know I wasn't very friendly when we first met, but you know that was about Daniel rather than you. As I got to know you, I could tell you were different from the string of girls he usually brings home and I found myself liking you more and more. After what happened with Amber, I never wanted to let anyone get close to me again, but I realised I'd take that risk for you. I wanted to say this on Saturday, but I screwed up with that game your friend started so I asked you out this week to try and recover it, but I lost my nerve then too. I wanted to ask if you'd go out with me. Properly. On a date. Not just as friends.'

What a beautiful, heartfelt speech. A tear slipped down my cheek.

Michael chewed on his thumbnail. 'I've made you cry! Was it that bad?'

I shook my head and wiped at the rogue tear. 'No. It was lovely. I'm sorry, though. It has to be a no.'

'Is it because of Daniel?'

'It's not Daniel,' I said. 'It's not you either, Michael. It's me.' I groaned. 'I can't believe I just said that. It sounds like such a cliché and I don't mean it to. I can't give you a proper reason right now and I'm really sorry for that, but I can't get involved. I should have said so last night. You're not the only one who chickened out of things.'

'I thought there was something between us that night at the car park.'

There was! But I didn't want him to cling onto that and turn it into a ray of hope. 'I do like you, Michael, but just as a friend. In the car park, I think I was just caught up in the moment. I was upset. You were there for me.'

Michael nodded. 'Is it that other bloke from Saturday night? Are you seeing him?'

My stomach clenched and I hoped Stevie had the humanity to stay in the lounge and not punish Michael with an appearance in the hall. 'No, I'm not seeing him either. He's a good friend, though, and I'd like to think you and I can be friends too.' I groaned again. 'Another cliché! I genuinely mean it, though. I really, really like you and I'd like us to be friends, but I understand if you'd rather not. I can't offer you any more than that, though.'

Michael nodded slowly. 'That's a definite no, isn't it?'

'Sorry.'

He shrugged. 'Friends it is, then. But I may need some space to get you out of my head.'

My heart sank. What had I done to the poor guy? He took one more long, sad look into my eyes. 'I'd better go. Goodbye, Elise.' He leaned forward and gently kissed me on the cheek.

'Goodbye, Michael,' I whispered as I closed the door.

'You went out with Michael this week too?' I jumped and turned round. Stevie stood in the lounge doorway, a strained expression on his face.

'You heard everything?'

He nodded.

'I'm sorry, Stevie. You both asked me out after the party. I agreed to see you on consecutive nights so I could let you both down lightly, but I chickened out.'

'So what you said to Michael applies to me too? You're not interested in me either?'

I leaned against the door and slowly slid to the floor, my legs feeling like they were made of liquid.

'I *am* interested.' Tears filled my eyes again. 'But I can't get involved with either of you. I can't allow myself to think about it and the reason I can't allow myself to think about it is the reason I can't get involved, and I know that sounds like absolute gibberish, but it's the best I've got right now so you can bloody well take it or leave it, but it's all you're going to get.' The last few words were barely audible as, for the first time since discovering

I was pregnant, the pain, confusion and frustration bubbled over into hysterical sobs.

'Hey!' Stevie dashed to my side and gathered me in his arms. He stroked my back and my hair and rocked me gently while I clung onto him and cried for my husband's betrayal, Daniel's betrayal, my fatherless baby, and the tangled web of deceit I'd weaved.

'It's all right.' He stroked my hair away from my face. 'I'm here for you.'

His face was so close to mine that I could see a spattering of freckles across his nose and cheeks. The tenderness in his eyes was beguiling and, next minute, his lips were on mine. Had I kissed him first or had he kissed me? Who knew, but I wanted him so badly and I could tell from the urgency in his kiss that he felt the same.

One of his hands reached into my hair and the other round my back, pulling me even closer until it felt like our bodies were moving as one just like it had felt with Daniel that night on the beach. *No! Daniel! The baby!*

I pulled away suddenly. 'I can't do this, Stevie. I'm so sorry. You'd better leave.' I scrambled to my feet, heart racing, breathing laboured.

'I'm sorry,' he said, standing up too. He looked at me with such an expression of sadness that I felt the tears welling in my eyes.

He shook his head. 'I shouldn't have done that, especially after what you'd just said. I really am sorry.'

'Please don't blame yourself. It isn't anything you've done wrong. Believe me, it's all me.' *And Daniel.* I pulled open the door.

Stevie took my hand in his and gently squeezed it, then tenderly pushed a tendril of hair away from my cheek. 'You know where I am if you need me,' he said softly, giving me an apologetic smile that didn't even show his dimples.

I nodded, fighting hard against the urge to pull him to me and kiss him again. 'I'm sorry,' I whispered.

Shoulders slumped, he stepped outside. 'See you around.'

I shut the door quickly and slumped against it, tears trickling down my cheeks. *Damn, damn, damn!*

30

✉ From Sarah
Hi Elise. Are you OK? I've left messages with
Auntie Kay and on your voicemail, but you
haven't returned my calls. I've been round a
few times and found nobody in. I'm worried
about you. Are you still poorly? Stevie says
he's seen you, but he's being cagey about it.
Has something happened between you two? Sorry
to pry and sorry to quiz you by text, but I
can't get hold of you any other way. Please
get in touch to let me know you're OK xxxxxx

✉ To Sarah
I'm fine. I promise. Sorry I haven't returned
your calls. Really busy week at school. I'll
come round on Wednesday if my slot's still
free! Xx

✉ From Sarah

Phew. My door's open for you any time. See you
on Wednesday xx

Early evening on Wednesday, I walked up and down Castle
Street four times before I felt brave enough to knock on the door
to Seaside Blooms. It was time to tell Sarah about the baby. I'd
cancelled on her and avoided her so much lately that she'd
probably thought I was still upset about her getting married
while I got divorced. It wasn't fair on her and it wasn't the type of
person I was. *Must tell Sarah about the baby. No more lies. Must tell
Sarah about the baby.*

'Elise! Thank God you're here. You won't believe what's
happened.' She pulled me into the shop and locked the door.

I followed her into The Outback and sat on the battered
leather chair while she heaved herself onto the desk. The last
time we'd sat at the desk together had been about ten months
before when she'd just taken over the shop. How things had
changed during that time. She was getting married in twelve-
and-a-half weeks and I was getting divorced and having a baby.

'What's happened, then?' I asked, eager to buy time before I
shared my news.

Sarah rolled her eyes. 'What hasn't happened? Serious wedding
trauma.' She told me a long convoluted tale about a double-booked
wedding car, out-of-stock favours, the suit-hire shop losing the
order for the men's morning suits, and the invite printers going bust
after she'd paid a deposit. To be fair to her, it did sound like she was
having a rough ride with pretty much everything going wrong that
could go wrong. I knew how important it was to her to get her day
perfect, but I couldn't fully concentrate. The only thing on my mind
was saying the words 'I'm pregnant' to her and, after what she'd
been through, I was worried that it might tip her over the edge.

'And to top it all,' she continued, 'Callie's only gone and
announced that she's pregnant.'

I sat upright. 'Callie's what?'

'She's pregnant. I've had to order her dress in a bigger size and then there was a huge panic because the manufacturer told Ginny they'd already made them and they'd have to charge me for both sizes which was going to be a financial disaster after losing the deposit on the invites.' She paused for breath and I bit my lip, realising I'd forgotten to ask Ginny about ordering me a bigger size. Looked like that was going to be a costly moment of forgetfulness.

'Could Callie pay?' I suggested.

Sarah shook her head. 'I wouldn't have asked her. Money's tight for them as it is and, with a baby on the way, they'll need every penny. Thankfully there's no need. Turns out I was just in time.'

'Crisis averted, then?' I made a mental note to send Ginny a message on Facebook as soon as I got home.

'Well, that part is,' Sarah said, 'but Callie's got terrible sickness so she might have to drop out of being a bridesmaid altogether if it doesn't improve.'

My eyes widened. 'You're sacking her for being pregnant?'

Sarah laughed. 'Of course not! As if I'd do something so mean. It was Callie's suggestion. She's terrified of standing at the front of the church and projectile vomiting all over my wedding dress so she suggested she'd be better off at the back of the church where she can make a swift exit if needed.'

Was now the right moment to throw another pregnant bridesmaid into the mix? It didn't feel like it. Although Sarah was making a joke of it, I knew how stressed and worried she'd be about getting everything perfect for her big day. Maybe if I stuck to the subject of pregnancy, a more appropriate moment would present itself.

'I didn't realise they wanted a family so soon,' I said. Callie and Rhys were about to celebrate their first wedding anniversary and I could have sworn she'd told me they wanted to be married for three or four years before trying for a baby.

Sarah fiddled with a pen she'd removed from a tub on the desk, clicking it on and off. 'They didn't, but apparently some friends have had an IVF baby recently after trying for five years to conceive naturally. They hadn't considered the possibility that it might take ages or might not happen at all so they decided to ditch the protection and, of course, it happened immediately. They're acting like it's the most unexpected thing in the world.'

I flinched. 'Unexpected pregnancies happen.'

'Yeah, when you're using protection, but when you're not using anything, what do you expect? And Rhys should have known better.'

'Why?'

'Because he knows he's fertile. He's already a dad.'

I frowned. 'Is he?'

'He's Megan's dad. Didn't you know that?'

'Megan who?'

Sarah shook her head, frowning at me. 'Are you having a senior moment? Izzy's daughter? Bridesmaid at Jess's wedding? Ring any bells?'

Izzy? Yes, she rang lots of bells. Especially the one marked 'Lock up your boyfriends'. I knew she wasn't entirely to blame for what happened at Jess's wedding because Daniel would have charmed the pants off her – literally – but she'd known he was my boyfriend so she should have kept them firmly in place. 'The subject of Megan's dad never came up and I never asked. None of my business.'

'Well, now you know.' Sarah put the pen back in the pot and stretched. 'Sorry. I've not stopped moaning since you arrived, have I? It's been a fraught few weeks and I promise I'm going to shut up about the wedding now. I think I just needed to offload, particularly after Callie's announcement. How are you? You still look a bit pale.'

Yes, and that probably had a lot to do with the bombshell she'd just dropped. I could hardly make my announcement now. 'Still not a hundred per cent,' I said.

'Did you go to the doctor's?'

'Yes.'

'And?'

I chose my words carefully. 'She said there's nothing wrong with me. I need to take it easy for a while and allow things to run their natural course.'

'Oh. Stevie said he saw you on Friday...'

My heart raced at the mention of his name. 'You've been talking about me?'

'In passing.'

'What did he say?'

'Not a lot. I'm guessing he asked you out and you said no. Or something like that.'

'Something like that,' I muttered. 'You might as well know that Michael asked me out too. Unless you already know that.' It came out a little snappier than I intended it to and I could tell from the guilty expression that she did know. I really didn't want to talk about it. The image of Michael's hurt expression when I offered him only friendship, followed by that brief moment of passion in the hallway with Stevie had been haunting me.

'And...?' Sarah prompted when I remained silent.

I shrugged. 'And I turned him down too.'

'I thought you liked him. And Stevie. I wondered if you going out with them both last week was about helping you decide which—'

I tutted loudly. 'For God's sake, is there anything you don't know about my comings and goings over the past week?'

'Sorry.' Sarah twiddled with her engagement ring. 'I wasn't prying, but where do you think both bouquets came from?'

'Oh! I never thought... Sorry.' I gave her a sheepish smile. 'I'm sorry for that outburst. I've had a tough week. I like them both, but I don't want to get involved with anyone right now. I want some time alone.'

'Because of what Daniel did?'

'You could say that.'

My phone rang. 'Sorry, Sarah. Kay, hi, are you okay?'

'Gary's here,' she said.

'Really? Why?'

'He wouldn't say. He's really upset. Can you get here?'

'Yes. See you in about ten minutes.'

I stood up. 'Gary's at Seashell Cottage. I have to go. Lovely catching up. Same time next week?'

She shook her head. 'Sorry. I can't do next week.'

'No worries. I'll see you a week on Saturday for your birthday meal, then.'

* * *

As I dashed back towards Seashell Cottage, my mind flitted between two things: why was Gary at Seashell Cottage and what the heck was I going to do now that Callie had announced her pregnancy? I'd felt relieved when Sarah told me about Callie and I realised I couldn't share my news. Why had I felt that way? I chewed it over for a few minutes before I found the answer. Because I still didn't know how I felt about the baby myself. Was I sad about it? No. Was I happy? No. I just felt so... so... I searched around for the right word... numb. Yes, that was it. Like it was happening to someone else and not me.

The front door opened as I headed down the garden path and Kay stepped outside. 'He's in the lounge. He's in a bit of a state.'

'Do you know why?'

'He wouldn't say. I hope I did the right thing by calling you.'

'Of course you did. Where are you going?'

'For a walk.'

'It's your house, Kay. We can't kick you out.'

'I could do with the exercise and I might get some nice photos.' She patted my arm. 'I'll be back in a couple of hours. Don't let him upset you, though. You look exhausted.'

'I am.'

I found Gary pacing up and down the lounge. 'She knows,' he said as soon as I walked into the room. 'We were so careful yet she knows. How does she know? Did you tell her?' Then he burst into tears.

I ran to him and held him tightly.

'I take it you mean your mother?' I asked when he'd calmed down enough to be led to the sofa to sit down.

He nodded.

'I didn't tell her. I said I wouldn't and I kept my promise. I take it you didn't tell her about you and Rob when I suggested it?'

He shook his head. 'The timing never seemed right.'

I nearly laughed at the appropriateness of that statement given the conversation I'd just avoided with Sarah. 'With your mother, the timing would never have been right. What did she say?'

He wiped his face with the tissue I offered. 'What didn't she say? The language. It was like she was possessed. She said I was as evil as Lloyd and that we were now both dead to her because of our sins. She started ranting about HIV and AIDS and how that would be God's punishment to me for my "abnormal behaviour". What sort of person would say a thing like that to her son?' Tears coursed down his cheeks again and I took his shaking hand in mine.

'I'm sorry,' I said. 'I really am. You know I've never been her biggest fan, but that's worse than I could ever have expected from her. Have you told Rob?'

'Not yet. He'd have stormed round and told her exactly what he thought of her. I'll tell him, but I need to be less emotional about it. The only person I knew who'd understand was you. I know it's asking a lot after—'

'Stop right there. You came to the right place. You were there during my mother's finest hour and I'm here for you during Cynthia's.'

I made him a cup of tea and we talked about his encounter with Cynthia, how guilty he felt for not making more of an effort with Lloyd who he now realised would have had a far rougher time at the receiving end of his mother's prejudices than he'd ever imagined, and how tough an existence his father must have had being married to such an opinionated, narrow-minded woman.

'What about you and Rob?' I asked. 'How's that going?'

Gary raised an eyebrow. 'You really want to know?'

Did I? Actually, I did. I'd accepted our marriage was over some time ago, but I think I'd also come to terms with the reason. Was that because of my fling with Daniel or because I had more important things to focus on now? 'Yes,' I said. 'I really want to know.'

'It's going really well, actually. We're... No, it doesn't matter.'

'Go on. I promise not to have hysterics.'

'No. You don't want to hear this. I shouldn't have said anything.'

'You can't leave it there, Gary. Let me guess. You're moving in together. Am I right?'

'We've been looking at a few flats on Sea Cliff.'

A couple of months back – perhaps even a few weeks back – that information would have floored me yet, strangely, it didn't. I actually felt happy for him.

'What are you smiling at?' he asked.

'You. Despite the trauma with your mother, you look so content. It's nice.'

He smiled. 'I *am* content. I thought you'd be upset.'

'So did I. A lot has happened over the last few months and I think I'm finally in a place where I can accept it and move on.'

'And have you moved on?'

'By which you mean is there someone else?'

'I suppose so. Is it that guy from Bean Cuisine?'

'It was, but that's all over. I think he was my Getting Over Gary prescription and, for a while, he was exactly what the doctor ordered. It's just me on my own for the moment and I'm quite happy with that.'

We sat there smiling at each other for a while. 'Are you okay, now?' I said eventually.

'I will be. I think my mum has shown her true colours and my priority right now is to get to know my brother and his family.'

'I'm so glad you've said that. I always wanted you to reach out to Lloyd and Zoe.'

'Did you? You never said.'

I shrugged. 'I never said a lot of things, particularly where your family were concerned, and I regret that now. I've been seeing Jem again. He says I shouldn't have regrets. I should have learnings. I've learned a lot from our marriage, and I've learned a lot since. I hope it's all made me stronger. Why are you looking at me like that?'

Gary had tilted his head slightly to one side, with an amused smile on his lips. 'You're different.'

'Oh. Good different or bad different?'

'Good different. I can see glimpses of the girl I knew at school and college, but with added wisdom and maturity. I like it. You seem stronger.'

'I feel stronger. Thank you.'

Gary stood up. 'I've taken enough of your time. I'd better go.'

I stood up too. 'I'm sure she'll come running back to you when she realises she's completely screwed up and she's a very lonely woman with no family.' I didn't care that it sounded harsh; she deserved it.

'I hope so,' he said. 'Thank you. You've been a great help. Does this mean we can be friends again?'

'Come here, you.' I hugged him. 'We've always been friends and we always will be. I think that's why our relationship worked for so long. It's been good to have some time apart while I got over the hurt. I'd like to think that we can find our way back to the friendship that started this whole thing off and that I'll be able to forgive Rob.'

'I'd like that.' He walked towards the front door then turned to face me. 'Thanks. You've shown great dignity throughout all of this. You're an amazing woman.'

'I'm not sure I handled it with dignity at the start but thank you.'

'Are you okay, by the way? You look tired.'

I smiled. 'I've had a bit of sickness recently, but I'm improving.'

'Have you seen a doctor?'

'Yes. I'm sure you'll understand that I've registered elsewhere, but I'm absolutely fine thank you, Dr Dawson.'

'You're sure? I want you to be happy too.'

'I know.' I took hold of his hand and smiled. 'And I really think I'm going to be. It's been a tough few months, but the future's looking bright.'

I reached around him and opened the door. We hugged again before he headed home to Rob.

As I washed the mugs, I reflected on our parting words. It really was going to be okay. I didn't feel quite so numb anymore. Talking to Gary about Rob hadn't hurt. Talking about being friends had felt like a real possibility. It felt like I'd closed a door on my old life with Gary and opened up a new one on my life with baby bean. I was going to have a baby and I was going to love it whether or not Daniel wanted to be in its life. And I would never, ever, show such contempt and disrespect for my child as Gary's mother had to her two boys, no matter what challenges or diversity it brought into our lives. We'd get through everything together because I would love this baby. In that moment, I also knew that, despite the concerns I'd shared with Jem, I would never, ever be like my mother.

I stroked my stomach. Gary's proposition to have his baby hadn't felt right, but somehow this scenario finally did.

31

The next week-and-a-half flew by – ten days of keeping my secret from everyone. I didn't hear from Michael or Stevie, not that I expected to, although butterflies soared in my stomach every time I thought about Sarah's birthday meal, knowing Stevie would be there.

I met Clare and Callie on the Saturday morning to finalise the plans for Sarah's hen do and to book everything. It was all very civilised, which was a relief, because I couldn't have faced a bust-up with Clare.

Sarah's birthday wasn't until the following Friday but she was providing the flowers for several events that weekend so had decided to have her birthday celebrations the week before.

'Happy Birthday to you, Happy Birthday to you...'

Sarah took her seat at the head of the table in Le Bistro – a cosy restaurant a few streets back from the seafront – while twenty or so friends, colleagues, and family members sang to her.

'Thank you so much for coming,' she said. 'It was my thirtieth birthday last year and I didn't do anything because I didn't feel like there was anything to celebrate. A year later, I have a new business, a fiancé, new family, and new friends.' She looked round the group, nodding. 'What a difference a year makes. Thank you all for being part of it.'

Yes, indeed. What a difference a year makes. Sarah had split up with her boyfriend on her thirtieth birthday, hopped on the train home, and had been presented with Kay's proposal to take over Seaside Blooms. Now she had a thriving business and was planning her wedding.

To stop me dwelling on how much my own life had also changed during that year, I retrieved the gift bag containing Sarah's present from under my chair, walked round the table, then crouched down beside her. 'Happy birthday,' I said.

She smiled. 'Thank you. Can I save it till Friday?'

'Of course you can.'

After hugging her, I returned to my seat opposite Jess and Lee. Ginny from The Wedding Emporium was seated beside me, which made me feel on edge. I'd messaged her about changing the size of my dress, telling her that I'd lost weight after the stress of splitting up with Gary, but had put it back on now and was worried the size I'd ordered wouldn't fit. I'd felt quite distressed at how easily another lie had materialised. It gave me some insight into Gary's world, though. Once you started lying, it was so hard to stop. You had to create new lies to cover old ones. I'd casually suggested that it may be a good idea not to mention anything to Sarah after so many disruptions to her plans already. Ginny had replied saying that I was just in time with the change and that she agreed there was no reason for Sarah to know. I couldn't help panicking that she might suddenly drop it into conversation over dinner. I knew it was ridiculous to worry about it, but I couldn't help it.

A burst of laughter drew my eyes further up the table to where Stevie was seated with Clare to one side of him and Ben to the other. The three of them were creased up with laughter. I watched as Stevie wiped tears from his dimpled cheeks and found myself wishing that I'd been the one to make him laugh like that. His sparkling eyes and dimples were such a turn-on. A hot flush creeping up my body, I grabbed my water and took a big gulp.

An oily olive bounced off my forearm, making me jump.

'Have you heard a single thing I just said?' Jess demanded.

I hadn't even been aware that she was talking to me. I took another glance down the table and caught Stevie's eye. He gave me a gentle, reassuring smile. At least he wasn't ignoring me. I turned back to Jess. 'Sorry. I'm all ears now.'

Ten minutes later, our starters arrived. Jess sniffed the air like a Bisto Kid and pointed to my plate. 'Hmm, soft cheese. Now that's something I can't wait to gorge on when these two appear.'

I laughed as I cut open my deep-fried Camembert, salivating as the warm cheese oozed out of the breadcrumbs, then her words actually registered with me. Soft cheese? Pregnancy? Oh no! How could I have been so stupid? I couldn't eat it. Yet I was starving. I pushed it around my plate then hid it under some lettuce leaves, hoping nobody would notice. I think I'd have got away with it if it hadn't been for a well-meaning waiter when it came to plate-clearing time. Was there something wrong with it? Was it not to my taste? I felt like everyone on the table was watching me.

'It was delicious,' I insisted, 'but I'm not very hungry. I need to save my appetite for my main course.'

'Please, madam, tell me if there was something wrong. I'll tell the chef.'

'No, no, it's lovely. Really, it is. It's just me. Please take it.' Thankfully he stopped debating and removed the offending item.

My stomach churned and I needed fresh air. I politely excused myself and tried to walk with dignity and grace away from the table, legs wobbling, stomach churning. *Mints.* I grabbed a handful from the bowl by the till and hadn't even made it out of the door before I'd unwrapped one and stuffed it into my mouth.

There was a chill in the air as I stepped outside, which probably explained why there was nobody seated at the metal tables. Taking a deep breath, I sat down at the furthest table, which was surrounded by wooden trellises covered in climbing plants. I sucked on my mint and waited for the nausea to subside. I unwrapped another one, shoved it in my mouth, then sat forward, resting my head in my hands.

'You're pregnant, aren't you?'

I looked up, startled, as Clare pulled out the seat next to me and sat down.

'Of course not. Why would you...?' But I stopped as I looked into her curious eyes. What was the point in denying it? I sighed, 'Yes. How did you know?'

'It was the cheese tonight. I heard what Jess said and I saw your face.'

I bit my lip. 'Do you think anyone else noticed? I don't want them to know.'

'No. I think your secret's safe,' she said, gently. 'How far will you be?'

'A little over ten weeks.'

'I'm assuming that, if you're avoiding drink and being careful with food, you're planning on keeping the baby?'

'Ending it isn't an option for me. I couldn't do that. It's not the baby's fault that it wasn't planned. You probably think I'm doing the wrong thing, don't you?'

Clare sat back and glared at me. 'Have you learned nothing from our fight? You really think I'd recommend a termination?'

'No. Not *recommend* as such. It's not a judgement about it. I just thought you hated kids so that's maybe what you'd do if you were in my situation.'

'I don't hate kids.'

'But Sarah told me you call babies gremlins and can't bear to be around them. I just assumed that—'

'It's easier that way. I don't have to—' She stopped and cleared her throat. 'Ten weeks, you say? Not Gary's. Unless...? Okay, stop shaking your head. Not Gary's. Daniel's?'

I nodded and chewed on my lip again.

'So you're ten weeks pregnant with Daniel's baby and nobody knows. What happens next?'

'Is that true?'

I jumped at the male voice and looked up into his pained eyes. My heart thumped.

'I asked you a question. Is it true that you're pregnant with my brother's baby?' His voice was thick with emotion, his face pale, his body shaking.

I stood up. 'Michael. I'm sorry. I...' But what was there to say?

'Don't,' he snapped. 'I don't want to hear it. Give this to my dad.' He thrust something into my hands, turned, and marched out of the seating area.

'Michael!' I glanced at Clare.

'Go after him,' she hissed, grabbing the item off me.

'Michael!'

He'd rounded the corner and was striding up Sandy Bank towards town by the time I caught him. 'Michael! Please talk to me.'

He turned round, his face pale except for a bright red patch on each cheek. 'I know you said we could only be friends, but I hoped that, with time, you'd start to think of me as more than that. I'm so bloody stupid. First Amber. Now you. And my bastard brother has to screw things up with both of you.'

'I'm sorry. I never wanted to hurt you.'

'And neither did Amber, yet somehow I'm stuck in Groundhog Day with two severe cases of unrequited love where the women I care about choose that two-timing shit over me, he ruins their lives, and I'm expected to pick up the pieces.'

I reached out and touched his arm, but he shrugged me off. 'Please don't touch me. I can't do this. I can't be friends with you.'

'I'm not with Daniel, though. I ended it.'

'But it's not over. You're carrying his baby. I wish you well, Elise, I really do, but I can't be there to watch you bring up my brother's baby.'

'I'm sorry you had to find out like this.'

'So am I.' He turned to walk away, then spun back to face me again. 'Does he know?'

I shook my head. 'Please don't tell him.'

'I won't. You do know he won't want anything to do with it, don't you?'

I nodded. 'I'm counting on it.'

My heart thumped as he held my gaze. Then he turned and disappeared up a side street.

'I'm sorry,' I whispered as I leaned against a lamppost, fighting another wave of nausea. It wasn't my fault he'd overheard Clare and me, but it didn't stop me feeling wretched with guilt.

A warm hand slipped into mine. 'I wanted to make sure you were okay,' Clare said. 'Are you?'

A tear slipped down my cheek. 'I'm not actually sure.'

Then, for the first time ever, Clare hugged me and in that one moment I felt all the bad feeling between us pale into insignificance. The woman holding me didn't seem like the bitchy man-eater I'd always put her down as; she seemed like a sensitive and warm person who I actually liked. At that moment, she was also a person who I really, really needed. Who knew?

32

October half-term couldn't have arrived soon enough for me two weeks later. I was exhausted. My first trimester had taken it out of me, not helped by the start of a new academic year and getting ready to complete on the house sale.

I'd realised it was unfair to expect Gary to pack up the whole house, so I'd agreed to spend most evenings during the last fortnight sorting, dividing up, selling or giving away our belongings. What an emotionally draining experience that had been, properly saying goodbye to our life together. It had also been good for my relationship with Gary. We'd talked more than we'd talked for years, and he'd managed to fully convince me that, even though he knew he was gay, he'd been happy as my husband for the first ten years thanks to the friendship we'd shared. It was comforting to know that our marriage hadn't been a complete and utter failure.

I'd told Graham about my pregnancy. As my boss, he needed to know for health and safety reasons. The hopeful look in his eyes that Gary and I had overcome our differences was painful, and telling him that Gary wasn't the father was embarrassing, but if he judged me, he didn't let on.

I still wasn't ready to tell anyone else, though. I'd come close to confiding in Gary, but I bottled it. Clare, as the only other knowledgeable party other than my midwife and Jem (and Michael, of course), had been true to her word and kept the secret. She'd even taken to texting me to ask how I was and when I was having my scan. I exchanged the occasional text with Curtis, but I didn't mention the baby.

My first scan was timed nicely for half-term. It was scheduled for shortly after two o'clock on the Tuesday afternoon. I awoke with butterflies in my stomach. The nerves didn't settle all day and I seemed to be permanently traipsing to the bathroom, even before I had to take on the obligatory extra fluid an hour before my scan.

Kay had gone to York for a spot of early Christmas shopping with her friend Linda, which was a relief as she'd have soon noticed that something was afoot. I was a little surprised she hadn't noticed already because usually nothing got past her. She did seem distracted with her photography, though. And Philip. She was adamant that it was just friendship, but I'd watched them playfully flirting with each other at Sarah's birthday meal and had seen them together several times since. She could deny it all she wanted, but love was definitely in the air.

As I arrived at the hospital, a thought struck me. What if they told me that something was wrong with baby bean? My legs instantly turned to jelly and I had to slow down to steady myself. I felt sick at the thought and suddenly regretted my decision not to tell Sarah, Gary, Jess, or Dad what I was going through in case I needed them to pick up the pieces. I didn't want to go through this alone. If there was a problem, I wasn't sure that I was strong enough to cope on my own. Stupid, stupid decision. Stupid secret. Stupid lies.

Arriving outside the ultrasound department, I pushed the door open, then burst into tears when I saw who was waiting for me.

'I know someone who went through this alone.' Clare hugged me. 'It was hard for her and she could have used some moral support. I thought you might feel the same and, assuming I'm still the only one other than Michael who knows about the baby, I'm the only one who can give you that.' She let me go and indicated that I should sit down.

'I'm glad you're here,' I said when she sat next to me. 'I'm having a panic. What if something's wrong with the baby?'

'Then something's wrong with the baby and we'll cross that bridge. You'll know either way within about ten minutes and there'll be nothing you can do about it. What will be will be.'

Normally I hated Clare's tell-it-like-it-is approach, but her words were surprisingly comforting and just what I needed to make me wipe my eyes, blow my nose, and pull myself together.

'Elise Morgan?'

It took me a moment to register that the young brunette holding a file and looking round the waiting room was calling for me. I hadn't officially reverted to my maiden name, but I planned to. I'd decided it would save complications later if I started my pregnancy as Morgan. 'Sorry, that's me.'

She smiled. 'We're in room two. My name's Dawn and I'll be your sonographer today.'

Clare followed me and sat by the bed as Dawn explained the process. When I lay down, she took hold of my hand.

'Is it your first baby?' Dawn asked, looking from me to Clare then back to me.

Clare giggled. 'We're not together, you know.'

Dawn blushed. 'Oh, sorry. You just looked very close.'

Clare and I looked at each other and grinned. 'Would you believe it if I said we hated each other until recently?' I asked.

'They say love and hate are very close emotions,' Dawn said, then blushed again. 'Not that I'm suggesting you love each other. I think I'm going to stop talking now and focus on finding this baby of yours. This might feel a little cold.'

The sensation of the cold gel on my stomach made me squirm, but all feelings of discomfort soon went as the sound of a steady heartbeat filled the room and a grainy shape appeared on the screen.

'Oh, this is good,' Dawn said. 'Baby's laid in a really good position today.' She pointed to various different parts of the image, telling me that we were looking at baby bean's head or spine or legs. I wasn't really paying attention to what she said. All I could think was that I was looking at a baby. My baby. The one thing I'd desperately wanted for so many years, but which my husband had refused to give me. Now I had the baby but no husband and I didn't actually care. All I cared about was that tiny little blurred being with the rapid heartbeat. My family.

I turned to look at Clare, but she wasn't looking at me. She was staring at the screen, mesmerised, a single tear running down her right cheek. I looked back at the screen, but I didn't feel tearful. I felt elated.

'Thank you,' I said to Clare as we left the ultrasound department. I was genuinely touched by her unexpected support. 'You've been amazing, both today and at Sarah's birthday. I really appreciate it.'

'I'll be sending you a bill,' she said. 'When will you be telling people? I won't say anything, but it would be good to know.'

'Not till after the wedding.'

'Won't you be showing by then?'

'Maybe, but I'm hoping it won't be too obvious. I wear maxi dresses a lot anyway so I should be able to hide it.'

Clare sighed. 'Maybe, but the bridesmaid dresses *aren't* maxi dresses.'

I grimaced. 'I know, but they're not tight-fitting and I ordered a bigger one to give me that bit more space.'

'It's your choice, but it's a long time to keep something like this a secret.'

'I know. I don't want to steal Jess's thunder with the twins and I don't want to steal Sarah's about the wedding so, if I can, I'd rather wait.'

'I hear you, but will you not be placing a heap of unnecessary pressure on yourself by keeping this a secret? I know most people stay quiet until the first scan, just in case, but you know the baby's well now. This is the time people usually make the big announcement.'

'I know, but Sarah got so stressed about Callie's pregnancy that I really don't want her to worry about mine too. And I mean it about not stealing Jess's and Sarah's thunder. There's no need for me to take the attention away from them when I can wait to announce my news after their big events. Does that make any sort of sense to you?'

Clare nodded. 'You are way, way, way too nice to people. I still think you'd be better off just getting the news out there, but it's your decision. I won't say anything, but I'd urge you to reconsider. People could get upset.'

'Thank you.'

We arrived in the lobby and discovered we were parked in different directions.

'I'll be going, then,' Clare said, 'but keep me updated and let me know if you need to talk. Apparently, it can be a pretty emotional thing, this pregnancy bollocks.'

I laughed. 'If I want to talk about my pregnancy bollocks, I'll be sure to look you up!'

I didn't feel like returning to an empty Seashell Cottage. Instead, I wanted some time to think about my pregnancy and telling people about it. Maybe Clare was right and I should make an announcement. Daniel had a right to hear first, though, and it was the sort of news that warranted a face-to-face conversation. A difficult one. And I still didn't feel ready to face it or to face him.

Driving to Lighthouse Cove, I parked so I could look out to the calm sea and clear blue sky. I fished the scan photo out of my handbag. 'Hi bean. I'm so relieved you're okay.' I ran my finger around the outline of his or her tiny body then propped up the image on the dashboard.

I leapt as someone knocked on the passenger window about ten minutes later, then relaxed when I saw it was Stevie... well, relaxed as much as I could with my stomach doing somersaults at the sight of him. I hadn't seen him since Sarah's birthday meal and clearly my feelings hadn't changed during that time.

'I thought it was you,' he said, poking his head through the window that I'd wound down. 'What are you doing here?'

'Just thinking. You?'

'I've been for a run. It's a bit nippy, though.' He shivered. 'Don't let that blue sky deceive you.'

'Get in before you catch a chill.'

'Thanks.' He settled into the passenger seat as I pressed the button to close the window. 'You said you were thinking. About anything in particular?'

I couldn't help myself. My eyes flicked to the scan photo on the dashboard. Stevie reached for the photo and studied it for a moment, nodding slowly. I held my breath, waiting for his reaction, heart thumping.

'I guess this answers my question,' he said, still looking at the scan. 'And it would explain why you turned down both Michael and me.'

I nodded. 'It wouldn't have been fair to get involved when I knew I was pregnant.'

Stevie stared at the scan, a wistful expression on his face, then he gently placed it back on the dashboard.

'I'm sorry,' I said.

He turned to me, looking surprised. 'What for?'

'For not telling you the truth at the time.'

He smiled, but his dimples barely showed. 'I know now. Do you want to talk about it?'

I bit my lip and shrugged. 'There isn't much to say. I'm nearly thirteen weeks pregnant with Daniel's baby. He doesn't know yet. I don't want anything from him, but I think he has a right to know. The only other people who know about it are Clare, Michael, Jem, and my Head and I'd like to keep it that way for now.'

'I understand your Head would need to know, and Jem's your counsellor, right?'

I nodded.

'So confiding in him makes sense, but Clare and Michael seem unlikely choices.'

'Tell me about it. Clare guessed when we were out for Sarah's birthday. Michael came to drop his dad's camera off and over-heard her. He kind of lost the plot with me.'

'I *knew* you were upset that night,' Stevie said. 'That's why, isn't it? Clare said you'd exchanged words with Michael outside. It was about the baby, wasn't it?'

I nodded. 'It wasn't pretty.'

Stevie glanced towards the scan again. 'How come nobody else knows?'

'Because my sister's pregnant and my best friend's getting married and I want them to enjoy their moments without me stealing their thunder with yet another unexpected turn of events. I think the gay husband was enough of a surprise without me announcing my pregnancy by a five-timing, friend-thumping, rebound-relationship cretin.'

Stevie smiled and, this time, his dimples showed. 'I take it there's no chance of a reconciliation with Daniel, then?'

'Gosh, no! Never in a million years. I always knew it wasn't love but, after what he did to you, I wasn't sure I even liked him. The... er... the deed was already done at that point.'

'How do you think Daniel will react?'

'Not well. I expect he'll want me to end it and, when I refuse to do that, he'll want nothing to do with the baby, which is absolutely fine by me, but a shame for the baby. I already feel bad that baby bean won't have a father figure in his or her life.' I sighed. 'But I'll try to do my best to make sure they don't miss out. You won't tell anyone, will you?'

'Of course not. How are you feeling?'

'The nausea has subsided a bit so that's a relief. I'm a bit scared, but I'm also really excited. I know I may not look it right now, but that's because I'm still a little shell-shocked at seeing baby bean for the first time. It's starting to feel more real.'

Stevie touched my hand and a shockwave passed through me, sending my pulse racing. 'Congratulations. I know how much having a baby means to you.'

'Thank you. It's not exactly the way I'd have chosen to do it, but I don't think anything that's happened this year is the way I'd have chosen.'

'Yeah, it's been a tough year for you.' We both stared out at the sea. 'Unexpected events usually make us stronger, though. They test us and they help us know ourselves.'

'Very profound, and very true.'

We sat in silence, still staring out at the waves.

'Can I ask you a question?' Stevie said after a while. 'You don't have to answer if you don't want to.'

'I'll try to.'

He turned in his seat to face me. 'If you hadn't found out about the baby, would you have considered... I mean, would I have stood any... erm... would you...?'

My heart raced so fast, I felt like it might explode, as I held his gaze. 'I would.' Was he going to ask me out anyway, despite the baby? What would I say? I wanted to say yes, but it was hardly fair on him, was it?

Stevie looked away and cleared his throat. 'I think I've imposed on your thinking time for long enough, so I'll head home and leave you to it. Your secret's safe with me. Look after yourself.' Then he exited Bertie and ran off down The Headland without a backwards glance.

I leaned back in my seat and sighed as I watched Stevie disappear into the distance, my heart sinking, then I picked up the scan photo. 'If it hadn't been for you, baby bean, Stevie and I might be together. I think we know that Michael was just a crush, don't we, and Stevie was always something a bit more special?'

Oh well, it wasn't going to happen now. He'd just proved that by running away. I suppose I had to give him credit for not running off immediately because he'd probably wanted to. 'From now on, bean, it's just you and me against the world.' I looked at the waves again. 'There's always hope, though. One day, maybe...'

I gently placed the scan in my bag then drove back to Seashell Cottage where I should have done some marking. Instead, I searched online for buggies, cots and Moses baskets. For the first time, I started to feel like a mum.

When I lay down to sleep that evening, though, all I could think about was Stevie and the hopeful look in his eyes when he'd asked me if he'd stood a chance. Before he fled, that is.

33

An unexpected text came through the next morning while I was eating my breakfast:

✉ From Gary
Solicitor just called to confirm that all's good for completion tomorrow. The house is nearly empty but I found a couple more boxes of your stuff

✉ To Gary
Thought I'd got all my stuff. What's in them? Can I come round to collect them tonight?

✉ From Gary
I can drop them off if you want. I'm not going to tell you what's in them, but I think you'll be excited

✉ To Gary
That's mean! I'm going to be thinking about

this all day now! Kay has a friend coming
round tonight, so it would be easier to meet
you at the house. Any time that suits you

✉ From Gary
See you there at 6.30pm. Happy thinking!

I put my phone down on the dining table and tried to resume my marking, but Gary had me intrigued. I'd be excited? What could he possibly have found that would make me excited?

I picked up a year ten English literature assignment and tried hard to focus on that instead of speculating on what Gary might have found. Unfortunately the assignment was a critique of *Romeo and Juliet*. A relationship that could never be, eh? Just like Stevie and me. I sat forwards in my chair with my head in my hands, and sighed.

* * *

I felt ridiculously nervous as I pulled onto the drive and parked Bertie next to Gary's car. I glanced across at the big red 'SOLD' panel across the 'For Sale' board, which still seemed so out of place outside my former home.

The front door opened before I had a chance to ring the bell. 'I can't wait to see your expression when you see what I've found.' His grin was huge and his excitement was infectious.

'I nearly didn't get any work done today, thanks to your little teasers.' My voice echoed in the hall – a clear indication of an empty property. I didn't like the sensation.

'Come through to the kitchen.'

'You look tired,' I said. 'Are you okay?'

'I haven't had much sleep recently, but I'm fine. Come on. I'm desperate for you to see this.'

I followed Gary down the hall and he stopped outside the kitchen door. 'Close your eyes.'

'Gary!'

'Humour me.'

I sighed but smiled and did as I was told. He took my hands and led me into the kitchen.

'No peeping.'

'They're closed.'

'Before you open them, did you guess what I might have found?'

'No. And I had to stop thinking about it because I wasn't getting any work done.'

Gary laughed. 'Sorry. I wasn't trying to put you off. Open your eyes.'

I opened them then gasped and clutched my hand to my chest. 'Is that...?'

He grinned. 'Open it and see.'

I took a step closer to the turquoise plastic crate in the middle of the island and lifted the lid off. Nestling inside was a pile of coloured exercise books and loose sheets of paper.

I lifted out a light blue book. 'Ashlea the Unicorn Whisperer,' I read off the front cover, then shook my head as my eyes skimmed over page after page of my neat teenaged handwriting. I reached for a few more books then turned to Gary. 'I don't understand. Mother said she'd burned these. Where did you find them?'

'In the attic.'

I shook my head, hugging the books to my chest. 'I thought we'd emptied the attic a couple of weeks ago.'

'So did I but it would seem not. I was packing away the last few bits in the spare bedroom when I heard a noise up there. I thought a bird might have got in so I decided to investigate. When I put the light on, I saw something glinting in the far corner and found the crate and this.'

He handed me a wooden unicorn figurine with a sparkling silver horn, standing about twenty centimetres high from hoof to horn.

I gasped as I took hold of Serenity. 'No way! I thought she'd been burned too. How did we miss them up there?'

Gary shrugged. 'Complete mystery.'

'It certainly is.' The scenario reminded me so much of re-discovering Sarah's lost clairvoyant CD last year. It signalled the start of amazing things happening in her life. Had Gary just found the start of mine?

'I hope you don't mind,' he said, 'but I read some of the stories. They're good, Li. Really, *really* good.'

My cheeks burned. I'd discussed ideas and plotlines with Gary, but I'd been too embarrassed to let him read any. I'd only ever shared them with my sister. 'You're not just saying that?'

'I promise I'm not. The characters are well developed and the plots are quite intricate.'

I placed Serenity down on the island and stared at Gary. 'How much did you read?'

He hesitated. 'All of them.'

'Seriously? There must be seven or eight stories in there. When did you find the time?'

'The early hours of the morning.'

'So that's why you look so tired.'

He nodded. 'I honestly couldn't put them down. There's nine of them, by the way. I hope you're not mad at me.'

I shook my head and smiled at him. 'How could I be mad when you've re-discovered Ellorinia for me.' I'd thought about it a lot since my conversation with Stevie, and even more since I'd doodled the sword, but I'd been unable to muster the energy to start over. Now I didn't have to.

Gary gently placed Serenity into the crate and put the lid on it. 'You know what this means, don't you?'

I grinned. 'I certainly do. We've just found me.'

34

The next few weeks seemed to whizz by. Much as I wanted to spend it reading my stories, I had to spend the rest of half-term in a flurry of marking work and lesson preparation.

The second half of the autumn term started with the usual frantic Christmas activities – rehearsals for the Christmas pantomime and the EGO equivalent, and planning the end of term party – plus parent consultations and an Ofsted inspection. I never seemed to have a moment spare, although any snatched minute I found, I spent re-discovering Ellorinia. The distractions kept me from doing the one thing I knew I had to do – talk to Daniel.

The week running up to Sarah's hen do arrived and, with it, a new determination. This was the week. I was nearly seventeen weeks pregnant and the father had a right to know. Clare had been in regular contact about the hen do on our WhatsApp group but had also set up a group for the two of us on which she repeatedly urged me to make the announcement. I knew it made sense, especially as the deception was wearing me down. Once I'd told Daniel, I'd just go for it.

I resolved to text him after work on Monday and see if he

could meet me one evening that week, but I picked up a voice-mail before I had a chance: 'Elise, it's Lee. Jess is in labour. We're on our way to the hospital.'

My heart thumping, I sat down heavily in the staff room.

'Bad news?' Graham sat down next to me.

'Jess is in labour. That's four-and-a-half weeks early.'

'My cousin had twins five weeks early and they were abso-lutely fine. I'm sure Jess's babies will be too. Do you want to go to the hospital? I can take your classes for you.'

I shook my head. 'No. It's fine. She could be in labour for hours.'

'And she could have a caesarean. Go to the hospital, Elise.'

Graham had been right about the caesarean. Three hours later, I gave my first hug to my tiny five-pound-two-ounces nephew, Oliver James Grainger, and then traded him for two-ounces-lighter Emily Hannah Grainger. Holding my adorable sleeping niece, my thoughts turned to baby bean and how incredible it must feel to hold him or her when holding my sister's babies felt so emotionally overwhelming.

'Hey, don't cry,' Jess said. 'You'll find someone else and have your own baby one day.'

Yes, in about twenty-three weeks' time, but this definitely wasn't the moment to share that news. Instead, I said, 'I know. In the meantime, I get two gorgeous babies to spoil and no sleep-less nights or stinky nappies to change.'

'I might let you off with the sleepless nights, but didn't you realise that it's in every auntie's job description to be on stinky nappy-changing duty?'

'As long as I get lots of cuddles as compensation.' I handed Emily to Lee. 'I think it's time I left you two to enjoy your babies alone. Is *she* coming in?'

'Mother?' Jess shook her head and tears glistened in her eyes. 'Lee phoned. She said she hates hospitals and she *might* come round when we get home. I think we can substitute *might* for *won't*, can't we?'

I knew she wanted me to say encouraging words and reassure her that of course our mother would visit but I couldn't do it because I knew she was right – especially after what I'd overheard Mother saying at the wedding – and I wasn't going to build any false hope.

'Don't let her get to you, Jess. You knew what she'd be like.'

'True. I know she's not exactly parent of the year material, but I thought she might feel differently about her grandchildren. Silly me. Lee's parents are already on their way down from Aberdeen and Dad will fly over from Spain at the weekend, yet she lives ten minutes' walk from here and can't be arsed.'

Taking care not to squash Oliver, I gave Jess a hug. 'I'm here too and I'm very proud of you both. I'll be such a great auntie that they won't miss their Grandma Morgan.'

'I know you will. Thanks, sis.'

'I'll visit again tomorrow after school, whether you're here or at home, but you may have to wait for presents because I was feeling superstitious about purchasing until I knew they'd arrived safely.'

I jabbed at the lift button and tapped my foot while I waited for the lift to arrive. Even though I'd overheard Mother expressing her disinterest in the twins at the wedding, I'd hoped she'd change her mind when they were actually born. Clearly not. What a stupid, selfish woman.

I was still muttering under my breath when I exited the lift on the ground floor and collided with someone. 'Sorry.' I looked up. 'Stevie? What are you doing here?' Butterflies flitted round my stomach at the unexpected sight of him.

'Are you okay? Is something wrong with the baby?'

I smiled. 'No. I've just been to see Jess. She's had her twins.'

Stevie's face lit up. 'Really? What's she had?'

Jess had decided to only tell family about the genders so I'd been sworn to secrecy. I'd become pretty good at keeping secrets. I told Stevie their names, weights and all the usual baby details. 'They're absolutely gorgeous,' I said. 'It was a bit strange thinking that, in about five months, I'll be holding my own.'

'How are you feeling?'

'Good. The nausea has completely gone now. I'm tired, but I think everything's fine otherwise.'

'Have you told Daniel yet?'

I grimaced. 'That's my task for this week. I've been procrastinating because there's no way he'll take it well.'

'Then he's an idiot.' Stevie frowned. 'But we already know that because he let you go.'

The butterflies went crazy as he looked at me intently. I gazed at his mouth and found myself desperate to kiss him again. That brief moment at Seashell Cottage had felt amazing. If only I hadn't had to stop it.

'Erm, I'd better go,' he said, breaking our gaze.

'Of course. Why are you here, by the way? Are you okay?'

'My Uncle George has had a minor op. I'm visiting him.'

'Oh. Have fun.' I shook my head. 'That was such a stupid thing to say. Sorry.'

Stevie looked at me intently again. 'Nothing you say is ever stupid. Look, I'd better go, but promise me you'll let me know if you need me for anything. I mean that. Anything.'

'I promise. Thank you.'

A moment of electricity passed between us. He seemed to move closer and closer ever so slowly then he pulled me into his embrace. 'Congratulations on becoming an auntie.'

He looked embarrassed as he pulled away. The lift door opened at that moment and he dived into it, almost colliding with an elderly man trying to exit with a walking frame. 'See you later,' he said, then averted his gaze, only glancing back up and catching my eye in the last millisecond before the door closed.

I bit my lip as my pulse raced. *Stop it! It's not meant to be.*

* * *

'Elise! I didn't expect to hear from you again.'

I sat in Bertie in the hospital car park and shuddered at the sound of his voice. 'Hi Daniel. Are you free to meet me one night this week? Any night except Friday works for me.'

'Meet me? Why?'

'There's something I want to talk to you about.'

'Let me guess...'

My heart thumped. Could Michael have told him?

'... You're missing me. You've realised that you can't bear life without me.' His voice dripped with self-assured arrogance.

'No, Daniel, that's not it. I just want to talk.'

'About getting back together?'

'No, but I would like us to meet up.'

'You're after a one-night stand, eh? Works for me.'

I sighed. 'You're not listening to me. I just want to meet to talk about something. Something important.'

'We're talking about something important now. I have to admit, I *have* missed you. You were pretty good company as well as a damn good shag. How about you come over tonight? We can catch up on old times.'

'Seriously, Daniel, what part of "we need to talk" don't you understand?'

'Talking's over-rated. But if you really must talk, we can do that after we get reacquainted.'

Who was this guy? Had I been so badly on the rebound that I'd fallen for a smarmy sex-obsessed idiot like that? I only hoped there'd been a less smarmy act put on by him when we'd met because, if I'd been taken in by the person on the phone, I'd had one serious lapse of judgement.

'Elise? Are you still there?'

'I'm still here.'

'When should I be expecting you?'

'I think you'll find it's me who's expecting.'

Silence.

'Expecting what?'

'Your baby, Daniel. I didn't want to break it to you over the phone, but you've given me no choice. I'm nearly seventeen weeks pregnant.'

'You're shitting me.'

'I'm not "shitting" anyone.'

More silence.

'It's not mine. We used precautions.'

'Precautions aren't infallible. It *is* yours.'

'No, it's not. Seventeen weeks? What's that in months? It can't be mine. It's your gay husband's.'

'You know full well that I hadn't had sex with Gary for at least eight months before I met you. Seventeen weeks is a little over four months. The baby *is* yours.'

More silence.

'I... I can't... I'm not...'

'I'm bored of this conversation, so I'm about to hang up. The baby's yours. I'm only telling you because I think you have a right to know. I don't want anything from you, though, because I reckon you'll be as crap a dad as you were a boyfriend. Good-bye.' And I disconnected the call.

It was a cheap shot. Perhaps I wouldn't have said it if I hadn't been wound up by my mother's don't-care attitude, but it was done now. I could relax and get on with my life although relaxing might not be the right word; it was Sarah's hen do at the weekend which meant more secrets and lies about why I wasn't drinking. I certainly wasn't going to take the focus off her on her own hen weekend by announcing my pregnancy. Maybe afterwards? I shook my head. Clare had been right; I should have bitten the bullet and made the announcement after the scan. Now I'd got too close to the big event and really would be stealing her thunder if I announced it, so, instead, I was in a tangled web of lies. Just like Gary. How easily it could happen.

35

✉ To Clare
Just wanted to thank you again for your
support in hiding my secret this weekend. I
don't know what I'd have done without you
these past months and those are words I never
thought I'd say to you! How things change.
Thank you so much. I really owe you one…
several, in fact xxx

✉ From Clare
Don't you be telling anyone I've gone soft.
You'll ruin my reputation! You know where I am
if you need to talk xx

It was a little after eight on the Tuesday evening after the hen
weekend and I was shattered. A combination of a long journey,
sleeping in a strange bed, and a full day outdoors at the adult
playground had taken their toll.

Lying throughout the weekend had been exhausting too.
Over the phone on the Thursday night, Clare and I had

concocted a story to explain why I wasn't drinking and why I couldn't drive any of the rough-terrain vehicles like the tank. I'd allegedly hurt my back moving the stage at school and was on some really strong painkillers which couldn't be taken with alcohol. Fortunately, fourteen women and lots of activities kept everyone distracted and nobody noticed when I forgot to act like my back was giving me gyp.

We'd decided to go for a more leisurely Sunday with a trip to The Metro Centre in Gateshead – a huge shopping centre and leisure complex – on the way home. We'd agreed to split up to do what we wanted. With no energy to traipse round shops, I'd opted for the cinema with a few of the other hens and had fallen asleep within minutes of the film starting.

Sarah had a great time, which was the main thing, although she'd given me and Clare a strange look when we announced we were sharing a room. I caught her looking at us with suspicion on a couple of other occasions and wondered if she'd guessed, but Clare assured me that it was just the unexpected sight of us not sniping at each other constantly after years of having to dive in and play referee.

I yawned then put down the paperwork I'd planned to complete. It was no good. My bed was calling.

My phone beeped and my heart thumped faster when I saw who'd sent the text:

⊠ From Stevie
How was the hen weekend? I bet you're exhausted. Did you manage to keep things secret? xx

⊠ To Stevie
Hi. It was brilliant but, you're right, I'm shattered. I'm off to bed now! Clare told Sarah I'd hurt my back and was on painkillers

so couldn't drink. She seemed to accept that
so my secret's safe. For now. Hated lying,
though. Thanks for asking. How was your
weekend? xx

✉ From Stevie
Good. Long walk with Bonnie on Saturday, beers
with Nick on the evening, then Sunday lunch
with my Uncle George and another long walk
with Meg while Uncle G slept in front of the
TV farting! See you soon xx

✉ To Stevie
I don't suppose you fancy

I shook my head and deleted what I'd written. Asking him
out for a drink? What was I thinking? He'd made it clear he
wasn't interested anymore when he'd fled after seeing the scan.

Putting my phone down, I got into bed. I could hear Kay and
Philip chatting downstairs, plus the occasional burst of laughter,
and smiled as I wrapped the duvet round me. Kay had confessed
over the weekend that she and Philip were an item. Apparently
it had started after the Bay Trade anniversary celebrations, but
they'd wanted to keep it quiet while they both adjusted to their
first relationship after losing the loves of their lives. They made
such a great couple and I was thrilled that Kay had finally
decided to let love in after shutting herself off to it for about
forty years.

Listening to another burst of laughter made me realise that
I'd completely and utterly outstayed my welcome. Kay would
never say anything, but the arrangement was only ever meant to
be temporary and I'd already been her lodger for... what? Four-
and-a-half months? It was time I moved out and found somewhere to start afresh; just bean and me. I had the money from

the house sale so there was nothing to stop me. In fact, if I didn't act fast, I could still be living at Kay's when baby bean made an appearance, which would definitely be pushing the boundaries of her hospitality.

House-hunting alone? Scary thought. Gary and I had looked at several properties together and I vividly remembered how useful it had been to have the two perspectives. I couldn't enlist Sarah or Kay without explaining to them why I was looking for a family home and, with the wedding fast-approaching, I really couldn't break the news. The timing had gone from bad to appalling.

There was only one person who could help me. But was it too cheeky? He'd said to let him know if I needed anything and it would be a great excuse to see him again, even if it was only platonically. Before I had time to talk myself out of it, I picked up my phone and typed a message:

⊠ To Stevie
Hi again. Please tell me if this is over-step-
ping the mark, but can I ask you a huge
favour? It's time I moved out but I'm nervous
about house-hunting alone and I can't enlist
anyone without giving up my secret. If I set
up some appointments for after school this
week and next week, is there any chance you
could accompany me & be my voice of reason?

⊠ From Stevie
I'd be delighted to. Of course it's not over-
stepping the mark. We're friends, right? This
is the sort of thing friends do for each
other. Just text me when you've set up any
appointments x

Friends? My heart sank at the affirmation that it was purely platonic. What was done was done. I'd had my chance and I'd blown it.

* * *

'It's nice,' Stevie said two nights later.

'Nice?' I raised an eyebrow. 'Nice is a word you use to describe a puppy or a cake. It's not the word I'm looking for to describe my future home. What's wrong with it?'

'It feels a bit... soulless. It's beautifully decorated, but there's no character to it. It's a perfectly functional three-bed semi, but I see you in something older. I don't think that new-builds are really you.'

'My last house was a new-build.'

'I know, but I think Seashell Cottage suits you better.'

In the second property, I turned in a circle round the kitchen. 'I like the kitchen. It's nice.'

Stevie laughed. 'Nice? Yes, it *is* nice. It's functional. It's clean. It's well-decorated...'

'But...?'

'It's just not you, Elise. As a house, it works perfectly. But as a home...? I just don't see it as the place of your dreams.'

We said goodbye to the estate agent and sat in Bertie for a while.

'What made you choose your last house?' Stevie asked.

'Pure practicalities. It was brand new so we could just get on with life and our careers without worrying about DIY.'

'Did you love living there?'

I shrugged. 'I thought so, but now you've got me wondering. What you said about a house versus a home... well, I think it was just a house which was why selling up hasn't really bothered me. Sorting our stuff out was emotional because of all the memories but, since moving out, I've missed my marriage and my friendship, but never the house.'

'Why don't we look at some older properties? You might be surprised.'

* * *

On Monday evening the following week, I had three back-to-back viewings lined up for older houses in very different styles, starting with a three-storey four-bedroom terraced house near town. Stevie was right about the feel of the property but I realised that three storeys, no garden, and no off-road parking wasn't the most practical option.

Property two was in a village called Cranton, about ten minutes west of Whitsborough Bay. It was pitched as, 'A charming cottage, ideal for a family, in need of a little TLC.'

'A little TLC?' Stevie whistled. 'Who are they kidding? It needs complete gutting. In fact, it needs knocking down and starting again.'

Even the estate agent looked embarrassed. 'I've not actually viewed this particular property before.' She shuffled some papers together, keeping her eyes cast down. 'Of course, the price does reflect the state of the property. You're getting a lot of property for your money.'

It had potential and would make someone an amazing home. But that someone wasn't me, not on my own with a baby. 'Sorry, but it's a no,' I said to the agent. 'I work full-time and I'm single. I can't take on a project like this.'

The final viewing was a 1930s semi. Stevie took my hand as we walked towards the front door. I liked the feel of my hand in his. It felt comfortable. Natural. Home. But I didn't like the house. It reminded me of my Auntie Maud's. I hadn't liked her. Like Mother, she'd been a drinker and her house had smelled of whisky, pickled onions, and damp dogs. She didn't even have a dog. I clung onto Stevie's hand as an old man showed us round. He told us that he'd lived there for sixty years but his wife had died after Easter and he'd made the decision to move into a home. I didn't want to live in that house with the air of sadness, death, and memories of my auntie.

'Drink?' Stevie said as we walked down the drive towards Bertie.

'Good plan,' I said, trying not to feel too disappointed at having no serious contenders.

I drove to The White Horse in Little Sandby.

'I've never been in here before,' I said. 'Am I right in thinking it's under new ownership?'

'About eighteen months ago. The new landlord and lady are brilliant. They've completely refurbished it and turned it around. The last lot drank their profits, I think, and their food was rubbish so they gradually lost all their trade. These two have worked magic.'

My stomach grumbled loudly.

'Have you eaten?' Stevie asked.

'Not yet. You?'

'Not since lunch. How about we get some tea and we can plan your next house-hunting move?'

'I haven't taken enough of your time already this evening? You're not sick of me yet?'

Stevie's eyes took on such a tender look as he said, 'I could never get sick of you.' My legs went a bit wobbly.

We placed our orders then took a table overlooking the beer garden, which was lit by a combination of spotlights, solar lights, and fairy lights. Very pretty.

I turned my gaze from outdoors to the inside of the pub. 'It's nice in here. You're lucky to have a local like this.'

'I know.' Stevie smiled. 'I try to support it whenever I can.'

I laughed. 'I bet you do.'

He took a sip of his lager. 'We've seen five properties now.

Am I right in thinking you've ruled out the new-builds and prefer the older ones?'

'Yes. Definitely. You were so right about older houses being more me.'

'Imagine that all the properties we saw today were done out in your taste, ready to move into, which did you like best?'

'Definitely the cottage. I could see the potential, but I haven't time to do anything with it. Even if I made an offer tomorrow, I'd be at least seven months pregnant before it goes through then I reckon there's several months of work to be done.'

'So we need to find you something like the cottage, but already refurbished.'

I screwed my face up. 'Financially that may be out of my reach.'

'There'll be something out there,' he said. 'I'm sure of it.'

'Fancy selling your cottage? I'd love to live there.'

'Would you really?'

'Of course. It's gorgeous.' As I said the words, I could picture us all living there together, watching cartoons with baby bean in the lounge while the log-burner glowed, dining in the kitchen and, well, I'd seen his gorgeous bedroom and I could just imagine... 'Is it hot in here?' I fanned my face. 'I'm just going to the ladies. Back shortly.'

Leaning against the sink, I tried to regulate my breathing. I had to stop fantasising about Stevie. He wasn't interested.

'Are you okay?' he asked when I returned to the table.

'Pregnancy flush. Sorry about that.'

'I was worried about you. You dashed off so quickly.'

'I'm fine, but it's nice knowing someone cares.'

We gazed into each other's eyes, butterflies going mad in my stomach. *Stop it, Elise! He lost his baby then his wife left him. Taking on another man's baby isn't exactly a much more appealing proposition, is it?*

'The vegetable fajitas?' a waiter asked.

'Me,' I said.

The moment was lost, but the electricity was still there. It crackled all evening, it fizzed in the car, and it took all my willpower not to lean across and kiss him when I dropped him back home later. Despite my best efforts to just think of him as a friend, my feelings for Stevie kept getting stronger and stronger. Damn!

36

Commitments at school over the next few weeks meant I couldn't squeeze in any more viewings before Christmas but, at lunchtime on the last day of term, I received a call from the estate agent to say a cottage in Cranton had just come back on the market and they could squeeze me in for a viewing late afternoon. With an early finish at school, I decided to go for it. Stevie was working to a deadline so couldn't join me but said he looked forward to hearing all about it at Sarah and Nick's wedding the following day.

The estate agent, Laura, unlocked the front door to the cottage and ushered me into the hall out of the wind and rain. 'The people who were buying it have lost the buyer on their house so have had no choice but to pull out.' She rested her golf brolly against the doorframe as she shut the door to the elements. 'Shall we...?'

I followed Laura round the two-bed cottage, then she left me upstairs to tour the property again on my own. It really was lovely. Although there were only two bedrooms, they were both large doubles and definitely provided plenty of space for baby bean and me. With careful planning, the lounge was big enough to house a desk and shelving units at one end, and there was an open-plan kitchen-diner, which had been refitted a few years previously.

'What do you think?' Laura asked when I found her in the lounge.

'It's a lovely cottage but I'd like my friend's opinion. I'm seeing him tomorrow so I'll come back to you.'

After Laura pulled away, I sat in Bertie for some time, staring at the cottage while the rain pelted against my windscreen. It was perfect. It was smaller than I was used to, but it certainly had enough room for the two of us. It had character and warmth. It didn't need any work. I even liked the colour scheme so wouldn't have to worry about painting. It was in a village I loved at a price I could afford. So what had stopped me from scheduling a second viewing immediately or even making an offer?

My phone beeped and my heart raced at the sight of Stevie's name on the screen:

✉ From Stevie
How was it? Do we have a winner? Xx

That was what was stopping me: Stevie, and the recurring image of baby bean and me living in Bramble Cottage with him.

Lying in bed that evening, I stared at my bridesmaid dress hanging from the top of the wardrobe and listened to the rain battering against the window. I hoped that the weather forecast was right and that the storm was going to pass. Even if it didn't, it would still be an amazing day. I was so thrilled for Sarah that she'd finally met the man she wanted to marry, and I was excited about the prospect of spending the day in Stevie's company, even though it could lead nowhere.

* * *

Tears pricked my eyes as I stood by the church entrance beside Callie and Clare, watching Sarah stroll along the winding path beside her dad. Pride flowed through me at the sight of my best friend looking so radiant and beautiful on the day she'd dreamed of for so long.

Her dress was perfect. A band of crystals across the sweetheart neckline and a band round the waist added elegance to what could have been a fairly simple bodice. Layers of light tulle sparkled with more crystals and the netting parted in the middle to reveal a panel of the lightest champagne tulle, which complimented our bridesmaid dresses perfectly. The effect was completed with a sparkling tiara and a long veil to below her waist before the dress opened out into a long train.

She stopped when she reached us. 'My face is already aching from grinning. I think I'll be in serious pain later.'

Clare reached forward and adjusted Sarah's veil. 'So all the champers you down at the reception will be for medicinal purposes to dull the pain?'

'Sounds like a great excuse to me,' Sarah said. 'Are we all ready?'

'Ready,' everyone chorused.

'Is my train spread out properly?'

'It's perfect,' Callie said.

Sarah slipped her arm back through her dad's. 'Let's do this!'

'The Trumpet Voluntary' started. Sarah turned round and grinned at us, then stepped into the church. We'd agreed between us that, as there was no chief bridesmaid, we'd walk down the aisle behind Sarah in alphabetical order by first name so I was last to step into the church. As we slowly made our way down the aisle, I smiled at the adoring looks Sarah drew from both sides of the congregation. I nodded to Jess and Lee, each holding a sleeping baby, and smiled at friends and relatives of Sarah on the bride's side of the church. Experiencing that sensation of being watched, I looked to my right instead... and straight into Stevie's eyes. *Oh wow! Serious thunderbolt situation.*

I couldn't concentrate throughout the service. I kept stealing glances across at Stevie looking ravishing in his navy morning suit. Each time I caught his eye, explosions set off in my stomach again. It was the suit. It was only the suit. And hormones. Yes, the suit, the hormones, the excitement of the day and a tiny sip of bubbly had turned me giddy. That's all it was. But as we posed for photos outside the church, stood so close to each other that I could feel the heat from his body, I knew it was more than that. And I knew I had to push my feelings aside.

Starting tomorrow.

37

It was like Sarah's birthday all over again when our meal arrived. Brie tartlet. I looked at Clare just as she looked at me. We both cried, 'Brie!' then cracked up laughing. I'd had so much in my head over the last few months that I hadn't given the food choice a second thought.

'What's for mains?' Clare asked.

'I can't remember.' I grabbed the menu and groaned. 'Field mushrooms stuffed with roasted Mediterranean vegetables and topped with goat's cheese. I can't eat goat's cheese either. Damn! I'm starving.'

'Pudding?'

'Tart au citron with raspberry coulis. At last! Something that's safe to eat.'

'I hope you like veggies,' Clare whispered. 'And bread. Yummy!'

'Are you okay?' Stevie knelt down beside me after they'd cleared the starters away with my brie intact. 'You didn't eat your starter.'

'I can't,' I whispered. 'It's soft cheese.'

'Of course. Stupid me.'

'I can't eat my main either. Thankfully there's no soft cheese in my dessert.'

'Poor you. You can have my dessert too if you like.'

'That's really sweet of you but I should be able to fill up on vegetables.'

'Just looking out for you and baby,' he whispered. That intense gaze was there again and my stomach flipped. What would he do if I kissed him right now?

* * *

Before coffee was served, Stevie excused himself and Clare immediately turned to me. 'You and Stevie,' she said, in a hushed tone.

'What about us?'

'You like him, so you do. And, when I say like, I mean fancy the arse off him. So will you be making your move tonight?'

I pointed to my stomach. 'What do you think?'

'I think he fancies the arse off you too and that the baby should make sod all difference to you getting together.'

'But it does. It makes a massive difference. I know he liked me before, but he's made it pretty clear since that he just wants friendship. The minute he knew about bean, things changed.'

Clare shook her head. 'Bollocks. People don't switch off their feelings that easily. Believe me, Stevie still adores you, but if I'm not mistaken, you made it clear that you just wanted friendship so he's probably holding back because of that. He might be worried about scaring you off if he tries to push for more.'

Could she be right? I'd been very clear that friends was the only thing on offer the day of the surprise visits. But I'd also said in the car that he'd have stood a chance if I'd never fallen pregnant. What I hadn't made clear was that he still stood a chance. What if that was why he'd fled? What if it had taken him all his courage to ask me the question then I didn't expand the answer to give him any encouragement? What if he'd been waiting for a sign from me all this time?

'He's coming back,' I said, spotting Stevie in the distance.

'Think about what I've said, won't you? Give him a sign and I guarantee he'll act on it.'

'What sort of sign?'

'I don't know. Just something to encourage him that you see him as more than a friend.'

Once the coffees had been served, the conversation turned to what everyone was planning for Christmas and New Year. 'What will you do, Clare?' Philip asked.

'Absolutely nothing. Christmas is family time. As far as I'm concerned, I have no family. Therefore I don't do Christmas and I've always hated New Year.'

Philip's face fell. I bet he wished he'd never asked. Although Clare sounded like she couldn't care less, I detected a slight shake in her voice and I really felt for her. My mother was a waste of space, but at least I had Jess and Dad. What must it be like to have nobody?

'What about you, Elise?' Philip asked.

'I'm going to my sister's for Christmas.' I pointed in the direction of the table where Jess and Lee were. 'Can't wait to spend it with my baby niece and nephew. My dad's across from Spain at the moment, so he'll be there too. Should be lovely. As for New Year, I haven't really thought that far ahead. What about you?'

We chatted round the table about our plans. Ben tried to convince Clare to join him for a party at a friend's house on New Year's Eve, but she was having none of it. He suggested she come to Whitsborough Bay and have Christmas with him and his parents, but she wouldn't hear of that either. 'It'll be strange with no Sarah,' he pleaded, but she stood her ground. I hoped she wasn't going to be lonely. It was her decision, though, and I could imagine it was frustrating having everyone nag you into trying to enjoy an occasion with which you really didn't feel at one.

'What are you doing, Stevie?' I asked.

'I'll go to my Uncle George's. He's the one who had the minor op a little while ago. He's the only family I have left now so we always spend Christmas Day together. Don't know about New Year yet either.'

The only family he had left? I hadn't realised Stevie's parents had passed away. Why didn't I know that? Had I been told and forgotten? I'd have to explore further, but now wasn't the time.

'What about you, Philip?' Stevie asked.

'Kay's invited me to have lunch with her family, then she's joining Michael and me for tea.'

'Then Philip's taking me away for New Year's Eve.' Kay couldn't hide her excitement. 'I've just found out, but he's keeping the location secret.'

'UK or overseas?' I asked.

'He won't tell me that, either.' Kay smiled widely. 'It could be the garden shed for all I care, as long as we're together.' She gazed lovingly at Philip and my heart melted. I had no idea things had moved on quite so quickly but they weren't getting any younger and they'd both known love before so were certainly going to recognise it when it came along again.

'Ladies and gentlemen,' a female voice announced over the microphone, 'we hope you've enjoyed your wedding breakfast. Mr and Mrs Derbyshire would like to welcome you into the bar area for about half an hour. They'll then invite you back into The Briar Room for their first dance as husband and wife followed by your evening's entertainment. Thank you.'

Clare stood up and grabbed her wine glass and a part-finished bottle. 'I'll be going to freshen up. See you later.' Without waiting for a response, she marched off.

'Is she okay?' Stevie said, staring after her.

I shrugged. 'Hard to tell. Sarah says Clare gets funny whenever the subject of her family comes up. She never talks about them. I suspect she said too much and needs a bit of time alone. Speaking of family, I'm so sorry about yours. I didn't know you'd lost your parents.'

He indicated that we should head towards the bar area so I walked beside him, wondering if he'd give any more information or whether I should change the subject. Thankfully he spoke. 'You don't know because I don't usually talk about them. It's not the first thing you can blurt out as soon as you meet someone and, after that, the timing never seems right.'

Bad timing? Now that was a concept I understood. 'You don't have to tell me now if you don't want...'

'No. I want to,' he said. 'Okay. Here it is. My mum lost her battle with breast cancer when I was fourteen. My parents were devoted to each other and my dad took it really hard. He couldn't bear to live without her so, two years later, he took his own life and, unfortunately, I was the one who found him hanging in the garage.'

I stopped walking and grabbed his arm, tears rushing to my eyes. 'No! That's awful.'

'Uncle George, my mum's brother, took me in. He'd never married or had children. It must have been tough for him to suddenly have a bereaved hormonal teenager thrust on him, but he was amazing.'

'I don't know what to say. I can't imagine how difficult that must have been for you.'

'He made a pretty good guardian actually.'

'I don't mean living with your uncle.'

Stevie smiled. 'I know what you mean. I'm being flippant. I'd like to talk about it some more with you, but maybe not today. Today should be a happy day. Do you mind?'

'Of course not. I just feel so bad that I didn't know. I've had loads of negative things to say about my mother and you've probably been thinking I'm a right ungrateful cow to feel that way when you've lost yours.'

Stevie put his arms round me and kissed the top of my head. 'I could never think anything like that about you. You're the most amazing woman I've ever met. I hope you know that.'

I felt my whole body tingle as he held me close. The urge to kiss him was overwhelming. I moved my head slightly. *I have to do this. I have to...*

'Sorry, but could we ask you to move into the bar,' said a voice. Stevie let me go, apologised to the waiter and did as instructed. *Damn! Moment lost yet again!*

We joined Ben, Skye and Stuart in the bar. I got chatting to Ben about my house-hunt and he told me about his new kitchen. The chit-chat seemed very lame after what Stevie had just told me. Clare appeared after twenty minutes or so and seemed to be back on top form. There was no point asking her if she wanted to talk about it because she never did.

Ten minutes after that, the wedding compere called us back into the main room for the first dance. The tables had been cleared to the sides, the curtains were drawn, and disco lights threw coloured patterns across the floor and walls. Sarah and Nick took to the floor for their first dance.

'Ladies and gentlemen, Mr and Mrs Derbyshire would love it if you could join them on the dance floor,' announced the compere as a second ballad played.

I thought about what Clare had said about giving him a sign and turned to Stevie to ask him to dance, but he was already looking at me. Without words, he took my hand, led me onto the dance floor then wrapped his arms round my waist. I put mine round his neck.

'You look radiant,' he said.

My heart raced. 'Thank you. You look pretty good yourself.' Very, very good. Weren't the chief bridesmaid and best man meant to get together? Well, the best man was engaged and there was no chief bridesmaid so how about the regular brides-maid and the usher? I liked the sound of that.

'Thank you,' Stevie said.

We moved slowly in silence for a verse. 'I should have complimented you earlier,' Stevie whispered. 'But I didn't want to embarrass you in front of everyone.'

My heart thumped faster. 'Thank you,' I whispered again. *Give him a sign!* I pulled him a little closer, laying my head on his shoulder. He responded by tightening his grip. Closing my eyes, I snuggled further into his shoulder. I heard his breathing quicken. I wanted to kiss him more than I'd ever wanted to kiss anyone before. And I didn't want to stop there. Was Clare right that he was waiting for a sign from me, something more than holding him more tightly? I'd have to say something, wouldn't I? But what if she was wrong? What if I suggested something and he turned me down? He'd done that once before and, back then, I barely knew him and certainly hadn't fallen in love with him. I opened my eyes, loosened my grip, and stepped back. Fallen in love with him? Had I?

'Are you okay? Stevie still had hold of my arms. He looked concerned.

'Just a little tired.' Oh my goodness. I loved him. Really loved him. I had to say something. But that scene in Stardust filled my mind again. What if he rejected me? I couldn't do it. Not now. I wasn't brave enough.

I stepped away from Stevie. 'I may just go to my room and have a lie down for a while. Would you excuse me?' I needed to think things through. Could I risk making a move tonight or not? Could I take it if he rejected me for a second time?

'Do you want me to come with you?' He laughed. 'To keep you company, not to have a lie down with you. Don't want you to think I'm trying to take advantage. Friends don't do that.'

My heart sank. So that was it, then. He really wasn't inter-ested. 'No, it's okay but thanks. I'll be back down in an hour.'

When I opened my eyes again, it was to see daylight pouring through a gap in my curtains and a note under my door from Stevie:

Didn't like to disturb you. You must have been exhausted. I have to leave early in the morning so won't be at breakfast. Happy Christmas xx

38

My stomach rumbled as I made my way downstairs to the dining room the following morning. The smell of bacon wafted up to me and, despite being a vegetarian for sixteen years, I could happily have wolfed down a bacon sarnie at that very moment.

'What happened to *you* last night?' I turned to see Clare descending the stairs behind me.

I shook my head. 'Disaster. Realised my feelings for Stevie were a bit more than fancying the arse off him as you put it. Went to my room to psyche myself up to doing something about it. Fell asleep. Woke up an hour ago to a note under my door saying he'd gone.'

'That's just bollocks bad luck, that is, especially when your man spent the evening moping around waiting for the love of his life to re-appear.'

'I'm not the love of his life. He just thinks of me as a friend.'

'Yeah right. Pull the other one.'

We reached the restaurant. Even though I'd received his note, I couldn't help scanning the room for Stevie in case there'd been a change of plan. No such luck.

Clare took a seat, but I apologised and headed straight for

the buffet table, grabbed myself a croissant, and eagerly took a huge bite on it. The nausea may have gone, but it came back if I didn't eat regularly and, after a rather sparse dinner last night, I was ravenous.

As I was about to take my next bite, a hand on my shoulder made me jump. Stevie? But it wasn't. 'Kay! You frightened me.'

'Sorry. I didn't mean to,' she said. 'Particularly given your condition.'

I bit my lip. There was no way I could deny it, especially as I knew my shocked expression would have given me away immediately. 'I ...' But no words came.

Kay sighed. 'Have you got a minute?' Without waiting for me to answer, she marched out of the dining room.

I threw a worried look in Clare's direction. She widened her eyes and shrugged. Taking a deep breath, I left the dining room and found Kay in a lounge area full of high-backed armchairs and leather sofas. She indicated that I should close the door. I couldn't read her expression. Was she angry? Disappointed?

'How long?' she asked.

'Twenty-one weeks.'

She paused. I could tell she was working out the date of conception. 'Daniel's?'

'Yes.'

'Does he know?'

'Yes.'

'Is he interested?'

'No.'

She shook her head and sighed. 'No surprise there, then.'

'Are you angry with me?'

Her face softened. 'Yes, I am, but not for the reason you think.' She looked round the room and indicated a pair of chairs in the corner of the room. 'Let's sit.'

I realised I was still holding the croissant, although it was now crushed. I lay it on a nearby coffee table and brushed the crumbs off my hands before sitting down.

Kay sat forward in her chair. 'I'm not angry with you for falling pregnant or making any sort of judgement about it so please don't think that for one minute. I'm actually really thrilled for you... if it's what you want. I'm assuming from conversations we've had that it is.'

'It is.'

She smiled warmly. 'Good. Then huge congratulations. You'll make a wonderful mum, Elise. You really will.'

Her kind words meant a lot to me, especially as I wouldn't hear any such praise from my own mother. 'Thank you. How did you know? I'd have assumed Daniel told Philip, but you wouldn't have needed to ask if it was his if that was the case.'

'Daniel hasn't breathed a word. I know I haven't been around much lately, but you don't live with someone in a two-bedroomed cottage and not notice things. There've been changes in your eating habits and your appearance. I've even heard you being sick. I didn't have to be Miss Marple to work it out but I didn't want to ask. I figured you'd tell me when you were ready.'

I fiddled with a loose thread on my jumper. 'Is that why you're angry with me?'

'Angry may not be the right word. It's a bit strong. I'd say... a bit miffed.'

'So is that why you're a bit miffed with me? For keeping it secret? I'm sorry, Kay. I should have told you, but—'

'I'm not talking about me, sweetheart. I'm talking about Sarah. This is *huge* news and you haven't shared it with your best friend. Yet, if I'm not mistaken, both Stevie and Clare know. And I believe Michael might too. A couple of comments he's made make sense now. Am I right?'

I lowered my eyes. 'You're right. I didn't set out to tell any of them. They all stumbled upon the news somehow. Nobody else knows. Not even my family.'

Kay reached forward and took my hand in hers. 'You're one of the kindest, most selfless people I've ever met, so I know that you'll have had good reasons for keeping this a secret and I wouldn't be surprised if one of the reasons was avoiding stealing the spotlight.'

I looked up, surprised. 'It was.'

She smiled. 'It's so like you to think about others like that, but secrets have a way of surfacing and, no matter how good your intentions were, this is one secret that should probably have been shared with your family and your best friend at least.'

'Has Sarah said anything?'

Kay let go of my hand. 'Not directly. She hasn't guessed you're pregnant, if that's what you're thinking. However, she has noticed the closeness between you and Clare and is confused by it after years of bad feeling between you both. She knows you've been confiding in each other and she suspects that Clare's opened up about her past. Understandably, she finds that hurtful. She has no idea it's you who has the secret.'

My stomach sank. Poor Sarah. I'd really screwed up. 'I was going to tell her after her honeymoon.'

'I think you should tell her now.' Kay stood up. 'Actually, I *want* you to tell her now. I can't make you, of course, but you should be prepared for the repercussions on your friendship if you leave it any longer.'

'You think it's that bad?'

Kay nodded. 'I do. Would you like me to see if she's come down to breakfast and ask her to come and see you?'

I stood up, shaking my head. 'No. This isn't the time or the place.'

'Will there ever be a right time or place?'

'Probably not, but there'll be better ones than this. I promise I'll tell her before she goes and hope it's not too late.'

* * *

'I shouldn't have left this until today.' Sarah planted her hands on her hips the following day and shook her head at the piles of clothes on the bed. 'I hate packing. Especially when it's last minute like this.'

'I thought you weren't driving to the airport till teatime.'

'We're not. I've got six hours, but I'm still feeling that it's too last minute.'

'To be fair, you have had a wedding to think about, a shop to manage, and Christmas.'

She rubbed her hands across her face and shook her head. 'What was I thinking, getting married so close to Christmas when I own a shop? Durr!' She moved a pile of clothes aside and sat down on the bed. 'I need to sit down and relax for a moment or I'm going to forget to pack something vital.'

She leaned across and moved a pile of clothes on the other side of the bed so I could sit down beside her. We both plumped the pillows and leaned back against the headboard.

'Where's Nick?' I asked, wondering whether he was likely to walk in on me mid-confession.

'I sent him out to The Old Theatre with Stevie for a full English. He's rubbish at packing. He somehow manages to fill a suitcase with only three items of clothing. It's quite a talent.'

My pulse raced at the mention of Stevie's name and I hoped Sarah wouldn't notice the colour in my cheeks. 'I bet he does it deliberately so you relieve him of his packing duties.'

'You may have a point.' She picked up her mug of tea and took a slurp. 'So what happened to you on Saturday night? Stevie said you were tired and had gone for a lie down, but I didn't see you again.'

'I managed to fall asleep and not wake again till morning. I'm so sorry, but I missed everything after your first dance.'

'No! Nightmare. You must have been exhausted to sleep right through.'

'I was. But there's a reason why I was exhausted.' I took a deep breath. 'I'm pregnant.'

Sarah's eyes widened. 'Oh my God! Who? Where? When? How? Actually, scrap the last one. I know how. But ... oh my God! I need details!'

'Who? Daniel. He knows, but he's not interested which is fine by me. Where? On the beach at Lighthouse Cove.'

The smile slipped from Sarah's face. 'On the beach? But that happened in the summer, which would mean you're—'

'Five months pregnant and a rubbish friend for not telling you sooner. I'm sorry. With the twins being born and you getting married, there never seemed to be a good time to share the news.'

She grabbed my arm and gasped. 'Your family don't know? You've gone through more than half your pregnancy on your own?'

I squirmed. 'A few people knew. Mainly by accident.'

She let go of my arm and twiddled with one of her curls. 'Oh my God! Clare knows, doesn't she? That's the secret you've been sharing.'

* * *

As I curled up under my duvet that night, I couldn't stop picturing the hurt expression in Sarah's eyes as I told her about Clare finding out and how she'd joined me for my scan. With Kay's warning that secrets had a way of surfacing heavy on my mind – especially with it being the same warning I'd given to Gary about confessing his sexuality to his mother – I'd told her everything about who knew, how, and what they'd done with that information.

She'd cried. She'd actually cried. She thought she'd failed

me as a friend if I felt I couldn't open up to her about something so important. I'd then jumped to defensive mode and reminded her of her reaction to Callie's pregnancy announcement. We argued. We cried. We argued some more. I'd never argued with Sarah, even as kids. It was hideous.

'It's been a heck of a year for both of us, hasn't it?' Sarah had said, hugging her teddy bear, Mr Pink. She wiped tears from her cheeks. 'I don't want it to end with me losing my best friend.'

'I don't either. I really am sorry. I wish I could turn back the clock, but I can't. I thought I was protecting you, but I think I was really protecting me.'

We talked some more then I helped her pack before driving back to Seashell Cottage. Peace was restored, forgiveness was granted, but damage was done. I prayed that Sarah would have such an amazing honeymoon that things would be back to normal when she returned. I'd certainly make every effort to include her in my pregnancy and my life in general to try to repair the damage I'd caused. No more secrets.

Then it hit me. I'd not mentioned my feelings for Stevie. Another secret. Even worse, it was another secret that Clare knew.

39

Christmas Eve arrived and, with it, my next scan. I was nearly twenty-two weeks gone by then but had wanted to wait for the school holidays before I booked it. Once again, Clare was in the waiting room.

'I thought you couldn't come.' I hugged her.

'I managed to move a couple of things around. I wanted to be here. As I said before, I don't think anyone should go through this alone.'

'Thank you.'

'Will you find out what you're having?'

'A baby, I hope. Or I'm in big trouble.'

'Ha ha.' Clare stuck her tongue out. 'You know what I mean.'

'I wasn't going to. The gender of your baby can be one of life's few genuine surprises if you let it be, but I'm far too practical for that. I want to know what colour to decorate the nursery and what clothes to buy because, as a single mum, I'm not going to have time to think about stuff like that once bean arrives.'

'I know it's a stupid question, but it's the question you have to ask all expectant mums...?'

I smiled. 'I honestly don't mind, but I have this very strong feeling that it's a girl.'

* * *

'It's a girl,' the sonographer confirmed ten minutes later.

Clare grinned at me. 'You were right.'

'She's lying in a really clear position so I'd say there's very little doubt.' The sonographer pointed to the screen. My baby girl.

'Thought of a name?' Clare asked.

'Not yet. I've always liked Hannah, but our Jess beat me to it. It's only Emily's middle name, but it wouldn't feel right. I suppose one of the benefits of being a single mum is that I get to pick the name. No compromises needed there.'

We walked to the car park together fifteen minutes later. 'Have you been in touch with Stevie since you ran out on him?' Clare asked.

'I didn't run out on him. I got spooked so I went to my room to think about whether I was brave enough to give him a sign, like you said, just in case he rejected me.'

'He wouldn't have rejected you.'

'How do you know?'

'I just know.'

'How?'

'A wee leprechaun told me.' Her eyes twinkled with mischief.

I gave her a playful shove. 'I give up trying to get any sense out of you. If Stevie and I are meant to be, it will happen despite me messing up on Saturday. Destiny will prevail.'

'I want to say bollocks to that, but I think, on this occasion, you might be right.'

I sat in Bertie five minutes later, looking at the new scan photo. 'Could she be right?' I whispered. 'I hope so, but no time to dwell on it right now. Your mummy has a mountain of

Christmas presents to wrap for your cousins so I'd better get home and get cracking.'

* * *

Later that evening, I wrote a text for Stevie:

✉ To Stevie
Quick text to say I'm so sorry for not making it back downstairs on Saturday night. I meant to, but pregnancy fatigue must have got to me and I fell asleep. I'm really sorry we didn't get to finish our dance. I was really enjoying it. Maybe another time? Hope you have a great Christmas Day tomorrow xxx

I re-read it. It wasn't blatant, but it was definitely a suggestion. *Let's see if he responds. Send.* I turned the light off and drifted into sleep.

* * *

I drove to Jess's house the next morning armed with bags of gifts. I'd gone a little overboard on the twins, but it had been so exciting buying for them while knowing that I had their cousin growing inside me. Their female cousin. *I'm having a girl! I'm having a girl!* And today was the day I'd tell my family. At long last.

As soon as I walked through the door and saw the 'Happy First Christmas' banners everywhere, I canned my plans. Damn! Why was it never the right time?

* * *

It was lovely spending the day with my family, or at least the ones who counted.

'What's your mother doing today?' Dad asked over Christmas pudding. I knew he was only asking out of self-preservation to make sure she wasn't about to pay a visit.

'Drinking herself into oblivion with her friend Irene I suspect,' Jess said. 'Why should Christmas Day be different?'

'I'm sorry,' he said.

'Dad, you have nothing to be sorry about,' I said. 'You tried to change her, but she didn't care enough about you or us to last more than a day without a drink or a fight. I don't know how you managed a year, never mind a couple of decades.' We both knew he'd only stayed because of us and I'd admire him for eternity for that. Even though the divorce had come through when I was fifteen, he'd stayed in the house until Jess was eighteen and old enough to leave home. As soon as she moved in with Lee on her eighteenth birthday, he moved to Spain and finally started living.

'What are you all planning for New Year?' he asked, tactfully changing the subject.

'Lee and I are planning a romantic night in with a candlelit meal and a film... if a certain pair of babies allow us, that is. Doubt we'll still be awake at midnight, though.'

'Elise?' Dad asked.

I shrugged. 'I've been so busy that I haven't made any plans. Are you still going to see Bryan?' Bryan was Dad's best friend from school. He lived in Liverpool and, like Dad, was divorced and hadn't remarried. They took it in turns to visit each other at New Year.

Dad nodded. 'Don't think we've missed a year since I moved to Spain. You make sure you get something planned. New Year can be a funny time and you've been through a lot this year with Gary. Make sure you're not alone and melancholy.'

'I won't be, Dad. I promise.' I stood up. 'Now why don't you all go into the lounge and relax while I clear this lot away?'

'I'll help you,' Dad said. 'No protests. Jess and Lee, you're under strict instructions to relax before my grandchildren wake up. Elise and I will do the washing up.'

'Can I wash?' I asked. 'I hate drying.'

'Be my guest,' Dad said. 'And while you're doing it, tell me how you are.'

My stomach lurched. 'I'm fine, Dad. Why?'

'You look tired and like there's something on your mind.'

I gulped. 'I'm really fine. I'm always tired after the autumn term. You know that.'

I thought he was going to protest and I'm not sure I had it in me not to confess all. Instead he said, 'Okay. Whatever it is, I'm sure you'll open up when you're ready.'

I wondered for a moment whether he'd guessed. I felt my cheeks flush. 'Let's get these pots done then put the kettle on, eh?'

We'd no sooner finished the dishes than my phone rang. I dug it out of my bag in the hall and my heart skipped a beat when I saw Stevie's name flashing on the screen. Was he going to respond to my suggestion? I hoped so!

'Hi Stevie, Happy Christmas!' I sat down on the bottom stair.

'Hi you. Happy Christmas too. Was Santa good to you?'

'Very good. They clubbed in and got me some gorgeous things for my new home – wherever that may be – and I feel quite spoilt. What about you?'

'Uncle George is the only one who buys for me and he gave me what he's given me since I was about six – a book token.'

My heart went out to him for only having one immediate family member. He just had to say the word and I could double the size of his family. 'How was Christmas dinner?' I asked.

'Delicious. It was a joint effort by which I mean Uncle George peeled one carrot and I did everything else. He overdosed on sprouts, though, so I've had to leave him snoring and farting in the front room and come into the hall for some fresh air.'

I laughed. 'That sounds very pleasant. I'm in the hall too so that's spooky. The twins are asleep, Dad and I have just done the washing up and he's making a brew. It's party central here!'

Stevie laughed. 'Have you told them about the baby?'

I lowered my voice. 'I was going to, but Jess had all these "Happy First Christmas" banners up and it didn't feel right.'

'It's your choice, but there's always going to be a reason not to say anything, isn't there? One of the twins has smiled for the first time or taken their first step.'

'I think bean will have made an appearance by then,' I whispered.

'Fair point. You know what I mean, though, don't you? Look, it's none of my business, but don't you think it would be lovely to tell your dad face to face?'

'That's why I was going to tell them today.'

'Then still do it. Don't let some banners put you off. I'm sure they'll all be thrilled for you. I'm going to stop lecturing you now.'

'It's fine, Stevie. You're right. I'll tell them.'

'Good. Believe it or not, my reason for calling wasn't to have a go at you. I wanted to ask whether you'd made any New Year's Eve plans yet.'

'Not yet.' *But I'd love to spend it with you.* 'Probably TV and an early night. Everyone I know seems to have plans.'

'Not everyone. I don't, although I'm hoping you'll change that. Would you do me the honour of dining at mine on the evening and seeing the New Year in with me if you're not too tired?'

'Just the two of us?' I asked, my heart racing.

'And Bonnie, of course.'

I smiled. 'Sounds good.' *Sounds amazing.*

'Brilliant. I don't like the idea of you driving back home when you're tired so the invitation extends to staying over. We could maybe take Bonnie for a walk round The Headland the next day.'

I hesitated. Stay over? What did that mean? In the spare room or with him? My stomach did somersaults at the thought of the latter.

'Elise? Are you still there?'

'Sorry,' I said. 'I... erm... I thought I heard the twins. It's a yes. The meal would be great. And the walk the next morning.' *And a night in your bed.*

'Is six too early?'

'Six is good. Enjoy the rest of your day and I'll see you next week.'

'Now go and tell your sister and your dad that there's another baby on the way.'

'Yes sir! Bye.'

I sat on the stairs for a few more minutes replaying our conversation in my head and grinned. New Year with Stevie? Lovely. I just wished it wasn't so far away.

Okay. It's time. I wandered down the hallway into the lounge where Dad was handing out cups of tea and coffee. *Here goes...*

'While we're all together, there's something I need to tell you that may come as a bit of a surprise...'

40

✉ To Stevie
I did it! You gave me the encouragement I
needed to tell Dad and Jess yesterday and they
were really excited for me. It was the right
thing to do. Thank you xx

✉ From Stevie
So pleased for you. I hope I didn't preach too
much xx

✉ To Stevie
I needed the push. The next conversation won't
be so easy…

✉ From Stevie
Your mum? I'm happy to come along as moral
support if you want

I couldn't impose on him with that, could I? But after her
scathing attack on me when I'd told her I was splitting up with

Gary, I really didn't relish telling her the baby news on my own.

✉ To Stevie
If you really mean that, I'd be eternally grateful xxx

✉ From Stevie
I really mean it. You tell me when and where. We'll face this together xxx

* * *

'This was a bad idea,' I said a few days later as a man in his forties burst through the door of The Flag Inn, fought through a crowd of smokers and vapers, threw up over the withered raised flower bed in the car park, wiped his mouth, then staggered back inside to cheers and pats on the back. It was only 1 p.m. What a state to be in already.

Stevie took hold of my hand and pulled me away from Bertie. 'C'mon. You can do this. I'll be right by your side.'

'She's not very pleasant, you know.'

'I know.'

'She brings out the worst in me. You might not want to spend New Year with me after you see us together.'

Stevie squeezed my hand. 'I know who the real Elise is and, if things get ugly in there, I know it's down to your mum, not you.'

I nodded and sighed. 'As long as we've got that crystal clear. Okay, let's do this.'

We walked towards the door.

'Did I warn you that she'll probably be wearing a nightie?'

Stevie stopped and stared at me. 'To the pub? In the middle of winter?'

I cleared my throat. 'I'm afraid so. She says they're cheaper and prettier than dresses.'

'Oh. Okay. That's certainly different.'

'My mother *is* different. As you're about to find out.'

I held my breath as we passed through the smokers and vapers then released it slowly as we stepped into the pub, knowing that the aroma inside wouldn't be much better.

'It stinks of BO in here,' whispered Stevie.

'I know. We won't stay long. I promise.'

At the bar, I ordered a pint for Stevie, a mineral water for me, and a double whiskey without ice for Mother. 'She's over there, next to the jukebox,' I whispered to Stevie. 'And she *is* wearing a nightie.'

Stevie gasped. 'So she is. Wow. That's... erm... pretty special.'

'Isn't it? Let's get this over with.'

I placed the drink down in front of her and she smiled without looking up.

'Hello Mother.' I sat down, indicating to Stevie that he should sit too.

She looked up. 'Ah! The divorcee. What a treat.' She pointed to the drink. 'From you?'

'Yes. Happy Christmas.'

'It is now.' She took a gulp. 'Who's the loser?'

I grimaced at her rudeness. 'This is my friend, Stevie. Stevie, this is my mother, Marian.'

Stevie held out his hand, but she ignored it. 'Pleased to meet you Mrs Morgan.'

'It's not Morgan. I'm not married to that arsehole anymore.'

'That "arsehole" is my dad,' I snapped. I reached for her glass and lifted it above my head. 'Can we drop the insults? Or should I tip this on the floor?'

Her eyes widened with fear as she reached for the glass.

'Can we, Mother?'

'Okay. I'll play nicely. Just give me my drink back.'

'Say thank you.'

'Ooh, we are feisty today, aren't we? Have you finally grown a pair?'

'*Say thank you.*'

Stevie placed a hand on my knee and gave me a reassuring squeeze.

'Thank you,' she snarled.

I placed her drink back on the table and took a swig of mine, wishing it was something stronger than water.

'So, your divorce isn't through yet and you've already found another mug. I guess some women can't cope without a man in their lives, can they?'

So much for dropping the insults, but at least she'd stopped attacking Dad. I toyed with retorting, but what was the point? A battle of words would frustrate me and give her great pleasure. 'Stevie's not a mug. We're friends. And I *can* cope on my own.'

She laughed and pushed a matted curl behind her ear. 'When's the big day?'

'I've just told you; we're not getting married.'

'Not even set a date yet? Scared of losing the deposit when it all goes wrong?'

I sighed. 'When what goes wrong, Mother?'

'Your relationship. I give it a year from now, if you're lucky. It won't last long enough to make it up the aisle unless... ooh, don't tell me you're knocked up. Because if you are, maybe you'll tie the knot out of duty, but mark my words, you'll both be miserable. Because that's what happens when people get married and have children. I should know. Ruined my life, didn't it?'

Stevie gasped. 'That's your daughter you're talking to. How can you be so cruel?'

'Oh, it speaks,' Mother slurred. 'And it's feisty too. I can see why you ditched the doctor for this one. I bet he's a bit of a go-er.'

'That's it.' I stood up and grabbed her drink. 'Don't say I
didn't warn you.'

'Noooo!' she cried

I poured the liquid onto the wooden floor. 'Oh dear,
clumsy me.'

'How could you?' she snivelled.

'How could I? Really? How could you, Mother? I've put up
with your bitchy and sarcastic comments for far too long now
and I'm not putting up with them anymore.' I stood up and
straightened my back, realising too late that I'd done a typical
pregnant-woman-standing-up action.

Her eyes widened. 'I was right. You *are* knocked up.'

'Yes, Mother, I'm pregnant.'

'I won't babysit for it, you know.'

'I wouldn't want you to or trust you to. In fact, I don't even
want you to *see* my baby. I know that won't bother you, though,
seeing as you haven't bothered to see Jess since she had Emily
and Oliver nearly seven weeks ago.'

'I've been busy.'

'Shopping for nighties and drinking yourself into a stupor?
Yes, I can see you have. Goodbye, Mother.'

I reached for Stevie's hand, but he stopped and picked up his
pint.

'Leave it,' I hissed.

'I don't want it,' he said. 'I'm just making sure *she* can't
have it.'

Mother grabbed my drink and gulped it then pulled a face
when she realised it was water and not a gin and tonic as she
must have hoped.

'I hope you're not expecting me to come to your wedding,'
she shouted as we paused at the bar for Stevie to hand over his
drink. 'Because I'm not sure you're worth the price of a new
nightie.'

'And you're not worth the price of a meal,' I shouted back, 'so don't wait for an invite.' I grabbed Stevie's hand and dashed for the door.

* * *

'Do you want to talk about it?' Stevie asked when we were safely inside Bertie.

'Can we go to your house first?'

'We certainly can.'

We drove to Bramble Cottage in silence while I re-played the conversation in my head. I hadn't handled it well, but she'd started it. My anger had started at Jess's wedding and had been steadily simmering since the twins had been born and she'd made no attempt to visit them. I found out on Christmas Day that she hadn't sent cards or gifts for their births or Christmas either. Jess broke down in tears when she told me that. Dad had just stared at her helplessly, a haunted look in his eyes. I suspect he'd been replaying the wedding conversation, knowing exactly why she hadn't bothered with the twins, yet unable to voice the reason.

'You put your feet up and I'll make you a hot drink,' Stevie said when we arrived back at Bramble Cottage.

'Thanks. I feel quite drained now.'

I must have dozed off because I opened my eyes to find a throw over me and the room in darkness, except for a warm glow from the log-burner and several candles. I stretched as my eyes adjusted to the light.

'Hi sleepy-head,' Stevie said, leaning forward in the armchair near the window. 'I brought you a tea, but you were spark-out.'

'Sorry about that. I only planned to close my eyes for a moment, but it was clearly longer than that. What time is it?'

'About half four.'

'I've been asleep for three hours? What must you think of me? This is becoming a habit.'

Stevie smiled. 'You and baby obviously needed it. How are you feeling?'

'Embarrassed about earlier.'

'With your mum?' Stevie put his book down and joined me on the sofa. 'Please don't be. I thought you were very restrained in pouring her drink on the floor rather than her head.'

I cringed. 'You have no idea how much I wanted to pour it over her, swiftly followed by your pint. I'm sorry that she was rude to you.'

'Don't be. She's obviously a bitter woman.'

'Very bitter. And I'm sorry she kept going on about us getting married. I lost the energy to keep correcting her.'

Stevie smiled and my heart melted at the sight of those gorgeous dimples of his. 'Please don't worry about it. Although if you start going out wearing a nightie, I might have to re-think our friendship.'

I giggled. 'If I start going out in my nightie, you have my permission to ship me off to Dignitas and put me out of my misery.'

'It's when *I* start going out in *your* nighties that we really need to worry.' He stood up. 'Let me go and get you a fresh brew.'

I stretched then gazed round the room. I could happily stay there and never leave. There was something about Bramble Cottage and its owner that felt so right. Was I brave enough to tell him that?

41

'Happy New Year!' Stevie took my overnight bag, closed the door, then gave me a hug. 'Come through to the kitchen. I've made some fruit punch. Non-alcoholic, of course.'

In the kitchen, he handed me a drink. 'On tonight's menu, we've got warm wild mushroom salad with feta, but I Googled it and apparently feta's okay in pregnancy if it's made with pasteurised milk which this one is. But I'll understand if you would rather not have the feta.'

I smiled. 'Sounds like you've gone to a lot of trouble. Pasteurised feta is fine, thank you.'

'For mains, I've made an aubergine and chickpea curry, and for dessert we've got raspberry and rhubarb crumble. I apologise that none of the courses go together. I got a bit carried away with the recipe book and only thought about the clash of tastes after I'd bought everything.'

'It all sounds delicious and I like variety in a meal so don't worry about it. Thank you for cooking. We could have just got a takeaway.'

'I enjoy cooking,' he said, 'and it's better for you and baby.'

I smiled and automatically stroked my small bump. 'We appreciate it.'

Stevie cooked the mushrooms while I laid the table, then we ate our starter and main courses.

'Given that it's the last day of the year, it's tradition to look ahead,' he said over our curry. 'So, what are your hopes for next year?'

'To find somewhere nice to live, to have a healthy little girl—'

Stevie dropped his fork. 'You're having a girl?'

I grinned. 'I had my scan on Christmas Eve and decided to find out.'

He sat back in his chair and smiled. 'A baby girl. Congratulations. Are you pleased?'

'I am actually. I'd had a couple of dreams about it being a girl so it was quite surreal getting it confirmed.'

'I'm delighted for you,' Stevie said. 'So, other than a place to live and a healthy daughter, do you have any other hopes?'

'Not to be alone.' What I really wanted to say was, 'To have you love me as much as I love you,' but I was nowhere near brave enough. That was the sort of thing I needed alcohol to say. But if I could have alcohol, it would mean I wasn't pregnant, which could mean Stevie and I would have got together long before when he was keen on me as something more than just a friend. 'What about you?' I asked.

'Not to be alone would be up there for me too. I was wondering—' A firework banged outside. He blinked and glanced towards the garden. *You were wondering what, Stevie?*

He looked back at me and cleared his throat. 'Other than that, I want to finish decorating my third bedroom, grow my own veg, and work more collaboratively with Nick. He's put some work my way and I've put some his way. I reckon we could do really well if we properly joined forces.'

'Sounds good. Nick's a great guy. I bet he's really easy-going to work with.' But I'd rather have known what he'd been wondering.

'He is.' Stevie stretched. 'Can you face dessert yet or shall we move into the lounge and have it a bit later?'

I pondered for a moment. 'Later, I think. I could squeeze some in, but I think it may push me over the edge so I'll let the rest settle. It was delicious. You're an amazing cook.'

'Thank you. It was my pleasure.'

We moved into the lounge and Stevie put on some soft music. 'Maddy and I would have had a girl.' He sat beside me on the sofa. 'We called her Rebecca.'

I lightly touched his arm. 'I'm so sorry. Do you want to talk about it now?'

He fixed his eyes on mine. 'I do, actually.'

We talked about everything: his parents, his Uncle George, my relationship with my mother, what went wrong between him and Maddy, what went wrong between me and Gary, and whether he'd seen much of Rob recently.

'Did you know they've moved into an apartment on Sea Cliff?'

I nodded. 'Gary phoned to tell me. He didn't want me to hear it from someone else.'

'I've never seen Rob look so happy. They make a great couple.' He put his hand over his mouth. 'Was that insensitive? Does it bother you?'

I shook my head and smiled. 'Not anymore. Gary seems like... another lifetime ago. My life has changed beyond recognition this year. Some of it's been bad. Some of it's been good. Although I was devastated when things ended with Gary – particularly how I found out – I can look back now and know it was for the best. Not because I have baby bean – although she's an added bonus – but because Gary and I weren't working. It was like treading on eggshells trying not to upset him. He needed out for obvious reasons, but I think I did too. I just couldn't see it at the time.'

'Do you ever see him?'

'We saw a lot of each other while we were packing up the house, but I've barely seen him since it sold. I miss him. We've been friends since school so it's strange not having him in my life. Maybe that's another hope for next year.'

'Does he know about the baby?'

'Not yet. I want to tell him in person so I'll probably arrange to meet him before school returns.'

'I've got another hope for next year,' Stevie said. 'I want to run a half-marathon. I might as well put all the running to good use. Sarah didn't have time to come as regularly in the run-up to the wedding so I started doing longer distances.'

'That's brilliant,' I said. 'You've really taken to running, then?'

'I never dreamed I'd like anything remotely athletic, but I'd actually call it my main hobby. I couldn't imagine not running now.' He got up and put another log on the burner. 'Did you manage to find a new interest?'

'I don't have to. I've been able to breathe fresh life into an old one.' Stevie listened intently while I told him about Gary's discovery in the attic. 'It needs a bit of work, but I think there are the makings of a series in there.'

'Will you try to get it published?'

'I think so, but I don't think it will be polished enough by the time baby bean arrives, so this could be a long-term project.'

Some loud bangs outside made Bonnie whimper and Stevie stroked her ears. 'She's not really scared of fireworks. She's just a drama queen and sees it as a chance for attention.'

A ping from a clock on the wall made us both look up. 'Midnight,' Stevie said. 'Happy New Year, Elise.'

'Happy New Year, Stevie.'

'I'd suggest we go out and watch the fireworks, but it's started chucking it down.'

'Then I'm happy to stay in here.'

'There's no need to miss out. I've got something for inside instead.' He reached over the side of the sofa and lifted up a box of Christmas crackers. 'Would you do me the honour...?'

'Ooh, crackers! I never win the prize, though. I'm always a little scared to pull hard.'

We pulled the first cracker and Stevie won a small sparkly pink notepad. 'More you than me, I think.' He passed it to me. 'Not sure it's quite big enough to write another Ellorinia book in, though.'

I smiled. 'Perhaps not.'

We pulled the second cracker. He won again: a mini set of screwdrivers. 'I don't wish to be sexist by giving you the pink notepad and pocketing the "man tools". Would you like these too?'

I laughed. 'No. They're yours. You won them fair and square.'

'One last cracker and you get to keep what's in this, no matter what it is, because you're my guest. Deal?'

I smiled. 'Deal.'

Giggling, I pulled the cracker with him. 'Yay! I won!' I cried as an object tumbled into my lap.

'What is it?'

'A keyring I think.' I picked up the silver fob and held it in front of me. Several silver charms hung from a chain.

'What's on it?' Stevie asked.

I studied the items. 'It looks like a dog, a buggy, a jigsaw piece, a blackcurrant, a house ...' Oh my goodness! My heart started to race as I spotted the connection and my hands shook slightly as I continued to separate the items. 'It might actually be a cottage rather than a house. And perhaps the blackcurrant is a bramble? There's an apple.' For the teacher perhaps? I swallowed on the lump in my throat. 'And there's a bean.' Tears rushed to my eyes as I stroked the kidney-bean shaped charm between my fingers. *Could this mean...?* I didn't dare finish the thought in case I was way off.

'That's a pretty random set of items,' Stevie said, reaching for the keyring. Electricity fizzed through me as our hands briefly touched. He lay it on his palm and spread the charms around. 'Or is it? What do you think?'

I bit my lip as I chose the right words. I needed to be brave. 'I think that they might initially seem a bit random, but when you put them all together, it's like the missing jigsaw piece has been found. What do you think?'

'I think you could be right. And if we add one more element...' Stevie pulled a shiny brass key from his pocket and placed it on his palm beside the keyring then released a nervous laugh. 'Sorry. I'm going to have to put these down because my hand's shaking.' He placed the key and keyring on the leg of his jeans instead. 'The first time you came here, you described it as a family home. It *is* a family home, but the family I expected to live here didn't quite materialise and Bramble Cottage has always felt like it had a missing piece of the jigsaw. I know two people – well, I've only actually met one of them so far – who could be that missing piece and could make it into the family home that it should be.'

I chewed on my lip as I waited anxiously to hear where Stevie's speech was going to take us.

'That same day,' he continued, 'I told you that I was scared of getting hurt again, or being the one to cause pain, so I'd been cautious with relationships, which was fine because I'd never met anyone worth taking the risk for. As soon as I met you, I knew you were worth taking the risk for. You were with Gary at the time so I put it down to a classic case of unrequited love that I'd get over eventually. Perhaps. With a lot of time. Then your marriage ended and I found myself alone with you in Stardust and you kissed me and... have you any idea how much restraint it took not to run after you that night?'

A warm tear slipped down my cheek. 'Why didn't you?'

'It was too soon. You weren't over Gary. I'd have pushed you into something you weren't ready for, and potentially lost you forever.'

I nodded. He was right. Much as I'd been hurt and humiliated at the time, I'd have resented him for taking advantage when I was so confused. 'How's the risk assessment looking now?'

Stevie smiled. 'I think I'm about to take the biggest risk of my life.' He took a deep breath. 'Sorry. I'm making a mess of it. This is harder than I thought. I'm so scared of saying the wrong thing.'

I wiped at another tear and smiled encouragingly at him. 'In the time I've known you, I don't think you've ever said the wrong thing. Whatever it is you want to say, please just say it.'

'Okay. Here goes. Big risk time. I want you to move in and make Bramble Cottage your home. When baby bean arrives, I want it to be her home too and I want to help you with her. I really hope you'll say yes and help turn this place into the family home it should be. However, I can't be certain that you feel the same way about me as I do about you. You said no once before, but I know why. I guess I said no to you too in Stardust too so we're equal in the rejection stakes.' He reached into his pocket again. 'I love you, Elise, and I want to be with you, but I love our friendship too and, if that's where you want the relationship to stay, I completely understand. I hope you'll accept the keyring and everything that means, and I'd like you to pick one more charm to add to it.' He opened his palm and arranged two more charms on it. 'The hands shaking are for friendship or you can go for broke and have my heart. Or you can tell me I've completely overstepped the mark and I can shove my keyring where the sun doesn't shine.'

I wiped my wet cheeks and slowly reached out my hand. 'If you're absolutely sure, I'd like to accept these.' I picked the keyring and key off his knee. 'That cottage I saw before the wedding was perfect, but I couldn't bring myself to say yes to it when all I could picture was bean and me living here with you and Bonnie. I'd love to move in.'

Stevie grinned, dimples flashing. 'That's a relief. I wasn't completely off the mark.'

'No, you weren't. As for the extra charm, I'd like to go for this one please.' I reached forward and picked up the hands shaking.

Stevie's dimples disappeared as he lowered his eyes to see the heart left in his palm. 'Oh well. It was worth a try.' He curled his hand into a loose fist and smiled weakly at me.

'Not so fast on jumping to conclusions,' I said, placing my hand over his fist. 'I've picked the friendship charm because I personally believe that a strong friendship is the basis for all successful relationships. I know it may not have ended well, but my marriage to Gary worked for a long time because we were best friends and my brief encounter with Daniel didn't work because we weren't. You and I have a great friendship, which is why our relationship is going to work. At the risk of being labelled greedy, I'd like this too.' I unfurled his fist and took hold of the silver heart. 'And I give you mine in return. But I have to be absolutely sure you know what you're doing. I'm carrying Daniel's baby. That's a huge ask. Have you really thought it through?'

Stevie reached out and tenderly stroked my cheek. 'I've done nothing but think about it since I found you at Lighthouse Cove with your first scan picture and you said you'd have chosen me if things had been different. That one comment gave me so much hope. I know I ran away like a startled rabbit, but it was only because I knew that, if I stayed any longer, I'd blurt out how I felt and I wasn't sure the timing was right for you to hear it. I want to be with you and I don't see your pregnancy as a problem. For me, that baby girl is an added bonus. Not only would I get to spend the rest of my life with the woman I love, but I get a baby daughter too. It doesn't get much better than that. So stop worrying that it's a huge burden, will you? Because you couldn't be further from the truth. Do you believe me?'

I nodded as another tear slipped down my cheek and Stevie wiped it gently.

'Are you sure I haven't pushed you into this?' he asked. 'Was the keyring too much? Clare said suggesting you move in here might scare you off but it was killing me viewing those houses with you when all I could do was picture you and baby bean here with Bonnie and me. I wondered if I should have just asked you on a date again, but I didn't think we had the luxury of time. You needed somewhere to live before the birth and I just thought why not let it be here?'

'Back up a minute,' I said. 'You mentioned Clare...?'

Stevie wrinkled his nose. 'I wasn't meant to say anything. Please don't be mad at her. All she did was give me a little hope at the wedding that you might feel the same way as me. When I got your text on Christmas Eve, I dared to believe that maybe she was right. Then she called me and pretty much ordered me to grow some and jump you. I decided to go for the gentler approach.'

I laughed. 'She is right. I love you too, Stevie. So much that it hurts. I really do want to move in and I really do want to be with you. Now can we stop talking because there's something I've been dying to do?'

'What's that?'

I leaned forward and wrapped my arms round his neck. 'This.'

For the third time, our lips met and this time neither of us needed to pull away. I closed my eyes as I melted into the most amazing kiss of my lifetime. Soft, sensuous, and absolutely perfect. Last year had been about getting over Gary and finding myself. With my re-found interest in writing, standing up to Gary's mother and standing up to mine too, I'd finally achieved that. This year was about starting over with Stevie and I couldn't think of anywhere I'd rather be or anyone I'd rather be with. Happy New Year? Yes, and Happy New Life too.

ACKNOWLEDGMENTS

Thank you so very much for reading *Finding Hope at Lighthouse Cove*. I hope you enjoyed Elise's journey through quite a turbulent time in her life.

This is the third book in the 'Welcome to Whitsborough Bay' series and was originally released under the title: *Getting Over Gary*. When I received my amazing publishing deal from Boldwood Books, I was thrilled that they wanted to take on several titles from my back catalogue including this series. It's been a joy to work with my editor, Nia, on tightening the manuscript for re-release under the gorgeous new title. And thanks to Dushi and Sue for their valuable copy editing and proofreading skills.

In my dedication, I thanked my mum, Joyce Williams. As well as proofreading and providing feedback on every book I've written, my mum is an invaluable one-woman marketing tool. I don't think anyone in the village where she lives has been spared from her polite... shall we say encouragement... to buy her daughter's books. And she always has a ready supply of my business cards to distribute when she's away in the caravan. What a superstar. I love that she keeps a track of my reviews and chart positions, sending me excited texts when there's good news. Thank you so much for believing in me and supporting me. It means a lot and I love you very much xx

Mum was one of my beta readers on the original version of this story, along with my sisters-in-law, Clare and Sue, and friends Liz and Nicola so a huge thank you goes to you all for that. My super-talented writing friends, Sharon Booth and Jo Bartlett were also beta readers and I must particularly thank Jo who read the original story several times as it went through quite a few major changes before becoming the story you've just read.

Thank you to my writing family, The Write Romantics, for your continuous support and encouragement and, again, to Sharon for tea, cake and friendship.

A huge hug goes to my husband, Mark, and our daughter Ashleigh. Ashleigh was nine when *Getting Over Gary* was released and is thirteen now. Throughout those years, she's shown signs of following in my footsteps, constantly coming up with new stories and eagerly typing away. She doesn't tend to get beyond the first few chapters before she gets bored or starts thinking of a different idea, but I'm sure she'll find the perfect story one day that fully captures her imagination and keeps her going. As for Mark, he's been pivotal in my journey to becoming a writer and never begrudges me time with my imaginary friends.

This past year as part of the Boldwood Books team has been, for me, a writing dream come true. The passion, enthusiasm and dedication of the team makes me smile every day and I constantly thank my lucky stars that I found my home with such a supportive, forward-thinking publisher.

Finally, thank you to you the reader. You have also made my dreams come true and I can't thank you enough for taking a journey into the world of Whitsborough Bay. If you've enjoyed your trip, please do tell your family and friends and consider leaving a short review online as it really does make an author's day to hear from readers.

Big hugs

Jessica xx

MORE FROM JESSICA REDLAND

We hope you enjoyed reading *Finding Hope at Lighthouse Cove*. If you did, please leave a review.

If you'd like to gift a copy, this book is also available as a ebook, digital audio download and audiobook CD.

Sign up to Jessica Redland's mailing list for news, competitions and updates on future books.

http://bit.ly/JessicaRedlandNewsletter

ABOUT THE AUTHOR

Jessica Redland is the author of nine novels which are all set around the fictional location of Whitsborough Bay. Inspired by her hometown of Scarborough she writes uplifting women's fiction which has garnered many devoted fans.

Visit Jessica's website: https://www.jessicaredland.com/

Follow Jessica on social media:

  facebook.com/JessicaRedlandWriter

  twitter.com/JessicaRedland

  instagram.com/JessicaRedlandWriter

  bookbub.com/authors/jessica-redland

ALSO BY JESSICA REDLAND

Standalone Novels

The Secret To Happiness

Christmas at the Chocolate Pot Café

Welcome To Whitsborough Bay Series

Making Wishes at Bay View

New Beginnings at Seaside Blooms

Finding Hope at Lighthouse Cove

Coming Home to Seashell Cottage

ABOUT BOLDWOOD BOOKS

Boldwood Books is a fiction publishing company seeking out the best stories from around the world.

Find out more at www.boldwoodbooks.com

Sign up to the Book and Tonic newsletter for news, offers and competitions from Boldwood Books!

http://www.bit.ly/bookandtonic

We'd love to hear from you, follow us on social media:

f facebook.com/BookandTonic

🐦 twitter.com/BoldwoodBooks

📷 instagram.com/BookandTonic

Printed in Great Britain
by Amazon